SHATTERED
Veil

THE VEILED SERIES BOOK THREE
ELIZA MODISTE

This is a work of fiction. Names, characters, businesses, places, events, and incidents in this book are either the product of the author's imagination or used in a fictitious manner. Any resemblance to actual persons, living or dead, or actual events is purely coincidental.

Copyright © 2024 by Eliza Modiste

All rights reserved. No portion of this book may be reproduced in any form without written permission from the publisher or author, except as permitted by U.S. copyright law.

Book Cover Design by Perrin of The Author Buddy

ISBN: 979-8-3325-8546-3

www.elizamodiste.com

SHATTERED VEIL

Content Warning: This book contains content that may be troubling to some readers, including, but not limited to, mentions of childhood abuse, suicide, stalking, and murder. In addition to those, there are depictions of kidnapping and methods of torture.

Contents

1. Chapter 1 — 1
2. Chapter 2 — 23
3. Chapter 3 — 38
4. Chapter 4 — 59
5. Chapter 5 — 84
6. Chapter 6 — 109
7. Chapter 7 — 132
8. Chapter 8 — 149
9. Chapter 9 — 169
10. Chapter 10 — 190
11. Chapter 11 — 214
12. Chapter 12 — 239
13. Chapter 13 — 263

14.	Chapter 14	292
15.	Chapter 15	313
16.	Chapter 16	338
17.	Chapter 17	368
18.	Chapter 18	389
19.	Chapter 19	414
20.	Chapter 20	436
21.	Chapter 21	460
22.	Chapter 22	478
23.	Chapter 23	505
24.	Chapter 24	505
25.	Epilogue	505
26.	Dear Reader	505

Chapter 1

It's strange how life can toy with a person. How the simple passing of time can change someone. How experiences can melt someone down as if they were made of metal and reforge them into something...new. And that something new could also be improved—it most certainly could—however, I often wondered if the reforging could render the metal brittle and breakable. If the reforging wasn't a step above but simply a weak attempt to give the metal new life without appearing outwardly damaged. If the reforging was simply a bandage to cover the ugly wounds that were once disgustingly apparent.

There was no doubt where I would place my metaphorical smelting. It had occurred months ago during a time that I prayed I could forget, and I was currently stuck in a strange, liquified purgatory that left me...lost. Day after day, week after week, I've been attempting to go through the motions of *sleep, eat, repeat.*

I've been doing so out of necessity because...that's what animals *do,* right? Sure, there's some occasional exercise, depending on the species. Some act playful; some don't. But that's the gist of it...sleep, eat, repeat. Animals do what they need to do to keep their bodies moving—to live—to thrive—until they die.

We're animals. *Humans* are animals, so I supposed that while I was trapped within the molten stage of my own purgatory, I could do just that...I could sleep, eat, and repeat.

But *no*. Humans need more than that. Our emotions...they go far beyond allowing us to simply sleep, eat, and repeat. They have the ability to make us run both hot and cold, twisting the monotony of what could be a simple existence into something far more complex. Into something that could bring us a joy so bright—so warm that it heats our body from the feeling alone. Unfortunately, the flip side of the coin of this is darkness. A hellish void that's freezing to the point that we could be pushed to end it all. There's love. Hate. Jealousy. Guilt. *Repressed Desire.*

That last one...*fuck,* that last one. I've felt all of the spectrums of emotion because I'm human, of course, but repressed desire is one that I've been growing increasingly familiar with. And that, in turn, is beginning to drive me mad because I'm a man that runs hot—I always have. I *emote.* My feelings are absorbed with the full extent of their power and worn on my sleeves for all to see, so to repress something out of what feels like necessity...it's unnatural to me.

And I *think* it's starting to affect how I outwardly appear to others. I *think* it's starting to make me look...bitter. *Grumpy.*

Even now, I was grumbling to myself as I hunched over my meal—a leftover plate of tikka masala from the night prior—desperately wishing that I could push my chair backward to ease my aching shoulders. The idea was impossible, of course, because the stool, along with all the other stools that surrounded the so-called dining space, were bolted to the ground. I wasn't sure if Corporate America thought that all of us were inbred criminals who would steal even the chairs in the kitchen space, but the thought of it irked me.

Truthfully, it had never bothered me before. The stools, I mean. But the tangent that I had unnecessarily ventured on within my mind regarding my molten state and repressed desire had suddenly made me sullen...and I was grinding my teeth together as my friend and colleague Shawn Brooks entered the break room. He strutted his way past me, turned to the left to walk around the peninsula of a white countertop, and beelined to the fridge. I watched as he grabbed an orange-tinged Tupperware that had a yellow sticky note adhered to the red top that read: *Brooks.*

"Turner," he greeted me as he popped the lid and threw it into the microwave.

"What's up, Brooks?" I replied, pushing my lunch around with a fork in my own plastic-ware.

The button-down shirt he wore had a blue checkered pattern, and it criss-crossed as he folded his arms over his chest, cocking his head at me. Shawn's light green eyes, which offset the dark tone of his skin in a striking manner, narrowed at me in mock accusation.

"You haven't answered my question from earlier."

I took a bite of chicken, which had turned cold, chewed, and swallowed. "What question?"

"Tomorrow—you goin' out with us?"

I nearly spat my next bite back in the plastic container. *"I thought you were joking?"*

His dark eyebrows rose. "About spending quality time with a good friend? *No.* Thanks for *that* reply, though—"

"Brooks," I scoffed. "Come on, don't do that fuckin' guilt thing you do."

"You look miserable lately, Jay," Shawn groaned. "It would do you some good to let off some goddamn steam."

I sighed, placed the top on my Tupperware, and snapped it shut. *"Letting off steam* does not equate to going to a *strip club,* Brooks."

He threw his short mess of thick curls back as he whined, "Yeah, yeah, James Turner doesn't *do* strip clubs. He doesn't *do* one-night stands. He's a committed man. Oh, *please,* Jay—you haven't been with a woman in months."

"Um...I don't share my entire life with you. You have no idea if I've been seeing someone lately or not."

"Oh. Have you been seeing someone, then?"

"I—*no, whatever*—look, going to a strip club has nothing to do with being committed to someone," I retorted. "I don't wanna walk into a place with loud-ass music, half-naked women, and dollar bills all over the floor—"

"Yeah," Shawn interrupted me in a sarcastic tone, "that sounds like a *terrible* time."

"Shawn—"

He gasped dramatically, his vibrant eyes widened, and the microwave dinged.

"You did *not* just first-name me. My first name is reserved for people who are so inclined to scream it out." His jokingly shocked gaze flashed to me. *"Unless..."*

"Brooks, *please."*

Shawn grabbed his meal from the microwave, walked over, and sat on the stool beside me. He shot me an uncharacteristically serious glance.

"Don't make me say it," he murmured.

"Say what?"

He sighed. "Fine, I'll say it. I mean this with *all* the love in the world, but you've been…*bleh* since you finalized the divorce with your wife."

"Dammit, Brooks."

I didn't think of her much—swear to God, I didn't, but his mention of my failed marriage *did* make my thoughts swing back to Allison.

I thought it would hit me like a punch to the gut at the time. Mutually ending a relationship with a woman whom I thought was the love of my life *should* have hit me like a punch to the gut, but the sparks had fizzled out long before we inevitably called it quits. The main issue was obvious—cliché, almost—we got married too soon. I mean, *so soon* that my parents assumed that her father was walking me down the aisle with a shotgun due to an unexpected pregnancy kind of *soon*.

I wasn't.

I was just filled with such an infatuation that I couldn't stop myself from diving headfirst into everything Alli. Into her long, blonde hair—her bright blue eyes—her tan legs—the way she'd moan my name and bite my ear when I was deep inside of her. It was a toxic high that I had once related to finding God.

I have since realized that *that* God has quite the morbid sense of humor, but that was beside the point.

Happiness with Alli was so long ago that even thinking of it felt like a fever dream. *That* was before we came to realize all of our irreconcilable differences. She liked going out to clubs; I hated dancing and loud spaces. She liked the great indoors; I tried to go camping as often as possible. She wanted to immediately start having children; I thought that was a terrible fucking idea considering her penchant for clubbing. The woman loved to shop; I was trying to save for the down payment on a house. She loved attention; I was jealous by nature. She bought a cat on a whim; I was allergic. *Okay,* that last one wasn't entirely irreconcilable, but I *really* wanted a dog, and she put her foot down—*anyway.*

We just didn't fit together, and we could only try for so long to force our respective puzzle pieces together. It was two years before the fire that once burned between us no longer had so much as embers, let alone any trace of heat at all, and we respectably went our separate ways.

Or, that was what I fucking *thought* was going to happen.

The divorce—the *legality* of it all was what really smacked me in the face. Her lawyer—the lawyer that I didn't even realize she had hired until it was too damn late to get a respectable one for myself—believed that, amongst many other valuables, she was entitled to our home. The whole. Goddamn. Thing. Not a dime to me. Now, I didn't give a shit about the money. I *had* money. I wasn't rolling in it by any means, but I wasn't about to put up a fight for who won the television that we previously had in our living room.

She did, by the way—she won the rights to that, too.

It didn't matter. It was in the past—*truly* in the past. It wasn't the divorce that had put me in such a shitty headspace. I didn't blame Shawn for assuming that—I also didn't correct him because I didn't care to speak of it.

"I am not *bleh*," I argued.

"Then come out and have a beer," he spoke through bites of spaghetti.

"At the strip club?"

Shawn swallowed and then nodded. "Yeah."

"Why do I need to go with you to a strip club? We can go get a beer *literally* anywhere else."

"Tommy suggested it," he noted.

"Tommy?" I said the name with an upward inflection, attempting to place him.

"He's in sales."

"How've I not met *Tommy from sales?*" I questioned. "That doesn't sound familiar at all."

"He's new," Shawn stated. "Started on Monday."

My eyebrows unintentionally raised. "And he's so bold to recommend that we all go to a strip club together for an after-hours event? I feel like I should talk to human resources."

Shawn laughed. "I thought it'd be good for you, so I said—"

"Don't say it," I muttered.

"That you'd tag along," he finished his sentence with an admission, smiling wide with not a single trace of guilt.

I griped, "Brooks, *why?*"

"'Cause you need to get your mind off of your ex-wife."

Oh, good God.

"It's been three…almost *four* months since the divorce was finalized." I assured him, *"Trust me,* my mind hasn't been anywhere *near* Alli."

Shawn set his fork down in his lunch, interlaced his fingers in front of himself pointedly, and made direct eye contact with me for two whole seconds before stating, "Prove it."

I exhaled. "I'll think about it."

His teeth blinded me, and he smacked me on my left shoulder twice.

"Atta baby, Jay. I knew you had it in you—"

"This feels like coercion at its finest," I retorted as I stood and snatched my Tupperware.

Shawn murmured, "Uh huh. Thank me later."

The remainder of my work day was as it usually was. My used Tupperware was stowed by my feet once I returned to my cubicle. I clicked the black button with an *up* arrow on the right-hand side of my desk, lifting it to the appropriate height, which allowed me to stand as I worked. I jiggled the mouse to wake the screen. My glasses, which I typically wore for late-night driving and computer glare, sat waiting for me next to my keyboard. I grabbed the silver, circular-lensed frames, brought them up to my eyes, and went to work.

Staring at spreadsheets day after day, analyzing data and various other reports to determine the financial soundness of companies that invested in our services, was...boring. There's no other way to put it—it was never a job that felt glamorous, but I liked it. I was able to put in my eight hours per day and not concern myself with the stress of working overtime. If I had to call in sick, there was no worry over who would cover for me because the work could wait. I had a decent salary. The benefits were good. The commute was only twenty minutes on a heavy traffic day. Like I said, I didn't have much room to complain.

And though today was a typical day, I found my mind wandering more than it usually did. Perhaps it was because Shawn had mentioned Allison and assumed that I was discontent over the lack of her presence in my life, but I was drifting off to memories that I seldom tried to visit while I drove back to my apartment—the apartment that I had taken from Claire Branson and Zoey Sheffield.

It was the day that I was told that the house I had bought with Alli was no longer mine—that was the day that I had moved into apartment 2A. I knew Claire and Zoey well...*better* than well. They were both part of the friend circle that we had built for ourselves here in Salem, Virginia.

Claire was my brother Luke's girlfriend. It had been approximately one year since I had teamed up with her, Luke, Zoey, and—for what seemed an inexplicable reason at the time—their across-the-hall neighbor, Liam Cohen. The skeletons in Claire's closet had come to roost, and save for a few wounds that were far from superficial, we had all come out safe on the other side. Traumatized and forever bonded by what we had gone through together, but safe nonetheless.

And *Zoey*—well, she's Claire's best friend. Her old roommate. *And* I had a bit of a fling with her a few months back. It all went sideways when she fell in love with Liam...that wasn't something that I dwelled on, for there are no hard feelings there. Not only was it months ago that Zoey had been officially seeing Liam, but it was impossible to hold a grudge when we had all been put through hell for a second time.

Just after Zoey had stepped aside from our casual fling, she and Claire had moved out of their apartment due to a break-in from Zoey's stalker. A horrifying event that was perfectly timed due to my recent homelessness, I shacked up in their apartment all by my lonesome because they were concerned about the threat and just...never left, I guess. In a long story *very* short, we all attempted to find the man after I had moved in—to detain him and call the police, of course—and don't even *ask* me how she did it, but when he began to threaten us all, Zoey ended him.

And I really do mean *ended him*. I saw the corpse. I helped toss him in the river. I watched him float away—we *all* did, along with Liam's sister, Cassie.

It was a moment that was pinpointed in my life. One that forever solidified my memories to be filed in folders labeled as *before* or *after* its existence. It was my metaphorical smelting...and the more I thought about it, the more I wondered if I really *was* liquid. If I really *was* waiting for a mold of some sort that I could be poured into so I could begin anew. Perhaps, instead, I had already been reforged. Perhaps I had been melted and left to solidify in a horrifically warped version of myself. Perhaps this was *it*, and I was just fucking damaged.

I shook my head to clear it, the reminder of the things that I had witnessed and the impact that it had on me an unwelcome one that I hadn't revisited in quite some time, and a glass of whiskey slid across the countertop to sit pretty in front of me.

After arriving home, I found myself wandering to Henry's, the bar just down the street from the apartment complex, as I regularly do. The space was small and the lighting dim. Music often played so quietly that one would have to strain their ears to hear it, and regulars would frequently wander in and out. It was a watering hole that I had grown to love, and it just so happened that Luke and Claire were two of the employees who manned the bar.

Luke stood before me, his grey eyes—*my* grey eyes—squinting at me. I knew the look. He didn't have to say anything to go along with it, but he did anyway.

"What's under your skin, Jay?"

I shrugged, reached for the glass, and brought it to my lips. The liquid went down smooth, and the taste lingered on my tongue, wetting the facial hair around my lips just enough to keep the scent fresh in my nostrils with every sip.

"Weird day," I told him bluntly.

"Yeah?"

"Yeah."

Claire emerged from a door to the back room on the opposite end of the bar. She held an unopened bottle of clear liquor that I couldn't discern, and she appeared wholeheartedly unbothered until her gaze quickly found mine. Her red hair was up in a messy bun, and the yellow light from the shelves of alcohol to the left of her shined through the strands, making them glow as she cocked her head to the side.

"What's up with you?" she asked, setting the bottle down in its appropriate spot on the lower-most shelf and walking over to us.

"Said he had a weird day," Luke answered for me, crossing his arms.

"Hmm." Claire mimicked his motions.

I glanced at Luke. "I can talk for myself, you know."

"Uh huh," he mumbled. "So, what's up?"

I chose the least prominent thought in my mind. "My friend from work wants me to go to a strip club with him."

"Has your friend *met* you?" Luke asked, his eyebrows high and his expression amused.

The bell from the entrance chimed overhead, and I ignored it.

"Don't get me started," I returned, holding up a hand. "Told him it wasn't my scene—he does *not* care."

Claire chuckled. "Tell him you're not going—he can't *force* you."

I groaned. "He made this whole fuss about thinking I'm hung up on Alli."

"Ooo," Luke voiced with a cringe as he ran a hand through his typically well-coiffed brown hair. "Yeah, no."

"Plus," I added, "he already told the guy who suggested the place that I'd tag along."

A high-pitched voice trilled from behind me, *"Oop, catch us up,"* and I didn't even turn to view her, for I knew where she was intending to go.

Her usual seat was to my right, and Liam normally sat beside her, on *her* right. The blonde duo did as such, and Zoey's tiny frame slid onto the barstool beside me.

Before I could answer, Claire spoke for me, "Jay's work friend invited him out to a strip club."

Liam let out a loud, *"HA!"* while Claire turned to grab his and Zoey's usual drinks. His mop of hair was thrown back, an arm wrapped around his upper stomach as he laughed, and he beamed as he stated, "That's *funny.*"

I watched as Zoey pressed her lips together to hold back her laugh, her green eyes shining at his amusement.

"You wanna sort him out?" I asked her in a grumble.

Zoey argued, "Hey, he's not wrong. You in a strip club is *hilarious.* What are ya gonna do? Ask a stripper to go on a date before she gives you a dance?"

"I'm not going to *ask* for a dance," I clarified, grabbing my glass and taking a quick sip. "I'll get in, get out, get back home. It's a visit of obligation."

"Uh huh, sure," Zoey countered as Claire slid her a bottle of cider and Liam a beer. "Which one you going to? Red Light? Gas Lamp? PT's? Rifle Ralph's?"

Liam lifted his beer, smiling widely at her until he took a drink.

"Are those real places?" I questioned. "The fuck is *Rifle Ralph's?*"

"All very real," Zoey noted. "Rifle Ralph's is full nude—*you should go to Rifle Ralph's.*"

I glanced at Liam. "Are you not concerned about how she knows this?"

"Nah," he replied in a snicker. "We already had the talk. If she wants to apply for a job at a strip club, I told her I'd do the same—"

"And I do *not* want the housewives or house*men* of this town or the ones surrounding it scraping their nails down his body, so that dream died about a millisecond after it was born," Zoey quipped.

"Dirty Dan's would've paid well," Liam remarked quietly, and Zoey elbowed him hard enough in the ribcage for her dainty force to cause him to cough and giggle simultaneously.

Luke and Claire laughed at their exchange, the entrance dinged overhead once more, and I peeked toward it with a smile on my face. My smile fell away quickly, and I took a large sip of whiskey because Cassie had just walked in.

She was tall. For a woman, I suppose—five foot nine, maybe five foot ten. Her brown hair was straight—like a curtain of rain that fell from her head down to her waist and fuckin' *shimmered.* Swear to God, it *shimmered.*

I mean, *fuck,* did she put *glitter* in it? I didn't fuckin' know—*doesn't matter.*

Her smile was…large. Blinding. It would scrunch up her slim nose and warp her freckles, pinch the corners of her brown eyes, and turn them into tiny slits. Due to it being early November, it was freezing as shit outside…and for whatever reason, she was wearing a crop top. It had long sleeves, but, y'know—*still*. The white fabric stopped just above her waist, showing off her stomach and a *very* tiny belly button ring. Her legs were long. Tan. I couldn't *see* that they were tan right now, considering that she was wearing jeans.

Thank God she was wearing jeans.

No, I just knew that they were tan because we had met over the summer, and every day that I saw her, she wore shorts. *Short* shorts. Denim shorts. Black, white, blue, every goddamn color imaginable—you bet your ass she had them. Wearing that along with a pair of black high-top kicks, she'd stroll into Henry's, say hello to her brother, and…I don't know…exist.

Whatever.

I sound bitter, I know. I can't fuckin' help it.

She waved a white-tip manicured hand at us all, held up an index finger to signify that she would be right back, and strolled directly to the women's room.

"Do you have to do that *every* time she comes in here?" Claire muttered.

"Do what?" I returned.

"Have a look on your face that screams that you'd rather her be literally anywhere else."

I sighed. "That obvious?"

Claire snorted. "You're not exactly a master of disguise, Jay."

I couldn't help but laugh at that.

Luke interjected, "Drop it, baby—he's just not a fan. It's all good."

"Cas can be a lot," Liam interjected in an understanding tone. "I get it."

Oh, Liam, you are far from getting it.

"She's *nice,*" Claire whined back.

"Claire's right," Zoey nearly sang, her pixie cut tilting to the side as she argued alongside the rest. "Cassie's nice."

"Yeah, she's plenty nice," I retorted. "No qualms."

"If you had *no qualms,* you wouldn't glare at her so much," Claire argued. "What's your deal?"

"So—*not* dropping it," Luke murmured.

"She's..."

I considered my words, and nothing came out. Instead, I buried my face in my whiskey and shrugged. Claire grumbled something about me needing to *play nice,* and she wandered off to check on the few customers who were sitting at the tables to the right of the bar.

What could I say? That she'd gotten under my skin? That she sends my mind somewhere I didn't want it to be? That I was wholly tired of seeing her?

No, I couldn't say any of those things because the insinuation would be damning. It wasn't that I didn't like Cassie. She was fine, really. More than fine. Nice girl. Good sense of humor. Attractive as all hell, obviously, and there was no doubt that some sort of chemistry lingered between us. I felt it constantly—it was a low simmering that had started off in the base of my gut and warped its way up into my chest over the past few months.

I wasn't an idiot. I knew what the feeling insinuated, and I wasn't averse to romance—quite the contrary. I had considered exploring this...this *crush* with Cassie. I had given it significant thought, as I typically do with all things in my life. However, she was...*young*...nearly a decade my junior. And she was *Liam's little sister*—so it could cause some sort of a rift within our tight-knit group.

Therefore, she was off limits...and that was *fine.* The crush that felt rather inappropriate at times would dissipate eventually. There were certain times that were more difficult than others to repress the desire that I held for Cassie Cohen, though...and for whatever reason, tonight was one of those times.

I felt rather than saw her slink into the stool on my left. It was where she usually sat—directly next to me, so close that I could feel the heat of her through my clothing.

Cassie reached for my glass, brought it to her lips, and took a large sip. The act was one that she repeated every time we were both at Henry's—she would steal my whiskey, drink the remainder of it, and buy me my next round. She did it with a teasing smile. A playful attitude that dared me to, I don't know, chastise her for it.

She did so just now, and even though I knew it was coming, the gesture twisted something up inside of me. It was the typical yearning that I experienced around her and, as usual, I had to stifle the urge to grab her by the back of her neck, yank her lips to mine to taste the whiskey on her tongue that she had stolen from me, and remind her that the next round is on her.

I closed my eyes for a beat, took a cleansing breath through my nostrils, and let it out—because *that* just couldn't happen. Normally, I would shoot Luke a glance and he would get me my next drink, but for whatever reason, I was feeling especially weak tonight. So weak that I just...needed to go *home.*

"You have such good taste," Cassie joked as she set my glass down in front of herself, taking it as her own.

"Cas," Liam admonished her. "Stop bothering him."

I sighed. "Uh huh. Good taste. Right. I'm, ah—I'm outta here tonight, actually."

"Oh, *come on,* Jay," Cassie complained. *"Stay.* Have fun. *Please."*

The last word came out as a playful beg, and she pouted out her lower lip in a way that made me want to bite it. I considered her last word for only a moment until my brain damn near screamed at me.

"Early morning at work," I lied, needlessly telling her, "Go ahead and drink my whiskey—I won't."

Luke and Claire griped from behind the counter, stating that the night was still plenty young. Zoey loudly agreed with them, and Liam mirrored similar thoughts aloud from the right of her.

I didn't listen to them, though. I paid my tab, began walking toward the front door, and caught Cassie frowning as I chanced a peek back at her. She waved goodbye, I waved back, and I returned home to sleep, eat, and repeat.

Chapter 2

I woke with a flinch of my entire body, my heart and mind racing. I immediately rolled over and tapped my phone, which laid on my bedside table, to check the time, and it glowed as it read: *2:00 A.M.*

On the goddamn dot.

I laid back with a grunt, placing my hand on my bare chest and finding it damp with a cool sheen of sweat. I grimaced, the feel of it along with the tremor of unease that ran in my veins an unwelcome one, and the memory of the dream remained vivid in my mind. I pressed the heels of my palms into my eyes until I began to see stars, blinked *hard,* and sighed at what replayed in my brain.

His legs were warm. Skinny to the point that my hands wrapped around them completely, my thumb overlapping my index finger on either ankle as I helped carry him. Pale. So pale that I wondered if it was due to the stoppage of blood flow to his extremities. But warm—that was the biggest thing that I remembered about it, for whatever reason—his legs were still warm.

I thought about it as I sat in Claire and Zoey's apartment a mere hour after we had disposed of him, watched him float away, and drove back to the complex. It was a ridiculous notion that we could all just go back to life as we all knew it, but that's what I felt as though I was expected to do. I sat on the couch with my head in my hands for...fuck, I don't know how long...and I was alone. Remarkably alone. Luke had Claire. Zoey had Liam—a fact that I was rapidly putting behind me. But as far as leaning on someone who could fully grasp the situation at hand, I had no one.

And it wasn't until then that I realized that Cassie was also home alone, battling her own demons just as I was.

I audibly scoffed at the idea the first time I considered it, for I didn't know her. It felt like I did, but I didn't, really. I had only met her twelve hours previously, and in those hours, she managed to immediately drive her way right under my skin, scared the ever-living shit out of me by going against all of our suggestions, made me think she could be dead in the woods somewhere, and actively helped us all consider how to dispose of a corpse. I didn't know her—but I was fairly certain that despite that, she and I were somehow trauma bonded just as the rest of our group was.

I mean, we dove toward each other while bullets were flying, for God's sake. She yanked me away from a line of fire. And now, both of us were sitting in our own abodes, wrestling with what I could only assume were similar dark thoughts.

The more that I thought about it, the crazier it seemed that we weren't in the comfort of each other's presence...so, after the seventh time that I eyeballed my car keys on the kitchen table, I stood from the couch to grab them. I drove to Cassie's place, which was straight north of me and directly into the woods. I parked in front of her tiny cabin of a house. I shut my car door loudly, as if I needed to announce my arrival, and I stood next to my vehicle for upward of a minute.

A full goddamn minute.

A full minute of attempting to talk myself out of being here. A full minute of telling myself that this was stupid. A full minute of wondering if sleep deprivation could drive someone insane.

And then, she opened her front door.

She stood on her patio in a flimsy pair of white shorts and an oversized navy t-shirt. Her hair up in a bun, her feet bare, her face tired, it was so quiet that she barely had to raise her voice to speak to me.

"*What are you doing here?*"

"Um..." I hesitated, my mind having gone blank, and I replied with a shrug, "I—I don't fuckin' know."

She crossed her arms. "I'm not a woman that needs comforting, if that's what you're thinking. I'm far from a damsel in distress—"

"I didn't think you were," I called back quickly.

"Then what?" she asked, her dark eyes narrowed in honest inquisition.

"I could use the company," I admitted. "Could you?"

Her arms fell by her side, her defensive stature dropped, and she nodded.

"Do you like whiskey?"

I felt my eyebrows pinch together. "I mean, yeah, but it's well before noon."

She threw her hands up. "I don't even know what time is right now, Jay. It's all relative, and no matter what the actual time of day is, I'm getting drunk. I don't want to talk about shit. All I want to do is blast these memories out of my skull with the help of my friend Jack Daniel's—and then, I'm sleeping for twenty-four hours."

Her words resonated through me, for diving into a void sounded damn near blissful. Even more, there was no mention of confiding in each other otherwise. It was an invitation to drink—to silently feel without inquisition—until we no longer could. And the more Cassie's words sank in, the more it felt like a necessity.

"You got another glass?"

"Only if you can keep up," she returned without a trace of sarcasm. "You're already here; don't make me black out alone."

I nodded in return, and she watched me as I lumbered my way up the stairs of her porch, moving to stand before her. She exhaled softly, the scent of fresh whiskey on her breath. The smell was hot—so much so that it stung my nostrils, and I considered that the liquor was most likely so recently drunk that it was still burning her tongue and lingering in her throat. I looked into her eyes, and though they were, without a doubt, exhausted, they still challenged me. I didn't know what for—they just did—and I had the desire to ask if she was alright. To inquire about her mental wellbeing after witnessing all of the horrid things that we both did...but there was no use for any of that. There was no point in asking because I knew we were both in a poor state. So, instead, I put my hands on my hips and spoke:

"You started without me?"

She shrugged. "Didn't know you were coming. You blame me?"

I shook my head. "Nah."

And so, she allowed me into her home, the rusty orange tile and dark green accents in the small kitchen familiar to me, for I had been here mere hours ago before we had all done the unspeakable. I sat at her circular dining table, all that rested upon it being a handle of Jack Daniel's that was mostly full and a single lowball glass. Cassie silently grabbed me my own glass, set it down before me with a clunk, and poured.

She sat across from me, and I looked to her, to my full glass, and then back into her eyes. She tipped her head toward my drink.

"Catch up."

I drank obediently; she filled her glass and did the same, and we continued until we were both most certainly succumbing to the effects of the alcohol. Occasionally, one of us would repeat the actions from before—grab, pour, drink—and the other would follow suit. What neither of us did, however, was speak. We simply sat with each other, drinking for the sole purpose of numbness, and the silence stretched on for there was nothing to say.

It was perhaps an hour later when we had both had more than enough. I felt my eyelids begin to droop, and the only thing that kept them open was Cassie's dark gaze turning to mine. The beautiful brown was glossed over, lost in a haze, and she threw me the tiniest of smiles. Her hand reached for mine that had been resting on the tabletop, and she squeezed. Patting it twice before letting it go in a gesture of thanks, Cassie stood from her seat.

It scooted across the tile with a grating noise, her tall body swayed, and her footsteps, which I had recently come to realize were typically graceful, were suddenly not. She stomped heavily—loudly down the only hallway that was in the house. I knew it led to a small bathroom on the right-hand side, and I could only assume that her bedroom was in the same vicinity down that hall.

"G'night, Jay," she called back to me with a not-so-gentle wave of her hand, and she disappeared into a door on the left.

Though she hadn't said I could use it, I helped myself to her couch. It was sat in the living area next to the front door, just before the kitchen. In front of a large, black, cast-iron fireplace, the brown couch called to me, and I sprawled across it. The memory of my bumbling steps toward my sleeping arrangements was lost to the liquor, but the thoughts that remained in my mind that night were not.

They were loud. Belligerent. They screamed at me to follow her—to join her in her bed, embrace her from behind, and allow us both to settle into the contentment of another's arms. To wake in several hours having not moved an inch and, behind the veil of a hangover, feel each other's bodies and distract ourselves with ecstasy. To drown out the noise in our minds by listening instead to the newfound sounds that either one of us made in the throes of passion.

My mind reeled with the thought, and she was so close that I could taste it—but even heavily under the influence, I knew that the choice would have been a poor one.

I left before she could wake the next morning, tip-toeing over the tile and closing my car's door so softly that I didn't even hear it click shut.

The memory was real—colorful and full of life despite the reminder of the event being somber. And I had no idea what spurred it. It had left me breathless, my chest tight with the feeling of longing that I had experienced months ago whilst in mental turmoil.

I attempted to shiver it away, but it remained. It, along with the sight of the man we had disposed of, lingered in my brain, forcing anxiety to drip over me and trail down my spine. My back arched at the sensation as I cringed away from it, and I stood from my bed with a groan.

I paced the apartment. Chugged a glass of water. Took not one but *two* showers—one hot and one cold—neither helped. No matter what I tried, the sensation hovered over me, and it stayed until it was time for me to ready myself for work. I did so slowly, allowing my routine to busy my mind as much as it possibly could. I cranked the radio as I drove, focusing on the lyrics of the songs and the rambling drivel of the commercials.

It was my work that allowed me to truly distract myself, though, and I had *never* been more thankful to see businesses in financial ruin via poorly invested stocks. I dove into it, took a short lunch, and worked late.

I most likely would have worked late regardless of my state of mind, though, because it was Friday. The day that I had agreed to go out with Shawn. I was told the establishment we were planning on visiting was only a stone's throw away from work, so I buckled down until 8:00, input the directions in the map app on my phone, and drove.

I eventually sat in my car, parked in the lot outside, taking in the view of the front. It was *busy*—so busy that I had struggled to even find a place to park. The building was nothing special, really. It looked like all the others in this area of the city—grey and single-storied. The only thing that made it stand out from the rest was the large, neon-red lighting that displayed the name in all caps right above the door:

GAS LAMP

Shawn stood with Tommy in waiting to the right of the entrance, and I grumbled as I began to make my way to them. I had met Tommy earlier in the day. Though seemingly fine while I had introduced myself, I couldn't help but notice his appearance—blonde hair that seemed to be styled with so much product, I could almost *hear* it crunch as he turned his head. A smile so unnaturally white, you would think he were a walking commercial for brightening strips. With the way that he spoke with several *bro's* and *chill's* interlaced into his sentences, I wondered if he were a part of a fraternity in college. If so, the persona had most certainly stuck to him like glue. He wore wraparound sunglasses with a blueish-tinted mirror finish, and I grimaced at the sight.

"Tats?" Tommy's obscured gaze trailed over my arms. The night was less chilly than anticipated, and I had rolled the long sleeves that I typically wear for work up to my forearms. *"Nice, bro*—lose the glasses if you wanna get laid."

I squinted at him. *"Yeah,* I don't anticipate meeting someone here."

"Are we ready, then?" Tommy ignored my notion, questioning me and Shawn with a wide grin on his face.

"Ah—yeah, ready," Shawn replied.

"What are *those?*"

I pointed to Tommy's face. Not toward his teeth; I wasn't *that* much of an asshole—to his eyewear.

He gestured to them with a wave of his hand. "These? Oakley's, man!"

"The sun has set," I reminded him bluntly, looking toward the night sky.

"It's an accessory," he told me offhandedly.

I retorted, "Mmkay, well, that *accessory* is making you legally blind, considering that it's *night time* and we're going to be *inside.*"

Tommy's blonde brows bobbled up and down, and he tilted his head downward to peek at me from behind the frames. "Well, I'll be able to *feel* plenty."

I fucking hate this guy.

I scoffed. "What, are you gonna grope the dancers as if you're trying to *read fucking braille?*"

Shawn interjected, *"Jay—"*

I held up a hand in his direction, an index finger and thumb pressed dangerously close together. *"This* close to abandoning ship, Brooks."

Shawn held up one finger. "You promised me at least one beer's worth of time."

"Yeah, man, chill—you gotta at *least* get a few dances," Tommy spoke.

I stared at Shawn, muttering, "Is this a test of my patience?"

Tommy chuckled, my annoyance a thorough amusement for him. The noise grated on my ears.

Shawn returned to me, *"Okay,* come on," as he patted me between my shoulder blades. "Let's go."

I whispered, *"You owe me."*

"Uh huh," Shawn replied instantly as we walked on. "I'm gathering that already."

A sign by the front door announced that it was *Cosmic Night.* The lights were dim in the club, and there were blacklights abound. Loud music blared overhead, and the girls wore glow-in-the-dark, strappy getups that shined to show off their greatest assets. We shouldered through what had to have been hundreds of men to find open seats, came across a few closer to the back of the club, and sat. The seating was booth-like in nature, curved, and arranged around a raised, circular stage. I watched the dancers warily as they wandered around us, every so often rotating the woman before us. I declined dances, shrugged away from suggestive grazes of women's touches on my shoulders, and sipped at the ten-dollar beer that I had purchased as I wondered how a bunch of thirty-something-year-old men sitting around watching each other get blue-balled was supposed to be entertaining.

After what was my one beer's worth of time, Tommy nearly shouted, "Yo, can someone buy Turner a dance already?"

I intended to tell him to shut the fuck up, but my words just...left me. My mind turned *numb*. I closed my mouth, for it had fallen open.

She was long legs and strappy heels. Her athletic body was barely covered by a string bikini that glowed bright green. Straight, dark hair hung down to her waist, and her makeup had flecks of luminescence along her cheeks that simulated freckles—the shining freckles continued down her abdomen, all over her arms and thighs, and it forced me to wonder if the beauty marks would exist underneath the makeup. A thin line of eyeliner made from the same glowing material was shining on her upper lids, and the small piercing in her navel was in a similar neon color.

Fuck. Cassie.

Even in the dark of the blacklights, I could tell that it was her. I struggled to gather my thoughts—to recall conversations that I had listened to over the past few months. She had said she was an accountant...*right?* An accountant who works at a call center with graveyard hours. *Not* an exotic dancer—*I would have fucking remembered that.*

I tore my eyes away from her, and Shawn elbowed me.

"*Her.* Get a dance from *her.*"

"I—what?" I stammered in an oddly high pitch. "No, no. I can't."

"Saw you lookin', Jay," he noted as he wiggled his thick brows. "C'mon. She's cute."

I exhaled heavily. *Apparently,* while the remainder of my close-knit group had thankfully mistaken my feelings for Cassie to be ones of distaste, Shawn saw right through me in one glance. No one else had ever witnessed me seeing Cassie half-naked for the first time either, though, so I ushered away the consideration that Shawn was a telepath.

"Brooks..."

I began to put together some sort of an explanation, but my words fell short. I didn't know what they were going to be in the first place—I would have figured something out eventually, I always do—but I didn't get the chance. Cassie was making her way toward us, I was thoroughly considering getting up and escaping through the back door, and Tommy reached out an arm to halt her steps.

And the room turned green. Not literally, of course, but the oh-so-familiar feeling of jealousy crept up my spine and forced me to sit up straight. I wanted to tell him not to fucking look at her. To not grab her hand and hold it—*like he was currently fucking doing*. And to not, for the love of God, ask her for a dance.

"Hi," Tommy spoke, and she looked down at him with a dazzling smile. *"Hi* there," he repeated, cash in hand extended to her. *"You* are gorgeous. Can I get a—"

"Oh, thanks, man." The words were out of my mouth before I could even stop them, and Tommy's head turned in my direction. I remarked to her, "He wanted to buy me a dance."

Cassie finally caught my eye, and her brows shot up into oblivion. The look was the embodiment of surprise—it was just as good as if she were to have stumbled backward on her stilettos, fell on her ass, and clutched at her metaphorical pearls in shock. She looked me up and down—thoroughly, I assumed, to ensure that I was, in fact, who she thought I was—and I offered her a smile that pulled up half of my lips. The look of pure shock fell off of her face, and I saw her shoulders slump down as she appeared to let out a long breath.

It was a moment shared only between us that lasted a split second.

"You want a dance?" she asked with an upward inflection.

What am I doing?

"Yeah," I replied with a nod.

Okay, seriously, what the fuck am I doing?

Chapter 3

I had no answer for my internal monologue as it sharply questioned my choice of action. I simply watched Cassie happily snatch the dollar bills that Tommy had extended to her and tuck them into the strings of her bottoms. She mouthed, *'Thank you,'* and the dialogue in my mind silenced itself.

Tommy laughed disbelievingly, shaking his head as he called to her, "Come back to me once he's done with you!"

She rolled her eyes, but her smile remained as she threw him a gentle wave, curling her fingers in his direction. Cassie grinned at Shawn, who had disbelief and glee written across his face, and as she strolled past me, she shot me a questioning glance. I didn't get a chance to respond—as I was sitting on the end of the booth, Cassie had whipped herself around it to stand behind me, a hand grazing my chest as she moved.

She leaned down, whispering in my ear, "Fancy seeing you here."

Vanilla. She was so close to me that I could smell some kind of vanilla-scented shampoo that lingered in her hair. *God dammit.*

All I could think to reply with was a softly chastising, "I thought you were an accountant."

"And I thought you had perfect eyesight, yet here we are," she teased me, grabbed my glasses on either side of my face, and pushed them up so they sat on top of my head.

"Astigmatism," I clarified. "I use them for driving at night and computer glare—*ah!*" I audibly gasped as Cassie's nails raked gently from my chest down to my ribs. "Fuck, I'm *ticklish-don't-do-that, Cas.*"

She laughed, and her breath ran over my neck. "You learn something new every day."

"Feeling like you're avoiding the topic at hand," I retorted quietly. "You work *here?*"

"Yeah...Liam doesn't know I'm a stripper," she stated plainly. "And I'd rather that he continues not knowing this tidbit about my life, if you know what I'm getting at."

"Mum's the word."

Cassie pushed on either of my shoulders, standing up straight, and spun around the edge of the booth to face me. Without hesitation, she placed a knee on either side of my thighs, her hair brushing against my shirt as she looked down at me.

Her hips rotated above my crotch, and I swallowed through a large lump in my throat. "You don't have to actually give me a dance."

We both continued to speak to each other in hushed tones, our conversation a private one not to be heard by others.

She cocked her head to the side. "It *is* my job—if I don't dance, I get reamed," she admitted in a mockingly dramatic tone. "There are cameras *everywhere*. Boss-man is always watching. So...I could make my way back to your friend who paid me, or..."

"Not my friend," I muttered back. "Was just trying to save you from him being an obnoxious ass."

"Ah, chivalry *isn't* dead, then," she murmured, and I couldn't help but let out a soft breath of a laugh through my nose. *"So*—dance? Or no dance?"

I considered the sight of her writhing on top of Tommy for less than a second.

"Stay."

Her smile was blinding, as usual. "'Kay." Cassie then rocked herself above me. I glanced down to witness the glory that is her body, squeezed my eyes shut for one tight blink, and she noted, "You could at least pretend like you're enjoying yourself, though. Put your hands on my ass."

If my mouth hadn't been stripped dry by this interaction, I would have choked.

"What?"

She laughed. "You look like you're in *pain*. Don't be so stiff. Just imagine I'm someone else."

"Fuck, that's impossible...I thought we weren't supposed to touch the dancers?"

Cassie grabbed my empty beer out of my right hand and glanced at Shawn, who had scooted down several feet to give us a wide berth.

She asked him, "Can you hold this for your friend?"

"Yes!" Shawn grabbed it from her almost immediately, his amused eyes twinkling at the sight before him.

Cassie stated, "Gas Lamp is dancer's choice as long as it's not *too* groping," and grasped both of my wrists. She placed the palms of my hands on either side of her hips, the glowing strings to the bikini bottom and the dollars tucked away there grazing my thumbs. Her skin was soft on my fingers, and I couldn't stop myself from giving the area a generous squeeze.

"There you go," she crooned.

Her tone—her *confidence*—tempted me. Called to me on a level that made excitement thrum through my veins—attempted to force the façade of my disinterest in her to fall the wayside as she was inviting me in. The feeling was dangerous, and I wanted with everything in me to fall right into it. To say that, *fuck,* I was in Rome—and I was to do as the Romans do and allow myself to relish in the feeling of her body on mine for as long as she would remain here.

Cassie's eyes sparkled as she rose up on her knees, brushing the tip of her nose up the side of my face until the fabric of her top was staring at me. The small, gentle curves of her breasts were but an inch away from my mouth, the freckled makeup spatters on her chest shining in the blacklight, and I had the burning urge to bite at the string that held the bottom of the two triangles of material together. Her hands tangled in the hair on the back of my scalp, pulling to angle my face up to hers, and any joking disposition that she had fell away. Cassie looked down at me; her hair shielded us from the world like a curtain, and suddenly, we were in a universe that was all our own. The movement of her hips stopped, her fingers flexed at the roots of my scalp, and her doe eyes turned serious. Our breaths mingled together within the confines of her beautiful, dark tresses, and it was there.

A connection.

A locking of eyes that felt as though it were tying me to the ground itself.

I had felt it before—not with Cassie, until just now—with other women in the past. It would have typically sent my heart racing, I'd yearn to deepen it all with the seal of a kiss or the clashing of our bodies, and I'd fall. *Hard and quick.* That was how it always happened for me when I'd feel...*this*. I hadn't experienced it in a long while—years, probably—but the connection I had with Cassie at this instant didn't send me reaching for the stars as it usually did. Instead, because of the boundaries I had set for myself combined with the raging sexual tension that I constantly experienced with her, it brought me some sort of twisted grief that I couldn't come to terms with, and I needed it to end.

Now.

My voice was hoarse as I said, "Get off me, Cas."

"What?" she whispered. "Why? I haven't finished. We've got more time in the song—"

"I don't want it. You're right—this *is* painful," I gruffly stated and quickly lied, "I don't want you on me. I shouldn't have even spoken up before. I wish you didn't *fucking work here. Please* fucking get off of me."

Cassie blinked rapidly. Her prior confidence—the one that she always wore—wavered, and my stomach sank because it wasn't my intention to be a gigantic asshole. I didn't mean to curse at her in an odd tone that made me sound as if I were being actively burned. It all just...fell out of me...and if there were any opportunity for me to pick it all up and shove it back in my mouth, I would have.

Her eyes darted away from mine. "*Shit,* um, sorry."

"Cassie—"

Cassie flipped her hair back, exposing us both once more, and her demeanor immediately shifted. She wore a soft smile, but her eyes had hardened—she traced her fingers down my chest, but she was stiff.

"If it looks like we're arguing, you'll get escorted out," she muttered with a brief flash of her teeth.

"I don't want to argue."

She returned sharply, *"Then don't."*

Her hands left me, she shifted slightly to gracefully move her body off of mine, and I couldn't stop—*wouldn't* have stopped even if I had the ability to do so. One of my hands whipped out to grab her wrist, and though she halted her actions and smiled down at me with what would have been a smoldering, enticing expression, all I could see in her gaze was...sadness. And *that* hit me right in the gut.

"I didn't mean it like that," I said just loud enough for only Cassie to hear. "I'm *sorry.*"

Cassie pulled her wrist from mine in a subtle act that came across as her coyly waving me goodbye, and she stood.

As if our interaction had never happened, she strolled away from me casually, and I stared blankly as she sauntered her way over to Tommy. Though comical to note that his teeth—which I had no doubt were cheap veneers—were glowing light purple under the blacklight, any trace of humor I could have had regarding that was whisked away. Cassie had bent at the hips slightly, placed a hand on Tommy's chest, and he tipped his head so far back that his sunglasses looked to the ceiling. Her touch traced its way up to his neck, and she spun to face away from him.

Our eyes locked, and for just a moment, I saw her anger. Her *hurt* at my unnecessarily harsh words. The expression washed off of her face, replaced with a mask of general seduction, and she lowered herself to brush the back of her body against his. My jaw clenched as I watched her. Watched her angle her face to his and whisper something in his ear. Watched her hips circle to the left and right on top of him. Watched his hands reach for her, find her ribcage, and squeeze.

He wandered, one hand up to her right breast and the other down to her left hip, and I felt my gaze widen, focused on his touch on her chest. Cassie's free hand flashed out to remove his hand from where I was glaring. She placed it pointedly against her other hip and continued on. One sashay to the right, one sashay to the left, and the grip that she had moved was gliding from her hip down to her inner thigh. It grazed along the seam of her bottoms on her crotch, and I was certain that my nostrils flared with the jagged breath that I took at the sight.

Cassie mouthed what I could barely make out as, *'Stop,'* Tommy's fingers flexed into her skin, and the metaphorical colored tinge of my sight shifted rapidly from green to red.

Jealousy foregone, I could feel blood boil through my veins as Cassie's seductive little smile was wiped from her lips and replaced with annoyance. She grabbed at each of his hands, pushing them aside as she clearly was moving to make her way away from him, and he wrapped around her tighter. One grip back on her top, his other arm reached across her lap and pulled her onto his.

"Tommy, *she said stop,*" Shawn called to him, but it didn't appear to reach his ears.

Cassie tried to scramble to her feet, having toppled off of them and onto Tommy, and she chastised him in words that I couldn't hear. She twisted her body sharply away from his hand on her chest, his grasp on the fabric remained strong, and her breast was exposed as it was yanked aside.

"Tommy!" Shawn yelled this time, and by the time his name left his mouth, I was standing.

I rushed to them in a matter of two steps, grabbed his fingers that were touching her, and yanked, twisting them backward with enough force for the digits to touch the tops of his hands. I heard multiple satisfying *cracks,* and Tommy responded angrily:

"*AH,* the fuck is your *problem,* Turner?!"

I grabbed Cassie by her upper arms and pulled her to stand.

"Jay," she spoke to me in a warning as she gathered her balance, quickly adjusting her top. I ushered her behind me, ignoring her call of my name.

I leaned down to Tommy's eye level. "She said *fucking STOP!*"

It came out in a scream that reverberated through my vocal cords, and before I could say—or *do*—anything else, I felt her hand on my shoulder.

"Jay—" Her words to me were cut off short, and she spoke to someone else, "Where the fuck were *you?!*"

I stood straight, staring at Tommy with an unspoken, *'Don't move.'* It didn't appear that he was intending to at any time soon, though, for he was grimacing at his fingers that looked to be immobile. A man replied to Cassie from my right.

"I was helping Skylar," he noted. "We good?"

"No," she retorted angrily, "we are not *good,* Trevor." I saw her throw a hand toward Tommy in my peripheral vision. "Fucker yanked my tit out."

Tommy grumbled, "We were gonna see them eventually—"

I couldn't stop myself from saying, *"Tommy,* I will *fuck you up."*

"James," Cassie admonished me.

"Alright, alright," the man, who I assumed was a bouncer, spoke again, and I glanced his way to see a bald man around my height and approximately one hundred pounds heavier than me. He held up a hand at us all. "No fights, guys—time to go."

"Yup," I replied quickly. "Let's get out of here—Shawn?"

"Uh huh," he immediately returned, pushing himself to his feet. "Leaving. Got it."

"Don't leave. You're my ride," Tommy complained.

"You're getting kicked out, guy," Trevor, the bouncer, told him plainly.

Shawn scoffed at Tommy. "I'm not your ride anymore. You can get yourself back to wherever you're going. Jay—leaving?"

He clapped me on the shoulder, and I huffed out a breath. "Yeah, ah..." I looked at Cassie, and she muttered a forcedly casual:

"See you 'round, Jay."

I pressed my lips together tightly, and nodded. "Bye, Cas."

Shawn and I walked on without a look back at Tommy, I genuinely hoped that Trevor would throw him out the back door and break his sunglasses in the process, and we shoved past the men who crowded the various other dancing stages as we made our way out of the establishment the exact way we came in.

The moment that we hit the chilly air of the outdoors, Shawn asked, "What the *fuck* just happened?"

"A lot," I replied succinctly. "I'm gonna find a way to get Tommy fucking fired." I pointed at Shawn accusatorily as our steps took us into the parking lot. "You *had* to take his suggestion. It *had* to be a strip club. It had to be *fucking this one—*"

"Okay, let's back up," Shawn interjected with a hand held up. "First off, I heard Tommy's fingers crack—if he comes to work with casts on his hands, he could say that you assaulted him. I'm *with you.* I'll fill out paperwork vouching for whatever you say, but getting him *fired* may be out of the realm of possibility with whatever you were planning since he's *injured.*"

"I don't fuckin' care," I griped. "I'll make something else up. Management likes me. Whose side are they *really* gonna be on?"

"That aside," Shawn continued, "who was that stripper?"

"Dancer," I corrected him.

"Dancer. Who was that *dancer?"*

"Ah." I glanced at him, saw that he was looking at me with raised eyebrows, and I spoke as if it were a question, "I don't know?"

"She knew your name," he remarked. "Had a little *private* conversation with you before she got off of you just as quick as she had hopped on. Called you *Jay,* not James—several times. You called her *Cas."*

"We exchanged names when she jumped on my lap and started grinding on me," I lied in a bitterly sarcastic tone. "Jay's a common nickname for people whose names start with," I gasped dramatically, *"the letter J."*

"Come on, man."

I groaned loudly, slowing my steps as I arrived at my car. When I turned to face Shawn and realized that he had no intention of letting down, I rattled off:

"My brother's girlfriend's old roommate? We had a...*thing*...a very brief thing a few months back."

"Uh huh," Shawn replied hesitantly. "You told me about her—Zoey, yeah?"

"Yeah. We called it quits; you know that. She's dating someone new—*that guy's little sister?* Is Cassie." I threw a hand back toward the building. "Dancer Cassie."

His eyebrows pinched together. "Oh. Are, uh—you guys even close?"

"Yeah." I immediately corrected myself with, "No," and then stammered, "It—it's complicated. I don't fuckin' know."

"From the look on your face earlier, you didn't know she worked here?" Shawn guessed.

I laughed sardonically. *"No, I didn't know!* I wouldn't have come near the place with a fifty-foot-fucking-*pole* if I knew that!"

His head tipped to the side. "You have a problem with her being a stripper?"

"Dancer," I corrected him for the second time.

"Dancer."

I sighed. "I—no?"

Shawn smiled. "You don't seem very confident in that answer."

"I'm not."

"What's the deal, Jay?" He asked and waited for me to respond. I couldn't find it in me to do so, and he finally deduced, *"Oh,* you're into her."

I rested my backside against the tailgate of my car. "She's driving me fucking insane."

"It would appear so." Shawn leaned in a similar fashion on my vehicle to my left.

I glanced at him. "I was a dick to her earlier."

Shawn's head bobbed backward. "You ripped Tommy's hands off of her, and it did *not* look like she wanted them there. How's that being a dick?"

Of course, he hadn't heard our quiet exchange. Between our hushed voices and the loud music around us, our conversation had fallen on lost ears.

*"No, no...*before that. She was on top of me, and it was all...I don't know...*intense* for a second...and I snapped at her."

"Snapped at her?"

"JAMES!"

I closed my eyes and sighed. "Shit."

I glanced toward the source of my shrieked name and saw Cassie walking toward the both of us with intent. An oversized black hoodie swallowed her, hanging down to her upper thigh. Flimsy sweat shorts just barely poked out from the hem of it, the sky-blue material blowing in the light breeze with every step she took. Her heels were gone, replaced with her usual black high-tops, which were absolutely stomping their way to us. Arms crossed over her chest and eyes narrowed in an accusatory stare, it was all too apparent that she was pissed.

Shawn had pushed himself to stand, but he remained stuck in place as he watched her approach me with wide eyes and a high brow.

I asked, "Why are you out here, Cas?"

"Why am I here?" she retorted as she stopped her steps in front of me, hands now on her hips. "The fuck do you *mean* why am I here? Why did you *come here?*"

Her outright anger made me initially stammer, "I—um—Brooks—"

"I dragged him out," Shawn quickly spoke. "He didn't even want to—"

Cassie held out a hand, palm facing outward to him. "You seem nice. You do, so...y'know, don't take this the wrong way, but *shut your trap.* Give us a minute."

"Easy, Cas," I attempted to assuage her, but she steamrolled on.

"Don't *easy Cas* me," she snapped, her squinting eyes now locked on me and bringing my attention to her makeup. The once glow-in-the-dark freckles were a light blue without the help of a blacklight, and I couldn't stop my gaze from tracing each one of them. "That was fucking. *Mortifying.* James."

Her admonishment hit me in the gut. "Cassie, I'm—"

I intended to apologize, but she interjected with a single index finger in the air, "No, no—*I'm* talking now. You show up to my work. You ask for a dance. *You asked for it, Jay.* I start to give you one...you *freak the fuck out,* tell me to stop, and fuckin' berate me for doing it in the first place. You tell me you wish I didn't work here." The hurt leaked into her voice at the last sentence, and she paused before sneering, "Is that what you wanted? Was that your *plan?* You find out I'm a stripper and show up to my work just to embarrass the shit out of me?"

"No," I replied, aghast. "God, no—I had no idea you worked here at all; I didn't mean to..." I thought back to how I had spoken to her earlier and exhaled heavily. "I didn't mean to be such a dick, Cas. I'm sorry."

"If you're gonna go all *protective brother* on me and get pissed over what I do for work, then don't ask me for a goddamn dance!"

Protective brother?

I blinked at the phrasing, allowing it to settle over me, and heard it once more in my mind.

Protective. Brother.

It forced my spine to straighten, and my tone dipped down deep as I questioned aloud, *"Protective brother?"*

Shawn, who had slowly backed away from our conversation yet was still watching from several feet away, muttered to himself, "Oh, boy."

"Yeah," Cassie returned sharply, "if I wanted that, I would have told Liam what I do for a living. And I'm glad ya cared enough to be *bothered* about the jackwagon that kept feeling me up, but—"

"But there are bouncers for that?" I interjected with grit in my voice. "Ones that were moving *way* too slowly, and I caused a scene? Yeah, I'm aware that I caused a scene, but it was *not* because I was feeling fucking *brotherly.*" Her big, doe eyes blinked slowly while she took in my statement, and the words that were on the tip of my tongue fell right out of me. "And I could show you *exactly* what I mean by that. I could make how I feel about you as clear as crystal, Cassie, but I'm not—"

"How you *feel* about me?"

The sentence could have been interpreted in several different ways when I spoke it, but my tone—my tone held an undercurrent of emotion that couldn't be misconstrued. My chest panged as the sentiment between lust and adoration hung in the air between us, but it appeared that Cassie had thoroughly missed the memo. Her reiteration of my blurted words was sneered in the same fashion as the rest of her side of the conversation, and I looked upwards as I questioned what to say.

Shawn called out, "Jay! Come *on.*"

He stood three cars away by a small, red hatchback—a vehicle that I most definitely knew was not his—and his eyes were wide and disbelieving as he stared at me with a look that screamed, *'The hell are you doing, Turner? Fess up.'*

"Brooks," I warned him, "now is *not* the time. Stop eavesdropping; I'll see you at work on Monday."

He rolled his eyes so hard that his head followed them. "James."

I bit out, *"Shawn!"*

Shawn nearly flinched at my yell of his name, and I saw his shoulders sag. "Fine, man—Monday."

He began to walk away, and Cassie complained, "So, you're just being a dick to *everyone* right now, or what?"

I spoke to the sky, "No! I'm *trying* here, Jesus!"

"Trying to be nice?" She asked with a cock of her head. "Well, you're doing a shit job at that…if you just flat out dislike me, then say it."

"No!" I groaned. "I don't *dislike* you, Cas. But *fuck,* it would be easier if I did."

She squinted at me. "What...what in the world does that mean?"

I shook my head. "Nothing. I'm being a dick—just take that at face value."

"I'm not just gonna say, *'Oh, well...Jay's being an asshole. That tracks!'*" Cassie scoffed. "That doesn't *track* for me because you're not. So...unless something *else* crawled up your ass and died, and you're deciding to take it out on me for some reason, that leaves me with *me* being the problem."

"Okay, fine. It's you."

Her brow pinched together as if she hadn't heard me clearly, and she laughed a quiet, "What?"

"I said, *'It's you,'*" I repeated bluntly, and her face fell. "It's *you* that gets under my goddamn skin. There is *no* other explanation. It. Is. *You.* And I don't want to get into it because this conversation won't end well. It just won't. So, *please,* just...go back to work."

She uttered, *"James."*

"I can't *do* this anymore, Cassie!" I snapped. "Go back to fucking *work!*"

I didn't even get a chance to catch her expression to my outburst. Cassie's hair fanned out behind her as she spun on her heel and stormed her way back into the club.

My stomach twisted as I watched her walk away.

I went too far. *Way* too far. The aggravation of constantly having to hold my tongue around her had caught up to me, and it was no excuse. But that, combined with her sheer presence, the pull she had on me that I had to continually deny, and her questioning my behavior...it was too much, and I broke.

Maybe I *was* just a dick.

With that thought and a crushing weight of guilt, I began to make my way home. My thoughts swarmed me as I drove, and I made no effort to ward them away. The radio remained off, and I allowed the berating within me to continue, the silent punishment of myself one that I knew was warranted. I was unable to escape it—the scene of me cursing at her simply played over and over until I began to feel as though my self-retribution had left me battered and bruised.

Chapter 4

I sat in Henry's in my usual seat. I had my usual drink in front of me. I could feel the cool glass against my palm and the sting of the whiskey on my tongue as I took a generous sip. I set it down, and it made a satisfying clunk against the wooden counter. The noise around me was a general, quiet hum of conversation that I was unable to discern, and the individuals who were speaking were all a blur. Liam and Zoey could have been to my right, and Luke and Claire could have been behind the bar, but I wouldn't have known...because my focus was wholeheartedly on the presence that was sinking into the stool on my left.

I could feel her as I typically could. It was cold out, but she radiated heat. Her shirt had black sleeves that covered her arms down to her wrists, and I saw the material as she reached for my drink. I honed in on it as she lifted it to her mouth, watched the liquid touch her lips, and saw her throat bob as she swallowed. I wanted to be that liquor. I think she knew that...and she smiled wide. For whatever unknown reason, the wall that I had forcibly placed between us in the past was notably absent, and I breathed a sigh of relief at the feeling of being unrestrained.

The glass remained in Cassie's hand, she lifted it toward me in a cheersing motion, and her dark eyes danced.

"I like this one."

"It's the same whiskey I get every time," I reminded her.

Her mouth stretched further. "I know." A full drink slid before me from the unknown blur behind the counter, and as I reached for it, she asked, "You're hanging around this time?"

I nodded, drained half of my glass in one gulp, and returned, "May as well."

"Good," she replied, "it's my night off."

"Night off from what?" I asked her in a tease.

"Work."

Delightfully unfiltered, I crooned, "And what do you do for work, Cassie?"

She set her glass down, dragged her eyes from my feet to my head, and said, "I think you know that already."

"I do."

"Are you capable of keeping a secret, James?" she questioned me in a tone that felt seductive, and I couldn't help but allow a smile to pull at my lips.

I looked at her, felt our eyes lock as she silently demanded my attention and kept it, and I replied, "Yes."

"Good," she said. "You smile as if you're picturing it."

"Picturing what?" I asked.

"Me," Cassie quipped, reaching for the glass that was once mine and tossing it back. "Working."

Images of her in a scantily clad, glowing getup that barely covered her flashed in my mind. I could nearly feel her breath hot on my face as I imagined her moving over me. My cheeks heated at the notion, and my eyelids were suddenly hooded with lust.

"Maybe I am," I admitted.

Her head tipped to the side. "What aspect of me working are you envisioning, exactly?"

"The one with you on top of me."

I said it with grit in my voice, and her eyes were alight with either entertainment or anticipation—I couldn't decide which.

She hummed a happy noise and voiced, "That's what I thought," and I seriously considered the latter.

Our back-and-forth banter continued on like none other. With the absence of my usual limitations toward her, our conversation and the wit that we threw toward each other was effortless. It was charming. Flirtatious. Brash. It went on for what felt like hours until Cassie sighed with a breathy laugh and quipped:

"Damn...I'm buzzed."

And, of course, she shouldn't drive. Couldn't drive. My apartment had plenty of space...and it was awaiting us both.

A gasp that stretched the capacity of my lungs and rattled in my throat ripped through me before I even had the chance to open my eyes.

It was a dream.

A fucking *bad* one.

Not bad in the sense that it gave me anxiety or sent my mind to a memory that I wished to erase—bad in the sense that I could see it all burned into my retinas. *Bad* in the sense that the star of said dream was Cassie. *Bad* in the sense that much, *much* more had occurred in that dream before I had woken in a sweaty puddle with a shuddering inhale.

Of course, I had thought of Cassie in a sexual manner in the past. Whenever she'd tease me, I'd want to kiss her in response. She'd use profanities in the middle of a conversation, and I'd consider how it would sound if she were moaning it. She'd wear *short* jean shorts, and I'd note that her legs were long—so long that if she were to bend over at the waist, I could fuck her from behind with ease.

They were similar to intrusive thoughts of, I don't know, steering off the highway with a rapid jerk of my hand...jumping from a bridge...biting glass...punching a window. I wouldn't do any of *those*, obviously, and I'd usher the sexual thoughts away just as quickly as I would the others. But *this? This dream?* It was different.

I couldn't stop picturing her legs wrapped around my head.

My face between her thighs.

Her shivering around me, screaming to the gods as she came on my mouth.

I could *feel* her convulsing on my tongue.

"Fuck," I moaned a miserable curse, continuing to heave large breaths as if I had just finished sprinting.

I tried to will the vivid non-memories away, yet they remained.

I had offered her the spare bedroom in my apartment. She asked if she could have a nightcap, and I obliged. We chatted on the couch. Our eyes met as we realized how close we were sitting. She smiled that *fucking* smile...and I went for it. She sighed against me, I felt like a god amongst men, two plus two equaled four, and then, her bare feet were grazing my back as I worshipped her.

I was painfully erect, now—to the point that I was concerned that moving the comforter that laid over my lap would finish me off—and shame was washing over me in a wave. It was just a dream...a harmless dream...but thinking of her in such a way felt wrong on so many levels.

And, *fuck me,* but that made the thought of it even *hotter.*

I sprang from my bed, thanked whatever god above that I didn't orgasm from the movement, and headed straight for the shower. The image was probably comical, really, and it was a goddamn *blessing* that I lived alone. My torso was angled slightly downwards in an attempt to reduce the strain of my dick against the fabric of my boxer briefs. My bare feet slapped across the cherry wood as I power-walked past the kitchen, and I groaned when I glimpsed the time on the stove that read 2:03 A.M. I rushed into the bathroom with an air of desperation, cranked the temperature in the shower to what I could only describe as *ice,* carefully peeled my boxers off, and stepped in.

"AH!"

I sucked in a breath through my teeth, my muscles stiffened, and I allowed the frigid water to pelt my body. I told myself that I would stand there for as long as was needed to remedy my *situation*...and the minutes passed. The initial shock of the temperature waned, my fingers and toes began to go numb, my skin—though typically a bit pale aside from the areas that were tattooed—seemed to have a blueish pallor to it, and my cock was *still* fucking hard.

I wondered bitterly if I would die here. If I would get fucking hypothermia from standing in this shower, waiting for my hard-on to abate.

Monday would roll around, and I wouldn't have the ability to call in for work, being dead and all. My coworkers, most likely Brooks, would be concerned because, if anything, I was a punctual and up-front person. The lack of my presence throughout the day without any alert of it—a *no-call, no-show,* as it could be called—would be alarming, and they would try to contact me. The phone would ring, and ring...or, perhaps, my phone would have died by then, as well...and *that's* when the police would show. They would bust down my door, the shower would still be running, and they would race to the bathroom.

And, there I would be. Dead. Blue all over, with the exception of my cock, of course, because I would probably *still* be fucking hard.

It would be an anomaly. The policemen would be perplexed—I could imagine it:

Policeman One stops in his tracks. "Oh shit, he's dead."

"Uh huh...for a while, looks like," Policeman Two replies. "Better call the medical examiner."

"Is he...is he erect?" Policeman One ponders aloud as he squints at my body.

Policeman Two grimaces. "Oh, Jesus. That he is."

"How the fuck is that possible?" Policeman One notes, "He's past rigor mortis, right?"

"Definitely," Policeman Two agrees. "No idea how he's hard right now...they're gonna want to do studies on this shit."

"An autopsy at the very least, right?"

"Oh, yeah."

Policeman One tilts his head to the side as he takes in my appearance even further, and then asks hesitantly, "...think it has anything to do with how big his dick is?"

Policeman Two nods emphatically. "I mean, he's enormous...probably. They'll want to study that, too."

I laughed loudly at my morbidly imagined scenario, looked down, and whispered, "Oh, thank God," because I was *finally* flaccid.

I turned the water to hot, regained the feeling in my limbs, and remained there until my skin was splotched with red from the heat. I exchanged my sexual thoughts of Cassie for the memory—the *real* memory—that had happened the night before. Remorse over what I had said, how she could have taken it, and why repeated over and over in my brain. I supposed that was natural—a *natural* thing to feel after essentially telling her to fuck off. It would pass, I told myself.

It didn't pass, though...and furthermore, I was concerned that the dream which had left me in a state of, erm, *distress* was becoming a recurring one. It *did* recur—both Sunday and Monday at exactly two o'clock in the morning, I awoke in a similarly shocked state. Eyes wide open and flat on my back, I was panting. Damn near covered in sweat, I groaned, realized the sins that I had unintentionally committed yet again, refrained from slapping my face as a form of punishment, and hopped in an icy shower.

On Monday morning, I had thankfully recovered from my brief bout of hypothermia, and as I drove to work, I—once again—thought of Cassie. Not in the lewd manner that I had been attempting to erase from my dreams, but with shame regarding my horrific behavior. I had considered contacting her, but I didn't have her phone number—I had never asked her for it, and I never intended to—and I was cursing myself because of it. I didn't know what I would *say,* but I still had the urge to reach out and talk to her. There were several routes I could take:

Erm, sorry, I can be a douche sometimes. We cool?

I'm definitely not friends with the guy who tried to rip your top off.

I didn't look at your tit when it happened.

Your, um, glow in the dark makeup was cool. Where'd ya buy it?

Stupid. All of those options were idiotic because they skirted around the actual matter at hand, and Cassie was too *smart*—too *inquisitive* of a woman not to see behind my false intentions. That aside, none of those words would have been near enough. I felt as though I needed to crawl on my knees for forgiveness. To tell her that I was shocked at the sight of her—frozen underneath her as she moved above me, and when our eyes locked, I had splintered and snapped. That pushing thoughts of her out of my mind was one of the hardest tasks I had ever been daunted with, and *that* was why I was an asshole—I was pushing her away for obvious reasons, and I was *so* fucking sorry. But I couldn't do all of that because...y'know...*the insinuation.*

There was no middle road that appeared to me along the lines of apologies. Not now. And I hated myself for that.

Monday was a distraction, at the very least, because work was...*interesting*. I was no longer drowning myself in the day-to-day monotony of my job. No—*now,* I had *workplace drama.* The moment that I walked to my cubicle, I saw Shawn's dark, curly head whip to mine from the adjacent workspace. He wore a cringe on his face as he watched me set my things down with care.

He leaned on the edge of his desk, greeting me with a long, drawn out, *"Heyyyyyy, buddy—"*

"Why are you *hey buddying* me?" I returned.

Shawn's green eyes darted to the left and right, finding the other cubicles beside us unoccupied. "Have a good weekend?"

"Shit weekend," I retorted. "And I feel like you *know* I had a shit weekend and *why* because you're alarmingly up to speed regarding my personal life."

"Is...now when I officially apologize about Gas Lamp?" he asked hesitantly.

"Yes."

He gave me a meek smile. "Sorry. Shit idea."

I exhaled heavily. "It's all good, man."

"I take it you didn't talk to Cassie," he remarked, glancing at the ceiling.

"No." I was going to be snarkier, but when Shawn looked to me with a tinge of sympathy, I backpedaled. "No, I, ah—haven't seen her. Haven't reached out. I don't have her number."

"Right, right," Shawn replied. "You should, though...mend bridges. Form bonds. *Ask her out."*

I barked out a laugh. "Fairly certain that she hates me at the moment, but thanks for the sage advice."

"Yeah, the tail end of that conversation wasn't exactly in your favor," he stated with a cringe. *"Yikes, man.* You have work to do."

"You *kept* eavesdropping?" I asked him with high eyebrows. He shrugged, and I chastised him, *"Brooks."*

"You were loud!" he defended himself. "It was impossible not to listen in. And I...*kinda* thought I'd end up hearing the beginnings of a feelings confession, followed by a kiss, *followed by—*"

"Shawn."

"I strained my ears to keep hearing, okay? *I'm sorry.*" He did not sound sorry in the least. Shawn carried on with, "I'm a sucker for a good love story. I was rooting for you...despite the fact that you were a total dick, dude. What *the fuck?*"

"Are you a love doctor, Brooks?" I asked bitterly.

He shrugged. "I root for love when I see it. Apologize to her. Buy her chocolates."

I stated plainly, "She's twenty-two years old. That's a little young for me."

"Who gives a shit? Your brother's girlfriend's whatever that you told me about...Zoey. She was younger, yeah? What's the difference?"

"Ah, *that* was a five-year age difference. *This* is nine."

"So? What's the rule for acceptable age to date...half your age, plus seven?"

The math in my head was lightning quick.

"Twenty-three," I replied. "My youngest acceptable age to date would be twenty-three—"

"You rounded up!" he retorted. "Twenty-two and a *half*. It's like you're making excuses *not* to ask her out. I mean, *fuck,* man—you're tense. I'd like to not see you walkin' around the office with *that* look on your face anymore—"

"What look?" I interrupted him. "I have a look?"

"It's like...you're a jack-in-the-box that's been cranked to *juuuust* before it's about to pop," Shawn explained.

I nearly snorted. Though his description was apt, I muttered, "I don't look like that."

"Maybe I just know you well." He shrugged. "Worked in the same space for a few years; I'd like to think so."

I sighed. "Fine. *Maybe* you have a point."

"So..."

"So...*what?*"

"So," Shawn pressed, "ask her out."

I grimaced. "Zoey's boyfriend's *little sister.*"

He cocked an eyebrow up high. "Lingering tension between you and Zoey?"

"God, no...that was months ago. It just feels...*wrong?*"

"Dirty," Shawn corrected me, and I threw him a quick glare.

"There's a—a bro code about shit like this, right? *Thou shalt not pursue a bro's sibling.*"

One of his dark eyebrows raised up. "How close are you with Zoey's boyfriend? He's a *bro* now?"

"Complicated friend circle," I stated. "Kinda."

Shawn immediately replied, "Mmkay, well, do you *think* Cassie's into you? Because *I* was up front and center for the tension bomb, and it was comin' from *both* of you."

I ground my teeth together. "We wouldn't work," I told him simply. "All of the other stuff aside, I'm a jealous guy—"

"Turner," Shawn laughed disbelievingly, "that's an understatement. I *saw* your face on Friday."

I exhaled. "Yeah, she makes me a little crazier than normal. *I get it.* Point being, even if she wasn't strictly off-limits, I don't want to be…I dunno…*toxic.*"

Shawn began to hum the Britney Spears song by the same name. His maroon sweater-clad shoulders bobbed from side to side, I allowed him to do so as I watched him with half-lidded eyes, and then he sang an off-key, high-pitched:

"I'm addicted to you; don't you know that you're toxic?"

"Shawn."

He beamed a smile at me. "I'll allow the first-name calling. You're stressed. You do you, boo...*speaking of* you being crazy—"

"Where's this going?"

"I swung by the sales cubes. Tommy got in early."

I threw my head back and groaned loudly, following it up with a hushed, "Couldn't he just have quit? Save me the misery of potentially seeing his face?"

"You broke his fingers, Jay."

I cringed at the news, though I had a sneaking suspicion of that already. "And you know this because..."

"Because he has splints on the index and middle fingers on both of his hands, James! He was typing like *this."*

Shawn then held his arms out to the side, pointing them down at ninety-degree angles, and began to individually click buttons on his keyboard with fingers that he kept forcedly straight.

I chortled at the sight. "That's funny."

He smiled at my amusement but replied, "It is not *funny,* Jay—"

"If you're tryin' to get remorse out of me for this one, it's not gonna happen." I added, "In fact, I should have done more."

He sighed heavily. "Bottle up the crazy, Turner. I know you can do it."

"Instead," I offered, "I should talk to HR and tell them that *Tommy* dragged us to an inappropriate venue for a work event and proceeded to assault an innocent woman."

"And then...technically...*you* assaulted *him*," Shawn stated. "That's not gonna end well for you. Like I said," he whispered, *"bottle up the crazy."*

He turned back to focus on his work, effectively ending our conversation, and I used the rest of the work day to ponder how I could render Tommy unemployed.

'Damn...I'm buzzed.'

Spoken in Cassie's voice, the words played over and over in my mind. They weren't *real*. They had never left her mouth outside of the confines of my brain—not to me, at least—but *damn,* did they feel like they were. Friday night, in my first forbidden dream, they were there. Saturday—yep. *Sunday and Monday?* You bet your ass. Tuesday, though? Somewhere between Tuesday night and Wednesday morning, my testosterone-riddled brain had made the connection. Mid-sleep, those cursed words left her lips, and they were my tip. My clue. My internal realization that I was, in fact, dreaming.

I *recognized* the dream. Unlike the nights before it, I was...*aware*. I felt as though I had control. I consciously told myself, *'You're dreaming, Jay, snap out of it,'* and despite all of it, I followed through. I bent the laws of my imagination as far as they would go. At some point, while unconscious, I had come to the conclusion that doing those things with Cassie in my mind wasn't...*forbidden*. It was just a dream.

And the things we did were *fucking filthy*.

It was waking that was the problem. Instead of flinching myself into reality, heavily breathing until I fully woke and racing to the shower, I was face down. Face down and bucking my hips into the fucking mattress. I didn't even get a chance to open my eyes—after what I believe were four thrusts, I came so hard that my hands fisted in the sheets, and I had the primal urge to *bite*. My teeth sank into my pillow, a sound came out of me that could have easily been mistaken as pain-induced, and I rode it out until my muscles ceased their clenching.

I opened my eyes, and the erotic haze was lifted. I cursed myself with a, *"God dammit,"* that was immediately followed with, *"Oh, no,"* as I realized the mess I had made of both my mind and my sheets.

One swat at my phone on the bedside table, I saw that it was—of course—two o'clock in the morning. It was *al-*

ways two o'clock in the morning when I would wake from my dreams of her. I threw my pillows to the floor, yanked the fitted sheet off of the closest corner of my bed, and used it to wipe myself clean the best I could. With the evidence of my most recent sins having somehow escaped through the fly of my boxers and splattered across my sheets and duvet, I contemplated the hours of the local laundromat. I flopped on my back onto the naked portion of the mattress and reached for my phone for a quick Google search, finding that all laundromats in Salem weren't open for several hours. Just south of Roanoke, though—there was a twenty-four-hour laundromat there.

Did I *want* to drive twenty minutes to the laundromat and twenty minutes back, spending several hours just to wash my bedding that was partially covered in my own sticky body fluids? *No.* Of-fucking-*course* I didn't want to do that—*especially* not at this hour. However, this hour, as unappealing as it was, would allow me to perform my walk of shame in the cover of the early morning.

So, I went. I rinsed off, packed up my things, and drove across town to the laundromat at two o'clock in the morning. My eyelids heavy and my mind buzzing with further thoughts of remorse, I fought sleep as I watched my sheets tumble in a circle through the glass door of a washer. By the time I transferred them to the dryer, I was in the process of berating myself. I was inflicting this self-punishment because even though it was just a dream, I knew what I was doing. I *know* how my mind and heart work and, *don't ya know it,* deciding to lucid dream-fuck Cassie Cohen and finish myself off onto my bed was mentally crossing a line.

And if I thought I was grumpy *before*...that wouldn't have even *compared* to my mood throughout the morning.

I arrived at work with palpable bags under my eyes. I set down my across-the-shoulder laptop bag at my cubicle. I began to fish my glasses out of the side pocket...and Shawn caught my eye. His head had swung on a swivel to view me, his eyebrows high as he noted:

"Jesus, Jay, ya look like shit."

I let out a long breath through my nostrils. "Brooks," I began slowly, "you know I like you. I *do,* man. But I will literally pay you not to talk to me today." I considered my last sentence and then rephrased to, "I'd literally pay not to have *anyone* talk to me today."

He frowned. "So, you haven't talked to Cas—"

"No," I snapped, gently placing my glasses on my face. "I haven't."

"Okay, okay," he replied, nodding. "I only take cash." I shot him a warning glance, saw the light-hearted joke in his eyes, and he held up his hands in defense as he smiled. "Or beer."

I sighed. "Beer. I'll get you a beer."

Shawn tapped both of his index fingers against his desk one after the other, as if he were playing the drums. They rapped the counter three times, he gave me a curt bob of his head, and he spun back to focus on his work.

It was uneventful; the remainder of my work day—quiet. My morning had mostly consisted of searching on the company-wide software to see if Tommy had been assigned any clients yet. He hadn't. My thoughts of sabotaging his success and inevitably getting him fired dwindled down as the day went on, and I was able to focus on my work. I popped my headphones in, listening to music that could only have been described as *Emo Grunge* to try to drown out the noise in my mind, and before I knew it, I was seated in the kitchen space eating my lunch.

Alone. I was eating my lunch *alone*...and though the lack of disruption further put my mind at ease, I was curious why I was given the opportunity of *alone time* in the first place. It wasn't until I saw Shawn out of the corner of my eye, swiftly redirecting Paula from accounts payable away from the break room, that I realized that it was his doing.

Shawn laughed a bit too hard, the sound itself not believable in the least. Paula, who is a *talker,* smacked his arm in a playful manner, and he glanced back at me quickly with a pinched expression on his face. I let out an amused breath at the sight of Shawn metaphorically stepping on a landmine by diving into a conversation with one of the most verbose middle-aged women I've ever met.

Paula was lingering by Shawn's cubicle when I returned. Her fire-engine red head was thrown back in laughter—*loud* laughter—and she invited him out to lunch. I heard the hesitation in his voice, which he quickly masked with a cough before agreeing on a nearby deli, and they were out the door.

Shawn didn't return for over two hours.

When I finally caught him slinking back into his chair at his desk, I removed my earbuds, stood, and made my way over. I leaned against the entrance to his cubicle with my right shoulder and crossed my ankles.

"Long lunch, Brooks."

He looked at me, offering me a small, bitter smile. *"Paula."*

"How is she?"

"Well," Shawn inhaled a long breath and, upon exhalation, rambled out, "her oldest daughter has been studying for finals—she's a sophomore in high school. The middle one just got her first girlfriend and *boy,* let me tell you, Paula is *opinionated* about her coming out as a lesbian."

He rolled his eyes heavily. "I wasn't about to debate with *Paula,* so I smiled and nodded and held my tongue, but *damn,* she's a bigot."

I shook my head, sardonically noting, *"That* sounds entertaining."

"Oh, I'm not done," he continued with a grimace, now leaning back in his chair and speaking to the ceiling. "Her youngest, the boy—is starting middle school. He's into theater, and she called him a fuckin' *dandy."* I cringed at the word and, without even seeing my face, he replied, *"I know.* It went on for *hours.* Anyway—I'm gonna work on filling out some paperwork with the state—county—whoever the hell I need to fill it out with. Get the process started to adopt her kids."

He said it offhandedly, and I laughed at his sarcasm. "I don't think that's how that works."

"I'll find a loophole somewhere."

"Mhm. That'll be great—three teenagers." I joked, "They'll call you Daddy Brooks."

Shawn glanced my way, still leaning back as he smiled wide. *"There* he is. I knew your usual sassy ass would be back at some point."

"Uh huh. So—you've been jumping in front of social-related bullets for me all day."

Shawn shrugged. "You requested quiet time. I delivered."

"Very chivalrous of you."

"You seem better," he remarked.

I wasn't operating at 100% capacity, of course, but I *was* better. And because that was partially due to his interference throughout the day—*and* because he legitimately seemed to care about my headspace as of late—I felt my hardened exterior soften even further.

"Mhm," I hummed. "You wanna get a drink later?"

"I was joking about the payment, you know," Shawn noted with a wry grin. *"This* bullet was free of charge."

I knew that already, so I simply replied, "Regardless."

Shawn nodded. "Where are you thinking?"

On an afternoon like this one—what should have been a run-of-the-mill Wednesday—I would typically relax at home after work. Henry's was great. I *loved* the bar, I did, and Wednesday was a day that Luke and Claire typically had off. It was common that they would frequent their place of employment on said day to enjoy the atmosphere when they weren't behind the counter—oftentimes with Liam and Zoey and, by default, Cassie. I did join them occasionally, but I had grown to appreciate my own space, as well. My own whiskey, if I were so inclined. The comforting sound of whatever music I desired to listen to, me placing a half-drank glass back on the side table as I lounged on my couch, and...*nothing else.* Maybe I would cook dinner; maybe I would order something in—it didn't matter. All that *did* matter was that I was within my own beautiful, quiet isolation.

This most definitely was *not* a run-of-the-mill Wednesday, though, and a visit to the bar was ripe on my mind. The quiet of the day had allowed me to take pause, and I itched to talk to Cassie—to apologize, know that we were...*okay*...and to force her out from under my skin. I had no issue with Shawn joining me on my excursion. Actually, the more that I thought about it, his presence could be a delightful buffer from all things Cassie after I got my apology to her out of the way. However, the knowledge that he had—not only of Cassie's work but of my feelings for her—couldn't be shared.

"Mind driving to Salem?"

"Salem?" he asked. "For what?"

"My brother and his girlfriend bartend down the road from my apartment complex," I explained. "They're normally off on Wednesdays. I figured I could grab a drink with them while they aren't serving me, for once."

His eyes widened, and he nearly flashed me all of his teeth. "Are you introducing me to your *family?!*"

I laughed. "I couldn't keep you a secret *forever,* baby. The bromance is too real." Shawn chuckled, and I added, "But I do have a condition."

"Conditional love," he murmured. *"I knew it.* Throw it on me; what's the condition?"

I stood up straight then, crossing my arms as I stated:

"You need to keep your goddamn mouth shut."

Chapter 5

"Nice place."

Intent on accompanying me on the walk to Henry's, Shawn paid me the compliment as I strolled through my apartment to quickly dispose of my work bag.

For the longest time, the apartment didn't feel like my own. It still had Claire and Zoey's furnishings—the wooden, rectangular kitchen table that greeted you the moment you opened the door. The grey couch to the left. The beat up, green chair adjacent to it. Either of their mattresses and the bedframes that accompanied them—those were still in their bedrooms.

Claire's looked as if it were nearly untouched. Her bedding having been cleaned at the nearby laundromat long ago, I remade her bed as if it were anticipating her return home. I bought a handful of colorful throw pillows to add some life to her ivory comforter, the coral and blue tones reminiscent of a beach house, and her door remained closed. She wasn't returning, of course, because she lived upstairs with Luke in apartment 3C, but I still ensured that her room remained tidy and inviting.

Zoey's old room, however—my room—had changed drastically. The sight of the white eyelet lace on her bedding had been making me cringe, unwanted memories of our brief fling springing to my mind, and because I truly, *truly* no longer thought of Zoey in that way, I had decided to redecorate. I *needed* to redecorate. Months ago, when she had decided to continue living with Liam across the hall in 2B, she had offered to put her things in a storage unit. She and Claire had *both* done as such, but I insisted that their things remained because it would save them the trouble of storing them, and, of course, I no longer had furnishings of my own to speak of. *Those* had stayed with Allison...and I had no desire to go shopping for such things. So...yes—I redecorated.

With Zoey's approval, I painted her light wash, wooden headboard and matching side tables black. I folded up her sheets, stored them in Claire's old closet, and bought my own. The mix of sage and hunter green combined with grey pillows gave the room a much needed shift, and it became my own.

I briefly considered explaining to Shawn that it wasn't *truly* my place. That Claire had lived here with Zoey, they both split off to room with Luke and Liam, and that I had simply taken over once Allison had claimed rights to our house. Going into detail could have brought up questions about the murky past, though...and after a few months, it really *did* feel like home.

Therefore, I simply nodded at his comment, throwing him a smile as I set my work bag on the kitchen table.

"Thanks—I like it."

He asked, "You said it was a short walk from here?"

"Oh yeah. Super short," I told him as we both made headway for the door.

I allowed him to exit first, locked the deadbolt behind me, and as I slid my keys into my pocket, Shawn appeared to be amping up for battle. His shoulders bobbled from side to side as we lumbered down the steps, and the moment that we reached the sidewalk, he spoke up:

*"Alright...*let me get this straight."

Dusk upon us, the air was brisk, and the rock salt that was sprinkled along the cobblestones to aid in melting the sheet of ice from Monday's storm crunched beneath our feet.

I sighed. "There's not much to get straight, Brooks."

"It's a little unfathomable that no one—no one in your *entire* friend circle—knows that she's a—"

I interrupted, "Remember when I told you to keep your mouth shut?"

"The street's empty, Jay," Shawn stated, gesturing with an arm thrown out wide in front of us both. "I'm not gonna spill your secrets. Don't worry, I'll be a *good boy.*"

He said it sarcastically, and I returned quickly, "Is that your fetish? Do I need to buy you a collar so you behave?"

Shawn snorted. "Hey, don't joke—I'm a very open-minded man. For all you know, I have a whole fuckin' closet filled with submissive shit."

"Okay, okay." I waved away his commentary. "Didn't intend to open Pandora's box. I'm not trying to picture you in leather."

"You are *now,* though, right?" His thick eyebrows bobbed up and down.

"Whatever makes you feel better at the end of the day," I quipped, swiftly redirecting to, "And *no.* No one knows. No one knows anything. They know I went to a strip club and nothing else...and they're not going to. I don't want Cassie any more pissed at me than she already is."

"Mmkay. And—"

"Stop," I interjected in a hushed tone. "There's not much else to know; we're here."

Shawn peeked upward to view the wooden, pinkish lettering overhead that read *Henry's,* and his head bobbed back in surprise.

"Huh—damn, that *is* close to your place."

"Yeah, yeah," I reached to open the door, and the bell dinged. "After you."

It was busier tonight—the dull murmur of voices was just loud enough to rise above the soft music in the background. Though the usual seats that our group occupied whilst Claire and Luke were tending the bar were empty, I didn't move to take them because we never sat at the counter when they were off the clock. It was the third furthest table from the entrance that we normally took. One edge of it butted up against the wall; we typically had two chairs on either side with a fifth at the table head—a sixth if Cassie joined us. Tonight, there were six—and Luke, Claire, Liam, and Zoey were all in their usual seats.

Luke caught my eye first as he was sat at one of the two chairs facing the entrance. He flashed me a surprised smile, gently elbowing Claire, who was on his left and lifting a short tumbler of clear liquid to her lips. She followed his gaze, quickly finished the sip of her drink, grinned at me, and threw me a wave. This alerted Liam and Zoey, who were sat directly across from them. Simultaneously moving their heads, Zoey smiled and waved similarly to how Claire had, and Liam ticked his head upward in acknowledgment of my arrival.

Though Shawn had walked in first, he trailed behind me as I led the way to the table, lingering just to my right when I stood beside my typical seat at the head next to Zoey.

"About time you showed up," Zoey remarked. "Out of sight since last week, what gives?"

"Busy," I lied succinctly. I wasn't busy. I was hiding away in my apartment for various reasons, all to do with Cassie. "Ah, Zoey, Liam, Claire, Luke." I pointed at each of them as I spoke their name and then gestured to Shawn. "Shawn Brooks. Brooks—everyone."

They all gave him a cheery greeting, Shawn waggled his fingers almost shyly, and Liam added:

"Grab another chair, Cas is comin'."

The mention of her name sent a nervous jolt through me, and I attempted to conceal my reaction by nodding and searching the nearby space for a spare chair. Shawn found one before I did, asking the women at the table just behind Luke and Claire if the empty seat was taken. They kindly told him that it was free, and we shuffled the seats just enough to allow room for him to sit between me and Zoey.

We sat, and Shawn pointed at Luke. "Brother?"

He smiled in return. "Uh huh. How do you know Jay?"

Luke began to lift a pale beer to his mouth, and Shawn happily stated, "Work."

Luke's light eyes narrowed mid-sip, and his head turned to me as he set his glass down.

"Is this the guy?"

"Oh God," Shawn cringed. *Am I the guy?*

I knew without further inquiry that Luke was questioning if Shawn was the work friend who had invited me to Gas Lamp.

"Yup."

He ground his teeth at my acknowledgment, and his judgmental gaze whipped to Shawn.

Shawn leaned backward under Luke's wordless scrutinizing, asking, "What did I do?"

"You dragged him to a *strip club?*" Luke said incredulously. "Do you know him at *all?*"

Claire's expression mimicked Luke's upon the mention of a strip club, Zoey snorted loudly into her cider and rushed to set it down, and Liam snapped his fingers once, his brown eyes alight with recognition.

He pointed at me with a broad grin and exclaimed, "That's *right!* Strip club! You went to a strip club on Friday!"

Zoey simply reached toward Shawn as if she wanted to shake his hand. He looked down, cocked his head in curiosity at her dainty digits, and took her hand in his.

"Nice job, man," she quipped as their hands bobbed up and down twice. "Hilarious. How was he?"

Shawn stammered, *"Um—"*

"Zoey, I'm *right here,*" I reminded her needlessly.

Her green eyes shot to me. "And there's no way you'll give us a realistic recounting of the night, now, *is there?*"

"Uh," Shawn's head bounced from Zoey to Luke. "For the record, I apologized."

"Oh, *please,*" Zoey spoke. "You don't need to apologize unless something went wrong." She gasped, and her smile blinded us all. *"Did something go wrong?"*

Liam chuckled at her excitement, and I internally squirmed as I said, "Nothing *went wrong.*"

"What...what could even go wrong at a strip club?" Shawn questioned aloud in an attempt to remain casual.

It did not sound casual.

"Yeah, that's not convincing," Zoey noted, amused.

Claire chastised her, "If he doesn't want to talk about it, he doesn't have to."

"So, which club did ya go to?" Liam asked.

Claire's red head snapped to the seat across from her. *"Liam!"*

I sighed heavily, looking down to the empty chair on my left that Cassie would soon be sitting in. Certain that she wouldn't care for the mentioning of her work when she was attempting to keep it private, I divulged as quickly and succinctly as possible:

"Gas Lamp."

"Nice," Zoey replied. "Y'know, they do a glow-in-the-dark night."

I exhaled heavily. "I'm well aware."

"Was it?" she pressed.

"Cosmic night," I returned. "Uh huh."

Zoey beamed. *"And?* How was it?"

"Dark."

Liam joked, *"Glow*-in-the-dark," and threw his head back in laughter at his terrible pun.

Zoey pressed her lips together tightly, patting his forearm as she muttered sarcastically, "Good one, Sweets."

"Dark," I repeated, "and depressing." Zoey looked at me with eager, questioning eyes, and I insisted, "There's no story there."

Shawn piped up, "We were only there for one drink. It was...not fun? And we, uh, left."

I grumbled, "Brooks, you're making it sound weird."

Shawn nervously remarked, "Remember how you said you'd get me a drink?"

Claire murmured, *"Oh,* I'll flag down Garrett," and hovered out of her seat to wave to the man tending the bar.

The conversation naturally steered away from my weekend's activities, turning to the group speaking with Shawn—Claire, Zoey, and Liam with general niceties, and Luke silently questioning whether Shawn appeared to be worth the time of day. Knowing Luke's penchant for holding a grudge and his first impression of Shawn being a poor one, I gently kicked to my left to reach his legs.

He looked at me, perturbed, and I mouthed a silent, *'Be nice.'*

Luke let out a quick exhale through his nose, looked back to Shawn, and plastered the tiniest of fake smiles on his face.

Claire, speaking to Shawn, lovingly brushed Luke's chest as she told him, "We met when Zoey and I moved here a little over a year ago—he hired me to work here, actually."

My brother's façade of a smile morphed into a real one as he looked down at Claire, watching her speak of their first introductions.

Garrett spoke from my left the moment he reached us, "Jay—usual?"

He was young. Tall. Blonde. Thin. Nice, though we hadn't spoken much, and truthfully, I was taken aback that he remembered what I typically ordered.

"Oh...yeah, thanks," I told him. I tapped Shawn on his arm. "What do you want?"

Without taking his focus off of Claire, who was still rambling on, he asked, "Stout?"

I looked up to Garrett, and he nodded. "Got it. Be back."

I glanced toward the door, expecting—*hoping*—to see Cassie. She wasn't there, though, and the voices around me turned to a dull murmur as I got lost in my anxious, anticipatory thoughts. Cassie would arrive, eventually. I would tell her hello. She would *probably* take my drink. I'd ask her—quietly so the rest of the group wouldn't hear, maybe whilst the remainder of them were distracted with conversation—if we could chat somewhere private. She'd roll her eyes, I'd shoot her a telling glance that would explain my need to revisit our encounter from Friday, and she would agree. She'd *have* to agree. We'd...I dunno...inconspicuously go to the bathroom one after the other, I'd meet her in the women's or she'd meet me in the men's, I'd thoroughly apologize for being an asshole, and she'd accept. It may take some work, but she'd accept. Without the guilt lingering over my head and knowing that she didn't think of me with hatred, the tension that I had built up in my mind between us would eventually melt away, and I could continue on with my life as I had intended.

Yep. That was the plan.

My fingers tapped on my thigh rapidly—pinkie, ring, middle, index; pinkie, ring, middle, index—until Garrett returned with my drink and Shawn's. I thanked him quietly, took a large gulp, and felt it burn all the way down to my gut. The bell chimed above the front door.

Truthfully, I have no idea how I heard it over the ambient noise of patrons—perhaps it was because I was hyper-aware. Regardless, I turned my head toward the noise, and my chest lurched. Her jeans were black, high-waisted, and tight. The maroon long-sleeve shirt she wore left her midriff exposed, the silver in her navel glinting out just above the fastening of her pants. Her hair was up in a high ponytail that rendered her neck bare, and though I expected her dark eyes to meet mine, they didn't. Instead, Cassie kept her attention raptly focused on Garrett, who had returned behind the bar. She gave him a cheery greeting, waving with a beaming smile, took one glance at the general direction of our table, and, without skipping a beat, looked back to Garrett and held up two fingers. He nodded, and I used all of my force of will to yank my attention away from their interaction because it felt as though I had lingered too long.

I stared at my drink, awaiting her fingers to wrap around the glass. The air to my left turned hot as she sat in the only available seat, everyone told her *hello,* and her well-manicured nails never appeared. I blinked as if my eyes were deceiving me, saw nothing different, and when I looked at her, she was smiling past me at Shawn.

"Hi. I'm Cassie—and you are?"

It was all too convincing, as if she had never seen his face, and Shawn stammered, *"Uh,* Shawn Brooks."

"He took Jay to a strip club," Zoey blurted, and my stomach dropped.

Cassie's smile faltered for the briefest moment—so brief that I believed I was the only one to see it because my eyes were trained on her face—and she hummed, quipping, "Nice." She looked at me, happy grin maintained but not reaching her eyes as she remarked, "Hope you had a good time."

"I didn't," I told her.

Cassie murmured, "That's a shame."

As quiet as it was, I was the only one who was able to hear that her tone was scathing.

"Alright, alright," Claire interjected. "He doesn't want to talk about it. We've been over this." I shot her a thank-

ful glance, and she looked to Cassie. *"So, Cassie...saw you saying hi to Garrett."*

Luke groaned. "This isn't gonna go over well, baby."

Claire waved a hand in his face, and he flinched backward to avoid it.

I pressed Luke, *"What's* not gonna go over well?"

Luke rolled his eyes, and Zoey spoke for him, "Claire thinks that *everyone* needs to be paired off."

Claire whined, "He's *nice.*"

"Garrett?" Liam grimaced. "Garrett and Cassie? Cassie and *Garrett?"*

Luke deadpanned, "That *is* the combination of their names, yes."

"He's, like...a *child,* Claire," Liam complained.

"He's twenty-one," Claire argued. "Close to Cassie's age—would you rather she date an *older* man?"

My intestines twisted, and I grabbed my glass as casually as I could muster to throw the remainder of the liquid back in one swig.

Cassie joked, "I have no problem being a sugar baby," the gulp I had taken got caught in my throat as I coughed, and Shawn gave me a single, rough rap on the back.

He leaned toward my ear to quickly mutter, "Pull yourself together, *Jesus."*

Zoey's eyes shined in Cassie's direction, and she approvingly exclaimed, *"Atta girl!"*

Liam looked down at her disbelievingly. *"Not* atta girl. The fuck, Zo'?" Zoey snickered loudly, and he grumbled, "Either way. Garrett's...twiggy."

Liam lifted his beer to his lips, and Zoey returned, "Maybe he's twiggy compared to *you,* ya big lug." Despite his annoyance, I saw him hide a hint of a smile at her joking reference to his large, burly stature. Zoey continued, "And who gives a shit? Don't comment on his appearance. *Maybe* your sister's into that."

"She can't date the bartender," Liam argued, albeit a bit softer. "They break up, what are Luke and Claire gonna do—fire him? I'm not gonna want to see him around."

"Because help is *so* easy to find in this town," Luke spoke over them both. *"Yeah*...no, I wouldn't fire him."

"You're assuming that I'm into him," Cassie interrupted, and I blew an exhale through my nostrils. "Who said I'm into him?"

"I didn't," Claire retorted, her hands up by her face in defense. "I didn't. Just...throwing it out there since I've caught him looking your way a few times."

Zoey laughed quietly, Liam groaned as he set his beer down, and Luke begrudgingly stated:

"He *has* looked."

Cassie took in everyone's commentary with a chuckle and glanced toward the bar, and if this conversation hadn't already made me practically grind my teeth down to the gums, I certainly was doing so now. I attempted not to appear as though my eyes were bulging out of my head as I followed suit and snapped my gaze to Garrett.

My thoughts on him, which had been all too positive moments prior, had suddenly shifted, and I couldn't stop my inner monologue from sneering, *'fucking string bean,'* as I fully took in his appearance.

Garrett really wasn't *that* thin—I was simply looking at him through green-tinted glasses. He was slimmer than Luke, who typically ran to keep his physique, but he wasn't entirely devoid of muscle. He could have been around my height—six-foot-one-ish. His hair was short—*very* short—and the bar lighting lit up his blonde strands as he moved. The features on his face were remarkably symmetrical now that I was *really* looking at him, with his nose pin-straight and his jawline sharp.

Shawn, who had turned to look at Garrett along with me, murmured an awestruck, *"Oh."*

"Eh," Cassie scrunched up her face in a manner of mild disapproval. "He's alright."

"He's *ni-ice.*"

Just as Claire sang the words, as if he were alerted to being the subject of our conversation, Garrett glanced our way. He lifted a lowball glass that appeared to be filled with whiskey, Cassie threw him a large smile, mouthing, *'Thank you,'* and he beamed back at her. Even from a distance, I could tell that his teeth were...bright. And well-aligned.

My eyes narrowed. *Stupid, attractive fucking string bean.*

"I know that he's nice," she told Claire. "We've talked before."

And just like that, my silence could be maintained no longer.

"You've *talked* before?" I inquired, looking at her with my eyebrows raised.

Thankfully, the remainder of the group was also wearing an expression of surprise, ranging from Liam's mild frustration to Zoey and Claire's delight to Luke's quiet, obvious contemplation of when they would have spoken at length.

"You guys really don't need to look so shocked," Cassie stated. "I've been with you here on Wednesdays. He *works on Wednesdays.* We've talked."

I retorted, "*'Thanks for the drink,'* and *'Can you get me my bill?'* isn't really considered *talking.*"

"You're not here *every day,*" she said to the table rather than me. "I've been here without all of you."

SHATTERED VEIL

Claire nearly squealed. *"And?"*

Cassie chortled, glanced over to see Garrett making his way toward our table with her drink in hand, and the moment he was within earshot, she sweetly asked:

"Did ya short me?"

He laughed as he set the glass down before her.

"I don't short you, Cas," he replied in a voice that I just now realized had a hint of a Southern accent. "You've watched me pour your drinks. I've *measured* them in front of you."

Cassie opened her mouth to reply in what I knew would be some sort of witty banter, and the thrum of unease under my skin had become too much.

Before she could speak, I interjected with a gesture at her drink, "Double Jack?"

Garrett answered, "Yeah."

I snagged Cassie's glass, brought it to my lips, and placed it before me with purpose.

"Mind grabbing us another one?" I asked.

"James," Cassie chastised me.

Liam shot me an appreciative grin, and I pointedly avoided it.

Garrett mumbled an agreeing, casual, "I'm on it," and turned on his heel to walk right back to the bar.

"You never order Jack," Cassie argued. "Seriously?"

"I'm not opposed to it," I returned in a curt tone.

Liam piped up happily, "Good interference, James."

Oh, Jesus.

"What *interference?*" Cassie complained. "Cutting off the shortest conversation of all time by sending him away? *Yeah,*" she glanced at me, "good interference, then."

"Don't date the bartender," Liam told her with purpose, leaning across the table slightly as he said it for further impact.

I shrugged. "Don't date the bartender, Cas." I said it as offhandedly as I could. Everyone in the group, with the exception of Cassie and Shawn, chuckled a bit, and I mumbled, "Bathroom, be back."

I moved as rapidly as I could without causing any undue concern, rushing away from the conversation that had rendered me foolishly jealous. I skirted past the single table that Shawn had borrowed a chair from previously, through the narrow hallway beyond it, and followed it until I ran smack into the men's room. The single, dimly lit stall was empty, and I was thankful that it gave me an immediate means of escape. I paced the room twice. I splashed water on my face and dried it with the brown paper towel roll hanging on the wall. I lightly smacked both of my cheeks as if to silently tell myself, *'Wake up!'*

None of it did any good, and I was just contemplating my next course of action when the door swung open from behind me. I hadn't locked it, unfortunately...and I immediately knew who had entered. As usual, I could feel her before I could even see her. Her burning presence was lingering behind me, silent while I feigned going about my business at the urinal.

"This is the men's," I spoke. "The women's is further down the hall. I thought you'd know that by now."

"Turn the fuck around, Jay, I can tell you're not peeing," she countered. I did so, met her disbelieving eyes, and she exclaimed in a hushed tone, "What the *hell* is wrong with you?"

I blurted out, "Don't flirt with Garrett."

"I was not *flirting* with Garrett," she responded. "I said all of one sentence to him."

"Did ya short me?" I repeated the single sentence she had spoken in a girlish tone that, for reasons even *I* couldn't decipher, contained an English accent.

Cassie snorted. "I'm British now, really? Is that what I sound like to you? A posh British girl?"

"I don't fuckin' know," I griped, looking to my feet.

"You're unbelievable," she sneered. "First, all the shit at my work—which was *bad enough,* my *God—*"

The reminder of my behavior made me groan a miserable, *"Cas."*

"And *now,*" she continued, "giving me shit over Garrett aside, you're here with the goddamn guy you brought to my work. You *told them* that you went to a strip club? Fucking *seriously*, Jay? I told you that I didn't want them to know!"

"Okay, wait." I held up a hand. "They only knew about that because I told them *before* I went. Zoey and Liam brought it back up. I didn't say a *word,* and neither will Brooks."

"Goodie!" she trilled with wide eyes, bitingly sarcastic. "Thanks *so* much."

I pressed my hands to my eyes. "Wait, *wait*...can—can we back up?"

"What, you want to *talk?*"

I exhaled heavily. "Yes."

"About?"

"Me being an absolute ass to you."

Cassie snorted. "Which time? When you embarrassed me after I did what you asked and started to give you a dance? When you yelled at me in the parking lot? *Oh,* or when you forcibly yanked me off of your friend and made a scene?"

"Fuck, first of all," I began, "don't call him my friend."

"The guy that got handsy, then," she attempted to correct.

"The man who exposed your breast," I stated the alternative phrasing, the reminder setting me on edge.

"You're so *courtly*. I'm a stripper, Jay—*exposed* is a weird word to use in this context."

"I don't give a shit."

Cassie paused, noting, "That actually bothered you, didn't it?"

"It bothered me enough to break his fingers," I confessed before I could stop the words from exiting my mouth.

Her dark eyes widened. "When did you—"

"When I pulled his hands off of you. Doesn't matter. We're not *talking about him.*"

"We're talking about *you?*" Cassie asked, irritation back in her tone. "You wanna talk about *you?*"

"Yeah—I was rude."

She crossed her arms over her chest. "Ya *think?*"

"I'm sorry, Cas," I muttered. "I'm *so* sorry."

Looking to the ceiling, she replied, "I don't—I don't *get it*. Do you have a problem with what I do for work?"

"No," I replied in a sigh. Jealously from the thought of what she did for money aside, I truthfully didn't. "I don't. Really."

She held her hands up in a shrug and let them fall by her side in exasperation.

"Then *what?*" she whispered.

"I..." I hesitated. "I was shocked, I think."

Cassie murmured under her breath, "Shocked, you think." She shook her head and returned, "I wrack my brain for the last few days, and it all boils down to that you were just *a l'il surprised.* Whatever. I'm just gonna..." she pointed at the door behind her, turned to begin to leave, and I rapidly moved to stop her by grabbing her wrist.

"Wait, I'm not—I'm not saying this right." I squeezed my grip on her. *"Please,* wait for just a second."

She let out a long breath, rotated to face me, and quietly replied, "Fine. What are you trying to say?"

I gathered my thoughts as well as I could, my fingers burned with the feel of her wrist against them, and I began, "I said it was you that was making me so..."

"Dickish," she offered.

"Dickish," I agreed. In the softest of tones, I said, "I wasn't lying. It's you."

Her shoulders sagged, and she stated, "You're not off to a good start here, Jay."

The undercurrent of frustration in her voice was laced with disappointment, and as much as I had been struggling to apologize without launching into a full-blown confession, it dawned on me that it wasn't fair for Cassie to be kept in the dark.

I breathed through the nervousness that clutched at my chest and admitted, "Not because I dislike you. Not because I have issues with your work. Because having you on top of me left me stunned, and I shouldn't think about you like that, but I did, anyway. I *do,* anyway."

Her anger appeared to have quickly withered away at my confession, and she breathed, *"Oh."*

"I've been a bit too busy holding back what I feel for you, and I snapped. I'm sorry."

"What you feel for me?"

Her recognition of the word was spot on, unlike how she had uttered it in disdain the last time I had seen her. When she repeated the phrase back to me, it was a whisper laced with such...such undisguised *hope* that it made my eyes flutter closed for a quick moment. I opened them, and it seemed as though we had gravitated toward each other. Cassie wore the look of a woman who wanted my lips on hers, and the mere sight made my chest wrench. Desire flooded my veins—desire to capture the strand of hair that had escaped from her ponytail and tuck it behind her ear—to cradle her jaw in my hand, pull her to me, and kiss her like I meant it.

And I *almost* did.

Instead, panic at my decision to verbally cross a line constricted my lungs, and I replied succinctly, "Yeah." Her response visibly churned in her mind, but it didn't get a chance to leave her lips because I wouldn't allow it. I pulled her wrist that was still in my grasp sharply to the left, she blindly followed my insistence to move, and I grabbed the knob as I dropped my hold on her. I ordered, "Stay here for a few minutes so no one asks questions, okay?"

I opened the door with a gusto that made Cassie take a large step back, and she called to me:

"*What?* Jay, *wait—*"

Her eyes were wide as the door shut, and I moved to distance myself from the bathroom as quickly as possible.

Chapter 6

Shawn stood at the bar, smiling at Garrett, who was sliding him a freshly poured stout across the countertop. I wasn't sure why he had chosen to make his way to the bar rather than have Garrett bring his next drink to the table, but I didn't care—and I don't think my facial expression showed that I was in the mood for conversation, either. Shawn took a sip, the foam from the head frothing his upper lip, and as he began to lick it away, he caught my eye and attempted to subdue his flinch.

"Ah—*hey,*" he tentatively greeted me, glancing to Garrett on his left and the table on his right where the remainder of our group sat. "What's wrong?"

"Finish your beer."

His brow furrowed. "Do I ask questions *now*, or—"

"*Shawn!*"

My interrupting chastise of his name nearly came out in a snarl, and he replied:

"Got it, *got it*—yes, sir."

He began to chug, and I turned to see Luke giving me a quizzical expression. Claire looked to him, to me, and tilted her head in curiosity. Zoey and Liam were, thankfully, lost in their own conversation.

"What's up, Jay?" Luke inquired.

"Work emergency, we have to go," I lied. "Long story, catch you up later—I don't have any cash. Think all these can go on a tab for me?"

"I got you. I'll keep track for later," Garrett spoke from behind, and Luke threw him a thankful wave. I again twisted back to Garrett, and he clarified, "Double Basil, Double Jack, two stouts?"

"The Jack was Cassie's," I replied.

His brow pinched together. "You took it from her, though?"

"She steals my drinks all the time, and I still pay for those," I remarked. "It's a thing—she takes my drink, she buys my next one."

Garrett glanced upward. "So...flip the cards, you're buying the second Jack I brought her? Which is the same thing?"

"I, ah..." I had intended to leave before Cassie managed to exit the bathroom, and the ticking clock in my mind had drowned out any remains of my common sense. "I don't—I don't know, just put them all on there."

"All? You want to buy all of her drinks?"

"I don't care, Garrett—*yes*. Sure."

"Mmkay," he replied. "You got it." Shawn set his empty glass down, panting for breath for a moment before covering his mouth as he belched, and Garrett remarked, "I do *not* envy you...feels like you downed a milkshake, huh?"

"Yes, yes—sorry, Brooks," I spoke up before Shawn could respond, turning him toward the exit and murmuring in his ear, "Leaving *now.*"

He waved weakly toward the table. "Nice to meet you guys."

Luke and Claire returned his wave, but Zoey and Liam looked up in confusion.

She voiced, "Why are you—"

"Work emergency," I repeated, for she clearly hadn't heard me previously.

"Can't you just...do your math later?" Liam asked with a tilt of his head that made him look *particularly* dog-like.

"What..." Shawn's steps slowed. "Wait, what do you think we do for a living? We don't just—"

"Not the time, Brooks," I rushed out. "Missing files, lost reports, important clients—*quick!* Before we get *fired.*" I pushed him ahead of me, calling over my shoulder, "Later, guys!" and we raced toward the exit.

The bell rang, the chilly air hit our faces, and the moment that the thudding sound of wood-on-wood was behind us, Shawn griped:

"*Fuck* you, man—do you have any idea how hard it is to chug a stout? My stomach's gonna explode."

All I did was grumble back an, *"Mhm."*

"Why, exactly, are we lying about having to rush off to work?" he asked as we took quick steps back to the apartment complex. "The hell happened? You came outta there like you saw a damn ghost."

"I fucked up," I murmured, a vice continuing to tighten around my sternum.

"What? What'd you do?"

I pressed both hands to my eyes and groaned, *"Oh,* I fucked up."

"Jay."

"I...may have insinuated that I have *feelings.*"

Shawn's eyebrows flew up. "What? I—when did you two even talk?"

"She caught me in the men's—she was *pissed.*"

"Sneaky, Cas," he muttered. "She said she was going to the bathroom, too. Super casual—convincing. Even *I* didn't think anything of it." Shawn rubbed his hands together briskly. "Mmkay, elaborate."

"Elaborate?"

In a scolding tone, he said, "Dammit, Jay! I want dialogue. I want feeling. *I want detail.*"

"I'm not gonna recount the entire conversation, Brooks."

"Well, give me *something* here!"

I recalled the expression Cassie had on her face when I told her I had been holding my feelings back—realization with slow-blinking, warm, brown eyes—and I told him:

"I...think she feels it, too? Or, I don't know, feels *something* for me."

Shawn let out a *whoop,* and I smacked his upper arm.

He whined, *"Oh,* come on—"

I retorted, "This is *not* a celebration."

"What are you talkin' about?" he shot back. "Yeah, it is!"

"I can't go there with Cassie," I reminded him. "I've told you this."

He snickered. "Why, 'cause it feels *taboo?*"

"Yes," I replied. "Exactly that."

"Whatever, man," he laughed disbelievingly. "She's into you, you're into her—I say you two *crazy kids* should give it a shot and not just torture yourselves. Life's too short, man."

I whined to the sky, *"Brooks—"*

"Nah, I'm not hearing your defense. I'm team Camie."

"Camie?" I repeated.

"Jas?" Shawn attempted a second amalgamation of our names. *"Ooh—Jassie.* I'm team Jassie."

"You did not just give us a name," I complained. "We don't need a *name;* we aren't a *thing;* I'm not *going there."*

Shawn shrugged, and his joking disposition waned as he said, *"Or* you do. Go there, I mean. Give it a shot—sounds like it's not only *your* choice now. It's hers, too. That's on you for spilling the beans."

The grip on my chest constricted further, and I sighed, for he may have been right.

I woke twice. The first instance was, I assumed, at two o'clock in the morning as per usual. I wouldn't know—I didn't check. What I *did* know was that I had dreamed of Cassie—*of course*—and a good chunk of my brain had deferred back to behaving like a caveman. A *horny* caveman who has no morals. The metaphorical line having already been crossed, the Neanderthal, which is normally buried in my mind, took control of the show...and I grabbed my dick and beat it like it owed me money.

I'm a sick fuck. *I get it.*

That being said, with no mess to clean due to the handy-dandy tissue box beside my bed, I did manage to sleep soundly afterward.

Until I woke for the second time, that is. Minutes before my alarm was ripe to go off at six o'clock, I opened my eyes to hear my phone vibrating with a vicious rattle against my bedside table. It was a quick, double-buzz that was meant to alert me of missed text messages, and I reached blindly to feel for it. Three pats later, I secured it in my palm, and I felt my face scrunch in confusion at what was displayed on the screen. It was several text messages, and the number was unknown.

910-510-9926
Today 12:15 A.M.

> You ducking ditched me

> Ducking

> DUCKING

> Goddamn auto-correct. You get the point. You have my number now. Call me so we can talk, you ducking idiot.

There's Cassie.

There was no question that it was her, though she hadn't even stated how she had gotten my phone number. I could see her, flustered and rapidly typing, perhaps cursing aloud to herself...and the thought of her reacting that way because of *me* made me smile. It shouldn't have, but it did. So, I contemplated my next actions as I readied myself for my work day.

I showered; I wondered how she asked for my number and from whom. I dried off; I thought about whether or not she was still at the bar whilst texting me at midnight. I dressed; I tried to picture how outwardly pissed she was when she realized that I had left with Shawn. I got in my car; I questioned if she had gotten home safe.

With the phone attached to the stand on the right of my steering wheel, I shook my head and tapped the phone number that I had recently added to my contacts under the name *Cassie*. I periodically glanced at the screen as it rang, the sound loud through my car's speaker. As the time of the call hit the fifteen-second mark, I began to mentally put together a script of what I would leave for a voicemail, and then, she answered.

"Hello?"

Her throat sounded scratchy, and I sighed out, "Hi."

"Oh," she returned, clearly surprised. "Oh, fuck." A rustling sound emitted through the speaker, and considering the sound of her voice, I questioned whether the noise was made by her bedding. "Um...hi, Jay."

"I woke you, didn't I?"

"Yuh huh."

I could practically hear her blinking the sleep out of her eyes.

"You can call me later if you—"

"No, no. I, um...I'm good," she replied.

"Okay." The line was silent, my response seemed like it hung in the air, and I spoke again, "You texted me."

Cassie groaned. "That's hazy."

"Hazy? Why?"

"Well, there were several hours after you performed a disappearing act in which I...drank."

The puzzle pieces clicked together, and I asked, "You're hungover?"

"Mhm...let's, er—bypass the text messages. Bypass last night."

It was an odd sensation, the combination of relief and disappointment...the emotions that I typically found to be polar opposites were now washing over me in unison, and I struggled to focus on the first, for I shouldn't have been *disappointed*. I laughed as if the action would force my former feeling to prevail over the latter, and though it sounded convincing, it did nothing of the sort.

"Bypass," I noted. "Got it. How much did you drink?"

"Unknown," she quipped bitterly. "I could check my receipt from the bar, but *someone* told Garrett they were paying for all of my drinks."

"Ah," I pressed my lips together tightly, remembering my stammering to the bartender as I moved for a quick escape. "*Right.* I think Garrett misunderstood that one."

"Did he, now?"

"Mhm...I'll send you a bill." Her returning throaty laugh at my sarcastic remark—which I had no intention of following through on—made me smile. I asked, "You make it home?"

"*Ah,* no," she returned. "Crashed at Liam's. Driving would have been a poor choice."

Though I knew she couldn't see me, I nodded. Comfort at her decisions from the night prior aside, nerves settled into the pit of my stomach at her admission. I thought back to how Cassie had greeted me, trying to remember if she had used my name. If so, Liam and Zoey would most likely be curious as to why I was calling.

I tentatively began to ask, "Are, uh...Liam and Zoey—"

"They're still asleep," she interjected, the reason for my questioning clear in her tone.

My unease dwindled down to nearly nothing, and I muttered, "Mmkay."

"So, I was thinking—you owe me."

I responded slowly, "Sure, I do."

"Luke and Claire made me aware that you could be of service to me," she noted casually.

A smirk pulled at my lips. "Is that right?"

"Which is why I have your number," she told me. "I have a bench."

"A bench?"

"Er—*swing*. I bought a bench-swing thing that I want to hang on my front porch."

"At this time of year?" I asked mockingly, "Are you going to sit on the bench when it's snowing?"

"I don't know! I wanted one ever since I moved in...never found the right one, and now that I did, I bought it on a whim." Cassie continued, "It's supposed to be nice out today...and there's a storm coming in by tomorrow."

"*And* you need help hanging it?" I assumed.

"Hanging it," she stated offhandedly. "Building it—"

"It's not *built?*"

"I've done half of it already! It's just *kinda* a two-man job to get it hung, and it won't take long to throw the rest of it together with two people. Liam said he's busy with class, so he's no help."

It wasn't at the forefront of my mind, but I did know that Liam was currently in school, studying to become a teacher for young children.

"Right...and it's supposed to snow tomorrow?"

"Mhm. Has to be today...or weeks from now, probably." Cassie whispered dramatically, "I'd *much* rather it be today."

"Cassie," I spoke her name in a soft laugh. "I'm working today."

"I'm aware that you're a typical guy with a nine-to-five job. I'm not working tonight—just come over after." Cassie added in a sing-song tone, "You *owe me...*"

I chuckled, her upbeat mood a rapid shift from our recent interactions that settled on me like a warm blanket, and I once again was inundated with an emotion that I felt the need to suppress. This time, instead of feeling the need to bottle up the feeling of disappointment at Cassie's unwillingness to discuss her late-night text messages, I was wrestling with what I could only discern as excitement. Excitement for potentially spending one-on-one time with Cassie.

It was...dumb. Silly. Juvenile, even, because I knew. I knew this could potentially lead me toward a path that I shouldn't venture down. That aside, the haze of excitement made me blind, and there was little time before I was replying:

"Twist my arm, Cas—I'll help you."

My Thursday at my place of employment was boring. Aside from the occasional dive into Tommy's work stats, which was rapidly becoming a daily activity, the numbers just...numbered. I sidestepped any of Brooks' inquisitions, the data I had to dive into, for whatever reason, was simpler than it typically was, and the hours dragged by. At exactly 4:45 P.M., I was entirely done waiting...and I figured that shaving fifteen minutes off of my shift would do no harm.

I drove with no music on, for my head was already abuzz. I cursed myself for that, and instead of careening down an expectant path that would lead me to rather ungentlemanly thoughts, I attempted to focus on the fact that Cassie had pointedly asked to *bypass* what had happened the night before. It was for the best, really. I told myself that on repeat as I made my way to her house, anyway, and by the time I arrived, I forced myself to believe that those words had stuck.

I strolled to her patio, walked up the few steps, and stopped in my tracks the moment that I saw Cassie's *bench-swing thing*, which was situated to my right.

Cream-colored and entirely wooden, save for the grey seat padding that rested against the siding of her house, it was half-built. Cassie had insinuated this already, but what she didn't describe were the approximately 1,001 steps that were remaining to complete putting it together. There were plentiful thin, wood slats making up the seat connecting on the left to an armrest, but the right was entirely disassembled. The slim panels were resting on the patio along with several pieces of similarly colored wood beside it, which I assumed were designated for the second armrest. A clear plastic bag with separate compartments for various screws, nuts, and corresponding Allen wrenches laid at my feet, and I bent down to pick it up with my eyebrows raised. It appeared that Cassie had cut open several of the sections to use the hardware within—much of it was left still unopened, but the areas that she had cut with scissors were entirely empty. It was then that I noticed a handful of large screws and wooden dowels scattered along the porch.

I glanced around me to ensure that none of them had skittered elsewhere, and the front door swung open. Cassie leaned herself against the doorframe. Her dark hair in a messy bun, she was dressed in a looser-fitting pair of jeans and a heather grey long-sleeve shirt.

She crossed her arms over her chest and smiled. "Hi."

I pointed at the pile of wood to my right. "Um...oh my God? When you said it was *half-built*, I didn't think you meant literally...or maybe that you meant it literally, but I didn't think it was entirely a do-it-yourself operation."

"Is that a problem?"

"Cassie," I laughed disbelievingly. "This is gonna take a *while.*"

"Well, thank goodness you're dressed for manual labor, then," she joked, eyeing me up and down.

I held my hands out to the side and looked down at my appearance—khaki slacks and brown loafers with a button-down shirt most definitely did not scream *carpenter*. My glasses, which I had nearly forgotten I was wearing, slid down my nose, and I grasped them by the stems to place them on top of my head.

I looked back to Cassie, who appeared to be thoroughly amused, and replied, "Yeah, I didn't anticipate having to woodwork. Thanks for the heads up."

She rolled her eyes. "It's not like you're, I dunno, sawing anything—it's just a few screws."

I chortled. "This is not just a few screws...and you spilled half of them on the ground! Are you missing pieces? This is the least organized operation I've ever seen."

Her head bobbled from side to side, considering my sentiment, and instead of answering my question, she simply offered, "I'll buy you pizza?"

"Thought I owed you," I noted wryly.

"Olive branch," she whispered with a smirk. "Are you a pepperoni guy?"

I repeated her action from before, tipping my head to the right and then the left and scrunching up my nose before saying, *"Eh...*sure."

The pizza was delivered and sat waiting for us on Cassie's kitchen table, but we remained outside. Pleasantly enough, in the time past, we had discussed what I do for work while we sat on the floor of the patio, putting together the second half of the bench. Cassie would hand me a screw, dowel, Allen wrench, or whatever else was necessary, and she would ask me a question. They ranged from, "You're a financial analyst, right?" to, "Do you like it?" and the rattled off combination of, "So, it's just looking at reports? Spreadsheets and stock activity? Do you get a lot of variety with what you see?" There were several more questions—all of which were followed with me answering her while holding whatever item she had given me in my hand. I'd wrap up my response, she'd nod and smile, and I would return my attention to the bench. Once the sun was beginning to set in the autumn sky and the chill in the air was growing brisker and brisker, I had legitimately lost count of the questions regarding my job, and I asked:

"Damn, Cas...did you think this was an interview?"

She laughed, glancing to the patio. *"No,* no."

"I mean, if it *were* an interview, it's going well," I mocked. "I'm like five seconds away from asking you about your salary requirements."

"Yeah?" She raised an eyebrow and jokingly asked, "You gonna hire me?"

A corner of my lip pulled up. "I, unfortunately, don't have that power...are you job hunting now?"

I had said it sarcastically, but she appeared to give the notion genuine thought.

"Nah, I'm good where I am," she paused. "For a while, at least. Few years, I dunno."

My head cocked to the side. "Are you...*actually* interested in my job? It's pretty bland subject matter for most people—I figured you were just trying to find something to talk about."

Or taking an interest in me.

I ushered the thought away as soon as it had occurred.

"Actually interested. Took some community college accounting classes."

I smiled. *"Oh."*

Cassie looked at me pointedly. "Do you think just because I'm a stripper, I'm *completely* uneducated?"

"Of course not," I replied as quickly as I could. "I'm aware that you're a smart girl, Cas."

Her subtle reaction spoke volumes. She was already glowing due to the time of day, the vivid pinks and oranges of sundown casting an ethereal hue across her tanned face, but when she registered my words, she appeared to light up from within. Her eyes pinched at the corners, her cheeks swelled as she seemed to be attempting to contain a broad grin, and I was certain that I saw her bite her lower lip as she cast her eyes to the ground. It was more than enough to give me the urge to say the words all over again. Instead, I looked down at the screw in my hand, placed it in the allotted pre-drilled hole that would secure the final slat of the bench seat to the armrest, and twisted my fingers to ensure it stayed in place.

Cassie silently extended her hand toward me to give me the appropriate Allen wrench, and I took it from her without even glancing her way.

"So," I began to slowly crank the screw into place, "do you just enjoy dancing for a living, then?"

"It's not so bad," she returned. "Schedule's been a little chaotic lately, but it'll come around."

"Chaotic? How?"

"Some of the girls went MIA."

"MIA?"

"Missing in action?" she explained the acronym with an uptick of her voice.

"I know what MIA means," I chuckled. "I mean, why?"

She casually replied, "I dunno. They're all flighty—it's not an uncommon occurrence for new dancers to miss a shift or skip off. Employee turnaround is...*high* in this industry."

I nodded. "Gotcha."

"Anyway. All our shifts got moved around...like I said...chaotic, but it'll come around. They'll hire more girls."

I asked, "So...you don't want to do anything with what you've studied?" Cassie hesitated, and I added quickly, "And I mean that in the least judgmental way possible."

I glanced to see her raised brow lower at my latter sentence.

"I would. Whatever an associate's degree in business administration could get me would pay *far* less than my current job, though."

"Right, right," I murmured. "Finished with school, then?"

She didn't respond immediately, and when I shifted my focus to her, she shrugged.

"Tried to get into a four-year school at first. Shit's expensive. May go back for more classes, I'm not sure."

The wood squeaked as I continued to tighten the screw, and I nodded. "Is that why you decided on the associate's instead of a bachelor's degree? The cost?"

Her happiness waned. "Ah, no. I couldn't get into any of the universities near me." I felt my forehead pinch in confusion, and she clarified, "Back in North Carolina. South of Wilmington."

I was well aware that she and Liam had grown up in North Carolina, coincidentally near where Claire and Zoey had lived—though they had never crossed paths with Liam or Cassie until they all resided in Salem. I was aware that he had moved here when he was eighteen and that Claire and Zoey had come along over a year ago. And though I had less intel about her, I was aware that Cassie was new here, having arrived sometime in the early summer of this year.

"I know where you're from," I replied. "You couldn't get in?" Cassie shook her head, and I questioned, "Can I ask why?" Her lips pursed together, and I quickly stated, "You can say no, I just—"

"I didn't graduate high school. I got my GED, but it threw a wrench in any acceptances since I didn't have a diploma or any significant high school experience."

I stopped cranking the Allen wrench. "Oh. You dropped out?"

"Flunked my freshman year," she corrected. "Twice. *Then,* I dropped out. Worked a bit as a waitress after I turned sixteen, started studying, and sat for the GED once I was old enough."

Her gaze was now stuck on mine, slightly hardened as if she were bracing herself for my rebuttal or, perhaps, waiting for me to inevitably question her intelligence. I did nothing of the sort, mentally or otherwise. I just nodded, extended my hand with the wrench, and she took it from me.

Without any inquisition from me, Cassie said, "Turns out, starting high school is a *real* bitch when your mom dies at the beginning of the semester."

I inhaled sharply through my nostrils, and my heart slammed against my ribcage for a single beat.

Fuck. How did I not know that?

"Shit..." I gently spoke, "Cassie, I'm—"

"You're sorry; you didn't know; you would have never asked about it otherwise to save me the discomfort?" She flashed me the smallest of smiles. "I know. You're good; don't be sorry."

My chest was heavy, and my mind was a blur with questions. Questions that I shouldn't voice aloud—most certainly not *now* and perhaps not ever. The first was to ask how her mother died. If she was sick and the illness had taken such a toll over the years that her body had simply quit, or if it was sudden with the trauma debilitating and lightning quick. The second was an inquiry regarding her father because one of the first things that I had learned about Cassie was that he was abusive. I had pushed the memory out of my mind, but I was there months ago when Cassie had seen Liam with a bloodied face—I had absorbed the information when she had incorrectly assumed that the damage was done by their father, Carter. The knowledge of his abuse weighed especially heavy on me now, as I wondered where Cassie had continued to live as a young teenager following her mother's death.

There were several other questions that paled in comparison, but those were the two that struck me the most. Because they were unspeakable at the moment, I replied quietly:

"I still am."

Cassie nodded. "Can we rewind a bit?"

Her voice was uncharacteristically meek.

"Of course."

She coughed as if to clear her throat. "Um—bench?"

"Just have to tighten a few screws, and it's ready to hang," I replied with as much enthusiasm as seemed appropriate, which wasn't much.

She briefly flashed me a grin that appeared to be of appreciation. "Let's do this, then."

Chapter 7

The somber reality of Cassie's childhood and subsequent teenage years hung over us like a dreary, overcast evening. It was dark, and though there wasn't a rainstorm present, our surroundings were still scented in petrichor. I didn't mind it while it lasted...on the contrary, I found myself sinking into it. Not in the way that a depressive episode can swallow someone whole, but in a way that almost felt bittersweet. Bitter with the recognition of what built her as a person...more than bitter—vile. Vile in that I wanted to scrub her past with disinfectant in the hopes that I could wash her pain away...and alternatively sweet with the realization that she had trusted me to be vulnerable, if only for a moment.

Thankfully, the metaphorical clouds inevitably cleared once Cassie made her way to retrieve a ladder from the shed at the backside of her house. We situated it where she wanted the bench to be—with respect to someone facing the house, on the far right-hand side, and perpendicular to the wall—and I climbed up to determine where it could be safely hung. The sun having quickly set, dusk was upon us, and Cassie watched me with a neon green drill in one hand and the other on her hip. Sliding a stud finder across the ceiling, I moved it toward the outer edge of the patio, searching for the joist beneath. It beeped loudly when I found it, and I reached into my pants pocket to grab the pencil Cassie had given me to mark the spot we intended to drill above.

I asked, "You got that string?" Cassie nodded, quickly handing me a blue piece of yarn and two thumbtacks. Because she didn't own a measuring tape—how she didn't ever have the need to buy one, I don't know—we had improvised to measure the width of the bench chains with some yarn that Cassie had in the depths of her closet. As she plopped both of them into my outstretched hand, I joked, "We are *so* lucky that you decided to pick up knitting on a whim."

I secured one end of the yarn right on the pencil mark with the thumb tack.

It was so quiet that I heard her blow an amused breath through her nose. "Yeah, I was shit at it...it's probably good for everyone's sake that hobby was short-lived. The Christmas sweaters would have been hideous."

I laughed. "I would've worn it with pride."

As I began to slide the stud finder across the ceiling once more, Cassie scoffed, "Who said I would have made one for *you?*" I stopped what I was doing, turning my focus to her but keeping my hand on the ceiling, and mockingly dropped my jaw open. She continued with a playful shrug, "*I* certainly didn't say that."

"Y'know what?" I quipped, "I take it back. You can keep your lumpy sweater." I held up the piece of yarn pinched between my fingers. "If you made it with this, it'd be itchy anyway."

She chuckled. "Oh no, that was my practice yarn. I'd bust out the big bucks for Christmas sweater yarn. I'm not saying it'd be pretty, but it *would* be soft...and warm. Probably loose-fitting since I wouldn't be able to get the sizing right, so it would be cozy, too. You could wear it by a crackling fire, watching the snow fall while you drink whiskey..." Her picturesque description was vivid in my mind to the point that I could smell the essence of Christmas, and Cassie paused. "Not that you'd ever know. 'Cause I'm not knitting one for you."

"That's fucked up," I replied with a loud snicker. "Don't make me want a sweater I'm never gonna get!"

Cassie gave me a devious grin.

I knew that was exactly her intention, and I shook my head at her as I returned my attention to the ceiling. I ran the stud finder along the expected path of the joist toward the wall of the house, adjusting forward and back as the light and beeping signifying solid material beneath occasionally petered out. I stretched the yarn taut, pushed the thumb tack into the ceiling, and glanced from point A to point B thrice...because it just looked *off*.

"Uh..."

"What?" Cassie asked.

I moved to slide the stud finder once more, confirming my internal thoughts, and then noted, "The joist isn't straight."

Her head tilted to the side. "What do you mean?"

I held up a hand, gesturing toward the house and then away. "The joists run this way, right? Should be straight...perpendicular to the wall. It's not straight—look at the string."

"Yeah..." she replied, tracing her eyes over the yarn, "I don't want it hung like that. It'll look weird."

I glanced at it once more, and nodded vehemently. "This house is crooked as shit."

"Hey," she admonished me sharply, "don't diss the house. I like this house. I *bought* this house."

My head snapped to hers. "You own this place? How'd you afford that?"

"It's a one bed, one and a half bath cabin in the middle of the woods—it wasn't exactly prime real estate." Cassie added, "And did you forget that I make good money doing what I do? You strip for a few years, you manage to save up for a decent down payment."

"A few years?" I responded. "You're twenty-two, how long have you been—"

"Since legal age, you can do the math," she stated quickly. *"Don't diss my house."*

Surprise aside, I told her, "I'm not *dissing* your house. I'm stating a fact—it's built crooked." She narrowed her eyes at me, and I spoke a bit more gently, "In this exact spot, at the very least. You wanna say it adds to the charm of the place? Go ahead." I pointed to the ceiling. "Doesn't change the fact that this joist isn't at a ninety-degree angle on the overhang. If you want the bench here, it's gonna be angled like the yarn is."

"So, crooked," she deduced bluntly.

I smiled wide. "Just like the house."

She pursed her lips together for a moment and then griped, "I don't want it to look like that."

"Eh, it's not *that* crooked," I reassured her and then joked lightly, "It'll add to the feng shui of the place."

Cassie chuckled, albeit a bit reluctantly. *"Feng shui?"*

"Oh yeah, I'm *all* about Chinese harmony. Balance. This feels right," I sarcastically remarked.

She rolled her eyes, and her grin grew. "You're so full of shit."

"Yup."

Her soft laughter made my smile stretch further, and she sighed. "Fine. If it's gonna be crooked, can we just lean into it and have it be catacorner? Like...hang it from two different joists and have it be facing out," Cassie held out her forearm at what depicted a forty-five-degree angle, "like this?"

I shrugged, pulled the thumb tack closest to the wall out of the ceiling, and threw it in my slacks' pocket, allowing the string to hang free. I climbed my way back down, shimmied the ladder forward, and once I was back up, I quickly swiped the stud finder across the ceiling until the high-pitched beep occurred once more. I kept it held in place, reaching my other hand down and flicking my fingers toward me as I spoke to Cassie:

"Hand me the string again."

She stepped forward quickly to assist me, reaching out to give me the makeshift measuring tape, and her fingers brushed mine as she placed it in my hand. While still focused on the space above, mentally examining the length between the other end of the yarn and where I held the stud finder, I reflexively grabbed her hand. Not the string—her hand. And that would have been fine if it didn't linger there—if the sensation of it in mine didn't make time slow to a crawl. I whipped my gaze to her, finding her dark eyes set on our touching fingers. They remained there for the briefest of moments, I squeezed them, and her hand fell away as she left the string in my grasp. We looked at each other, and for just a beat, we were stuck. Locked in place.

The rational part of my brain screamed at me, *'Cut it out and hang the goddamn bench!'* and I inhaled sharply as I quickly brought my attention back to the stud finder. I moved it along with the string until it was pulled taut, and I saw Cassie take a few steps back in my peripheral vision.

I retrieved the thumb tack from my pocket, shoving it in the ceiling to hold the yarn, and she asked, "There?"

I looked to her again, swallowing to mentally push past our brief, tense moment, and nodded. "What do you think?"

She cocked her head, her eyes tracing the string along the ceiling and then out into the space before us. Cassie moved to stand below me, angling herself as if she were examining her potential view, and she glanced up at me, throwing me a beaming smile.

"Feng shui?"

I chuckled. "Feng shui as hell."

I exhaled in relief as I leaned my backside on Cassie's green and white checkered kitchen counter, biting into a slice of cold pepperoni pizza. The bench was finally hung, the clock to my right on the stove read 8:07 P.M., and we ate in a comfortable, relaxed silence. Cassie sat at her kitchen table, chewing through a bite of her own slice, and she threw me a tight-lipped smile as I caught her eye. She finally swallowed, set her pizza down with purpose, and interlaced her fingers on the counter in front of her.

"So—are we gonna talk about it?"

I felt my head tilt to the side. "About what?"

"Your feelings."

Her bluntness made me cough through the pizza I had in my mouth, I somehow swallowed without choking, and I gritted out, *"Shit."*

Cassie spoke, "Sorry—you know me. I'm not *coy*...and neither are you. So, now that you're here...let's chat."

"I thought you wanted to—to *bypass* all that?"

She chuckled bitterly. "Yeah, *at the time*. When I was hungover and felt like I couldn't completely process sentences, I figured it wasn't the best time to discuss it all."

I opened my mouth, glancing to the front door and back, trying to figure out a way of escape because this morning was...different. This morning, when I had returned her text messages with a phone call, there was the distance of a speaker and several miles between us. If she had asked me to talk about my feelings then, I could have done so—that was my intention, at the very least. Despite the odd excitement I had felt upon receiving the messages, the plan was to pointedly tell her that I wasn't going to act on them. That the emotions I'd been stuffing down would dissipate over time, and ask her to, I dunno, give me some space. *Now,* however, with her beautiful brown eyes staring me down, I was struck with the sensation of fight or flight. Just as I began to question whether or not I should finagle my way out of this conversation, Cassie spoke again:

"If you try to leave right now, I will *literally* tackle you."

I had the urge to laugh—*loudly*—because I could picture her hitting me like a linebacker from behind. I couldn't find it in me to do so, though, because I felt as though the internal battle within myself was coming to a head.

I just murmured, "I'm not going anywhere." I silently placed my pizza on the paper plate that was waiting for me on her countertop, stepped to the seat beside her, and sank into it. I exhaled, nerves having crept up to the base of my throat, gathered my thoughts for the briefest moment, and began, "I...normally have an enormous amount of restraint. I'm a planner...with most things, I mean. I lay everything out in front of me and make calculated decisions—always have. Even when I'm doing something spontaneous, it's...not. Plan A changes, and I quickly think of options B through F, you know?"

Cassie's brow furrowed. "I don't understand, what does that have to do with—"

"But *you*," I interjected to continue to my point. "There's something about *you* that throws all my options—all my *plans*—out the window. You make me tick, and I...I don't have any plans for that, Cas. I'm a fuckin' blank sheet of paper when it comes to you, and I don't know how to deal with that."

Her head moved from side to side, a tinge of sadness reaching her eyes. "What does that mean?"

"Oh, fuck it," I said under my breath. My chest pounded as I confessed, "It means that *I want you*, but I can't do anything about it." Cassie's gaze widened. The beginning of the admission out of me, the remainder was poised to erupt—and I let it out. *"This,"* I rubbed at my sternum with my palm, "has been going on for...a while. But you're," I considered how to phrase my qualms and decided on, "a friend's little sister, amongst many other things…which feels a little more than wrong. I tried to shut it all out of me a long, *long* time ago, but you're…you're always there, Cas." She remained silent, allowing me to speak further if I were so inclined, and I reiterated in a whisper, "You're always there. In my head…under my skin…in my dreams. And *fuck,* when I was at Gas Lamp, you asked me if I just disliked you? I don't dislike you. Hell, I never did. I've been trying to keep myself in check, and I think I'm *fucking. Failing.*"

Our gazes locked on each other in the same intense fashion as they had in the past, and I glimpsed at her mouth as it just *barely* opened. It sent a thrill through me that felt forbidden, and my inhale trembled through my nostrils.

"My turn?" she offered in a breath.

I nodded, and she moved swiftly. Rapidly leaning across the table without a trace of hesitation, I barely had the chance to gasp before she kissed me. Her lips were soft. Plush. And the feel of them against mine made any thought of denying this moment immediately fall to the wayside. A low noise rumbled from my chest, and I reached my hands up to the sides of her face. Her mouth opened, our tongues touched, she sighed against me, a metaphorical checkered flag waved in the air before me, and we took off. Our grasps on each other were suddenly insistent. My grip was in her hair beneath her messy bun; she leaned forward enough to throw her arms around my neck. My touch grazed down to her waist and squeezed; she stood to situate herself between my legs. I rapidly scooted the chair back, and it scraped against the tile loudly; she took the step to close the distance between us, and I pulled her body flush to mine. She stretched across me, and it was only three smacks of our lips before I forced myself to break away. Her head angled down to me and mine up to her, and we were panting, our heavy breaths lingering in the air.

Her pull on me had historically been akin to quicksand, dragging me down into the depths the more that I fought it, threatening to drown me. It was only when she kissed me that the metaphor had come to fruition because the moment that I stopped fighting, it was as if the grit was forcibly pulled from my lungs. I could *breathe*...and it was so simple. All I had to do was stop fucking struggling.

At that realization, my will to maintain my distance from her was leached from my blood.

I brought a hand up to brush my thumb against the freckles on her cheek, and Cassie leaned into my touch. She glanced to my lips and back, I found myself doing the same, and I spoke in a voice that could barely be heard:

"Okay."

Cassie crashed into me, I caught her with my lips, and the usual repetitive mantra within me was silenced. The typical internal reminder that Cassie should be a no-fly zone was...gone. It was lost in a haze of *her*. The vanilla in her hair. The weight of her as I pulled her to straddle my thighs and take a seat on my lap. Her soft gasps when I pulled away to kiss her neck. Her removing my glasses from the top of my head so she could run her hands through my hair and pull at the roots.

The only noises surrounding us were our respective delicate moans...until the sound of a rattling engine and squeaking brakes forced our actions to slow. Our lips quietly separated, we each turned our heads toward the front door, and what appeared to be headlights shined through the front windows and onto the living room tile.

I breathed, "Is someone here?"

"Fuck," Cassie hissed, pushing on my shoulders to separate us and leaving me cold. She sprinted out of the kitchen and to the entrance, peering through the window to the left of the door for all of two seconds before saying, "That's Liam's car; he just turned in."

A jolt of shock ran through me, and the feeling of being caught committing a crime seeped into my veins.

My stomach dropped, and I groaned, "I thought he said he had *class?*"

Cassie paced the space between where I sat and where my cold pizza remained. She reached into her jeans pocket as she walked, checking her phone with a quick glance, and threw her head back in exasperation.

"God dammit, he texted me that he was swinging by, but I missed it. *Bad idea,*" she muttered. "This was a bad idea—*this,*" she waggled her finger between us as she stepped my way, "didn't happen."

At those words, crime be damned, my intestines returned to where they belonged. My back straightened. I felt my head cock to the side, and my jaw hung open as I disbelievingly took in what she said because *that*—erasing what had just occurred from existence—was not on the expected roster for me.

"Didn't *happen?*" I repeated slowly.

"It's forgotten, okay?" she insisted. "Us making out? Rug. Swept under it."

"Oh, it's forgotten already?" I asked sardonically, feeling as though a rug had been pulled out from under me rather than having memories hidden beneath it. "That was quick."

"You know what I mean," she whined, moving away from me and then turning on her heel to spin right back around. She rushed out, "I just got...carried away. I am *not* explaining what just happened to Liam."

"Cassie."

"If he gets weird about it, this could fuck the *whole* group dynamic up—"

"Cassie."

"Oh my *God,* you *dated Zoey!"* she exclaimed in a whisper. "What the fuck was I—"

"Cassie, *hold up,"* my voice turned deep, and her relentless pacing stopped. Once I was certain that I had her attention, I continued, "I wasn't gonna act on anything because of *all* of that shit, but when you point blank ask me about my feelings and then *kiss the life out of me..."* I paused and shook my head. *"That shit* feels damn near irrelevant to me after that, and now you want to forget it?" My tone rounded the corner from annoyed to frustrated, and her eyes widened as I asked, "You think that's *possible?"*

A car door shut from beyond Cassie's front door—Liam's car door, no doubt—and her head whipped from the entrance back to me. I eyed my glasses that she must have placed on the table in the midst of everything, and I placed them on my face.

Her shoulders sagged as she exhaled softly. *"James."*

I stood, and she watched me as I walked to her. I stopped once I knew that she could hear my hushed voice.

"Didn't happen," I repeated her words back, though mine held a sharp edge to them. "It's forgotten."

The front door began to creak open, and Liam's heavy steps thudded on the tile. I reached around Cassie to grab my paper plate behind her and took a large bite of my pizza as I strolled to the other side of the kitchen. I leaned against the counter next to the sink, chewing slowly.

Liam spoke in an upbeat tone, "Cas! How'd you get that bench up? I texted you, but you must not have gotten it...you got company or wha—" He froze at the sight of us, eyebrows raised into his blonde fringe. "Oh...I, uh, thought I knew that car out front." His dark eyes were speculative as he asked me lightheartedly, "What are you doin' here?"

Pulling Cassie onto my lap.
Sucking on her lower lip.
Licking the pulse point on her neck.

I covered my mouth as I finished chewing and swallowed my food. "Bench."

"Aw, *Cas.*" He redirected his attention to his sister, and I bent down to open the cabinet beneath the sink, throwing away my plate along with the remainder of my pizza in the small trash can there. Liam told her, "I could've helped—that's why I stopped by after class. I was gonna see where you wanted it, I," he paused, glancing at me. "Thanks, man."

"It's all good; I was paid in pizza."

And the taste of your little sister's tongue that she requested to be redacted from my memory.

Liam smiled in the same lopsided way that Cassie occasionally does. "How hard was it to hang?"

An anxious lump formed in my throat, and I shrugged, lying, "Quick work. You just caught me on my way out, actually." Without looking her way, I threw Cassie a casual wave. "Later, Cas."

I felt her eyes boring into my back as I headed for the door, Liam gave me an appreciative quick pat on the shoulder as I sidled past him that carried an all-too-heavy guilty weight, and I was gone.

Chapter 8

The night just...passed. I drove home in silence. I went straight to bed. I dozed off in a state of teenage-like angst, but the dreams that I sank into stripped me of the feeling completely. The blur of darkness had the occasional glimpse of light, but it still pulled me into the gloom as I slept. Images played before me like an old Hollywood reel, one short clip following the next:

Zoey, shaking from sheer shock, cradled in Liam's lap as he sat on the grass, mere feet away from a corpse with a mangled skull.

Thin, pale ankles clasped in my hands.

Cassie's body—mostly naked, sweaty, and writhing above mine, colored in sepia tones—hedonism incarnate.

An unknown woman, bloodied and bruised.

Cassie, once again, this time fully clothed and giving me a soft, somber smile as I held her face in my hands.

Claire, shrieking from the depths of her guts as a knife was thrust in her thigh.

Luke in a hospital setting, shirtless with streaks of iodine across a long gash on his ribs as he watched a doctor stitch the wound closed.

Save for those of Cassie and the woman who looked to have been beaten, they were all memories. Horrible memories. They weaved in and out of each other with the daunting fluidity of a rushing river encapsulated in ice—quiet, deadly, and cold...*very* cold.

I woke with the foreboding feeling that typically lingers after nightmares, staring at the ceiling with eyes wide open. It was only a few seconds of trying to make sense of the visions that were leaving me like condensated breath on a winter's day when I realized why I had woken in the first place.

My phone was vibrating on my bedside table, the screen alight with not only the time of—*fuck me*—2:09 A.M., but also with Luke's face. Wearing an amused yet annoyed gaze, I had taken the shot with quick fingers while he was wearing a Santa hat—it was a picture I took nearly a year ago at our Christmas visit to our parents' house. I reached for my cell and swiped to answer his call.

"'S'late."

Luke spoke through the speaker and into my ear. "Are you alone? Are—are you home? Are you home and alone?"

I was certain that I could hear him pacing while he said it—the pitter patter of his quick feet was hollow upon what could have been hardwood, and his tone was inherently anxious.

My chest squeezed. "Um, *yeah*. It's two in the morning, what do you think I'm doing? What's up?"

He rushed out, "We have a problem."

I sat up quickly. "What is it?"

"Can you come down to Henry's?"

"Yeah, I, ah—just give me a few?"

He exhaled heavily. "Yeah, okay. See you soo—"

"Wait, wait, what's wrong?" I asked. "You sound nervous."

"Not over the phone, Jay—just get here." His voice went faint, as if he were pulling the speaker away from his ear, and I heard him speak rapidly, "Did anyone call Cas—"

The line clicked, my head swam, and I looked at my phone in my palm, perplexed. I could have hypothesized endlessly about why he desperately needed me to meet him after closing time at Henry's or why he was asking if anyone had called Cassie, but I didn't. I *couldn't* because the panic in his voice was all too clear, and it was all I could do to spring out of bed, yank on whatever clothes I could find, and half-jog my way down the street.

I was careful to mind my steps as I moved. The ground was covered in at least an inch of powder, and thick flakes were clinging to my hair by the time I had made it. My hands were already throbbing with cold, and when I went to allow myself inside the bar, the front door wouldn't budge.

"The fuck?"

I pushed and pulled with more force in case it was somehow jammed, and by the time I was considering reaching into my pocket to call Luke and question it, he was opening the door for me from the inside.

He stood in the entry, his hair sticking up on all ends and his eyes wild.

"Get in."

I followed his instruction and crossed the threshold. *"Jesus,* you look like hell."

The music was off. As he strode away from me, Luke's steps echoed much like they had minutes ago through the speaker of my phone.

He ran his hands through his hair in agitation and insisted, "Lock the door behind you."

I glanced to the door and back to him. *"Um—"*

I heard an aggravated sigh, and the sound drew my attention to Liam, who was sat our usual table to my right. Claire and Zoey were with him, Claire watching Luke with a forlorn expression and Zoey's gaze remaining peeled on a glass of water that sat before her and appeared to be untouched.

"Just leave the door open," Liam told me with an altogether tired expression. "Cassie should be right behind you."

"Okay," I murmured. Luke began to pace in front of the table, running his hands through his hair, and I remarked lightly, "Brother, you do that anymore, and your hair's gonna start to fall out. What's going on? Why am I here?"

Luke finally took his seat on Claire's right, but I could see that his leg continued to bounce underneath the table.

He exhaled heavily and looked across the table. "We didn't want to be at the complex. Ah...Liam?"

Liam's face pinched together. "Let's wait for Cas, I don't want to have to do this shit more than I have to."

The way he said it made my stomach roll. The air around us all was fraught with a tension that caused the oxygen to strip from my lungs and a steady stream of anxiety to drip along my spine like cold water from an unfiltered, disease-ridden tap. I cringed away from the sensation and beelined to my chair on the right side of the table head.

Just as I began to sit, the bell chimed from the entrance, happy and upbeat—starkly contrasting to our collectively gaunt expressions—and we all turned to see Cassie stroll inside with a curious smile on her face. The only difference in her appearance from a mere few hours ago was that snow had flecked her messy bun, and despite my concern for whatever was troubling the remainder of our group, my mind still replayed the events from our night in quick flashes. The bench, the pizza, the kiss, the weight of her body on mine, the feel of her tongue in my mouth, the sound of my name on her lips after she told me that everything was *forgotten*—it was all there.

Cassie took one look at me, and I wondered, for but a moment, if the reel of events had played in her brain, too…but that all disappeared when she glanced to her brother and saw the expression on his face. The color drained from her cheeks, and she asked in a strained voice:

"Oh, Jesus Christ—*what?*"

She moved as quickly as she could to the empty chair beside me, sinking down into it with her back straight and her eyes wide.

Liam inhaled so deeply that I was certain his lungs had overinflated to the point of pain, let it out through his nose, closed his eyes to gather himself, and when he attempted to speak, nothing came out. He closed his mouth and looked to the ceiling, and Zoey's focus snapped from her water up to Liam.

"Lee, if you don't just show them the video, I am going to *lose it.*"

His dark eyes were soft on hers. "Zo', I have to explain a little—"

"They'll get it off of context clues. Just play the *fucking video, Liam!*" she whisper-hissed.

He mumbled, "Okay," several times over as if it were a prayer while he reached for his phone, which was face down on the table between them. After tapping on the screen a handful of times, he set it between us all. It was obvious that everyone else had already seen whatever Liam had on his phone, for Cassie and I were the only ones to sit forward at attention. He tapped the white *play* button in the center of the screen, and I felt my head cock to the side in confusion.

"Is that the hallway at the complex?"

I saw Liam nod in my peripheral vision. "Put up a security camera after everything. It's by the stairwell. Good angles."

There was no need to elaborate—*after everything* was referencing what had happened months ago with Zoey's stalker. I didn't blame him in the least...and I agreed with what he said—where he had placed the camera did offer good angles. 2A and 2B, my apartment and Liam's, respectively, were in plain sight. The two doors that followed them, 2C and 2D, weren't obscured in the least...and after watching what seemed to be a still image for upwards of ten seconds, a man appeared that made both Cassie and I suck in a quick breath.

Grey-haired, short, and wearing a pea coat that covered most of his body, the remainder of his features were obscured due to him facing away from the camera. That didn't matter, though. We knew who he was. And we hadn't seen Mister Milkovich in months.

Unbeknownst to us, while Zoey was living in apartment 2A, he had generously subleased 2D to his nephew, Peter. Neither Peter's presence nor his identity were clear until he began to stalk Zoey, the realization of who he was became known far too late, and, in an act of defense, Zoey inevitably murdered him. Struck him with a rock on the backside of his skull after he threatened all of our lives until he was no longer. The news had reported his death—declared it some sort of hiking accident to the public—and we had put it behind us. We knew that Mister Milkovich would return to his apartment at some point...that time had never come, though. Approximately four months had passed, it remained vacant, and his existence had simply evaded my thoughts...until now.

He most certainly was not evading my thoughts now.

My vision briefly clouded with the sight of Zoey's stalker. His body infiltrated my mind, thin and pale, dead and maimed, as I clutched his ankles and assisted Liam with chucking him into an overflowing river, and I blinked rapidly to usher the memory away.

I watched the video play as Mister Milkovich slid a key into the knob, unlocked the door, and strolled on in. The door closed, the video once again looked like a still image, and Liam tapped the center of his phone with his index finger to stop the feed.

"When was this taken?" Cassie asked.

"Earlier tonight. *Way* earlier," Liam told her. "I had no idea he had even come by the complex until I decided to check the feed 'cause I couldn't sleep."

"*Okay,* um…so he finally made his way back to his apartment," I confirmed aloud, my voice shaking slightly at the mere sight of him. "That was bound to happen…he probably wants to clean it up and find another tenant."

Zoey's gaze snapped onto mine, and the alarmed look in her eyes harpooned me in the chest.

"And what will Mister Milkovich find in his apartment, Jay?"

"Cameras," Liam answered for me.

I knew that already. We *all* knew that already—the explanation for *how* we knew that was long and arduous, but during the attempt to figure out who the man was that was on Zoey's tail, we *did* learn that he had placed what appeared to be nanny cams in several locations. One was in her apartment—*my* apartment, once she had left. Another was in the hallway in a similar position to where Liam had now placed his. I had taken these two cameras, and, at first, I had simply removed any footage that was recorded on them. It seemed like a solution that was easy enough...but the thought nagged me to the point that I essentially curb-stomped them to hell before tossing the leftover bits into a fire at a campsite in the woods.

Those cameras were fully taken care of. The ones left in 2D, however—the ones in which we had oh-so-briefly stumbled upon their live feed—one that was surveying the Milkovich's living room, and the other looking over a very ominous room covered in what appeared to be soundproof padding—those remained. The knowledge that he could have been intending to use that empty, padded room for...only God knows what with Zoey was nausea inducing. That part of the nightmare was behind us, though. I reminded myself of that as I pushed the memory out of my mind.

"The cameras don't have anything on them," I replied. "Not with any of us. The other two I had are, um..." *Destroyed?* "Wiped, crushed, and burned in a fire."

All heads whipped to mine, and Cassie asked, "You did all that?"

I twisted to look down into her wide, brown eyes, our shoulders touched with the motion, it was as if I were hooked up to an electrical current that set me on *fucking fire,* and because my yearning for the burn had never stopped since I left her house, I had to subdue the urge to lean into the sensation.

"I was a bit anxious at the time," my reply came out in a breath, "so...*yeah.*"

It was a millisecond. A goddamn millisecond that, honestly, I shouldn't have given a shit about because this exact second was akin to a shift in the tectonic plates beneath our entire group. I felt it regardless—felt our eyes lock how they have in the past and reveled in the sensation of lustful bliss, ragingly obvious mutual attraction, and plain old, straight to the point, *need.*

"The cameras are just the start of it," Liam stated ominously, and both Cassie and I shifted our attention rapidly to him. "I mean, *okay,* there's nothing of us on the cameras, but they're still *there,* and one of them is in that creepy-ass padded room."

Cassie replied as calmly as she could, "We knew that Mister Milkovich would see all that eventually. Nothing's changed."

"Yeah," I agreed. "The cameras and the room are creepy. I'm with you. But the guy *was creepy,* and there's no avoiding that being found out. And seeing Mister Milkovich again gives me the heebies, but none of this points fingers anywhere...I don't think any of this is a problem."

Liam leaned forward, slid his finger across the screen to fast forward the video, and just as he tapped to play it once more, Cassie groaned:

"Fuck, there's more."

With a phone pressed against his ear, Mister Milkovich had exited 2D. He shrugged up his right shoulder to hold his cell in place as he locked the door and spoke:

"Soundproofed the guest room and added a lock on the *outside* of it—door was open, but the closet's locked, and I can't get in." With a hand on his hip, Mister Milkovich was facing the camera as he let out a loud sigh and threw his head back. "There were handcuffs and a *gag* in the corner of the room, Artie. It looked like the beginnings of a torture chamber."

I whispered, "What the fuck," because we hadn't seen those on the camera—of course, not all angles of the room were displayed when we had seen the live feed months ago.

Zoey cleared her throat beside me, and Liam gently placed a hand between her shoulder blades, grazing his way up and down her back in a gesture of comfort.

The video continued on with Mister Milkovich saying, "I can't tell Barb about this—no—*no*, Artie, that would be horrible for her—she doesn't need to know that her son was...could have been some sick *freak.*" He began to walk toward the camera, toward the staircase. "I have no idea. I'm sure Peter had plenty of enemies...I just didn't expect *this.* Called a locksmith to open the closet—mhm, tomorrow afternoon—*exactly*—only Lord knows what's in there."

My guts metaphorically left me as he said it, dropping so hard and quick that the noise I made was as if the wind had been knocked from me. The room spun. My throat tightened. The instinctual sensation to *fucking run* struck me, but I knew that it would be no good.

All I could strangle out of my constricted throat was, *"Oh. Fuck."*

Liam reached for his phone once again and tapped on the screen to stop the video.

Cassie whispered, "What's in the closet?"

I voiced, "What was that, *'Exactly,'* that he said? What—what's exactly?"

Luke voiced timidly, "I don't fuckin'—" We all glanced at him, he shook his head so hard that three bulky pieces of his hair fell over his forehead, and he quickly whipped them back with a swipe of his hand. "We don't know, obviously. I—I don't even want to *say it,* but what if he had, like, pictures of you or something, Zoey?"

Cassie stated bitterly, "I'm betting this fucker made a goddamn shrine or some shit—"

Liam scolded her sharply, *"Cassandra!"*

"Mmkay, *sorry,"* she returned to her brother with a high brow, "but do you really think I'm *wrong* on that?"

"That's the conclusion *I* came to, anyway," Zoey muttered. She pressed her palms to her eyes. "I think Mister Milkovich is gonna start digging around."

Claire's blue eyes were shockingly wide as she said to Zoey, "If there's literally *anything* that has to do with you in that closet, you bet your ass that someone's coming to ask you questions."

"Hence," Luke spoke, drawing my attention back to him, "what I said before—we have a problem."

"Okay." I took a deep breath. "Let's...assume the worst and say there's shit that points to Zoey."

"Shrine," Cassie piped up somberly, and Liam shot her a quick glare.

"Even if someone...I dunno, brings it to your attention, comes by to ask you questions, whatever...what else are they gonna do?" I questioned the entire group. "There's no evidence. The rock is gone, the cameras are gone, *he* is gone."

Zoey appeared to be chewing on the inside of her cheek, and then she asked me quietly, "Do you know what they do during autopsies, Jay?"

"Uh," I hesitated, "decide on a cause of death?"

She hummed. "Mhm. Evaluate any obvious wounds, determine when and how death could have occurred, check out their teeth," Zoey swallowed, "potentially scrape their fingernails for DNA."

It was the briefest of pauses—brief, but the potential gravity of the situation had sunken in for us all, nonetheless.

"He had me by the hair," Liam stated gravely, and nausea bloomed in my gut. "Had his hand in Zoey's mouth."

"We...we have no idea what they found. What they *have.*" Zoey added in a rapid run-on sentence, "If they did find anything, it would've been tested against potential criminal records, and they turned up with nothing because we're not *in* the system, but if he has anything in that *fucking closet* that leads to me, they could bring me in, I could be a suspect, they could question Liam too, they could match *both of our DNA's* from that scraping, and then we're both..." She took a rattling breath. "We're both fucked."

Claire's voice shook. "He—he was in a river, that all had to have washed away—"

"Probably not dried blood underneath his nails, Claire. I had that cut on my head. He had me right," Liam reached a hand up to grip his mop of blonde hair by the roots, *"right here."*

"And I felt his nails in my gums," Zoey clarified. "I—I don't remember if I bled."

"Okay," Cassie spoke with purpose, "we need to get in that apartment before he comes back."

"Uh huh," Zoey replied quickly, *"ya think?"*

Claire straightened her spine. "I know how to pick a lock."

Cassie's disbelieving gaze whipped to her. "When the hell did you learn how to do that?"

She sighed loudly. "Long story."

Hands now over his face, Luke blurted out, "No."

"Luke."

"No, Claire," he retorted, letting his hands fall. "Not *you,* not *any of us.* What if we—what if there are other cameras we don't know about? What if someone *catches us in the act of tampering with what could be evidence?* Fucking *none of us* are going."

The silence was heavy as we absorbed his words because he was right. He was right, but none of us wanted him to be. I suspected that we all were pondering the same thing as we wordlessly deflated into our seats:

Do we have to risk it all, anyway?

I had wracked my brain with the question for upward of a minute when the front door to the bar opened once more, the metallic sound of the bell overhead happy and light.

Luke damn near growled, "We needed to lock the *goddamn* door," before he sharply called, "We're closed!" to the entrance.

I looked at whoever had strolled into Henry's. He wasn't large by any means—perhaps Cassie's height, wearing a black hoodie with dark jeans. I'd place him at about Luke's age. Though appearing to be in his mid to late twenties, his expression screamed that life had run him over. His hair, which was as dark as his hoodie, was scruffy and hanging down to his cheeks, damp from snow. He pushed it off of his forehead, the bar lighting cast shadows across his face that almost made him appear gaunt, and when his line of sight met ours, he began to reply in an irritated tone:

"Ya don't look close—" His words stopped, and his eyes widened when he seemed to *actually* see us all. His jaw fell open, and he murmured a mystified, *"Oh my God."*

"Closing time's at two!" Claire called out. "We can't legally serve—"

She finally looked at the man and gasped—I mean, *really* gasped—and I, along with everyone else at the table, glanced at her with a silent, questioning concern. The whites were visible around her blue irises as she took him in, and I swear the color drained from her face to the point that her freckles were the only feature on her skin with notable color.

Luke gave her the quickest of appraisals, scanning her expression for but a moment until he looked back to the man standing with his arms hanging by his sides at the entrance to the bar. He cocked his head, his gaze suddenly alight with an alarmed understanding, and he placed both of his hands flat on the table, pushing himself upward with a significant gumption. His chair shot backward and fell to the floor, and the rest of us, save for Claire, flinched at the sound. Luke took three rapid steps in the man's direction, and he stabbed his index finger toward him as he gritted out:

"Get the *fuck* out of my bar!"

I don't know why it took me so long to realize who he was.

Maybe it was because his hair had grown out, and he had a hint of stubble that was absent the last time I had seen him.

Maybe it was because it had been almost a year since I had been graced with his presence.

Or maybe...*maybe* I had tried to stuff everything that had occurred back then as far into the back of my brain as I possibly could. So far that I was initially dumbstruck as to why my brother was storming toward this man with an obvious, harmful intent.

It was only when the man hissed out, *"Shit,"* as Luke made his way that I was able to connect the dots because he was so shocked that I could see the color of his eyes. It was remarkable that I was able to do so from this distance, but that could have been because they were unsettlingly familiar. The icy blue was so light in color that I distinguished it from where I sat, and the realization felt like a sledgehammer to the chest.

Cassie was barely able to voice, *"Um..."* before Zoey screeched:

"What the fuck?!"

I shot out of my chair, and Liam cursed as he did the same—I was certain that it was both of our intentions to stop Luke in his tracks.

We didn't.

Our respective hesitation while we both came to regarding the identity of the man before us, as short as it was, was too long. Instead, Liam clambered behind me, I took two running steps in their direction, and Luke's fist managed to hit the left side of Colton Langdon's face with a loud, skin-on-skin smack that resonated throughout the bar.

Chapter 9

"Deep breath, brother." I attempted to hold Luke back with my arms around his stomach, yanking him backward as he grunted and fought my hold on him from behind. *"Goddamn—Luke!"* He jerked forward in an attempt to break my grasp, and despite our difference in size, he was nearly able to break free. I called behind me, *"Liam!"*

"Yeah, yup, I'm here," he rattled off, jogging to take my place. I stepped back as he grabbed Luke from me quickly, bear hugging him with his brawny arms around his shoulders and his hands clasping over his chest. He spoke to Luke calmly, "He's on the ground, bud. What are you gonna do?"

I glanced at Colton—Liam was right. Knocked on his ass, Colton was gingerly touching his face and wincing, and he didn't appear to be going anywhere.

"Ya didn't even give me a chance to *say* anything," he grumbled, blinking hard as if he were warding away stars.

"I'm not here for Claire. I'm not fuckin' nuts." His eyes flickered behind me to the table we were all once sitting at, and he offered everyone a weak wave. "Uh, hi, Claire."

I looked to find both Zoey and Cassie standing out of their seats with wide eyes—Zoey assessing Colton's sincerity with a clenched jaw and Cassie's expression one of bewilderment. Remaining seated, Claire tore her eyes from Liam, who was still containing a now stationary Luke, eyed Colton, and replied with a large exhale:

"Hi."

There was nothing but heavy breathing from the direction of Luke and Liam and a quietly whispered, *"Ow,"* from Colton as he traced along his cheekbone with his fingertips, until Cassie spoke:

"Who...who the fuck is this?"

The question could have been assumed to be directed at me because she was staring my way with an inquisitive, dark gaze as she said it. It wasn't, though...it was for the entire group because it was clear that everyone aside from Cassie was either alarmed or enraged—or both—at the mere sight of Colton. Despite that, I still debated how to respond for there was much that Cassie simply...didn't know.

She didn't know that when Claire had moved to Salem, it was as a means of escape from her criminal past. She didn't know that said criminal history was interwoven with her ex-boyfriend, Colton. And she *definitely* didn't know that he had inevitably blackmailed her into returning to her hometown. It was nearly one year ago that Claire had left Luke behind to sort out her old life, all of our newfound group came to her aid, and, in the end, several of us were far from worse for wear. Claire had been drugged, held for ransom, and a knife was lodged deep into one of her thighs. Liam's clavicle was shattered after a bullet went clean through him—the details of which he had, no doubt, kept from his sister. Luke was grazed in the gunfire along his ribcage. The man who was responsible for the injuries was gunned down by the police. Colton, however...was off scot-free.

It was all history that I didn't care to revisit, for we had healed since then. Well, we had healed enough to deal with the *next* traumatic event—the one that had rocked us all to our very core and seemed to be currently resurfacing. But we had healed, nonetheless...and, no, we didn't tend to speak about it. That was Claire's story to tell if she were so inclined to do so, and Claire was *not* one to speak about her past, so it remained behind us—assumed to be dead and buried. *Colton* was assumed to be metaphorically dead and buried to us. Yet, here he sat, quietly speaking to Cassie from the floor with a gritty:

"*Ah*—red's ex." Cassie glanced quickly to Claire and then back to Colton, and he introduced himself, "Colton Langdon." Colton looked at her curiously, as if he were trying to place her. "Who are *you*?"

The way he asked the question wasn't malicious in the least, but for some reason, it still made my chest sink.

Liam thumped Luke on his chest twice and asked, "You good?"

Luke nodded, the murderous glare still in his eyes, yet he remained in place, and Liam hesitantly released him.

Liam then snapped at Colton, "Don't talk to my sister. Fuckin' *leave.*"

"Liam," Cassie argued, looking to her brother incredulously.

He pointed at her and chastised, *"Don't."*

"Fuck off!" she retorted. "I can take care of myself!"

Liam groaned to the ceiling, "You think I don't know that? I just mean—"

"Not to interrupt the whole fam-damily," Colton interjected, slowly moving to stand, "but this was not what I intended."

"Was there something that you *did* intend?" Luke sneered from behind Liam, and Liam held out a hand as if to warn him not to move.

"Ah, *Luke,*" Liam spoke to him in a murmur that was all too clear within the quiet of the bar, "I thought you wanted him *out* of the bar. May not want to open a can of worms on this one—we're *kinda-fuckin'-busy.*"

"*Are you?*" Colton returned with high eyebrows.

"Yeah, I'm not enjoying the worlds colliding here, either, Liam," Luke hissed, ignoring Colton's remark. *"Five minutes."*

Claire spoke, "Why are you here, Colton?"

"*Here,* here?" he asked. "To drink. I had a long night, and—for the record—I didn't realize it was past two in the morning. *That was my bad.*"

"Why the *hell* are you in *Salem?*" Claire returned with more bite.

The initial shock that was painted on her face had washed away, and it was now replaced with something far beyond mere frustration.

Colton glanced to the front door and back, looked at all of us with a rather contemplative expression, and began to ask, "Are...are y'all *good?*"

"*Nope,*" Zoey spoke this time. "As far as I'm concerned, you can go buy yourself a one-way ticket deep into hell's asshole."

"We've never been on the best of terms, have we?" Colton returned, an odd, Cheshire-like grin growing on his face.

"Colton," Claire stated his name quietly, but it was as if it rang through the air.

Colton held up a hand in Claire's direction. *"Uh-bup-bup,"* he voiced. "Give me a quick l'il minute here. I haven't had the chance to absorb all this." I was priming myself to say that he didn't need to *absorb* anything when he cocked his head at the table we were once all sitting at and continued with, "Y'all are *tense*...past close at a bar," he gestured at Luke without turning toward him, *"your* bar...but not a drop of alcohol on the table between the six of you...and when I first walked in, it did *not* seem like you were leavin' any time soon." He squinted at Claire. "You're nervous...*really* nervous...and it's not because of me." His eyes narrowed even further as he murmured, *"What did you do?"*

"No." Liam said, "I'm not having you up in Zoey's business—"

Colton gasped dramatically, whipping his focus to her. *"Zoey! You?!* What'd you do?!"

His candor that had morphed from initial shock to confident, cocky, and questioning shot directly under my skin, and I yelled:

"For the love of God—we need to know that you aren't here to fuck any of us over. Just tell us *why you're fucking HERE, Colton!*"

Colton looked at me with eyelids halfway over his gaze. "If it makes ya feel any better, it has absolutely *nothing* to do with any of you."

I muttered, "Why do I have a hard time believing that?"

I had meant my question to be rhetorical, but he murmured in return, "You *may* be right," in a way that came across as mystified. Colton glanced around the room, asking, "I'm assuming that y'all live nearby?" None of us answered, and he seemed to take our nonresponse as a confirmation. "'Kay...*anyway*—this cute, sleepy li'l town has women going missing out the wazoo. Cue my arrival."

Wait, what?

Cassie spoke my exact thoughts aloud, "Wait...*what?*"

Colton looked at her with an interest that was piqued to the point that it unsettled me, and he inquired, "Are y'all *really* not in the loop on this?"

Cassie's question and my internal concern were sidestepped as Luke sharply spoke, *"No, we're not in the loop on that.* What, are you looking for more women to trick into being rescued?"

He used his fingers as quotation marks on the last word, and Colton's eyes hardened ever-so-slightly.

"Luke," Claire warned him with a pointed gaze.

"I'm feelin' some tension from ya," Colton retorted back to Luke. "Do we need to clear up that I never *tricked* Claire into any of the shit we did?"

"Yeah, until you fucking *blackmailed* her!" Zoey exclaimed disbelievingly.

"Hey, my life was on the line." Colton looked to Claire and said seriously, "You know that. I would've never—"

"None of us want to hear an *apology,* Colt!" Zoey returned.

"Well, fuck, I'm aware of that," Colton stated. "Tried to apologize once before, and pretty boy here punched me." He gingerly touched his cheek, saying to himself, "Don't think this one'll bruise..."

Luke's eyes widened. "You showed up at the goddamn hospital after Claire was stabbed, and Liam and I were *shot!"*

Cassie, whose pretty head was ping-ponging between everyone as they spoke, nearly vibrated as she took in Luke's admission.

Just as Luke was beginning to say, "Of *course,* I punched you," Cassie shrieked at her brother:

"You were *shot?!* What in the actual *fuck,* Liam?!"

Liam threw his blonde head back as he let out a loud groan. "A whole *year* ago—"

"A year?" she questioned. "That—*that's* what happened with your shoulder?! You said that you dislocated it, you lying *fuck!*"

"Now's not the time to get into it, Cas," Liam admonished her.

Cassie sank with a thud and the heaviest of eye rolls back into her chair, crossing her arms as she sat.

I shook my head rapidly because Colton's initial confession was still ringing in my ears.

"Do we wanna, like, address the fact that Colton said women are going missing in Salem?" The room fell silent once I spoke, and then I ordered Colton, "Tell us how you know that, why they're going missing, what that has to do with you being here, and then *get out.*"

Colton nodded slowly, chewing on the inside of his cheek as he seemingly thought to himself, and eventually replied:

"Yeah...*yeah.*" He clapped his hands once, as if he had internally come to a conclusion on something. "Yes, I *can* do that, 'cause I think y'all are makin' me start to smell fate." His eyes oddly bright, he took in a large breath through his nostrils and, upon letting it out, asked, "Is anyone else smellin' fate?"

Claire's elbows audibly hit the table as she held her head in her hands and grumbled, "Oh, good God, we don't have time for this."

"*Oh*, I'll be quick. Can I..." Colton pointed at the bar; his unfinished question went unanswered, and he strode past a dumbfounded Luke and Liam to take a seat. He sighed as if the load off his feet was a necessity, swiveling on the stool from left to right. *"Alright*—how do we wanna do this? Can this be like an *I show you mine and you show me yours* type of deal, or what?"

All of us simultaneously spoke different variations of, *'We aren't telling you jack shit,'* and he waved us away.

"I'll go first," he remarked. "I know about the women because, over time, I've come to know of some *very bad men*. These *very bad men* are taking these women—I'll stop there with the details to save your virgin ears. *Anyway*, this all loops in with *me* 'cause what they're doing is fucking disgusting, and I'm trying to stop them."

Luke tilted his head to the side as if he couldn't quite hear him correctly. "I'm sorry...someone's, what, paying you to..."

"Oh, no-no," Colton waggled an index finger in the air. "No one's paying me to do anything—ya see, I *thought* I hit rock-the-fuck-bottom after all the shit with you guys with my debt and the, ah, *everything else*. I didn't. Long story. I'll save ya the trouble. Point is—badder and badder work acquaintances equals more and more money." He snapped as he shot a finger gun at Luke. *"I've got money, now.* But all that *also equals* badder and badder shit to do and a shittier and shittier conscience." Colton concluded, far more somber than I expected, "Just…just tryin' to clean my slate. That's all."

I scoffed. "We're supposed to believe that you've been doing vigilante shit?"

Colton beamed. "Vigilante shit. *That* chicken soup has been good for the soul, man, *fuck.*"

"Okay." Luke stated disbelievingly, "Sure. You're a vigilante. *That tracks.*"

"What are you, twelve-stepping your way across the eastern side of the United States?" I sarcastically retorted. "Did ya find a narcissist's anonymous group? *Did they give you a program for recovery?*"

"Guys," Claire interjected, gesturing to herself, Zoey, and Cassie, "We're women. We all live here. Color me concerned regarding the potential missing women." Luke exhaled heavily, and Claire added, *"And* why you're so fucking eager to tell us all of this."

Colton wryly asked, "I'm not allowed to catch up with friends?" All of us collectively groaned—some with profanity and some without—and Colton's voice hitched up higher as he alternatively noted, "It always feels good to tell people that you're tryin' to better yourself?"

Claire admonished him with a biting, *"Colton."*

"What?" he chuckled back. "I *am*. Is that so hard to believe?" None of us had a response to that, and he sighed, his voice dipping deeper as he said, "If your reputation is squeaky clean in this town, you're safe, okay? Most of the missing women were in cahoots with some cartel, or...or they were prostitutes or strippers."

It was far from what I had anticipated, and my heart leaped out of my chest. I quickly glanced at Cassie to find her staring at Zoey's water. I took a deep breath as quietly as I could manage, let it out through my nose, and repeated the action over. When I saw that Colton was peering at Cassie as if he were awaiting her to speak, dread settled in my gut.

"As to why I'm telling you anything at all...like I said...*fate,*" Colton continued, moving his focus to Claire. "You think I *wanted* to run into you guys? You have so much fuckin' dirt on me, you could *whisper* in the cops' direction and I'd be behind bars. But, coincidentally, I'm here...and so are you." His tone turned from serious to grave as he admitted, "The situation's fucked, and I'm on the outside lookin' in here. If any of you have anything—*anything*—that you could tell me...now's the time."

The situation's fucked.

Colton, of all people, was saying that the situation was fucked.

The situation was fucked, and amongst many women, some exotic dancers had been taken for only God knows what. In this area of Virginia. Where Cassie secretly works as an exotic dancer. At an establishment that Cassie had oh-so-briefly mentioned was understaffed due to dancers going, as she had termed, *MIA.*

I desperately wished that I could toss everything he had told us out of my brain. That I could say, *'Welp, that's just simply not true, and it's time for you to go now, 'kay bye,'* and usher him out the door. As much as I didn't want to believe him, though, it was all too coincidental. The puzzle pieces fit, and furthermore, I couldn't think of a single reason that Colton would have to lie to us with the amount of conviction that I saw in his eyes—and *that* made it all the worse.

My hands shook, and I thrust them into the pockets of my jeans. My stress-induced tachycardia remained, and though the very real threat that Liam had announced to us all earlier was still unresolved and fresh in our minds, this knowledge still felt dire. Insane as the feeling was, and as much as I hated the fact that he was here at all, I suddenly felt as though I needed Colton to stay. To give us more information so I could be assured that Cassie wouldn't be in danger...or, conversely, so Cassie would realize that she had to...I don't know, quit her job? Distance herself from the clubs? Lay low while the dust settles with whatever he's involved in before going back to her life as normal?

That assurance couldn't be obtained—not without completely outing Cassie to the entire group. She would hate me for it, of course, because this was her life and she was living it the way that she wanted to, but keeping my mouth shut wasn't a viable option. Ushering Colton right out the door he had strolled in minutes ago without any further explanation was...impossible. I mentally gathered my words, preparing myself to speak on the matter, but Claire asked first:

"What about you scratch our back, then we scratch yours?"

The way she said it was all too casual. I felt my head tilt to the side as I tried to understand her intention, and everyone else remained silent until Colton slowly replied:

"Not what I was *hoping* for, but I'm listening."

"No questions asked?" she requested.

He shrugged. "Sure."

Claire announced, "We've got a lock to pick."

The swift return of our conversation regarding 2D was forced by her hand, and I pulled a sharp, surprised breath through my nostrils. What sounded next was entirely simultaneous:

Luke exclaimed, "Are you out of your goddamn *mind?!*"

Liam groaned, *"Oh,* God," and lifted both of his palms to press them to his eyes.

Zoey's gaze turned bright with a desperate hope, and her jaw hung slightly agape.

Cassie simply raised her eyebrows.

Colton glanced to Claire. "Why can't you do it? You've got muscle memory. I'm sure you'd pick it no problem, whatever it is."

She said nothing while Luke rolled his eyes heavily and threw a single hand in the air just to let it fall against his thigh with a *smack*.

"She just can't," Zoey snapped at Colton, "but *you* can."

Liam murmured, "Zoey," whilst Luke simultaneously barked:

"Fucking *no!* Are you kidding me?"

Her expression near crazed, her high pitch trilled back, "Would you two rather commit fucking arson and *burn* the complex down?"

Luke and Liam's complaints halted in their tracks. Liam mumbled a reluctant agreement at the obvious severity of the situation, and Colton murmured, "Complex?" while Zoey continued:

"I'm not letting this shit ride. The point is that *someone* needs to get in that apartment."

"Y'all need to break into an apartment?" Colton asked, eyebrows high as he crossed his arms over his chest. *"Whose?"* Our collective hesitation to that question, brief as it was, made him whisper, *"Interesting."*

"It is *not* getting interesting," Zoey bit back. "And as tired as I am of seeing your mousy-ass face—"

Colton muttered, *"Mousy?"*

"It's in the nose," she clarified. "And the ratty personality. Like I said, as much as I don't want you here, *you are.* Therefore—apartment. Break in, potentially snag a few things while you're in there." She bluntly stated, *"Scratch.* I, personally, think we've done enough for your ass to not need to figure out how we can scratch your back in return."

"And no questions?" He asked with a grimace. "Yeah, I'm not super keen on that idea; picking the lock on a residence and stealing shit out of it is a *big fucking ask."*

"Uh huh, because you're a total stranger to thievery," I sardonically snapped.

"If you think it's too big of an ask, then *leave,"* Claire told him with a challenging gleam in her eye. Colton visibly sighed, and she crossed her arms defiantly. *"Oh,* I'm *sorry*—is that not a good option for you?" Claire asked him in a sickly-sweet tone, "Are you worried about what you're getting into because you're grasping at straws? Do you think that asking us a few questions could be *beneficial?* After all, we do work at a bar, and drunk people tend to talk. Maybe we heard a name that you know of being mentioned, and it could give you a point of direction—I dunno. Does that sound like something that could be helpful to you, but you don't have anything to hold over our heads and *make us talk?* Is there nothing you can do to *force* things to go your way?"

Colton's expression twisted at the last two sentences of her sneering monologue, conveying his remorse for the past, and he returned in a raspy tone, "Fuck...I really am sorry, Claire."

What had appeared to be pride at Claire's harsh words had comingled on my brother's face with his prior anxious frustration, but that all washed away and turned to disgust as his focus high-beamed on Colton. The left side of his mouth pulled up in a silent snarl, but he held his tongue.

Claire hesitated, her jaw clenching before she said, "I don't need your apology. I need you to break into this apartment for us. You can ask us questions after—about your shit, *not ours."*

Colton pursed his lips as he took in her words and began to bounce his head from side to side as if he were regretfully debating the pros and cons of assisting us.

"Is no one else concerned that he'll just hold this shit against us and threaten blackmail *again?*" Luke asked as devil's advocate.

"How in the *fuck* would I do that?" Colton returned, throwing about an arm to gesture between himself and Claire. "We have dirt on *each other.* That's why we can peacefully cohabitate on the same *goddamn planet.*" He then pointed to the ceiling, moving his finger in a circular motion as he said, "Let's circle back—if I'm nabbed for breaking and entering, I'm getting five to twenty years—"

Zoey exclaimed, *"That much?!"*

"Yup!" he replied, popping the *p.* "My point is if I help you—*if*—that risk is on *me,*" Colton tapped his chest, now speaking to Luke, "not any of *you.* And that's a pretty fuckin' big risk. So...do you want that on you?" He paused, and then waved in Claire's direction. "On her?" Luke's reluctance waned at the mention of a threat to Claire, and Colton concluded, "Then, *please...*tell me that you have something for me aside from potential bar gossip, 'cause as sorry as *I am* and as much as I'd love to do this out of the goodness of my heart, I don't know if that's enough. *Help me help you.*"

Claire and Zoey both pressed their lips together tightly, and that was when I caught Cassie's eye because I was anticipating her to speak up with an admission. An admission that, of course, didn't reveal all of the details that Colton would crave, but enough to usher him into assisting us. I watched her as she opened her mouth, bracing myself for a raucous reaction from the group—mostly Liam—and then, she promptly closed it. Colton glanced at her with a raised, expectant brow that said he was ready for her to prove him right in his assumption of *fate*.

Cassie's focus flickered from me to him and back again. The remainder of the group was too occupied elsewhere in their thoughts to notice the split second of her hesitation, but I most certainly wasn't. Her dark eyes met mine, I saw the hint of a plea within them, and without bracing myself to so much as think, I blurted out:

"I was at a strip club about a week ago—Gas Lamp."

Cassie's shoulders lowered as she let out a long exhale, and I was sure that Luke, Claire, Liam, and Zoey's heads had all turned to me, but I paid them no mind. I solely waited for Colton to pull his eyes from Cassie, and when he did, he appeared to be assessing me with a generous scrutiny.

"Gas Lamp, really? I was casing that place a few days ago."

"Mhm," I told him. "It's understaffed."

He nodded. "That it is."

"I was told some of the dancers skipped their shifts."

Colton squinted. "They ever come back?"

I shrugged. "Don't know, but I can find out."

He asked, "How?"

The question was an obvious one, and it was directed at me from not only Colton, but everyone else with the exception of Cassie. Their confused, questioning expressions caused me to sigh, and I noted vaguely:

"I'm close with one of the dancers. We can talk later."

The bewilderment abound was immediately replaced with surprised understanding. I had no doubt that the questioning regarding said closeness and what that entailed would bombard me at some point, and I was ever-thankful that this was *not* that time.

Colton gave me a curt nod, and I pressed, "Is that *enough?*"

"Dammit," he groaned. "Yes. It's enough."

Zoey spoke again quickly, as if she were concerned that he would change his mind, "We don't have much time."

Nervousness at the upcoming events aside, relief still swarmed me to know that he would stay. That whatever Peter Milkovich kept in that closet could be known only to us. That the opportunity to speak with Colton further had been created, and he wouldn't simply disappear into the night, never to be seen again. I glanced at Cassie, saw my sentiment reflected back to me in her eyes, and she held my focus. Without having to say a word, she recognized my inner thoughts and subtly—rapidly—mouthed a silent, *'Thank you.'*

I blinked, and the moment was gone. Our eye contact broke, I pushed the thought of the potential danger in her life aside, and forced the current threat for us all to the forefront of my mind.

Chapter 10

Only minutes had passed since we had deduced that Colton's assistance in everything would be akin to an oddly necessary third-party demon sent from hell. It goes without saying that the trust that I had in him—that the rest of the group had in him, for that matter—solely existed because we were operating with a mutual benefit. We needed him, and he needed me. Well, truthfully, he needed *Cassie,* but that was a fact that obviously hadn't been spoken aloud. As often as he would glance at her with a brief questioning eye that appeared to be judging her familiarity, I had started to wonder if the secrets that she kept from our friends and family were known by him. It was a thought that I didn't have the chance to fully process for, as a group, we were…rather busy.

With the knowledge that Mister Milkovich was returning to his apartment later in the day—assumedly in the afternoon with a locksmith per the short snippet of one-sided conversation that we had heard on Liam's security camera—we knew that we had to act quickly. *How* quickly, we didn't know...it *was* his apartment, after all, and he could legitimately return at any minute. The only advantage we had was that it was still what most would consider to be sleeping hours. As urgently as we needed to act, though, we still needed time to lay out a plan. Taking our seats back at the table with Colton remaining at the bar facing us, we did just that.

Colton rubbed at his eyes and then let his hands fall to his lap as he opened them wide. The whites were bloodshot, and it offset the cool iciness of his eyes in a manner that almost made him appear more spent than he was. There was no doubt that he was exhausted—we all were, as it was nearing three in the morning—but he was tired in the sense that he looked manic. I supposed that one would typically behave as such, considering the circumstances.

It was good that he was worried. If he didn't succeed in getting into apartment 2D, scour the place for anything that could lead back to our entire group, and then leave without being caught...he would most certainly be in prison for a very long time. On top of that, if Colton didn't manage to remove the potential evidence in 2D, both Liam and Zoey could be, as she had so eloquently worded earlier, fucked. *Very* fucked.

So...yeah. We, as a group, weren't calm in the least, but I supposed that how he was acting seemed...apt. Especially because we were now going over final details, ironing out our necessarily rushed plan, and searching for any possible wrinkles before springing into action.

"Okay, okay-okay," Colton spoke. "So, 2D—it's not occupied." We all shook our heads *no.* "The guy who lives there is presumably coming back at some point today." General nodding from all of us. "And I'm," he squinted as if he were confused, "...taking down cameras that are *inside* the place?" Nods, once again. "This is feeling like evidence erasure," he grumbled.

Claire said, *"Colt."*

"Not asking," he remarked rapidly. *"Not asking.* 'Kay—cameras and..."

"Anything that seems out of place," Zoey finished. "Or looks like it could have anything to do with us, specifically in a closet that we know is locked."

"And you...don't know what could be in this closet?" Zoey shot him a glare, and Colton spoke slowly, *"Right...*ah, phone call. Keep me on speaker on your end. I've got some headphones in my car that I can use to keep you in my ear...I'll relay everything back, you tell me where to go and what to grab or leave behind. Who's gonna look out? Are there multiple entries?"

"One staircase, second floor," Claire explained.

"We'll probably just watch through the surveillance cam feed, right?" I asked the room.

"Surveillance cam?" Colton inquired. "Where's that?"

"Hallway," I replied.

"Yeah," Liam mentioned, "it's on my side of the hall, same as 2D, but it's angled—"

Colton's dark eyebrows flew up. "The fuck do you mean *your side of the hall?*"

Liam's mouth hung open as if he were intending to say more, but his mind had drawn a blank.

Luke held his head in his hands and griped, *"Liam,"* and Liam's jaw snapped shut.

Zoey sighed heavily. "Yeah, thought that one was gonna come out."

Colton noted, "So...you live there?"

The question was directed to Liam, and he *did* respond with a quick, succinct, *"Uh,* yes," but the way that the remainder of the group collectively squirmed made Colton cock his head to the side in curiosity.

"I'm...gonna pretend like I'm not assuming that you *all* live in the same apartment complex as this infamous 2D," Colton quipped. *"Moving on...*camera's in the hallway?"

Liam replied, "Mhm."

"'Kay," he stated hesitantly. "We need a second means of surveillance. That'll only give you enough time to say, *'Colt, someone's coming,'* before someone's walking through the door."

"What are we supposed to do," I chimed in, "have one of us posted up at the bottom of the stairs? There's a *blizzard*. It'd look mighty suspicious to have someone visibly on the lookout."

"Well, I need *something*," he argued, his tone sharp. "*Someone*. Your camera's not gonna cut it."

"That's all we have," Zoey retorted with narrowed eyes.

Colton bit back, *"All you have* is not *enough*. I'm not goin' in blind—I'd be asking to get caught without a more reliable lookout. Look, I'm down to help, but if that's *all you have,* I'm fuckin' out. I get that I have risks in this, but I'm not slitting my own throat here."

"*Okay,* okay," Cassie spoke. "Like Claire said—one entrance to the complex. Let's just all pile in a car or something and keep an eye from down the street. I've got the Jeep...we can all fit."

"*Thank you.* Jesus," Colton said as he let out a large breath. "That's much better...and you're right. One entrance is good. You only have one area to look out for, but that also means that I may only have one exit. If anything *does* happen and it looks like there are cops en route or some shit, I'm fuckin' bookin' it. I'm takin' a quick glance and grabbing what I can, I'm taking off, and I'm laying low."

Liam's brow pinched together. "Why do you have to take off? I live next door. I'll leave the door unlocked...if it looks like someone's coming, we could warn you, and you could be in my apartment before you're even seen."

Colton shook his head so hard that a few inky black strands of hair fell across his forehead. He pushed them back and countered, "No, no, no. That implicates you."

"Not if they don't see you," Zoey remarked.

"You have a security camera up," Colton reminded both of them. "If a cop's smart enough, they'll ask for footage. They catch me on tape going in and out of 2D? Whatever, I'll make sure my face is covered. They catch me going to *your place*...you're an accomplice."

"His camera can be easily taken down," I stated.

"And then none of whatever you have to grab out of 2D is just floating around wherever you have to run," Luke spoke up. "Take down Liam's camera, get in, get out, get back to Liam's apartment," he added in a bitter murmur, "get out of our lives."

"I'm not out of your lives until I'm chatting with *you*," Colton pointed at me with purpose. "That aside—any other tenant could have a security camera. *So* many people have them on their doorbells and shit now. It's too risky."

Barely loud enough for me to hear, Luke whispered down to Claire, "2C?"

She murmured a quiet, "Don't think so," back to him, and just as he was about to speak to her once again, Colton voiced:

"Secret-secrets are no fun, guys—you got somethin' to share with the class or what?"

Their nearly silent, two-sentence conversation didn't need to be explained to me—2C was the only other apartment on the second floor aside from mine, Liam's, and 2D, and it was obvious to me that Luke was questioning if our neighbor had a security camera.

Claire begrudgingly said, "I don't think they have a camera up, but I'm with Colt."

"Claire," Luke complained.

Claire shrugged, his bothered tone not outwardly concerning her in the least. "Too risky. Even if there aren't any other doorbell cams or whatnot, there are too many other factors. Walls are thin—downstairs neighbors could hear foot traffic if they're awake. 2C could literally watch through their peephole since they're right across the hall. Anyone in the entire complex could walk by and see him moving from 2D to Liam's. All more reason why *we're* not doing this shit." Colton nodded emphatically as she spoke, and Claire looked to him. "Liam's camera'll stay up so we can keep an eye on the hall, and we'll watch the entrance from down the road. We are in your ear and nothing else."

"I'm with ya," Colton replied quickly. "All goes as expected, we wanna just meet up here after?" All of our heads bounced in agreement, and Colton murmured, "'Kay...and for anything *un*expected...if I take off, don't try to distract whoever's coming. Don't try to intercept—that just points fingers back at you guys."

"Alright," Cassie murmured, "so...you run for it. We call you later?"

"Oh, no," he said. "If I take off, my phone's *gone*. I'm losing it however I can."

"Wait—what?" Zoey asked with high brows. "How are we supposed to get back in contact or know if, *I dunno,* you're on the run?!"

"Are you worried about me?" he cooed with a wry smile. *"Zoey!* I knew I'd grow on you."

Liam snapped, "You're not growing on anyone."

Zoey patted Liam on the forearm without taking her narrowed gaze off Colton.

"I'm not worried about you, you fucking *butt plug!* I'm *worried* that any shit that you grab from that closet will be in police custody or—like Luke said—just floatin' around wherever the hell you have to run off to!"

"See, it's shit like *that* that makes me want to question this situation more," Colton remarked. Zoey's nostrils flared in silent response, and he held up his hands in defense. "I'm not gonna! Building trust," he waved at himself and then the remainder of the group, "we're *building trust here.* Anyway...you're not gonna want me to keep my phone if the cops are after me. If I have that on me and the police see that you were the last point of contact and realize the call aligned to the time of the break-in..." He allowed his sentence to trail off without completing it because the insinuation was clear.

"Can't you just delete your call history?" Luke questioned.

Colton returned, "From displaying on my phone? Yeah, but I'm gonna be a little preoccupied with getting the hell out of there—and that wouldn't permanently remove it from my cell, either. If the cops want to plug it into a computer and do a deeper dive, it's still gonna be there. All that data just gets hidden somewhere else unless you nuke it...like, wipe it clean, give it a factory reset as if you're trying to sell the damn thing. I can't exactly do that in a rush, so I'll just ditch it somehow. Chuck it out a window, stab the screen with my keys a few times, try to flush it down the toilet—I've got options there. *Anyway,"* he continued without skipping a beat, "I'll plan to come back here—right away if all goes to plan. After the dust settles, if shit goes sideways...probably a few days, maybe a week. I dunno. I'll feel it out."

"So, what," Cassie asked him, "we just have to wait? You may just...*disappear?*"

"That's the name of the game sometimes," Colton told her with a shrug.

Everyone else remained silent, and I glanced to see Cassie shaking her head. It was the slightest movement, but I caught it nonetheless, and I assumed it was because she intended to speak privately with Colton afterward. The tone she had questioned him with was casual enough—well, it most likely *sounded* like a casual tone to the others who weren't privy to the threat that Colton had presented earlier. It wasn't casual in the least to me, though. I could hear anxiety laced in her voice...and though we had shared several moments in the past that were far more than tense, I had truthfully never heard that from her. Fear, I had heard—downright, to-the-bones terrified, I had heard. But anxiety—a hidden worry over what was to come—a nervousness over a loss of control—I had never heard that from her in the least. It was a fact that used to be astonishing to me.

I mean, she was beautiful, sarcastically witty, and stoic in the face of all things traumatic—what *wasn't* there to be astonished about?

Now, however, as I heard the nervousness that she attempted to hide beneath the surface, I could *feel* her anxiety. Somehow, it surpassed all reason of biology, coursing through her skin and under mine.

Cassie and I had slightly adjusted our seats so we weren't constantly craning our necks backward at Colton, but our legs were still under the cover of the table. I reached out with my fingertips to brush her knee, intending it to be a brief nudge that simply told her that I understood. That I knew that she held a silent fear of the unknown regarding Colton's reason for being here and the missing women that could be closely linked to her life. The moment that I touched her, though, I heard the quick breath she pulled through her nose. I was the only one that was listening—thank *God,* I was the only one that was listening—and, just like that, the gesture that I had meant to be one of solidarity morphed into something that was so much more. Electricity pulsed in my veins. I squeezed the grip I had on her lower thigh, and the current coursed through me.

"'Kay," Colton muttered, looking to Claire. "Last thing...what kind of lock are we dealing with here?"

"Round knob," she replied. "Just a jagged key."

"Deadbolt locked?"

Claire's shoulder bobbed up. "Don't know for sure."

"So, you're saying I may be able to get away with just shimming it?" Colton laughed. "Give me a challenge, *come on.*"

I released my grasp on Cassie's knee. She let out the breath she had dragged into her lungs as quietly as she could manage, and as my hand returned to my lap, it was as if a string were tied between us. I moved, and so did she—slightly. Ever so slightly, but enough for me to sense exactly where her leg was placed as her body angled toward mine.

I shook my head quickly, looking to Colton and asking, "You wanna speak English?"

Colton tilted his head to the side. "What about that wasn't English?"

"Shimming," Claire repeated the word, and I turned to see her. Her blue eyes were tired, and Luke was watching her with a clenched jaw as she said, "It's basically forcing something against what works as a lock...like, it'll push the mechanism aside." She mumbled to Luke, "I've never broken into someone's *home,* baby—only locks on protected merch we took out of stores. Take a breath."

Luke sighed. "I'm fine, Claire."

"I'll explain—door knob," Colton spoke over them, "meet the trusty credit card that I haven't used in years." He held up an index finger and shifted onto his left side to reach into his back pocket. Retrieving a worn, brown wallet, Colton flipped it open and dug out a plastic, blue card that was marred with scratches. He held it between his fingertips in his right hand and noted, *"Like this,"* as he moved the card forward and back.

Luke squinted at him. "I don't get it."

"Of *course,* you wouldn't," Colton said with a loud exhale as he looked at him with a pointed gaze. He gestured with his left hand up and down. "There's a slight crack between a door and its jamb, yeah?"

I looked back to Luke, saw him grimacing in Colton's direction, and he grumbled, "Yeah."

"Card." Colton held it up with purpose and then smacked it flush against his other hand, which represented where the door met the jamb. "Opening." He repeated his motion from seconds ago, rubbing the card against his hand in such a fashion that he would have been able to feel the grooves from the numbers tickle his palm. *"Shimmy.* Right where the latch is to push it aside."

"Oh...*kay,"* Luke's eyes went wide as he began to understand the act itself. "It...can't be that easy to break into an apartment." His nervous face whipped down to Claire. *"Right?"*

Claire shrugged, and Colton remarked, "Pretty damn easy if the deadbolt isn't locked."

"And if it *is* deadbolted?" Zoey inquired.

He told her confidently, "Get me something thin and blunt that can fit in a keyhole. I'll get in there, no problem." Colton added offhandedly, "The lesson here is to always lock your place with something that's only on the *inside* of your home—sliding chain, flip lock, what have you. *Safety first, kids.*" He then glanced at both Cassie and Claire, "Either of you ladies have bobby pins in your hair?"

"You're planning to unlock a deadbolt with a *bobby pin?!*" Luke's light eyes were now bulging from his head. "That—that doesn't seem very failsafe."

"Ah, *two* bobby pins," he clarified, holding up two fingers. "And it's not ideal, but y'all are low on time, and it works in a quick pinch." Colton patted the outside of his hoodie down to his jeans as if he were searching for something in his pockets. He comically noted, "I don't have lock-picking necessities on me at the moment."

I could practically hear Luke grind his teeth together, and Claire reached to comfortingly touch his shoulder.

She waved to her ponytail, mumbling, "I'm not using any," and eyed Cassie's messy bun. "Pins?"

Cassie quickly snagged two pins from the base of her bun, releasing a few strands of hair to fall and frame her face. As she held them up for Colton's examination, he leaned forward to stretch a hand out her way. She placed them in his palm, and he narrowed his eyes at them as he slinked back into his seat. He gave them what appeared to be a quick stress test, taking the time to pinch one pin between his thumb and forefinger and gently flex the material before moving on to the second.

Colton nodded, smiling wide. "That'll do."

It was only a handful of minutes later that Colton had connected his headphones via Bluetooth to his phone, the buds were secured in his ears, and the call between his cell and Claire's was connected. Without so much as a goodbye, he walked down the road. Liam rapidly pulled up the live feed footage from his security camera as we all raced to Cassie's Jeep, and we piled in.

Cassie had conveniently parked approximately a block away from the complex—nearly a halfway point between the apartment and Henry's. Keys in the ignition to turn on the battery but engine and headlights off, our collective breath was clouding before us as we watched and waited.

Cassie twisted the knob at the end of the lever on the right side of the wheel, the windshield wipers swiped once, the snow was whisked away and drifted off into the wind, and she turned the knob back to its original location.

Colton was visible from where we were parked, walking directly away from us with his hood over his head and the neck of the shirt beneath his jacket pulled over his nose. Strolling through the snowstorm that was seemingly progressing into a whiteout, I supposed that the full coverage of his face wasn't one that would be questioned by any random passersby. There were none to speak of due to the time of morning, but I considered it, anyway.

Liam was seated directly behind me, the light from his phone illuminating his face, and he spoke, "Camera feed's finally up—hallway's clear."

Colton's voice rang out from Claire's phone, which rested in her lap in the back seat. "As it should be. What is it, almost four in the morning? Place is ghosty." He narrated his anticipated movements in a murmur, *"Up the stairs, right side of the hall, 2D."*

I watched Colton's body disappear from view as he trudged his way up the stairs. We all waited for what felt like an excruciatingly long silence, and Zoey voiced:

"Are you sure that feed's live?"

I kept my eyes glued on the entrance while the rest of the crew in the back seat shifted to the right. Zoey was already practically in Liam's lap due to lack of space, and she was peering down at his palm. Claire looked over Zoey, Luke looked over Claire, and Cassie spun around from the driver's seat to glance behind her, stretching her neck in an attempt to see Liam's phone. Unlike the remainder of the group, it wasn't visible without her crawling over the center console, and she huffed out a quiet breath through her nostrils as she righted herself back in her seat instead.

"Yeah," Liam muttered. "'Course."

"There's probably a second or two delay on that, big guy," Colton spoke. "I'm up the stairs."

I counted out the seconds, and by the time I made it to *three,* Claire was speaking once more.

"There you are—see you on the feed."

"Three second delay," I noted in what came out as a grim tone.

"That was really more like one second," Cassie remarked. "You must have counted fast."

"I *one Mississippi'd* it," I countered. "It's three seconds. Three seconds is *long.*"

"Because counting *one Mississippi, two Mississippi* is the most reliable way to track time," Cassie argued.

Luke stated, "Even if there's a one second delay, it's fine—"

"*Three seconds,*" I corrected anxiously. "That's *way* longer than you think."

Cassie griped, "Not a chance in hell that it was three—"

"*Christ,* you two bicker like a fuckin' married couple," Colton complained. "It's super short. It's *fine.* Just keep an eye."

He could barely finish his last sentence before Zoey exclaimed, "Holy *shit,* are you..."

"In," Colton finished for her.

Cassie's head whipped to the back seat. "Already? *How?*"

Colton replied, "Shim."

"It's like you just swiped your card after buying groceries," Zoey noted. "That was fast."

"Quick fingers and muscle memory," Colton told her with a hint of pride.

"No deadbolt," Claire whispered in disbelief. "I can't believe—"

The following sound cut off all of our voices in their tracks.

The wind blew. A wave of snow washed over the windshield. I listened intently, anticipating the noise to stop, but it didn't. An odd beeping—one that was repetitive in nature, holding a tone for a beat before falling silent only to sound once more—was playing from where Claire sat. The low pitch didn't seem to be loud nor grating as it emitted from her phone and into our ears. In fact, it was an altogether friendly noise. It felt anything but, though, because the sound insinuated that something was, for lack of a better word, *wrong*.

"What's that noise?" Zoey muttered shakily.

I whispered, "Is that an—"

"*Alarm,*" Colton replied back in a haste. "Fucking motion-sensored *bullshit* in the entryway."

"What does an alarm mean?" Cassie asked nervously. "No—no one's home, so the neighbors may hear some beeping, so what?"

"They could wake up," Luke said. "Come out to see what's going on. Could call the cops—"

Claire stated rapidly, "The alarm probably already called the police—"

Each subsequent response was nearly spoken over the last until we heard the door to 2D shutting through the speaker.

Colton's words flew out in a rush. "If it sends out an alert, it goes to whoever put it up, and then they're asked if they think it's a threat, and *then they call the cops.* Or the alert to whoever put it up goes unanswered, and the cops fucking show up anyway." He exhaled heavily. "Small ass town like this, I've got five minutes—*tops.*"

Liam blurted out, "Okay, fuck the cameras—closet, Colton! Get to the closet."

No doubt tearing his way throughout the apartment as rapidly as his legs could move him, he returned quickly, "Yeah, yeah. Looks like two bedrooms. Which one?"

"The one with the *locked closet in it!*" Zoey yelled. "It'll be pretty obvious once you see—"

"What in the *ever-loving FUCK* is this room?!" Colton's exclamation was kept to a hushed level, but the shock was still evident in his voice.

"Ya found it," Zoey murmured grimly.

"Uh...handcuffs?" Colton questioned hesitantly, mentioning what we had heard Mister Milkovich speak of. He audibly grimaced, *"Ugh*—ball gag? Am I grabbing kinky shit?"

Liam snapped, *"No!"*

Colton quipped, "Thank *fuck,* I'm only comfortable with my own shit like that—"

Luke hissed, "I'm gonna kill him," while Claire spat out:

"Colton—closet!"

"I'm already on it," he spoke quickly. "I—*ah,* you've gotta be fuckin' *kidding* me."

He said it with a level of defeat, and I groaned, "God, *what?*"

"It's a keypad lock on the closet. Nothing to pick, just a knob with numbers, and...maybe a fingerprint scanner?"

Claire let out an exasperated, breathy, "Fuck," just as Colton told us:

"Okay—*one sec.*"

It was literally *one sec* later that we all heard a loud, speaker-grinding *crash!* Our collective flinch at the noise shook the car on its shocks, and Cassie shouted:

"The *fuck* did he just do?!"

I glanced at her with eyes so wide that I felt the cold air stinging them, and she returned the same expression back to me as the rest of the group waited with bated breath for any further sound.

Colton whined, "I hope y'all are *fuckin'* happy. My shoulder's gonna be bruised to hell after that."

"Colt, did you just bust the door down?!" Claire exclaimed. "The neighbors are gonna hear!"

"Y'know the phrase *in for a penny, in for a pound?*" Colton rhetorically asked with grit. "That. I'm bookin' it in less than two minutes at this rate, anyway." The last word faltered, twisting into a tone that turned...nervous. The insinuation made my stomach coil, the sound of Colton's breath straining as he whispered, *"Oh, God,"* made nausea rise to the base of my throat, and he asked, "Who lives here?"

If we weren't all sitting at attention before, we most certainly were now. I turned in my seat to look directly at Zoey, who was sandwiched between Claire and Liam, and she looked as though her mouth had gone dry. Jaw agape and a thousand-yard stare, she shook her head vigorously as I caught her eye. Her gaze shifted to Cassie, who had also turned to silently peek just as I did, then around the seating to Luke and Claire. Liam had placed his left hand on the back of her neck in a sympathetic gesture, and when she finally looked to him, I saw the muscles work in his jaw.

"Why?" he asked for us all, though his eyes stayed on her.

"Feelin' like I shouldn't be here," Colton muttered. "What—what did you guys do?"

Zoey's head whipped to Claire's lap as she snapped, "What's in the *fucking closet,* Colt?!"

Colton's swallow was audible. "Vials of meds, syringes, and a laptop." I tried not to picture it or assume whatever purpose they all served, but I failed. I failed *miserably,* and the thought made my head swim. "No clothes," Colton clarified. "Nothing else. It's...*very* neat."

A light caught my eye—not bright because it was from afar, but still present enough to draw my attention—and the red and blue hues made me gasp with a dramatic wheeze. Several others in the vehicle replicated the noise, though I couldn't have been sure of who.

"Laptop!" Zoey shrieked. "Leave the other shit."

"Grab and go, Colt. You have to leave," I called out. *"Cops.* Pulling up. *Now."*

Luke spoke to the ceiling, "That was *not* five minutes."

"Fuck," Colton cursed. "Grabbing. Going."

There was a general rustling over the speaker as I assumed that Colton rapidly moved. The air in the car felt as though it had turned even icier than the blizzard had already made it, and we all watched as the single police car leisurely stopped. A man exited the vehicle, beginning a slow descent for the stairs.

Claire yelled, "Where the fuck are you, Colt?!"

"It's been four *fucking seconds,"* he retorted. "I'm passing the kitchen."

"Cop's on the stairs," she warned him, her tone deep. *"Make a call."*

"God *fucking dammi—"*

With an odd, static noise that was akin to a vicious *crunch,* Colton's voice was cut off.

The wind blew once again—this time, with a gnarly howl—and then, for a moment that I would likely revisit in a future nightmare, all was silent.

With the feel of everyone's rapid heartbeats thrumming in the air, we stared at the entrance of the complex with an anxious anticipation. Snow continued to fall. The windshield was occasionally needed to wipe the accumulated flakes away.

Per Liam's surveillance, the hallway remained empty. The policeman had entered 2D, the only sounds to be heard on the camera from him were indeterminable murmurs of code numbers into his radio, and then, after what felt like a mind-numbingly long amount of time, Mister Milkovich made an appearance. We saw him slowly begin to hobble up the stairs—heard him on the camera feed grumbling about the cold, the break-in, and the general time of day—and he wandered inside. Not a word was said between us all as we just...waited.

And waited.

And waited.

And then, Mister Milkovich left along with the police officer.

Colton, however, was nowhere to be seen.

Chapter 11

We had several theories, all of which were discussed within the confines of Henry's as we awaited Colton's potential return. Claire thought that he had found a place to hide within 2D, and Liam and Zoey agreed. I brought up the possibility that he found another exit from the apartment, perhaps via a window, despite the space being on the second floor, and Cassie wordlessly nodded. Luke bitterly rambled with gumption that Colton's personal road to redemption could have led him to be in cahoots with the police, and Colton could have placed evidence directly in the cop's hands along with the mention of all of our names. His scorned viewpoint was quickly dismissed upon Claire's stern reminder that Colton was currently, in her words, *'fucking missing,'* and that he hadn't, *'waltzed on out of 2D skipping and holding hands with the cop.'* Furthermore, we rewatched the camera footage and realized that neither Mister Milkovich nor the policeman were carrying a laptop upon their exit.

Our back and forth nervous ponderings eventually petered out, and regardless of how adrenaline coursing through my veins had forced me to be alert, exhaustion hovered over me in a heavy cloud, and my eyes felt as though they were bleeding. Even the dim bar lighting burned my retinas as we occasionally glanced around our usual table seating. Purse-lipped, defeated looks were all we exchanged with the exception of when I would look at Cassie. Her dark gaze was guarded, our eyes would linger for far too long, and she would break our contact with a rapid downshift of her head time and time again.

Over an hour had passed by the time that we all decided to call it for the night or, rather, the early morning, and we all said our adieus because there was nothing to do at this point other than wait. Liam offered Cassie to sleep on his couch due to the questionable condition of the roads. She insisted that her Jeep would make the short trip with ease, and he argued with her for but a moment before Zoey nudged him with her elbow and gave him a curt shake of her head. Cassie set off, and I watched her as she trekked through the snow back to her vehicle—she didn't bother to look back as she went on her way.

It was when I had returned to my own abode, sitting on my couch without having even taken my snow-soaked boots off, that I realized the similarities between this very moment and the one from months ago. The one after Peter was no longer. The one when I had raced to Cassie's house so we could simply exist in one another's presence and not be alone. The thought made my pulse race—not because of the skin crawling, stomach sinking feeling of the memory of Peter that would never die. Not because I was thinking of her, though I most certainly was. Because this moment, as similar as it was to the one that I tried to push out of my brain, was *so* different.

Of all the reasons that I had yearned to be around Cassie—the simple companionship in the face of terrors past, the itch to know her...*really* know her, and the thought of all things steamy, hot, and unattainable—*this* was the worst. The threat of potential evidence being outed regarding Zoey's stalker's murder wasn't gone in the least. It wouldn't be unless Colton turned up and whatever he found was inevitably destroyed, incriminating or not...and because that had now turned into a waiting game, I was entirely focused on his reasoning for being in Salem. The idea that Cassie was linked to women who have gone missing and could potentially become one of them herself was tearing me up from the inside out.

It was a disjointed thought. I mean, for all we knew, her work was a perfectly fine place of employment despite anything we had heard from Colton, but the nagging thought of her reality being tied to his with an invisible string was gnawing at me. Truthfully, I knew nothing for certain, and neither did she...but I had felt her nervousness earlier, and that made the idea feel real. So very, *very* real.

And it was because of *that* that I was only sitting for approximately five minutes before I stomped right back out into the cold, praying that my car would muster the drive. Just like earlier, when Luke had called, I hadn't even bothered to grab a jacket or my glasses. I just left. I drove sitting on the tip of my tailbone, peeling my eyes to follow the road that was obscured by the storm. With each gentle turn making my tires spin out from beneath me, the drive was slow with my grip on the wheel white-knuckled, but it was all pushed out of my mind the second that I arrived.

The alarm on my phone went off as I pulled up to the left of her Jeep. The sound of a gently played piano rang throughout the car, and I let out a ragged exhale because that noise was typically the start to my day. From Monday through Friday, the quiet tune would wake me at six o'clock on the dot. It called to me now as if this morning were no different, and I groaned an exasperated:

"Oh, Jesus Christ."

I quickly removed my cell from my pocket, dismissed the alarm, and opened the door to be greeted with a brisk, icy breeze washing over me. I shook my head, wiping the snow from my face and leaving a damp trail in its path, and before I was even able to shut the car door, I saw her.

The light from inside her home illuminated her porch. She was barefoot despite the cold, standing just beyond the several inches of snow that had already piled high. A baggy orange t-shirt draped over her body to her upper thighs, black shorts peeked out just below, and she had let her hair down. With her messy bun having left the long strands kinked and frazzled, the air condensating in front of her with every exhale, and her eyes wide as she watched me, her expression was one of shock mixed with something wild.

I took slow, purposeful steps through the snow, and it wasn't until I halted directly in front of her that she asked:

"What are you doing here?"

The question was quiet, but it was as if she were hooked up to a goddamn microphone.

I replied, "Ignoring my alarm that's telling me to get up and get ready for work."

"And why are you doing that?"

"Because I'll have, like, *maybe* half a brain to use since I haven't slept much. And that half a brain is thoroughly occupied."

"With?"

"With?" I repeated the word incredulously. *"With?* Women are going missing at your work!"

"We don't know that," she replied in a clipped tone.

I asked with a heavy weight, "Did the MIA girls come back?" Cassie pressed her lips together tightly, and I stated definitively, *"Yeah,* I'm coming inside."

She stepped to the right to block my path. "For what?"

Sleep deprivation and stress from the reality of the now had burrowed under my skin tonight—that was certain—and her accusatory tone made the bugs that had settled to roost come alive.

I snapped, "The *fuck* do you mean, *for what?"*

Cassie crossed her arms, dismissively replying, "You should go home, Jay. Get some sleep."

"Sleep," I scoffed. "The fact that you think I could just *go home and sleep* right now is *hilarious."*

"Jesus," she sighed, looking to the porch ceiling before placing her dark gaze on me. "Fine. I'll bite. Why won't you be able to sleep?"

"I—*fuck,* Cassie, I'm sorry...but that question is asinine." The cheerful ringtone on my phone went off once more, and I frustratedly smacked the outside of my pocket three times to silence the alarm. It somehow worked, and I repeated what we knew with purpose, "Women are going missing. Your work may be a place that is compromised with that, and the *one* man," I thrust an index finger toward her face, "that we know of who can give us more information on that is presumably on the fuckin' run."

"This is *my shit,* Jay," she retorted. "As much as I appreciate you covering for me at Henry's, *you* are not involved in *my shit.* If Colton comes back, you can just send him my way."

I barked out a bitter laugh. "Oh, *okay. Sure.* I'm not involved...and neither is anyone else!" I exclaimed, throwing a hand out toward the abyss of snowy dawn behind me. "No one else that we know—*none of our family*—is aware of any of *your shit.* And y'know what? That would have been fuckin' *fine.* Completely fine—you don't want anyone else who's close to you to know about your work? Cool. Great. *Grand.* But *guess what,* Cas? *I* know. It's not a secret to *me,* and I'm not gonna sit on my ass and ignore all the shit that we learned about tonight."

"What do you wanna do right now, Jay?" she asked sharply. "Barge on into my house, sit down, and have a nice little chat about all the potential fuckery that could go down with whatever Claire's ex said that he's involved in?"

"No," I returned. "I don't want to talk about *any* of that shit. I'd just go in circles about it all, and I don't—we don't know enough, anyway. Not right now."

"Then *what?*" Cassie asked, her face pinched in exasperation. "What do you *want?* Why are you *here?*"

"I'm here for *you!*" I yelled.

"God dammit, I don't *need* you to be here! I am perfectly capable of taking care of myself!"

"I'm well-the-fuck-aware that you don't need me here. I have the feeling that you haven't needed anyone but yourself for most of your life." My words seemed to have stunned her, her head bobbing back for a quick moment as her mouth clamped shut. Her gaze stayed glued on me, and I took a breath to steady myself. "When I say that I'm here for you, I mean that I need you." I placed a hand on the center of my chest and stated, "*I* need to be around *you*—not the other way around. I need the *tangible. Proof.* That you're okay and that you're not...not missing like these other women."

Her defensive demeanor suddenly left her, her arms hung at her sides, and the hardened look in her eyes softened.

Cassie whispered, "Oh."

"Look...I am...*fried.* Everything that's happened in the past few hours has been a *lot.*" I exhaled heavily. "I'm *cold.* I'm *tired.*" Cassie's brow pinched together sympathetically, and I concluded softly, "I care about you, and I'm worried. Please...for the love of *all* that is holy...let me inside, Cas."

As quietly as they had exited my mouth, the last few words still felt like they came straight from my chest.

Cassie took a single step forward to softly wrap her arms around my waist, tucking her head into the crook of my neck. The act was so unexpected that for just a moment, I froze. My hands hovered in the air in a split-second hesitation, and her grip on me tightened. Her nose nuzzled along my neck, her forehead dropped to my collarbone, and when my brain fully recognized what was happening, I returned her embrace. I pulled her close, one hand on the back of her head and the other around her waist, and I squeezed as I rested my cheek against her hair.

It warmed me despite the weather blustering around us, for the hold she had on me was unexpectedly gentle. Vulnerable, even—*raw*. I found myself holding my breath because I knew that the moment would be fleeting. I didn't know for sure, but it appeared that Cassie may have been doing the same for her body was still with the exception of her fingers that would occasionally flex against my back. She did so one last time, finally drawing in a long inhale that forced her shoulders to rise, and she let it out against my neck. I breathed similarly in response, and she murmured:

"You really mean all that, don't you?"

"I really do."

My response came out raspy, and her grip tightened on me. Cassie looked up, her pretty brown eyes locking on me, and I knew that a quick tilt of our heads or a flex of my grip in her hair could pull her lips to mine. I could feel the heat of her face. Taste her breath on my tongue. The feel of her kiss from just hours ago had made me throw any concerns of my feelings for her into the wind, and I yearned for it once more, but because she had told me to *forget,* I ushered the thought away.

Her grasp on me loosened, and with a tiny tug on the front of my shirt, she said, "Come on," tipping her head to the inside in a quiet invitation.

I followed her in, and the first step that I took onto her tile made my boots squeak and my feet slip out from underneath me. I spun to the right, the arm of the couch breaking my fall so I didn't tumble ass-first onto the floor, and I cursed under my breath at the sensation of twinging muscles in my back.

I grunted, rotating gingerly to test my range of motion, and muttered, *"Ouch."*

Cassie was watching me with her arms crossed, no more than three steps away, with high brows and a questioning expression.

"You alright?"

She retraced her path before me to the entrance, doing what I had planned and shutting the front door for me. Her wrist flicked as she quickly turned the deadbolt, and she glanced back at me with inquisitive eyes, for I had yet to answer her question.

I stretched my spine upward, twisted slowly to the left and then to the right, and replied, "All good."

Cassie pointed to the floor. "Slippery when wet. Take your boots off unless you're trying to throw out your back."

"Right," I grumbled.

She turned an about face, and I watched her with interest as I did as she asked, touching my toes to my heels one by one to remove my boots. Directly next to the door that she had just locked was one of her wicker kitchen chairs. Cassie gripped it by the seat, dragged it across the tile to be situated in front of the door, and angled it to force the back of it underneath the knob. She jammed it into place, tested its strength with a quick wiggle from side to side, and turned back to me when she appeared to think its placement was satisfactory.

I must have had a skeptical look on my face because she threw a thumb over her shoulder, explaining:

"Makeshift lock from the inside. I have to buy a chain for the door or something." I nodded, somber that we had to even think of such things but thankful that she had the wherewithal to have done so. Cassie looked me up and down and asked, "Do you want to sit with me? I was trying to wind down when you got here."

She tipped her head toward the fireplace in front of the couch. It was just barely lit—too little to crackle and have called my attention previously, but enough for me to feel its slight heat against my shoulder—and a small stack of wood sat to its left. The table in front of it, which looked as though it could have been made from a cross-section of a large tree trunk, held a short glass that I knew for a fact contained Jack Daniel's.

"My, ah, brain wasn't turning off," she admitted. "Alcohol helps."

"Well, if you're gonna pour me a glass that big, we could use another log on the fire," I remarked.

Her lips pulled up in the smallest of smiles. "I'll be back, then."

While she bustled to the kitchen, I took it upon myself to tend to the fire. Situated in front of the cast-iron to protect the room from any errant spitting embers stood a three-sided standing screen. Grabbing the black fire poker that rested against the wall by the wood, I nudged the screen aside that was sure to be white-hot. With a precise drop of my hand so as not to burn myself, I laid another piece of wood into the flames. I adjusted it just so with the fire poker, the heat caught up to it quickly, and just as I was pushing the screen back into place, it let out a satisfying *pop!*

As I was leaning the fire poker back against the logs, Cassie quipped from behind me:

"You're gonna make me have to clean up more ash than normal, aren't you? You chose the biggest log. That's gonna burn for forever."

I turned to find her already sitting on the couch, watching me with a small smirk on her face and her glass cradled in both of her hands that rested in her lap. My own drink sat on the table in waiting for me.

"I'll stay up for a bit," I told her. "And I'll sweep up the ash in the morning."

"Just giving you shit, Jay," she spoke gently. Cassie gestured to the seat on her right with a tilt of her head. "Come sit."

I did as she asked, settling myself on the center cushion with my whiskey in my palms, and took a sip. She did the same, and we were quiet for a bit, watching the flames flicker and occasionally taking another drink. I eventually noticed her fingers tracing the edges of her glass in what appeared to be a nervous manner, and I nudged my shoulder with hers.

"Penny for your thoughts?"

Looking to her hands, she murmured, "Ah, my *thoughts*...there's a lot goin' on up there. Does the phrase *this shit's fucked* cover it?"

"No." I smiled a bittersweet smile. "It doesn't."

"I..." she hesitated, "learned a lot tonight."

The knowledge of Claire's history and how it had impacted the remainder of our group was a tale to be told, indeed—and she had only gotten the abbreviated version.

"That you did," I replied. "Are you asking for the full story?"

"No." She laughed without humor. "*God,* no. Y'know, I normally like details, but, ah..." Cassie waved her hand around her forehead and then allowed her arm to relax once more. "Like I said, my mind's a bit full for the moment."

"Yeah, mine's like that, too," I murmured.

She seemingly thought to herself for a beat. The fire crackled, we both took another small sip, and then she asked, "Do you ever feel like you're stuck in between?"

I felt my brow pinch together. "How do you mean?"

"Like the world is gearing up for something and you can—you can *feel* it. You can feel the shift...but it's not quite there yet. So...you're just waiting. Stuck in between."

I hummed in acknowledgment. "I think that's called purgatory."

She disagreed, "Pretty sure that's the waiting room between heaven and earth. I'm talking about one that's between two hells."

"Yeah..." I begrudgingly said, "I know the feeling."

"I don't know if there's a word for it. I'll call it purgatory, but it's...it's not that." She blew out a rough breath through her nose. "I don't want there to be another hell, Jay."

The whisper of a sentence left her, and I felt its gravity. It sat on my sternum, heavy—dirty—*sticky,* and unable to be washed from me. Her voice had wavered on my name. It was so slight that I could have chalked it up to vivid imagination, hope, or sleep deprivation-induced auditory hallucinations...but I didn't. I knew it was there.

"It could be nothing," I reminded.

She admitted in a meek voice, "It doesn't feel like nothing to me."

"Me either."

The conversation itself was nowhere near romantic, but the intimacy was there. The *closeness* was there, and just like that, the topic of our respective worries withered away to nothing. They were still there in our minds—I knew they were—but they had been tucked away because we were stuck once again. In a routine played several times over, we were locked on each other in a slow-moving gravitation, and I breathed, long and slow.

She finally said, "I meant what I said before...about forgetting."

I knew that already, but hearing it was a kick in the gut. The reiteration made me want to turn my head—to look away from her—but I couldn't. And it appeared that neither could she.

"I know."

"Because we could be messy," she clarified.

I nodded. "I know."

"For several reasons."

"I know."

Cassie's eyes remained on me as she shifted forward to place her glass on the table. She snagged mine as well and set it beside hers with a quiet clunk, and she sat back on the couch, turning to face me fully with her legs tucked underneath her.

She whispered, "They're irrelevant, though...aren't they?"

It was the same word that I had used the night before to describe my hesitations toward her—her relation to Liam and Zoey, her profession, our age difference, though my concern on that was long gone—it was all irrelevant. My feelings—shit, *her* feelings—made it all irrelevant.

Her usage of it made my chest burn, realization sinking in at the purpose of the softness in her gaze, and I exhaled a quiet, *"Oh."*

"Thanks for joining me," Cassie murmured. "In purgatory, I mean."

The tipping point was placed between us, and the edge metaphorically scraped my feet as I balanced upon it. I lifted a hand to her cheek, tracing her freckles with the pad of my thumb, and the burn in my chest spread as she leaned into my touch. With all the honesty in the world, I told her:

"I'd be here in hell, too."

The warmth in her eyes told me that she knew that I meant it, but she still blinked twice, slowly, as if she were attempting to absorb the words.

"Good." Her voice was nearly inaudible. "I like you here with me."

I melted into the couch—my body remaining still as I relished the feel of her beneath my palm, but my mind oozing into a delightful goo that would never leave the fabric beneath me. My face turned hot as I realized that she was so close that her breath was mingling with mine, and though I'm sure it was wholly unnecessary to say, I muttered:

"Me too."

Cassie asked softly, "Is now when I say that I officially want to take back what I said?"

"About forgetting?" I muttered.

"Yes."

I laced my fingers into her hair. *"Yes,"* I replied. "It is."

"Because I don't want to forget," she said in an exhale.

The mere sentence lit me up, sending a thrumming energy straight into my blood that made me squeeze my grip. She gasped quietly as I angled her head further upward with the guidance of my grasp, and, as if on cue, the fire crackled loudly.

"Kiss me," she whispered. "Please."

"Yes."

I brushed my nose against hers, she shuddered in response, and in a way that I had imagined several times over, I pulled her mouth to mine. To be honest, it was less rough than I had intended, for I wanted to kiss her with such force that I could feel my teeth press into the backside of my lips *hard*. Instead, the moment that I felt her against me, we both sagged heavily in relief, and our motions were deliciously soft. Cassie reached forward, fisting her hand in my hair, and pulled with a silent insistence to deepen our kiss. We did, tasting each other with patient touches of our tongues, emitting soft gasps and quiet hums of appreciation until our magnetism that I thoroughly hoped would never cease to steal my breath had escalated to sparks. Electricity. The word was simple enough, and I was certain that many before had used it to describe their attraction to another. This electricity, however, was stored in clouds that lingered above, primed to be released as lightning and set the scene around us ablaze.

Our movements rendered us shimmying for her to straddle me, grinding her hips over my cock that was forever hard at her existence and forcing profanities to fling from my mouth. She moved down to lick at the hollow of my throat, dragging her tongue up and biting just where my facial hair began. It elicited a moan from me, and she ordered:

"Take off your shirt."

Though she was the one who had asked, she completed the task for me, grabbing at the fabric and pulling it over my head. Cassie leaned back as she threw my shirt to the floor, raking her eyes from my abdomen up to my chest. She placed her hands on my stomach gently, and I immediately tensed.

"Ticklish, right?" she asked.

Her touch remained where it was, and I breathed out half a sigh of relief.

"You remembered. Please, don't scratch me."

Cassie hummed in acknowledgment, bending down and wandering with her lips. When she reached the crook of my neck, she whispered:

"What about this?"

I exhaled, "Yes." She sank her teeth into me just hard enough to leave a significant sting, and I arched into her. My cock throbbed, and I groaned, "Ah—*I like that.*"

She kissed the area with an open mouth as if to soothe, sweetly questioning, "You like me biting you?"

"Yes."

"Mmm."

She trailed her mouth to where my tattoos began at the curve of my shoulder and back over my pectorals, continued to sink lower, and nipped at the first rib she came across. I writhed under her, my fingers flexing against the leather of the couch. It was delicate torture, watching her go further and further, gently catching my skin with her teeth wherever she pleased, and I was her masochist. Watching her. Craving more. My ribs, my waist, my hips just above my pants—she gave deft attention to them all. So much so that by the time she fully knelt to the floor and licked from the button of my jeans up to my navel, I was flexing my pelvis in anticipation, my voice rough and cracking as I cursed to the ceiling.

The button was yanked open, and the zipper pulled down. I aided her in removing my clothing down to below my knees, and she looked up from below, tracing her gaze over my length that stood at attention for her.

I expected more beautiful torture. Perhaps a trail of kisses along my inner thighs—a bite to the back of my knee—anything that was sure to make me squirm. Cassie didn't do any of those. She placed a single, chaste kiss on either one of my hipbones, wrapped her lips around the head of my cock, and sucked.

I threw my head back. *"God,* fuck!"

She took more of me, her saliva leaving me glistening as she slowly moved up and down. I felt the base of her throat with every iteration, and it was too much—*far* too much for me to simply watch. I itched to guide her mouth. To feel her jaw flex or her cheeks hollow as she pleasured me. I reached out, touching the edge of her face, and moved in time with her rhythm. Her dark eyes met mine, and the sight of her watching me—watching me *watch her*—with her mouth filled, my hand now gripped on her neck for guidance as I gently fucked her face...it was...*fuck.*

It was enough to bring me to the precipice of my own release, and I was *not* allowing that to happen yet. I wrapped my hand in the roots of her hair, tugged to usher her off of me, and with lips so wet that they were dripping, she smiled wide.

Christ.

I stretched my other arm to cradle the left side of her face as I pulled her up my body and yanked her mouth to mine. Her tongue was slightly salty, the evidence of my abundant arousal clear as day, and my chest nearly vibrated as I spoke:

"Fucking *dirty girl.*"

I didn't give her a chance to respond. I tugged her top overhead, throwing it to only God knows where. I moaned at the sight of her bare breasts that looked as though they would *perfectly* fit in my palms, and, desperate to make her as needy and wanton as she had made me, I moved in. I licked across her chest, focusing on every curve, grazing my teeth in areas that I just couldn't resist. Her breath turned ragged, and her grip on the back of my head guided me to her nipples that I had pointedly avoided. I fought her, allowing myself to skim the area with the tip of my nose, only to place my mouth elsewhere.

"James," she complained. "Stop teasing me."

I looked up at her and simpered, "You want more of me?"

"Yes."

"Here?" I finally followed her touch and took one of her nipples in my mouth, dragging my tongue across it.

"Yes."

Smiling against her chest at her lust-filled tone, I grabbed her waistband.

"Here?"

"Lower," she breathed.

I kissed across her breasts, going where she led me, and licked her other taut peak as I reached under the fabric of her shorts and underwear. My fingers brushed against her smooth skin, and she shivered when I touched her where she so desired. I slid them forward and back, bringing her own lubrication up to her clit.

We simultaneously moaned—her, wordlessly, and me with a, *"Fuck,* you're wet."

Cassie rotated her hips, working herself against my hand as I wandered over her chest until she tugged on my hair to usher me upward. She kissed me voraciously, leaning her body into the motion, and with our tongues still tied, one of her hands left my scalp and pressed against her shorts where I was touching her underneath.

"In," she murmured against me.

"Mmm."

I tested one finger, and it slid in and out of her on her own volition as she rode it.

She ordered, "Two."

I did as she asked, she let out an alluring high pitch on my lips, and her hand fell away. Cassie wrapped her fingers around the base of my erection, and I flexed my hips to rock in time with her motions. We moved like that, slowly increasing our speed until every panted exhale was a passion-filled groan, our kisses turned to attempted consumption of one another, teeth were clashing, lips were being bitten, the still-burning fire and our rapid motions left our bodies hot, and we were fucking each other's hands with desperation.

I wanted inside of her—to flip our positions and pin her to the cushions—to feel her squeeze around my cock as she rode out her own release—but escalating any further in that sense meant a conversation about birth control options. And we were both too far gone for that.

"You'll make me come like this," I rasped. "Is that what you want?"

"*Yes.* Fuck, I—I'm so close."

"*Shit,* Cas." My muscles began to contract, she rode my hand harder, and I followed her tempo. "Right—right fuckin' there, *yes.*"

"James!"

She screamed my name, her head fell on my shoulders, and her pussy clenched my fingers *hard*. Profanity and nonsensical words alike, I shouted to the ceiling as I came, my face screwing tight while I ejaculated onto my stomach between us. Our motions slowed, her repetitive squeezing against my hand stopped, and when I removed my fingers from her, she placed a small kiss on my neck.

My heart was still hammering when I quietly spoke into her hair, "You okay?"

"Very okay," she spoke gently. Lifting her head and sitting back on my thighs to look at me, she traced the evidence of our sexual acts with her eyes from my groin to my chest. Gaze hooded, warm, and soft, Cassie leaned forward as if she couldn't resist returning, hovering over me to avoid the mess, and sweetly spoke against my lips, "Ya look good, Jay. Let me clean you up. Purgatory suits you."

I internally repeated the latter sentence to myself as she pressed her mouth on mine, and I smiled into her kiss, for I had never considered that purgatory could be a source of...happiness. Pleasure. Joy. An opportunity to bask in the now while I could for the unknown ahead seemed daunting.

Damn. Purgatory suits me.

Chapter 12

Wind ran through my lungs, rattling as if it were my last chance to taste it, and I was entirely upright before my eyes even had the chance to open. A clacking noise sounded to my left, my fingers clutched at my bare chest, and I attempted to slow my breathing with repetitive inhales and exhales as I glanced to the side table beside me to see...pancakes. And bacon. Cocking my head at the square, grey plate, I absorbed its appearance for all of two seconds before I looked upward to see a wide-eyed Cassie with her own plate of pancakes in her left hand.

She looked to have just flinched in shock, awaiting further surprises other than me waking in her bed as if I were a vampire rising from a coffin and she were my next meal.

Cassie gently asked, "My *God*, are you good?"

I legitimately debated my well-being as I recalled the details of the hours past—the time spent after I had arrived at her home, that is—after the acts that had occurred on her couch. Cassie had retrieved a wet hand towel, ensuring that I was thoroughly clean of my own mess, and we abandoned the remainder of our whiskey and the majority of our clothing to retire to her bed.

And though I was atop a plush mattress and thoroughly comfortable with the fact that we had succumbed to pleasures within each other and shared sleeping arrangements afterward, I wasn't, as she had asked, *good*.

My recurring dreams seemed to have shifted to a new topic—one that clenched to my bones as if it were bestowing upon me the weight of an impossible clairvoyance. For the second night in a row, memories had blended with unexperienced visions in my dreams. Flashes from the night of Peter's murder came first. Then, Cassie in the throes of passion above me—a dream that had come to fruition mere hours ago, the sepia ambiance of the fireplace and all. Scenes that I hadn't witnessed with my own eyes came next—a blonde woman who appeared to be badly beaten, followed by Cassie's bittersweet expression angled up to mine by the force of my own hands. The visions of the injuries I had witnessed being sustained when Claire's past had come to bite her were after that. Liam, whose wounds were missing from my last nightmares, was last—he was still alarmingly visible in the dark of night, screaming as he fell to the ground and clutched at his left shoulder.

It was at that point in my nightmares that I was woken by his sister, and the sight of her brought a light that attempted to break through the fog of it all. Trepidation still clung to me, though. I had thought nothing of it the night prior, but the events, if the others were to occur, were horrifyingly out of order in my life's timeline. Though I didn't believe in any sort of precognition, my mind still churned as to why this would be the case, and the cold sensation of dread remained in my bloodstream.

"James?" Cassie quietly called to me.

"Fine," I told her. "Got startled."

She tentatively sat on the mattress, and I shimmied my way out of the blanket to sit up beside her and swing my legs over the side of the bed. Cassie set her own plate on her lap, and she pressed:

"You sure?"

I blew out a last, loud breath. "Yeah."

Finally able to fully take her in, I noticed that she was dressed and ready for an outing. Or, rather, her makeup was prepared for an outing. While her clothing announced to the world that she was having a night in with black leggings and a maroon top that looked to be made of a comfortable, stretchy material, her face was done up. Much to my dismay, her freckles were concealed. Her eyes, though—black eyeliner rimmed her upper lid in a fashionable wing, and her eyelashes were, somehow, longer and fuller than usual. They drew me into her warm gaze in such a way that I had to blink twice to collect my thoughts.

"You, um," I stammered, "brought me food?"

A corner of her lip tugged upward. "You were out like a light, but it felt unfair for me to only make myself a meal. It's been almost a whole day since I last ate...figured you were hungry, too."

The gesture made my chest warm, and I truly meant it as I replied:

"Thank you."

She briefly showed me her teeth. "Mhm."

"What time is it, anyway?"

"Four o'clock."

"Four o'clock?" I returned disbelievingly. "In the afternoon?"

"If it were the morning, I'd be concerned that you fell into a coma," she remarked as she cut into her pancake with a fork.

I deduced aloud, "I slept for nine hours?"

"Warm fire, a little whiskey, what looked like some *vivid* dreams." She glanced sideways at me, skirted past my nightmares, and offhandedly said, "Mutual masturbation." She smirked, placing a bite of pancake in her mouth. "Mhm." She chewed, then swallowed. "That'll do it."

Her casual mention of our fireside activities would have been a joy, but my thoughts were still swirling about from my rapid wakeup. I shook my head quickly, looked back to where I had once laid and then to the side table, and quickly muttered:

"Shit—has anyone called? Luke? Liam? Where's my phone? I had it before we went to bed—"

"Charging," Cassie replied as she reached for a piece of bacon. It snapped as she bit into it, revealing that it was exactly as crispy as it appeared. "In the kitchen. No one from the group called either of us."

My body sagged in relief.

'Purgatory,' I internally reminded myself. *'We're in purgatory.'*

"Oh."

"Your friend, Shawn, however..."

I rubbed at my eyes. "Fuck. *Work*. I didn't even call in."

"Don't worry, he knows you're not dead," she murmured.

I felt one of my eyebrows cock high as I watched her slowly chew the remainder of her bacon.

"You went into my phone?"

Cassie held up an index finger while she swallowed, and then replied, "In my defense, it was vibrating so much, it was about to start a fire on my kitchen table. Took a glance at your notifications to make sure it wasn't Luke or anyone else and saw, like, ten missed texts from him." Her tone softened. "It's sweet, actually."

I admonished her gently, *"Cassie."*

"I didn't...*go into* your phone," she stated. "Wouldn't have been able to regardless, it's locked—I just...answered a phone call. I let the first three calls ring through to voicemail, and I *only* answered after the preview of his text sounded overly worried since you weren't responding."

I sucked on the inside of my cheek to withhold a grin, nodding all throughout her defense.

"Okay, okay." I reached to pick up my plate, feeling the warmth of it through the thin layer of my boxer briefs as I rested it on my lap just as she had, and grabbed the fork to stab into my breakfast. "What exactly did you tell him?"

Cassie joked, "Before or after he finished squealing like a pig when I answered, *James' phone, this is Cassie*?"

I pursed my lips together. "After."

"You think you caught a stomach bug," she told me with a smile.

"Mmm. Stomach bug. Got it. Did he ask why you were with me?"

"Uh huh—didn't answer him. Told him you were sleeping and hung up. He has since called three more times."

I chuckled as I lifted my fork to my mouth, tasted syrup before anything else, and grimaced when I began to chew for the texture was mealy, and the flavor…lacking.

"Angh," I groaned through my teeth and forced myself to swallow. *"Oh, that's bad."*

She incredulously laughed, *"What?"*

"Your pancakes—as much as I *do* appreciate them—are bad." Trading my fork for a slice of bacon as a palate cleanser, I quickly broke off a piece between my fingers and popped it into my mouth. "Can't fuck up bacon, though."

Cassie shoved my shoulder. "You *ass!*" I snickered along with her as she said, "You're full of shit, my pancakes are totally fine."

"I sincerely wish I were," I replied. "Sorry, Cas—your pancakes suck."

"They aren't *my* pancakes; it's not like I have a recipe. I followed the instructions on the back of the box—"

I interjected, "That was your first mistake."

"What are you, a pancake enthusiast?"

"The trick is to make sure you have buttermil—"

She deadpanned, "You're a pancake enthusiast."

"Can I show you how to make *actual* pancakes?"

"Why?" she simpered. "Because you're old and ripe with wisdom?"

I beamed. "Uh huh."

"Another time. Maybe." She pointed her fork, prong-end at me the moment that she finished slicing off another bite with purpose. *"Maybe.* I have to go soon. I'm running out of time."

My brow pinched together. "Go?"

Despite my complaints regarding her pancake making abilities, I continued to eat, but my chewing slowed when she succinctly responded:

"Work."

Reality of the now gut-punched me, and I coughed to clear my throat, my half-masticated, dry bite sticking in my esophagus.

"Beg—beg pardon?"

"My shift starts at five."

I waited for a punchline to her terrible joke, but it never came. "Your shift at *Gas Lamp?*"

Cassie peered at me with a single, high eyebrow, "You have a problem with my work, Jay?"

I chastised, "Don't do that, Cas."

She innocently returned, "Do *what?*"

"Act like my issue with your work has nothing to do with finding out that dancers are going *missing.*"

As if that weren't altogether alarming, she quipped, "Do you have an issue with it aside from that?"

My jaw hung open. "Are we really doing this right now?"

"Speak now or forever hold your peace," she sang, splitting the last word into two husky syllables.

I rolled my eyes heavily. "Okay, fine, *Jesus*—as a person, no. As someone who's one half of whatever *this* is..." I waved between us, and her face pinched together as I murmured, "Problem is the wrong word, but I'm not, ah, thrilled about it."

She set her fork down with a clack against her plate, turned her body to face me, and with a tone that just slightly turned hard, she said, "Please don't say you're about to give me the *I can do better* speech."

"I'm not. *Trust me*, I'm not." I sighed in exasperation and quickly stated, "I'm just a jealous guy. It is a *me* problem, not a *you* problem, and I can deal with that, but we have bigger fucking *fish-to-fry-here!*" Her brief defensive demeanor was whisked away, and she pressed her lips together tightly as I continued, "My mind is nowhere *near* the subject of you just being a dancer, Cas. You aren't dumb. Don't pretend like you're being ignorant because you're not."

"Okay, okay." Cassie eyed me sympathetically. "Straight up? We don't know anything for sure with all the stuff Colton said."

"Come *on,*" I retorted. "Women. *Dancers.* Have gone *missing.* In and around Salem."

She sighed. "I'm aware of the rumor mill. I was there for the origination of it last night, remember? I slept on it—just because we heard something from *one* man—"

My eyes widened, and I interjected, "The *rumor mill?*"

"One man," Cassie went on as if I hadn't spoken, "who none of you seem to trust all too much, for good reason—I'm gonna keep my skepticism on this one."

"Okay," I acquiesced. "You have a point, but our lack of trust in him aside, it's all a little too coincidental, don't you think?"

"James...I'm not up and quitting my job. Not before I know without a trace of uncertainty that something's up. It's not fair to my work, which is *already* short-staffed. It's not fair to the other dancers who'll inevitably have to pick up the slack." I opened my mouth to argue that her reasoning was insane. That a job is just a job. That if she were to drop dead tomorrow, Gas Lamp would recruit a new dancer to replace her as quickly and efficiently as possible. That her livelihood—hell, her *life*—should be put far above a job. Cassie stopped my planned interruption with a blunt, "It's not fair to *me*. I make really good money. I have great benefits. I've never had either of those things."

I exhaled softly. "I get that being financially comfortable is nice, Cas, but—"

"But I don't think you grew up poor," she argued, and I silenced myself for a beat because she was right.

My parents still lived in their upper-class, suburban home in Roanoke—it wasn't a mansion, and Luke and I weren't driving luxury cars at sixteen, but we were not, by any stretch of the imagination, poor. My college tuition was paid off. I landed a job right out of school and life never gave me a chance to so much as worry about money.

"I did not."

My confirmation was meek, for I was unsure of exactly how much she had to struggle as she grew up. Aside from being aware that her father was a shithead and her mother passed away when she was a young teenager, I knew very little. Through context clues within casual conversation at Henry's, I had gathered that they weren't well-off, but Cassie—and Liam, for that matter—were both quite good at skirting conversations regarding their childhood.

"Don't look at me like that," she muttered. "We still had a roof over our heads and food to eat, but once my mom left, it was *kinda* a fend for yourself situation." I focused on the word *left* rather than *died,* but I chose not to question it. Cassie continued, "Comfortable doesn't describe the peace that the paychecks give me, okay?"

"Yeah...okay, but—"

"And no one's up and going missing at Gas Lamp," she added. "Anyone who's skipped their shift did just that—*they skipped their shift.* There are security cameras all over that place, and if you recall, it's pretty damn public. If women *are* being taken, it's not gonna happen there."

Her words were a comfort, but wariness was still surrounding me as I murmured a slow, "Okay."

Cassie threw her last bite in her mouth, forcing it down before I could gather any further response for argument's sake, and she noted, "I have to get going."

She stood, taking her plate with her as she bustled out of her bedroom and, assumedly, into the kitchen, and I called out, "Wait—we're not—" I set my plate down on the side table and stood from the bed to stride after her. "We're not done talking yet."

By the time I reached the kitchen, she was gently placing her plate to the left of the sink. Moving to the table to gather her belongings, she looked at me with a raised brow, holding up a small, black backpack in her right hand before returning it to the table.

"I carry pepper spray in my bag at all times. I know how to use it safely. I'll call you when I get there."

"Will...I..."

"And I already shared my location on my cell, per your request...*remember?*"

I blew out an exhale through my nostrils at her apt reminder of the brief conversation we had so recently exchanged in her bed. "Can I at least drive you?"

"And leave me carless at two in the morning when my shift ends?" She returned with a slight smile.

"I'll pick you up, too," I offered.

"I'm not making you pick me up," she returned with a laugh. *"Come on."*

"You wouldn't be making me."

She grabbed the overcoat that was hanging on the back of a chair that matched her maroon top and began to pull it on.

"You're not driving me to work, Jay. My Jeep works just fine—I already cleared the snow off of it, *and* it's cranked and pre-warmed."

I sighed. "It's not about the state of your Jeep."

Cassie secured her jacket with a loud twang of the zipper as she pulled it up to her chest. Slinging her backpack over her shoulder, she looked at me with soft eyes, walking directly to me, and she placed a hand on the left side of my chest. I was sure that she could feel it nervously beating away with the sympathetic expression that she gave me. With the smallest of stretches onto her toes, she placed her lips on mine. It was a patient kiss—all slow-moving mouths and quiet smacks. Her arms wrapped around my naked waist, I hummed as the tightness in my chest eased ever so slightly, and when I touched my palms to the sides of her face, she pulled away.

With a smile, she assured me, "Look, I'm not jumping ship quite yet, but if anything seems wrong at Gas Lamp, I'll quit."

Any fight I had in me had abruptly left at the feeling of her lips, but I was still dissatisfied as I mumbled, "You will?"

She tilted her head into my left hand, and my fingers curled against her cheek as she quietly replied, "I won't even give two weeks' notice. I *do* still have a sense of self-preservation."

Her response could only aid my tension so much.

I asked, "Call me when you get there?"

"Mhm."

"And when you leave?"

"It'll be two in the morning, but *sure.*"

I further demanded, "And when you get home."

"And when I get home," she confirmed. "Yes."

"Thank you," I whispered.

Cassie's eyes gave me a silent *no problem,* and she stated, "I put my spare key on the table by your phone. Lock up for me when you go and just take it with you—I'll grab it from you later."

I nodded and insistently pulled her mouth back to mine. She leaned away after two chaste touches of our lips, and I griped, *"Stop that,"* before ushering her back to me. Cassie smiled against me, wedged her hands between us, and gave me a soft push once they reached my chest.

"I'm going to be late; I have to go. Eat your pancakes." Cassie reached up to give my beard a gentle tug, and my cheeks swelled in a begrudging grin as she cooed, "They're *really* not that bad."

She planted a last kiss on me—a hard one that I prayed would leave a bruise so I could feel her linger there—she bounded away, and in the blink of an eye, she was out the door.

I wasn't sure why, but I stared at the entrance as if I were anticipating her to walk back through it. My feet blindly brought me to the front door, and my eyes stayed glued on the wood until I heard the closing of her Jeep's door and tires crunching through the snow. I finally turned to find my clothing that had been stripped from me laid across the arm of her couch.

The sight of them alerted me to the cool temperature of the tile against my bare feet. I shivered, and I snagged my jeans to pull them on over my boxer briefs. After dressing quickly and finding that Cassie had neatly deposited both of my socks inside my boots, I took her advice and returned to my breakfast.

I ate the bacon first, of course, chewing it slowly. I had been unable to absorb the details of her bedroom until now, for my mind was otherwise occupied, and I found myself doing so as I made up her bed. It was small, much like the rest of her home, but rather than feeling cramped, it was cozy. The size of her bed allowed just enough room for the single nightstand where the remainder of my breakfast resided, and the headboard matched its color in a rustic, distressed white. The comforter was a camel brown, autumnal and akin to a dried leaf that had fallen from a tree and drifted to the ground, and it had the feel of suede on my fingertips. A pocket door to what was clearly her master bathroom was directly to the right of her nightstand—I paid it no mind, as the light was turned off.

Once Cassie's bed was sufficiently made, I walked the plate and fork back to the kitchen. Before sitting, I cut myself a bite, grumbled the moment it touched my tongue, and forced myself to swallow.

I shook my head. *"Nope."*

Deciding that I would fare far better with food of my own making at home, I promptly opened the cupboard underneath her sink where her trash was located and scraped the plate clean. Placing my plate atop hers on the counter to the left of her sink, I turned and found my cell on her dining table as promised. I unplugged it, letting the cord to the left of the table fall free to the tile, and peered at the screen.

I was less than shocked at the sheer number of texts from Shawn. Oftentimes, if I were out sick or on vacation, I would find my phone buzzing with his messages. They would typically contain random remarks regarding the day, and it would, truthfully, be as if I hadn't been away from work at all—in a good way. These messages were no different, but because I was typically a quick text responder and, furthermore, I had never been absent from work without notifying management, Shawn's tone had quickly changed as the day went on.

Shawn Brooks

Today 8:32 A.M.

> You're laaaaaate. I'm telling on you.

Today 10:04 A.M.

> Sleep through your alarm?

Today 12:13 P.M.

> Lunch is lonely without you, boo.

> Paula tried to ambush me with one of her long convos. I had to hide in the bathroom to escape.

> I'm still in here. It's been ten minutes. Think that's long enough?

Today 1:36 P.M.

> Okay, now I'm concerned. You didn't even put in PTO for today?

Today 2:20 P.M.

> You're not answering your phone either?

> Jay, come on. I'm all sweaty and nervous.

Today 3:25 P.M.

> A STOMACH BUG, MY ASS!

The next two messages that I received no more than one minute later contained a bevy of emojis—the first displaying balloons, confetti, and cake, and the second an eggplant, droplets of water, and a peach.

It was amusing, really—to the point that I blew out an exhale of a silent laugh. And, yes, despite the fact that we hadn't discussed our newfound closeness and what that meant, there was a part of me that was swarmed with what I could only describe as *butterflies*. Considering the circumstances and everything we had come to know within the last twenty-four hours, they felt rather inappropriate...but they were there. I shook my head gently, deducing that my mind was simply not up for verbally—or textually—explaining my current relationship with Cassie and any potential lying that would go along with it.

Today 4:23 P.M.

> Yes. Very sick. Talk Monday.

My phone almost immediately buzzed with:

> She's taking care of you, huh?

I sighed heavily. I *so* wished that were the case—I yearned for simplicity...and *this* was not it.

> Not now, man. Catch you up Monday. Sorry I ghosted.

> All good. Feel better. Long live Jassie.

His continued use of the amalgamation of our names still made me quietly snort. I shook my head, bringing my focus back to the present, and tapped through my phone to find my text message thread with Luke. I sent:

Today 4:26 P.M.

> **No updates?**

The message was left unanswered for only the amount of time that it took to return to the sink and wash both my dish and Cassie's. The vibration caused my phone to scurry across the tile on the countertop, and I glanced at it as I stacked the two clean plates carefully beside the cleaned mixing bowl and pan that she had clearly used earlier. It read:

> **Nope.**
>
> **Fucking hate this.**

I was uncertain if no news was good news in a situation like this. No news meant that Colton was still missing; therefore, potential evidence was still out of our hands. No news meant that neither Cassie nor I had any means of speaking with him regarding the MIA dancers at Gas Lamp. But...no news also meant that the police hadn't been back to ask questions about the break-in at 2D. No news meant that it was possible that, though he *was* missing, Colton and that laptop may not be in police custody.

The remainder of our conversation was lightning-quick:

> I know. Me too.

> I'll call you if we hear anything.

I let out a rather loud breath, pushing the thought to the back of my mind by the time I was locking Cassie's front door.

The blizzard had passed, leaving behind several inches of lumpy snow that would occasionally blow from the trees in large clumps, rapidly dissipating into the air in a glittering breeze. The roads were surprisingly clear as I drove, the warmth from the sun having melted whatever had stuck to the concrete below whilst I was sleeping. The apartment complex was quiet. I took a shower so hot that it blissfully stung my skin, and upon exiting into the steam-filled bathroom, I saw that my phone was glowing with a notification.

Cassie Cohen

Today 4:48 P.M.

> Made it to work.

I smiled softly, content that she had messaged as she had said she would, and it buzzed once more:

> X.

X?

X?

The single letter made the butterflies swarm, and my eyes locked on the screen as if I were convinced it would disappear, but it remained. *X* as in the universal symbol for a kiss, right? Or...*X* as in her fingers fumbled and sent me a text typo? I picked up my cell and unlocked it, simply holding it in my palm as if that would settle my thoughts, and eventually began to type back:

X?

I deleted it, of course, and replaced it with:

You mean to send that?

I deleted that, as well.

That's a nice letter.

That was fucking dumb, and I deleted it. What I finally managed to send was:

> Thank you.

Quickly, because I knew that I would talk myself out of it if I lingered on the notion, I followed it up with:

> x.

The moment that my thumb touched the screen and the *x* was sent off, I practically threw my phone back to the counter and bustled to my bedroom to clear my mind.

I dressed myself slowly—not for comfort, but just in my typical jeans and a t-shirt—and wandered back to the kitchen. I cooked the chicken breast that sat defrosted in my fridge, eating it with a bowl of pasta topped with canned vodka sauce.

I knew that it was okay. Not great, but okay—it was a go-to meal for when I just didn't want to bother with slicing and dicing. However, despite the fact that I could taste the array of seasonings that I used on the meat, the buttery pan-sear had left a pleasant browning, and the pasta was just to my preference of al dente, it all sat in my mouth like cardboard. I ate it, regardless.

I washed my dishes with a pensive mind circling solely about all things Cassie, and when I returned to the bathroom to retrieve my phone that I had so anxiously ditched, there were no notifications. That made sense because it was after five o'clock, and her shift had started, but I felt a slight twinge of disappointed nervousness nonetheless.

I sat, watching television and absorbing very little of it for what ended up being hours on end, but naturally, my entire being was wide awake. My legs were restless. My phone was devoid of additional messages. The sheet of paper in my mind symbolizing the remainder of my night read various to-do items such as:

Relax.

Stop thinking about her. She's fine.

No, really. Stop.

By the time the clock struck nine, my list was, as per usual with things to do with Cassie, wiped clean. With no reason other than an endless case of rational jitters alongside a heart-eyed teenage dream, my paper went entirely blank, and my restless legs were put to use as I stood to leave.

Chapter 13

I could have gone to Gas Lamp. I could have stared at the entrance of the establishment from my car, assessing its security from the outside. I could have gone inside and found her, either watching her from afar or alerting her to my presence, biting my tongue regarding any impending jealous thoughts at the sight of her in action. And I *desperately* wanted to make the last thought a reality. With the way that Cassie had willingly lowered her usual defensive walls, her forever insistence that she could *take care of herself*, and my desire to maintain and strengthen her trust in me, though, I forced myself to drive in the opposite direction and simply returned to her house.

It wasn't lost on me that I was chasing her. I was, somehow, *always* chasing her. Hours after we had just met, I was racing to her house. Even when I was trying to avoid whatever connection we had, the stars had aligned and forced me to show up at Gas Lamp while she was working. The dominoes of whatever our relationship was began to fall after that, and I went after her again when Colton inevitably returned. And, here I was, pedal to the metal down the same bumpy, snow-covered road that led to her home...chasing her. She wouldn't even be there for several more hours, and I was *still* chasing her because it felt like I could do no less.

Bones feeling as though they were trying to jump through my skin, I put my nervous energy to good use and searched for a shovel to clear her front porch of snow. It was easy enough to find—kept within a shed on the backside of her house that stored various other tools—and I was cursing that fact as the task at hand only took about fifteen minutes. I paced the kitchen afterward, body and mind restless, and upon realizing that it was only just past ten o'clock, I took it upon myself to light a fire. I returned to the shed to find a stack of wood kept beneath a blue tarp. There were smaller logs beside her fireplace, but they would burn quickly, and I knew that I was far from sleep. What was under the tarp was thick—far thicker than the pieces intended to burn inside—and I would have been remiss to immediately toss them in her fireplace.

So...I found an axe in the shed, and what had begun as an honest intention to replenish her chopped stack turned into an exertion that was needed. I swung at the logs for far longer than necessary and ended up sweaty with an absolute pile of splintered wood, most of which inevitably returning to its original location beneath the tarp. But...my anxiety that had dwindled with strenuous effects had returned full force. With exhaustion from my mental state and the exertion of chopping wood, I should have been primed to snooze away just as the fire managed to catch and crackle. However, as expected, sleep was evading me. I was simply watching the flames contort and flicker while I waited for her call.

The fire eventually reduced to embers, and two o'clock came and went.

And 2:15.

And 2:45.

The GPS location that she promised to share with me was shining bright on my phone, signifying that the last trace of her was at Gas Lamp, and my feet were pounding the floor—through the kitchen, to the fireplace, down the hallway, and back. By the time three o'clock came around, I was standing next to her couch, frantically tapping her name under *Recent Calls* to ensure that she was alright. I placed my cell against my ear, and there was no subsequent ringing. All that came through the speaker was Cassie nearly singing:

"Hi, you've reached Cassie! Sorry I missed ya. Here comes the beep."

The high-pitched tone sounded, indicating that my voicemail was being recorded, and I should have just hung up...but because my pulse was palpitating in my throat, I bit out in a shaking voice:

"You said you'd call when you got off. Your shift ended at two. I'm waiting for you at your house, and you're not *here.* Where the fuck *are you?!*" There was no response, of course, but I still paused as if she were listening on the other end of the line. I exhaled heavily and added, "If you aren't here in fifteen minutes, I'm coming to find you, and I swear to *God,* Cas, if you're totally fine and just chatting with your work friends after hours or some shit, I'm going to *kill you myself!*"

The last few words came out in a growl. I nearly smacked the glass face of my phone to end the call, and just when I was sliding it back into my pocket, her front door behind me was creaking open. I whipped around to see her standing in her doorway, eyeing me in curiosity. Dressed exactly as she was when she left with her maroon overcoat protecting her from the cold and black backpack slung over her right shoulder, she cocked her head to the side and quietly asked:

"What are you doing here? Did ya just never leave?"

I didn't answer her question—I just stomped in her direction. Her gaze widened as she took in my anxious state, and I threw my arms around her shoulders before the feeling of relief was even able to sink in. Cassie took a single step backward to steady herself, I buried my nose in her hair, my over-filled lungs deflated as I let out a loud breath, and her arms slowly wrapped around my waist.

"Fuck, you scared me," I whispered into her neck. "What happened to calling?"

"Phone died," she apologetically mumbled. *"Breath,* Jay, *shit."*

"Should I, um...*go?"*

A second woman's meek voice sounded from behind Cassie, and I lifted my head to see her illuminated beneath the porch light. Though I was positive that we had never met before, there was something about her that screamed familiarity. She wore all black, the remainder of her a stark opposite with her skin naturally pale and almost powder-like complexion, and her long hair was nearly white. Her eyes—large, and the irises so light in color that I was sure they could reflect an image like a mirror—were bouncing across my embrace on Cassie hesitantly. Cassie and I had spoken to each other so quietly before that I was certain she hadn't heard a word, but she still appeared to deduce that she had interrupted an important moment when she stated:

"I'll go."

Our hold on each other loosened, and Cassie lifted a hand to pat the left side of my chest, shooting me a quick, questioning glance that wordlessly asked if I was alright. I nodded rapidly in response, and her palm fell away as she spoke over her shoulder:

"You're fine, Sky."

"I—are you sure? I don't want to be in the way—"

She spun on her heel, sweetly chastising, "You're *fine*, Skylar," and then turned right back around to walk across the threshold.

I took a step backward to allow her inside, and Cassie's touch briefly found my waist as she casually waved for Skylar to follow her. She did, though the timid expression on her face remained as she walked past us and further into the living area, and Cassie shoved her front door shut.

"Um...hi." I waggled my fingers at Skylar. "I'm James."

Skylar smiled shyly. "Sky. Erm—sorry I barged in."

Cassie rolled her eyes. "You didn't *barge*, Sky. I invited you over. You're physically incapable of barging." She looked back at me. "Sorry I didn't call. The battery on my phone's shot...gotta get a car charger or something. Was just gonna charge it and call you, but," she gestured at me grandly, "you're here."

"I am," I unnecessarily concurred.

Our eyes locked. I saw Skylar's head moving back and forth between us in my peripheral vision, and she remarked, "I can *really* just go, I—"

Cassie turned her head to place her gaze on her, replying in an admonishment that came across in a pleasant tone, "You don't have a *car.*" Skylar's lips pressed together tightly as she looked to the floor, and Cassie explained to me, "Sky works with me at Gas Lamp—I was giving her a ride home since her car wouldn't start, and her bathroom's, ah, all screwed up. Um—flooded. She's staying here tonight."

I narrowed my eyes at Cassie's stammering, but Skylar appeared to be too lost in apologizing over the inconvenience to notice that it was unlike Cassie to behave as such.

"I don't know how that happened," Skylar cringed. "It was completely fine when I left to go to work."

"Yeah, well—bathrooms can be tricky. Chalk it up to old pipes," Cassie dismissively remarked. "I'm gonna go get ready for bed. I'm beat," she murmured. "Jay...a word?" She quickly called over her shoulder as she walked, "Blankets are in the basket by the couch, Sky—make yourself comfortable."

I watched Cassie move to the hallway, and as she disappeared into it, I stated to Skylar without looking her way, "*Ah...*be right back."

I walked straight to her bedroom, allowed myself in, and saw Cassie sitting on her bed with her coat beside her. The pocket door to the right of her that led to the small master bath was slid halfway into the wall, the light illuminating the tile at her feet. To my surprise, she was looking at me with a hesitant expression. I felt my head shake in mild confusion, but before I could ask her what was wrong, she blurted out:

"I fucked up Sky's bathroom."

I gently replied, "What?"

"I fucked up. Her bathroom. *James.*" Her irritated tone made me finally conclude that the situation was far from dire. My previous anxiety abated, and I smirked as she asked, "The hell do you mean *what?*"

I chuckled out, "What'd you do?"

She whispered, "Get in here. Close the door."

I did as she asked and pulled the door shut. Crossing my arms, I suggested:

"Let's back up a few steps...*that's* why it took you so long to get home?"

Cassie drew a long breath through her nose, letting it out of her mouth as she said, "I was trying to convince Sky to just stay over here tonight since she needed a ride home, anyway...she wasn't really listening. I had no choice."

"You messed with her bathroom on *purpose?*" I asked with a single raised a single eyebrow, and she nodded. "You missing out on precious girl time or what?"

"No," she snapped. "I am not missing out on *girl time.* Sky's apartment has, like, no security. The girl barely remembers to lock her door at night. I just..." Cassie peered to the floor. "I don't—we don't know anything, and I still stand by that. Work was...fine. Totally fine. Absolutely unsuspicious. But..."

Her words faded off, her sentence remaining unfinished as she glanced left and right as if she were searching for a sign, but her point was ever clear—she was concerned.

I sighed. "You're worried about her?"

"Uh huh." Her dark gaze landed back on me, and she defeatedly threw her hands up only to place them in her lap, continuing with, "She's my friend. I feel like I have to say...*something.* I can't have her just going on with her life having zero guard up, but I don't—I don't know what to tell her, Jay. She's bound to ask questions, right?" Pressing the heels of her palms to her eyes, Cassie groaned, "I'm at a fuckin' loss here."

Seeing her so bothered yanked at my heartstrings, and I moved to sit next to her on the mattress. I lowered myself onto it slowly, the padding plush beneath me, and I looked at her as I softly noted:

"Well...she's here for the night and she has no means of leaving. You bought some time to think, so that's a plus."

Her pretty face turned to me, and she let out a quiet, bitter laugh.

She voiced in a timid rasp, "I had to shove a hand towel down her toilet...flushed it until it overflowed."

"Cassie."

It came out as an adoring admonish, and her lips quirked up.

"I *may* have also yanked on her showerhead until it started to leak for good measure."

"Very creative," I cooed. "I would have paid to see that."

Her smile grew and then faded, and she muttered, "What the hell am I supposed to tell her?"

I shrugged. "We know a dude who thinks Gas Lamp could be shady, but we have no idea about that for sure, so just be alert?"

"And then she asks, *'Shady? How shady? How do you know? Who is this guy? How can you trust him? Shouldn't we just tell the police?'"* The last question was one that particularly struck me because speaking with the police when the concerns regarding Gas Lamp were interconnected with Colton seemed to be a poor choice. With him being missing and having just helped us remove potential murder evidence, I truthfully didn't want to be anywhere *near* the police. Cassie looked to share the same sentiment, and she murmured, "Sky's more of a *go-with-the-flow* type of girl, but...no *way* she wouldn't question that. And I—I don't think we should be answering questions right now."

"Yeah, me either," I returned in an exhale. "Well...you've got the night to mull it over, at least?"

Cassie nodded, paused for a moment, and then asked quietly, "Are you staying?"

I knew that question was coming, but it still caused my heart to flinch in my chest. I reveled in it, for it was yet another obvious reminder that things had shifted between us. It wasn't a dismissive, *'Okay, you can go home, now,'* or, *'Made it home, Jay. I'll lock up behind you. See ya later.'* It was neither an invitation nor a demand. It was asking what I wanted despite the fact that I knew. I knew that *she knew* that I wasn't intending on leaving her home—and that sentence comforted me more than anything because if she didn't want me here, she would have sent me packing the moment that she saw my face.

She wanted me here—*welcomed* me here—and that meant far more to me than any touch of our lips or brazen wandering of our hands.

"Yes," I replied.

"'Kay." Cassie smiled softly. "I was gonna head back out and do it myself, but, um...do you mind locking up for me? Tell Sky I'll just see her in the morning. I don't really think she's up for socializing right now, anyway."

"Since it's past three in the morning?" I questioned lightly.

Her smile grew. "Yuh huh."

"I'll lock up," I confirmed. "Be back."

I was up and ambling to go about the task at hand by the time she quietly called out, "Thank you," and I casually waved it away without a look back.

Skylar's head peeked over the couch when I exited the hallway, her expression pinching together as she remarked:

"I feel like I'm interrupting something. Am I interrupting something? I'm like five minutes away from calling an Uber."

"Call an Uber to bring you back to your apartment with the flooded bathroom that Cas just told me about?" I quipped. "Don't be silly." I moved past where she sat cross-legged on the center cushion, noting to myself that she had yet to grab the blanket that Cassie had mentioned. "And no—you're not interrupting anything. Cas didn't even know I was here."

"No?" Skylar questioned. "She mentioned you."

The butterfly infestation in my gut grew.

I kept my focus on the front door, locking it and then grabbing the chair to its right, similar to how Cassie had when I was here previously.

"Did she?"

She hummed in acknowledgment. "Something about how you've been around, *erm*...what are you doing?"

I shoved the back of the chair beneath the knob, ensured it was jammed tightly into place, and offhandedly said, "Oh, the lock on this door's shit—a good, strong breeze'll blow it open."

It was a terrible lie considering that one of the locks was a deadbolt, and she should have questioned it much like Cassie had anticipated with the mention of anything awry with Gas Lamp, but she did nothing of the sort. I turned to see Skylar nodding with what seemed to be an appreciative grin. There was no concern. No silent interrogation. Not a trace of unease in her light eyes...and the descriptor *gullible* came to mind. Nice, timid, and gullible—and though I had only met her minutes ago, I could thoroughly see why Cassie was wanting to protect her. Skylar covered her mouth as she yawned, and I took it as my cue to announce:

"Ah, I can get out of your hair...Cas is going to bed, too, I think." I pointed at her. "You like pancakes?"

She shrugged. "I have nothing against them."

"When we're all up," I stated. "Pancakes. I'll cook. Don't let Cas cook for you. Her pancakes are shit."

Skylar laughed. "Sounds good. Night."

I threw her a wave. "Night."

I returned to the hallway, willing the absolute horde of butterflies in my stomach to abate, and told myself that this wasn't a big deal. I was casual. Casual and walking into Cassie's bedroom, where I was intending to sleep for the second time. Everything was *fine*—and it needed to be. I *needed* to keep whatever wits I had about me lest Cassie's defensive walls snapped back up, and the trust that she had seemingly placed in me came crashing down.

This is fine.

Totally fine.

Upon closing the door to her bedroom, the creaking of water pipes and telltale splashing against a plastic curtain reached my ears, and my head snapped to her bathroom door, which was now slid mostly shut. A tiny sliver of light peeked through, and though I wasn't attempting to examine what was occurring beyond the space, I still saw it.

Her, I mean.

There was nothing distinguishing about the sight. It was simply a flash of her bare flesh as she moved from one side of the bathroom to the other. I hadn't, by any means, seen her naked body—nor was I looking for her naked body—but it still made my entire being flinch, and the notion of *playing it fucking cool* was obliterated from my brain in a quick *poof!*

I blinked several times, my vision turning fuzzy as I cocked my head and stared at absolutely nothing. Water audibly dripped to the floor in louder, weighted splashes—no doubt due to the rivulets that were now rolling off of her body. A humid waft of something I could only describe as *vanilla spice* made its way into my nose, my eyes went heavy, I unlocked my knees to take the few steps to the door, and I rolled it aside enough to poke my head through the opening.

"Cas?"

The master bath was white and small—room enough for a toilet to the left, a sink and small vanity smack directly in front of the door, and a shower to the right with an ivory curtain.

"*Ah,* you found me," she spoke from behind the fabric with the slightest of humor in her voice that made me bite my lower lip as I smiled.

"That I did," I replied.

"House all locked up?"

"Mhm."

"Is Sky good?"

"On the couch where you left her last."

"Mmm. Good. You comin' in?"

No, no—surely, I hallucinated that.

"Huh?"

Cassie peeked around the curtain, her face fresh—*clean*—and her cheeks flushed from heat. Her hair slicked back and entirely wet, she was looking at me with a wide grin.

"Come on—shower with me?"

Yes, ma'am.

I nodded enthusiastically, clawing at the back of my shirt and the remainder of my clothing to pull them off with haste. Cassie watched me for a moment and then chuckled as she pulled the curtain back to its original position.

She was facing away as I stepped in, her head angled up to the showerhead as water rained to her chest and rolled down her slight curves. It was clear where the stream had already traced over her as I eyed the long, pink, heated streak of her skin. It was just wide enough to nestle between her shoulder blades, running from the base of her neck to the dimples on her lower back. I placed my hands on either side of it, flexing my fingers into her shoulders, and dropped my head to touch my mouth to her spine. Cassie hummed happily as my lips damn near burned, and I murmured:

"The water's scalding you."

She quietly noted, "I like it hot."

I trailed my hands down to her hips. "I see that."

Cassie rested her head back against me, rolling it to the right against my clavicle, and I wrapped my arms around her waist to fully embrace her from behind. As expected, her body was radiating heat, and I fell into the flames, softly kissing her neck that she had stretched and left exposed before grazing my nose along her jawline.

In the most casual of motions—as if she had done the act several times before—Cassie grabbed my right wrist and brought it up to her lips, nipping the inked skin along my pulse point. I could hear her smile rather than see it as she made a contented noise, and she held my arm to her eye level as her fingers lazily traced along the dark marks. She eventually lowered it back to place my hand on the swell of her hip, but she continued tracing along the ink on my right arm as if she had memorized the lines.

"Do your tattoos mean anything?"

It was a simple, everyday question, and I relished in it.

I released my grip on her to extend my arms, looking as if I had forgotten about them. The marks on my upper half were all in a dark, monochromatic color scheme. The designs were mostly abstract, ranging from looking as though someone had taken a paintbrush and carefully dragged it across my skin in calculated strokes to flinging the same bristles at my body to create a harsh splatter. There were no letters...nor were there depictions of Latin or another language that I would have to translate for those who asked.

I embraced her once more, finishing my thoughts aloud with, "Nah. Just art."

Cassie nodded, her head lolling against my shoulder as she noted, "The artist made them look messy."

The way she said it was complimentary, and her tone made me smile softly.

"Messy art," I told her.

"James-the-planner is covered in messy art...I like that."

I chuckled into her neck because, somehow, she just...*got it*. It *was* messy. The ink had the outward appearance of a madman who had thrown paint at a canvas and then haphazardly tried to make sense of it all, but, in reality, it took dozens of hours and a talented artist to sink it into my skin. I always thought that it was somehow beautiful that what was covering my arms from shoulder to wrist—and similarly on my thighs, though those were in more vibrant colors—was a visual contradiction. I thoroughly enjoyed the thought of being a canvas for something that appeared to be *messy* when my life was typically so well thought out.

Cassie's speaking on my tattoos fell to the wayside, then, and it was pleasant. Far more than pleasant. The steam gathered and relaxed my muscles, we sank into the feel of each other, and it was just...*right*.

I had wondered if joining Cassie in the shower was to be a hot and heavy, lustrous, heavy-petting affair. I had no qualms if it *wasn't*, of course, but with her invitation and prior devilish smile, I had, naturally, expected it. I had thought that we would immediately explore each other's bodies to a further extent with quick, insistent, greedy grasps, the steam along with our actions stripping our breath away and leaving us spent. And it wasn't that being with her here, naked and wet, wasn't alluring in all definitions of the word. It was...but there was a sensual sort of care that hung heavy in the mist and shifted the aura of the room the moment that we touched. I felt it in the way that she relaxed into my arms—in the way that she reached up to brush the side of my face while I nuzzled her cheek—in the way that she twisted her neck to look into my eyes, holding my gaze for the longest of moments as we listened to the deafening sound of the water splashing against the tile.

Cassie was the one to close the distance between us, kissing me with a gentle purpose. With slow movements that turned my bones to jelly. With sweet, quiet, appreciative noises that forced my grip on her to tighten. She reached for my right hand with hers again, guiding it away from her hip and down to between her legs.

"Just like this?" she whispered.

The water cascaded down her chest, over her arm and mine, onto our hands where they met at the apex of her thighs, and mixed with the slickness of her that covered my fingers. Her breath hitched as I slowly moved with her touch, over her pussy, up to her clit in a circle, and back.

No...*hot and heavy* wasn't the descriptor that I would use for this. Hot and heavy, to me, meant pinning each other against walls—giving into depravity and all things dirty—gasping for breath and shrieking to whatever God above whilst seeking an explosive release.

Hot and heavy had its time and place...and *this* was not it.

This was...comfort. Passion. Ardency.

Unlike all things *hot and heavy,* pleasure wasn't the only reason for our actions. It was an impending outcome, sure—a glorious side effect—but it wasn't what was driving us forward. The sole purpose was *connection*. I could see it in her eyes—feel it when she sighed against me—taste it on her tongue.

And, *fuck,* it was heady.

I returned her hushed tone, "Show me how you want it."

"Yes."

Following her languid motions, I went down, up, and around; down, up, and around. I kissed her with the same patience—the same delicious tempo, at certain times with an open mouth on hers and others with a lazy lick along her neck when her head would fall back on my shoulder. My erection was hard against her backside by the time she was ushering my fingers inside of her, and I couldn't help but moan along with her as I moved in and out.

"You like it like this?" I crooned into her ear as her head lolled back.

"Yes," she breathed.

I nipped at the space between her shoulder and her neck, and she gasped.

"Just like this?" I asked.

"More."

"Mmm." I placed my lips against the area that I had bitten, her sweat caused by the heat around us salty on my tastebuds. "Faster? Harder?" My voice deepened. *"Both?"*

"No," she panted, and I slowed my movements to a crawl. "I want—I want *you.*"

I stilled completely, and Cassie turned to seal her mouth on mine, kissing me with fervor as she hummed a noise that could only mean *please.*

Pulling away from her, I inquired, "Are you on any—"

"Covered. IUD," she answered my question before I was able to finish it. "Are you..."

"Clean?" I presumed.

"Yes."

I rapidly replied, "Yeah, wouldn't have let you go down on me yesterday if I wasn't—you?"

"Yes—" Her response was cut off with a sharp inhale as I undulated my fingers once more, her head falling back against me as she moaned a loud, long, low, *"Jaaamesss."*

"Fuck," I groaned quietly into her hair. "Look at me." She rolled her head, our eyes locked, and I crashed my lips to hers before saying, "I fucking *love* how you sound right now, but your friend is on the couch, and you're echoing."

In an exhale, she said, "I don't care."

"I do," I told her. "Even if it's just your friend, those noises are mine to hear." I continued pumping my fingers in and out, and she nodded quickly, her mewls obediently turning quieter. I whispered approvingly, *"Mine* to hear. That's my girl."

"Your girl," she repeated my words. *"Yes."*

Goddamn.

I had been considering leading her back to the bedroom because it felt appropriate. Because I wanted her between the sheets. Because a stereotypically accepted area for metaphorically melding your soul to another's was a mattress. With her reiteration of my possessiveness having gone off like a flashbang, the idea of conventionally bedding her was swept away, and I was left blind to it all, for I wanted her *here*.

Right here in the humid air that was swirling amongst our palpable connection.

I removed my fingers from her gently as I murmured: "In here? Like this?"

Her back arched, her ass rubbing against me in a way that made me suck in a breath through my teeth.

"Yes."

Cassie's response came out as a plea as she shifted ever-so-slightly to bend at her hips, arms outstretched to the tile at her front to steady herself. The shower rained down between us, over my chest in hot streams and falling to her backside. I followed the droplets' path, gliding one hand over her spine and the other down to my cock to position myself against her, and just barely pushed inside.

"Ah, *fuck,*" I groaned at the feel of her—wet, hot, and tight—and leaned forward to wrap around her once more.

Reaching to where we met between her legs with one hand, I gripped her jaw with the other to angle her lips to mine, drank her in, and we both let out a quiet, *"Yes,"* as I slowly buried myself. Her pitch went high as I moved, whimpering a combination of my name and words that I couldn't comprehend. The water was at my scalp, soaking my hair and dripping down my face—onto hers—caressing the front of her body.

"I...I..." Cassie stammered with each breath, and I cajoled:

"Talk to me."

"Feels so good," she whispered. "I won't last."

I squeezed my grasp on her jaw, quickening my pace, and spoke against her mouth, "I'm right there with you." The splashing of the water that had found itself between our bodies was rhythmic, occurring in time with each thrust, gaining in speed and volume. *"Shit."*

My voice turned hoarse as the pleasure coiled within me, and Cassie hungrily kissed me with an open mouth. She took one of her hands from the wall and tangled it in my hair, fisting it tightly, and I moaned on her tongue.

"Like that," she softly cried as my pace became frantic. "Baby...*fuck.*"

Baby.

Baby.

The endearment repeated over in my mind, snatching my soul and leaving me breathless.

"Call me that again," I begged.

Her legs grew unsteady, wobbling beneath her. "You're going to—*shit*—baby, you're going to make me come."

Ready to snap, I pounded into her, biting at her neck, holding her close by her hair just as she had me, and I groaned into her ear, "Come for me." She silenced her scream by sinking her teeth into me in turn—on my left, just below my facial hair—and I felt her pulsing squeezes on my cock when her knees went weak. I kept her upright with the hold I had between her legs, and as I raced toward my own release, I praised, *"That's my fucking girl."*

Her returning, *"Yes,"* was slurred and weak, but it shot through me nonetheless, and I was gone.

Obliterated.

Exploding inside of her with a final thrust and a gritty moan into her neck, I was forced to let my grip on her hair go to steady myself with a smack of my palm on the wall.

Our exhausted breaths rose above the water as we came down. We stood up straight. Cassie turned in my arms, lazily lacing hers around my neck, and kissed me deeply. We rotated so I was fully beneath the shower, I tilted my head back to allow the water to run through my hair, and, without saying a word, Cassie reached to the inset shelf on her right that I hadn't even noticed previously. Grabbing a circular, squat, brown bottle that I assumed was shower gel, she squirted a generous amount into her left palm, returned it to the shelf, and rubbed her hands together to create a lather.

The vanilla scent swarmed me as she placed her hands on my chest. I felt my lips pull up into a deliriously contented smile, and she cleaned me slowly. She took great care, lingering especially over my arms and tracing the outlines of my tattoos, and stopped completely when she knelt before me and rubbed at the color on my thighs. I ushered her back upward with a gentle touch to her face, she returned to me, and between light brushes of our lips, I asked if I could return the gesture and wash her, as well.

Her nose skimmed mine as she shook her head, mentioning that she had already done so before I joined her, and upon the remark that her skin was turning *pruny*, we made a leisurely descent for the bedroom.

We sufficiently dried and dressed ourselves, me in the undergarments I had kicked to the floor and Cassie in just a pair of navy boyshorts that I more than approved of. I used her toothbrush. We had a brief, altogether playful argument regarding her belief that I needed to apply lotion to slow the formation of worry wrinkles on my forehead. I inevitably allowed her to smooth said moisturizer over my face.

It was beautifully comfortable, and the gratified upturn of my lips remained as I lay with her under the sheets. We rested face to face, her eyes closed as I toyed with her damp hair, running my fingers through the strands softly as if I were searching for tangles to tame.

Because I knew that she was yet to be asleep and the thought had crossed my mind, I murmured:

"I have a confession to make."

Her right eyebrow flickered upward for a split second, but she seemed entirely unconcerned with her eyelids still shut as she responded, "Mmm?"

"I *may* have left you a…rather uncouth voicemail."

Cassie finally looked at me, amused. "Did you now?"

"Mhm."

"And what, exactly, was *uncouth?*"

My hand had stroked to the ends of her hair, and I started again by her temple. "Can I preface with the fact that I left it while I was concerned that you had gone missing?"

A corner of her mouth pulled up in sympathy. "Yes, you can. Go on."

I drew in a long breath, and then let it out as I admitted with an upward inflection, "I was telling you that I was at your house?"

"Mmm."

"And talking about how you hadn't called."

"Right."

"And that your shift had ended a *while* ago."

"That's all ringing a bell."

"And that if you didn't get home within fifteen minutes, I'd come to find you." I paused, squeezing my eyes shut as I ended with, "And that if you weren't *actually* in danger, I'd kill you myself."

Upon repeating it, the words sounded...*bad*. Controlling, even. I opened one of my eyes to peek at her reaction, and Cassie giggled in a girlish fashion that made all my concerns fly *right* out of the room, through the hallway, past Skylar, beyond the chair that was forcefully shoved underneath her front door's knob, and into the abyss.

"Oh, that's *so* unlike you," she sarcastically sighed as she caught her breath. *"So* unlike you to be rude and snappy when you're stressed."

"Am I known to be rude and snappy when I'm stressed?" I repeated her words back to her.

"Mhm." Her gaze sparkled as she said, "That's James Turner energy, for sure."

I scoffed, *"James Turner energy?"*

"Oh, yeah." Cassie quipped, "Even if I *had* gone missing, I have a feeling you'd have shown up wherever I was in about ten seconds flat, though...you *do* tend to show up, don't you?"

What had meant to be a casual, offhanded joke hit me square in the chest. My delight in our banter was whisked away, and my swallow through the lump in my throat was audible.

"That's not funny, Cas. If you disappeared, I'd lose my goddamn mind."

I said it in a quiet mutter that made her tense, and when I looked into her eyes, I no longer found any trace of humor in them.

She whispered, "Sorry."

I blew out a rough breath through my nose. "'S'okay...you're right." I continued to brush through her hair with my fingertips. I murmured, "I'd find you, Darlin'."

The name for her had simply waltzed out of my mouth. I hadn't meant to say it—had never internally tested the word in my thoughts—but I uttered it, anyway. And there was no awkwardness. No teasing, questioning, *'Oh, I'm Darlin'?'* There was only her soft exhale before she leaned forward to kiss me gently, and we plummeted into our familiar magnesis.

Chapter 14

I'm a simple man. I put in my time at work, but not overly so. I love my friends and family. I thoroughly enjoy the company of a woman who is enjoying said company with me. I relish in the beautiful, comfortable laziness that life can provide. The latter two were currently leaving me in a happy, drunken buzz, though I hadn't drunk a drop of alcohol.

I had yearned to naturally wake, and I did—to a blissfully cold room, lying flat on my back with the heat of Cassie on my front. Her head on my chest, her arm around my waist and leg hitched up to wrap around my nearest thigh, I was holding her while she continued to snooze away. I had no recollection of my dreams, nor did I have any intention of mentioning the drama of everything involving Colton—whether it be 2D, the laptop, or the missing women of Salem. There was no need to speak of it now. With no lives on the line and no urgent notifications on either of our cell phones that I had glanced at upon first awakening, I had deduced that I was going to revel in the now.

In our purgatory.

Cassie would eventually stir, and we would rise from her bed with slow, blissful movements on this quiet Saturday as if it were a Christmas morning. We would go to greet Skylar, who, of course, was still on the couch. We would speak of breakfast. My bare feet would be cold on the tile as I walked back and forth throughout the kitchen to make them both pancakes. It would be simple. It would be *happy*...and for the briefest of moments, I sincerely thought that was a possibility.

I actually had a shred of fucking *hope*.

I was holding onto that shred until my phone began to vibrate on Cassie's bedside table, and I removed my hand from her naked waist to blindly reach for my cell. In one glimpse, I saw that it was Luke, and my hope dissipated into the air like smoke, leaving no trace of its previous existence whatsoever.

Trading the grip on my phone from left to right, I begrudgingly began to unravel myself from Cassie. She whined sleepily as I moved, rolled herself over, and stretched as if she were anticipating me to wrap my arms around her from behind. Her hair cascading over her bare back before me made me let out a quiet sigh, and if it weren't for the apprehension that I held over awaiting a call from anyone in our collective found family, I would have just silenced my cell.

I *almost* did, ever-present nerves aside, because the sight of her was calling to me like a damned siren...but because that would have been foolish, downright dumb, and, above all, *selfish,* I didn't.

Crawling over her and out of bed before the call could cease its ringing, the moment that my feet touched the floor, I slid my thumb across the screen to answer it. Before I could so much as speak my hello or walk to the bathroom as I had intended, Cassie called to me in a half-asleep, near-slurred:

"Come back to bed, baby."

What was most definitely Claire's voice shrieked through my cell that I still held in my palm, and I rapidly deduced that it was *not* just my brother who had rang.

Cassie's repeated use of the endearment—when we weren't even in the throes of passion, no less—was far, *far* more than welcome. In fact, if I hadn't made it abundantly clear already, I fucking loved it. *Now,* however, with the other end of the call clearly being on speakerphone, was not the time for her to be using it. The only thing I could be thankful for was that she sounded far from her own usual tone. Though it still maintained the typical deep huskiness that I enjoyed, it held a significant rasp. It was sleep-filled. Content. And, unfortunately for me, because I felt as though I was about to suffer from a stroke, *well-fucked*. She sounded well-fucked.

I glanced at Cassie, who seemed to be obliviously blinking the sleep from her eyes, and I looked from my phone and back to her with an alarmed expression that I hoped conveyed, *'Please, dear God, stop talking.'*

Claire's shrill, "AH—*fuck, TMI!*" was so loud that it was able to be heard by both of us, and Cassie appeared to fully wake—thoroughly and abruptly—as she sat at attention and smacked a hand over her mouth.

I pointed to the bathroom, signaling to her that I was going there to take the call, and she let her hand fall as she silently mouthed a frantic, *'What's going on?'*

As rapidly as I could manage, I lifted my phone to my ear and rattled off, "Is anyone dead, dying, or in danger?"

Luke called back, "No!"

My usual anxiety—the one that had nothing to do with my and Cassie's romantic involvement—eased, and I sighed before crooning, "In that case—*one moment, please.*" I pulled it away from my ear to purposefully hit the *mute* button, and spoke to Cassie in a surprisingly reassuring tone, "I muted myself; sounds like they're fine."

"Who's *they?*"

"Luke and Claire."

"Okay," she exhaled. "Okay…think, ah…do you think they knew that was me?"

I shrugged. "They heard *a woman*…not necessarily *you*." I listened to my phone once more, hearing glass sliding across granite and the murmurings of Luke offering Claire a towel to clean up spilled coffee. I concluded, "There'd be a touch more screaming if they knew, I think."

Cassie grumbled, "Probably…just—just don't say anything, okay?" She anxiously added, "I'm not trying to sweep us under the rug. I—I'm *not*, really."

I hadn't thought that in the least, but the reminder that her opinion had thoroughly changed on burying any of our feelings still made me feel shockingly light.

"This is far from a rug-sweep, Cas," I replied gently. "You think I want to up and announce that I was in your bed when we haven't even had a chance to talk about us? *Of course not*."

Her shoulders sagged in a quiet relief. "Talk about us later?"

"Talk about us *soon*," I corrected.

Cassie gave me a small smile, and it appeared as though she were about to speak once more, but a loud buzz sounded from the side table. Her focus was pulled to her cell, her grin waned, and she told me:

"It's Liam."

"His timing is impeccable," I said in an exhale. I gestured once again to the bathroom. "I'll take the bathroom; you stay out here?"

She nodded in agreement, picked up her phone, and answered it, "Hey, what's up?"

Walking the few steps to the bathroom, I rolled the door closed, strained my ears for a beat to ensure that Cassie's voice was relatively inaudible, and finally re-tapped the button to unmute the call.

As casually as I could, I said, "Good morning, brother."

"Hey," he spoke slowly, "bad time?"

"There have been better times for you to have me on speakerphone," I remarked. *"Hi, Claire."*

"Ah—hi, Jay." Her voice came out in a squeak.

I chuckled, "What's going on, guys?" My mild amusement at their timid responses immediately fell away when I heard Luke audibly take in a loud breath, and let it out in a ragged sigh. I pressed, *"Guys?"*

"It's Colton."

What felt like an electric shock ran through my body as my brother spoke his name in disdain. My body froze, and I questioned, "What about him?"

He replied bitterly, "He called Claire from an unknown number. He'll be at Henry's in an hour."

"I thought you said that no one was dead, dying, or in danger?" I retorted in a snap. "You let me put you on *mute?*"

"No one *is* dead, dying, or in danger," Claire argued.

"Oh, *by all means,* take my question literally!" I mocked, my voice coming out in a hiss in an attempt to keep the volume at a minimum. "Ya *probably* should have led this call with: Colton's reappearing in *broad fucking daylight* to a *public establishment!* You made it sound like everything is *fine!*"

"This is *to plan,*" Claire reminded me. "Everything *is* fine. Broad fucking daylight shouldn't matter to someone who is keeping up the appearance of having nothing to hide, and that public establishment doesn't open for another two hours." She added with gumption, "Luke and I are scheduled to open today, Garrett's not even on the work calendar until tomorrow, and Henry's out of town. Colt said he has the laptop. This is a best. Case. Scenario, Jay." Claire stressed, *"No one is dead, dying, or in danger."*

The details of the situation sank in, albeit slowly, due to my disbelief and subsequent hesitant relief, and I quietly responded, "Oh...I...*okay.* Where—wait—how'd he get out of 2D?"

"He hung up pretty damn quick; he didn't say."

Luke noted, "Not out the front door, obviously. Liam's been watching his camera. He said he didn't see him on any of the footage."

"Right, the camera," I muttered, considering for the briefest moment that Liam—and Zoey, Claire, and Luke, if they had discussed it—had known that I had been home very little as of late.

It didn't matter. Not now, anyway.

After a short pause, Claire spoke, "Colt's going to want to pick your brain about whatever he's involved in."

"Yeah, yeah," I sighed. "I'll be there soon. I don't really know that much, but my, ah—my friend might. I can give him her number; don't worry, it'll be a *later thing*."

It was the only workaround I could think of to keep Cassie's means of work in the dark. Thankfully, both of them murmured their agreements and had no further inquiry. However, I could only assume that they had realized that I was in bed with my *friend* who works at Gas Lamp. The dots there could only be so hard to connect, after all, and they left me feeling rather torn. The relieved half of me knew that, despite the severity of our current situation, the rumor would spread. Naturally, the entire group would be on my side for arranging to speak with Colton at a later time because bringing another person into the mix with the situation with 2D would be *alarmingly* dumb. Our two problems—if we were to deem them as something as trivial as that—would remain separate, and Cassie and I could speak with Colton as we saw fit.

It was good. It was a *good* thing. Really.

But the other half of me—the romantic that was still reeling over the second night that we had spent together—was both disappointed and guilt-ridden. The nature of the way I had fallen right into her was just as I had anticipated it could be—*hard and fast*—and the intensity of my feelings for her was only snowballing with every kiss. Every sigh of her against me. Every look into her warm, brown eyes. Truthfully, if the timing were right and our lives less chaotic, I would have already been contemplating if we should announce our seeing each other to the group and, more importantly, her brother because I wanted her. I wanted her hand in mine at Henry's, my fingers toying with hers atop the bar. Double dates with Luke and Claire. Jesus—dinner with Liam and Zoey, even, once the dust settled from the dropped bomb that is our relationship.

There was no uncertainty about it.

I wanted her *publicly*.

And I knew without a doubt that, for several reasons, *that* couldn't happen right now. *Shouldn't* happen right now. My brow furrowed in dismay at the notion as I stared at my phone in my palm after Luke and Claire's quick goodbye, and I moved to roll the door back into the wall. Cassie was already up and dressed, having thrown on her same clothes as the night before.

Her eyes whipped to me, and she murmured, "Good morning."

Her hair was not the usual straight, shiny drape that fell over her shoulders, wavy with a halo of frizz. The right side of her face was pinker than the left due to having rested on my chest, and the area underneath her warm, brown eyes was puffy. Though she was reflecting my own anxious anticipation, she still offered me a slight smile with a drowsy, trusting gaze.

Goddamn, she was a sight to behold.

"Good morning," I returned quietly, placing a hand on my hip as I asked, "You got somewhere to be?"

"Yeah...I have a feeling we both just got invited to the same party."

A corner of my lip pulled up, but only just. "That we did."

My clothing was on the floor before me, still in a heap from when I had stripped to join her in the shower. I stepped into my jeans, and just as I was pulling them over my hips, she noted:

"So...Colton's back."

"He is."

"With the laptop."

I hummed in agreement and snatched my shirt from the floor. "And he'll want to talk to me—and by *me*, I mean *you*," I pulled my head through the neck hole, put my arms through the sleeves, and smoothed the fabric over my abdomen, "about the MIA girls at Gas Lamp."

"Is this when we debrief about my work so you can do the talking for me?" Cassie pursed her lips, and then muttered, "Sorry you're a middle-man."

"Ah-ah." I waggled an index finger in the air. "None of that. I'm in the middle of it regardless because I want to be, right?"

Cassie exhaled, "Right."

"Anyway, we, ah…" I hesitated. "Don't need to debrief."

She squinted. "Why not?"

I spoke with an upward inflection, "Because I told Luke and Claire that I was going to let Colt meet up with my, erm, *friend* himself?"

"Oh." Her pretty face turned to an expression of relief, but it only lasted for so long. Her freckles warped as her nose scrunched up in distaste, and she repeated, *"Oh."*

"Yeah…"

Cassie rapidly and monotonously deduced, "They think you're fucking a stripper. *Great.*"

"I *am* fucking a stripper," I returned. "Though I don't care for *that* phrasing—"

"Jay!" Cassie threw her head back as she whined, "They're gonna know!"

"About your job or about me?" I asked with a single high brow.

She huffed out a breath, looking at me pointedly. *"Job.* Probably have to keep us under wraps, right? The timing is..." With a soft roll of her eyes, she bitterly chuckled, and I understood her sentiment without her having to explain further. I nodded in agreement, knowing just as well as she did that there was simply too much going on to even consider saying or hinting at anything about us. "Forget the bad timing of it all; they may think that you have a *stripper girlfriend.* And it's not me."

My mind stuck on a single word, everything else fell to the wayside, and I felt my head tilt as I questioned, "Girlfriend?"

Any frustration she had seemed to melt away, and she smirked at me as she bit her lower lip.

"Well, unless you're a *very* good actor or I'm bad at reading the room..." Cassie whispered dramatically, *"And I'm not bad at reading the room."* Stepping toward me, she reached forward to grasp at my shirt, pulling me into her as she looked to me and wrapped her arms around my waist.

"I had assumed that this was *not* a no-strings, casual fling. Y'know—off of context clues."

I found myself smiling as I draped an arm over her shoulders.

"I'm not usually a no-strings man, Darlin'." I attempted to smooth the frazzled pieces of her hair, tucking the strands behind her ear. "You make me feel especially...stringy."

Lowering my head, I had said the last word against her lips.

She said a wispy, "Stringy, huh?"

I nodded. "Very stringy."

"Good," Cassie replied quietly. "Me too."

We were attached at the mouth, then, and it could have been argued that it was either of our doings. The gentle, soft movements, along with the tightening in my chest at our verbal acknowledgments, had me immediately yearning to walk her back to bed. To strip our clothes, bury ourselves under the covers, bury myself in her, and murmur in her ear that she was mine as our bodies worked us up to ecstasy.

There was no time for that, though, and we both seemed to come to that realization with a disappointed exhale as our lips parted.

"Meet you at Henry's?" I breathed.

"I'll be right behind you," she murmured. "Have to drive Sky home; she said her apartment maintenance would be by at some time today."

"Mmm, right," I replied. "I had told her I'd cook you both pancakes. I'll have to apologize."

Cassie chuckled. "Another time, baby."

I flexed my fingers that had wound their way around the back of her neck, kissed her deeply, and allowed ourselves a last, brief moment before we willingly left our purgatory.

Colton was late.

As Claire had reminded all of us, he hadn't set an exact time to arrive—a simple, *'I'll be there in an hour,'* was all that she said was given—but as it was approaching fifteen minutes over that allotted hour, *late* was the descriptor that we were all using. Despite Claire's insistence that his inevitable return was *good news,* the passage of time made us all restless, and the anticipation for Colton to arrive was palpable amongst us.

Zoey was far from her usual boisterous self, staring at the wood grain of our table and seemingly stewing in her own emotional hell. Liam was beside her, taking turns between carefully examining her expression for traces of distress and snapping his dark eyes to the entrance.

Cassie had sat next to me, as per usual. Upon the mention of the word *late,* she began to occasionally check the time on her phone, glance to her brother, and then fidget with her fingers in her lap under the table. On the third iteration of this, I blindly reached for her hands with mine, finding her scratching at the edges of her cuticles, and her motions stilled when I squeezed her right palm. I avoided looking at her, and she did the same, but the interlacing of her fingers through mine and quick exhalation through her nostrils showed me her silent thanks. My heart skipped as her grip remained strong, and both of our pulses secretly thrummed in time beneath the wood.

Claire seemed to be the least concerned of us all—an elbow on the table, she was simply resting her head on her hand as she watched Luke with an expression of sympathy. My brother was the only one not sitting in his usual spot, his feet tapping along the hardwood of Henry's as he walked in front of our table and back.

"This is a set-up," Luke murmured. "This has *got* to be a set-up."

Claire sighed loudly. "It's not a *set-up.*"

He stopped in his pacing for a moment to look at her pointedly. "All of us gathered in one place? Waiting for him to show up with potentially incriminating shit on us? He's gonna bust in with the cops and get us all fucking arrested."

She sagged further into her seat, head thrown back as she let out a none-too-patient groan. "Colt hates cops, and he has no reason to blindly fuck us over. I know you're anxious, baby, but you need to try to take a breath—"

The front door swung open so quickly that the bell chime had a near-angry appeal.

All of our heads whipped to the entrance, Luke's pacing halted directly in front of our table, and he exclaimed:

"Where the fuck have you been?!"

Colton stood stock-still in front of the door as it clunked shut, holding what appeared to be the infamous laptop under an arm by his side. He squinted in Luke's direction, cocking his head to the side so far that his inky hair left the right side of his face and hung from the roots.

"What ever happened to *hello?*" Colton retorted snippily. *"How are you?"* He turned an about face, gave the door a quick once over, and flicked the deadbolt shut. As he faced us once more, he griped, "Thanks *so much* for risking your livelihood for us, Colt—it means a *lot.*" Colton stomped his way toward the bar, past Luke, who was now appraising him with crossed arms, and began to wave his free hand about as he complained, *"No,* don't bother with any of that! My shoulder *did* get fucked when I rammed the closet door, by the way." He gently set the laptop down on the bartop and rotated his right arm in a circular motion as if to test his shoulder's mobility, grumbling, "Stupid, *goddamn* keypad lock."

Colton took his seat with a shocking amount of grace, inhaling a long, seemingly cleansing breath and letting it out with an audible exasperation. Claire was the one to respond:

"How'd ya get out of 2D, Colt?"

She spoke with a lackluster sigh, and it wasn't until that very moment that I realized that Claire *wasn't concerned*. Yes, her eyes had bounced around the entire group, lingering on Zoey and, most often, Luke, care and worry held within her gaze...but she wasn't concerned about *Colton* in the least. It was as if she knew, without a doubt, that he would return. That he had the ability to avoid the police and snake his way back, and the only caveat to that was time.

It was a blunt reminder of her past, and I wondered how often she had been placed in a similar position to lead to this level of trust in him to skirt the law.

He glanced at her, and his frustration eased, if only slightly.

Colton shrugged with his unwounded shoulder. "Fire escape through the window outside of the kitchen. Just glad I found it quick enough."

I nodded, and so did Claire and Zoey, for the Milkovich's apartment was a reverse layout of 2A—their old apartment and my current abode—and we were more than familiar with it. We all knew that the building was dated, and the old metal fire escapes attached to the outside brick were still the only means of fleeing from a blaze within. The ladders were rusted—janky—and I could almost picture Colton hanging from the bottom step, dangling before he dropped to the snowy ground and sprinted off into the distance.

"Are we gonna talk about this shit?" Colton flicked a hand toward the computer.

I felt all of our bodies stiffen, and we looked at each other before Claire began to reply, "You agreed to not question—"

"Oh, we are *so past that,*" he chuckled sardonically to the ceiling. "Jesus *Christ*, guys. You had no sense—no *goddamn* sense—no fucking *clue* to. Warn. Me?!"

Luke sharply began, *"Hey,* we didn't know about the alarm—"

"Oh *no-no!*" Colton exclaimed, waggling an index finger in the air. *"That* was an assumed risk—a shitty one, but still assumed. I didn't give a second thought to you knowing about the alarm, and I still don't think you did because I'm pretty damn good at sniffing out lies. But the room?" He paused. "The. *Fucking. Room?*"

We all fell silent for a beat, and I glanced to Zoey to find that the color had drained from her face. Liam placed a hand between her shoulder blades, tearing his eyes off of her to glare at Colton as if he had no right to mention it.

With a clenched jaw, he nearly spoke through his teeth, "Why does that even matter?"

Colton blinked several times over. "Why—why does that *matter?* Ya didn't think to mention the empty torture chamber? It's the *one* thing that y'all seemed to know about in the whole damn place."

Zoey's elbows hit the table, and she groaned as she held her head in her hands.

Liam snapped, *"Watch it,"* with such bite in his direction that Colton's head flinched backward.

Claire consolingly murmured across the table, "Zoey?"

"I'm *fine,* Claire," Zoey returned with significant grit in her voice.

While Cassie and Luke simply held their tongues, bleak expressions all around, I watched Colton. Head tilted to the side, his expression was slowly turning. His irritation—or, perhaps, anger—at our unforthcoming dispositions melted away as he first took in Claire's concern for her friend. What seemed to be morbid curiosity came next, but I couldn't have been certain of that, for it was remarkably fleeting. The final emotion that lingered was a dawning realization that seemed to punch him in the gut, and his face blanched.

"*Fuck,*" Colton whispered, his attention on Zoey as he softly spoke, "I thought that maybe you had, I dunno, beef with a neighbor or something...*then,* I saw the room...I—I figured you were just putting your nose somewhere it didn't belong or something. I—"

"We aren't telling you what happened," Liam snapped.

"I connected the dots. You don't need to tell me what happened," he murmured, shaking his head as if he were sad to say it. "Listen...I told you that there are women going missing."

"Yeah," I took my turn to speak because I assumed his words meant a swift change in direction to the current threat at hand. A somber shift with an unnecessary reminder that he desired information from me. "Prostitutes, exotic dancers—"

Cassie squeezed my hand, and Colton interjected:

"Right—*usually*—but not everything in life is one hundred percent," he replied quickly. "My point is that I told you guys all of that. That women are being taken—going missing—in and around this town. I *told* you that...and you had no thought to mention that Zoey could be one of them and that our shit could be related?"

A hollow pang hit my gut.

Cassie's nails bit into my palm.

Luke's arms hung limply by his side as the gears visibly cranked in his mind.

Claire pushed herself to sit up straight.

Liam simply squinted as if he weren't sure of the insinuation of Colton's words.

Zoey's head whipped to Colt's, her hands still upright as if she weren't sure of where to place them.

Everything had occurred simultaneously, and we all stared at Colton with wide, dumbstruck eyes because, for whatever reason, none of us had considered that the hell we had endured could be entwined with his. I closed my eyes as my head swam with the notion, and I forced myself to focus on the aggressive *thump-thump, thump-thump, thump-thump* of Cassie's pulse beating with mine against our palms as I waited for the inevitable chaos to unfold.

Chapter 15

Our voices all clashed together in a horrified cacophony, most of us in a state of denial, speaking our disagreements aloud with noncontextual stammering. Believing that the hell that brought Colton to Salem was linked to what we had all gone through months ago was a jagged pill—uncoated, bitter, and large. And the way that it was presented to us were as if it were angrily forced down our esophagi. There was no softening of the blow. No metaphorical water to drink and ease the scraping along the inside of our throats. It just...hit us...and the ramifications of the possibility being true were causing us to descend into bedlam.

Absolute, utter bedlam.

"Okay, *okay*—guys—*guys!*" Colton's exclamation rose above the noise just enough for our near panicked discussion to halt in its tracks. *"Calm down.* Ya gotta loop me in, here—"

Luke, now sitting next to Claire with his hair standing on all ends, interjected, "Jesus Christ—*no, we don't.*"

"We don't have to loop him in on shit," Liam agreed with purpose, his freckled face pale and his dark eyes wide as he pointed at Luke across the table, "because *none of this is related.*"

"Liam," Claire spoke to him gently, "now isn't the time to be purposefully ignorant."

Looking at her hands that were knit before her atop the table, Zoey grumbled, "He's not being *ignorant.*"

"Zoey...*connect the dots.*" I leaned slightly to my right, telling her in as vague of terms as possible, "2D did...all the shit that he did. The shit in his apartment—in that room—looked like it was prepped to keep someone captive."

"*2D,*" Colton stated with disgust, "had needles and injectable meds in that closet."

He shifted to reach into the front pocket of his hoodie, pulled out a small, brown bottle that he gently held between his thumb and forefinger, and placed it on the bartop with a purposeful *clunk.*

My jaw hung open as I absorbed its appearance. Cassie dropped my hand beneath the table to spin in her seat and stared at it with wide eyes, and the remainder of the group groaned as Claire waved a hand before us all and asked:

"What the fuck is *that?*"

"Acepromazine," Colton replied as if it were the most obvious answer on Earth.

"What," Liam shook his head as if his eyes were deceiving him, "what is that?"

"Snagged it from the room. After a quick Google search, it turns out it's a sedative." Colton pointed to the bottom of the bottle, tracing the text on the white label with his index finger. "This here says that it's only intended for veterinary use. Regardless—the effects are the same. *Sedation.* Easy to find for someone who's—"

"A veterinarian," Luke choked out. "Mister Milkovich is a vet. *Was* a vet—thought he was retired by now, I don't—I dunno, maybe he isn't?"

"Who's *Mister Milkovich?*" Colton asked with narrowed eyes.

Claire rapidly asked, "Why, does the last name ring a bell to you?"

Colton shook his head. "Not even a little."

"It doesn't fucking *matter!*" Zoey shrieked, seemingly coming to a breaking point and honing in on Colton. "This shit is over and done with—"

Claire interrupted, *"Zoey,* if it has anything to do with what Colt's talking about, *it might not be."*

Zoey hissed, "They aren't *related,* Claire!"

"Tox reports on women who went missing showed sedatives in their systems," Colton pressed. "If it's—"

"Tox as in *toxicology?*" Cassie asked with an alarmed gaze, "As in they were dead?"

He replied in an exhale, "Yeah, as in they were found dead."

A lead weight dropped in my gut, and I voiced, "How do you even know all this?"

Luke murmured an anxious, *"Thank you, Jay."*

Colton pulled his focus from Cassie to me. "It's public record. I'm not saying it's plastered all over the news—it's not—but a quick search for articles with the keywords *Virginia, young woman,* and *death* pulls up enough."

Claire murmured, "No, no, *no,*" and rapidly began to dig in her jeans pocket for her phone. Luke watched her over her shoulder as she tapped away at the glass face, his nostrils flaring with every seemingly shaking breath. She whispered, "How have we not *seen* this?"

"It'll be smaller media—it's not like the bigger ones are going to report a random woman dying here or there," Colton told her. "But add *illegal substances, suspected prostitution,* or *exotic dancer* to the search bar...they'll pop up."

Claire's voice quavering as she stared at the screen, *"Jesus Christ,"* and Luke's Adam's apple bobbing in his throat as he swallowed were all that we needed to see to know that Colton's accusations were true. She murmured disbelievingly, "These go as far back as May—Salem, Hanging Rock, Bennett Springs—"

"Did ya not fact check me the last time I was here?" Colton questioned her.

Claire tossed her phone to the table, signifying that she had seen enough. Cassie's focus remained locked on Claire's cell, no doubt considering what she had just seen, and while everyone continued to speak, she reached for her own phone. A single glance downward confirmed that she was, indeed, searching what Claire had—her search bar read:

Virginia exotic dancer death.

"We were a *little* busy with our own shit, Colt," Claire stated in a groan.

"So," Zoey spoke with an edge, and I glanced down at her, "women have gone missing. So, they had sedatives—or drugs, or whatever—in their system when their bodies were found. So, 2D had sedatives and that room. Coincidental? *Yes.* Related? *No.*"

Liam quietly uttered, "Zo'."

She looked up to him and snapped, *"No,* Lee."

His eyes landed on Colton. "Why are the women being taken?"

"Liam," she admonished him, and he gave her a quick shake of his head.

Colton replied somberly. "Lots of reasons. Forced work, mostly. Drug ring shit. Sex shit."

Claire asked, "If they're being forced to work, why are they being found dead?"

His unhurt shoulder bobbed up and down. "Repeated sedation would take a toll on a body, right? That or they're just, ah," Colton's tone turned meek, "not of use anymore."

The noise that came out of me, unbidden, was gravelly and rough, and I reached up to rub at my eyes while Zoey nervously trilled:

"Well, good news there! I don't think I was going to be forced into slavery; I'm pretty sure the guy just wanted to take me and *fucking rape me.* He tried plenty of times to make his message *crystal* clear."

Liam miserably groaned, *"God,* Zo'."

She continued to rattle off, "The sedatives don't shock me. I don't give a shit how he got them. This shit is heavy enough. 2D was just—just fucking *crazy.* I'm *refusing* to believe that—"

Colton told her with purpose, *"He knew about the women going missing, Zoey."*

Our collective gasp was audible, and Zoey squeaked, "What?"

As if he were sorry to be confirming it for us, Colton's torso sagged with an exhale, his expression pinched as he said, "It's in the laptop. Old search history...he looked up those articles. Repeatedly, actually." Colton muttered, "Obsessively...and then, he stopped," before grabbing the computer and extending it to the table. Being the nearest person to it, Luke grasped it in his hands, hesitating for a beat before quickly setting it on the table in front of Zoey. We all stared at it as Colton near-apologetically remarked, "Listen, I wasn't trying to get in your shit. I just—that room felt wrong, and then I saw the closet, I just—I felt like I needed to know. All I did was charge it and look at the search history."

Green eyes large, Zoey blinked at the laptop several times and finally murmured, "Oh. That, um—that doesn't mean—"

"Oh my God."

Cassie's voice was just above a whisper, wavering from her pretty mouth as if her chest were being rattled from the inside. My attention snapped to her; everyone else followed, and I looked at Cassie's cell to see that she was slowly scrolling through a news article. The header of the local news outlet, *'The Salem Pulse,'* remained at the top of her screen in dysfunctional, clashing greens and reds. The colors grated on my eyes, but not so much as the content that was displayed beneath Cassie's trembling fingers.

The woman in question was named Delaney Pierce. Her face was smiling up at us—eyes full of life, deep dimples in each cheek, and a head of short, black hair so curly that it stood up on end. Though it was clear that she was surrounded by friends, the image was cropped to the point that no other person was shown, and she was gone as quickly as she had appeared when Cassie scrolled downward.

"Ah," Colton spoke, having peeked at Cassie's phone from over her shoulder, "Delaney, she's a recent one. It's fucking disturbing, right? Stripper with no close loved ones, no next of kin—it's targets like *that* that get swept under the rug...I mean, they *all* have been, but—"

"Um—I—*fuck,*" Cassie stammered, "e-excuse me."

She stood from her chair so quickly that everyone flinched, and she all but ran toward the bathroom.

"Shit." I didn't think—I just went after her. In the midst of standing and striding my way across the bar, I quickly told the group, "I got it; I got her."

It didn't matter if they thought anything of my racing to Cassie. Perhaps they wouldn't, because the situation was dire enough that we were all dancing on eggshells...and that was what we *did* as a family, after all. Through the craziness, trials and tribulations, murder and all, we inevitably leaned on each other. Ran toward each other rather than away.

But, like I said, it didn't matter.

All I knew was that my heart was lodged in my throat as I approached the women's. I half-jogged down the dim hallway, tore around the corner, and when I yanked at the knob to find it locked, I exhaled a string of profanity before calling quietly against the door:

"It's me, Cas—open up."

I heard her flip the lock, but it was me who opened the door. Phone still in hand, Cassie was pacing away from me toward the toilet. She spun ninety degrees on her heel to face the mirror above the sink, briefly looking at her own horrified face before meeting my eyes. Her usually tanned skin tone ashen and her breathing progressing to hyperventilation; she was the picture-perfect expression of panic.

Just as the latch on the door clicked shut behind me, she whimpered, *"Jay."*

The way her face contorted as she nearly cried my name gutted me, and I closed the distance between us in two short steps.

"Shhh," I consoled her, one grip on her nape and the other hooked around her waist. Her arms remained between us, curled into her chest, and her body vibrated as if she had caught a chill. "It's a lot to take in. I know—"

"I knew her," she murmured into my neck.

My entire being stilled. *"What?"*

"Delaney. The woman in the article I found. I knew her."

Relaxing my hold on her as quickly as I had pulled her in, I took only half a step backward to look into Cassie's frantic gaze. I rested my hands on her biceps, shaking my head as if that knowledge couldn't possibly be true.

"Knew her?" I asked as gently as I could.

"She was one of the dancers when I started working at Gas Lamp," Cassie admitted, and a sledgehammer struck my chest. "I didn't talk to her much…wouldn't have even noticed that she stopped coming in if my schedule didn't get moved around because of it."

My mouth hung open for a beat, and I replied, raw and ragged, *"Fuck. No. No.* What else did the article say?"

"Reported as a drug overdose," she said. "It didn't list what kind. Mostly talked about the rising drug problem in the city. She was found in some random back-alley close to Roanoke, I—I didn't know her *that* well, but I'm pretty damn sure she didn't use. And this article's only from two weeks ago...it would have been a *long* time between when she stopped coming to Gas Lamp and when she was found. I—I feel like this could check out, Jay, and...I don't know. I had to get out of there to take a breath." Cassie inhaled, long and slow, but it was anything but calm as it hitched in her throat several times over. She exhaled, "Figure out what I need to do here."

My usual verbose nature was stripped from me as my throat went dry. My eyes burned as I forgot to so much as blink. I attempted to swallow, but my saliva seemed to have escaped me along with any words, and all I could let out was an anguished, *"Angh."*

"I, um," Cassie began, "well, I don't feel comfortable being anywhere *near* Gas Lamp, now. I have enough saved up to get by for, um, a while...my mortgage is low, at least."

"Quit," I managed to say. "You'll quit. That's good."

"Call Sky after this, tell her about Delaney, keep," she paused to steady herself, "keep the details to a minimum, obviously, but she's skittish. She'll probably quit, too."

"Good." I nodded. "Good."

"And we can have Colton meet with us later for anything he wants to know—"

Her intention hit me, and my arms fell to my sides. *"Wait.* You're—you're telling the group...right?"

Cassie's face twisted as if she had tasted something bitter. "What? No, I can't. You know that."

"Cassie," I spoke her name disbelievingly. "You *cannot* be serious. This is bigger than your brother finding out what you do for a living—"

"I'm *quitting,* so that point is moot—"

"Moot?!" I loudly exclaimed.

Cassie held up both of her hands, palm facing out. "Shhh!"

I rambled, "It is not *moot,* Cas. Quitting doesn't just—just remove you from existence entirely if someone had their eye on you. Nothing about this entire fucking shitshow is *moot.* We just got *more* evidence that dancers from. Your. Work. Could be getting used, abused, and fucking murdered...and you think it's a good idea to keep up the façade?"

"Jay."

"I'd normally be right behind ya on the decisions you make with your own life, but this is bigger than...than *everything!"* Cassie opened her mouth, and I held up an index finger to stop her. My voice went low as I said, "I. Will. Be. *Damned.* If something like keeping your ex-work-life in the dark ends up getting you hurt or worse because we don't *all* have our guard up." Her face fell, her defense seemed to abate, and I added, "I'm *sorry*, Darlin', but they need to know."

She groaned, "I *so* don't want you to be right about this."

A bitter smile tugged at the corner of my lip. "Are you saying that I am?"

Her face pulled into a grimace. "Liam's gonna freak."

"To be fair, he'd freak *more* if you somehow still went missing, and I end up having to tell him everything myself."

I phrased it—and spoke it—as gently as possible, but she still squirmed as if I had snarled the words.

"God—*fuck,* okay. *Okay,"* she acquiesced.

My shoulders slouched, my knees nearly going weak with relief, and I sighed out, *"Thank you.* Out we go?"

Cassie nodded, albeit hesitantly, and I ushered her out the bathroom door with a hand on her lower back. It gave me comfort, somehow, to allow my fingers to linger there until we rounded the corner to the public, and forcing myself to keep my hands by my side near after was damn near impossible.

Conversation rang through my ears as I trailed behind Cassie:

"Look, I work in *retail,"* Zoey told Colton with purpose. "I don't exactly see why I would have been a target—I'm pretty far separated from anything that you're talking about."

"It doesn't matter *why* you would have been a target at this point, Zoey," Claire interjected softly.

Colton thought aloud, "Just proximity, maybe? I'm *assuming* you live in the same complex as 2D, too?"

Zoey waved his comment away. "Yeah, yeah—that's not—it wasn't like I was being slowly tailed, waiting to be *taken*. Guy was crazy. He tried to assault me in the street. Broke into my apartment. Followed us all to North Carolina—"

"Fucker," Colton murmured. "He wasn't subtle about it, but he could'a been high. That would explain a lot."

Zoey nodded, muttering something that was too quiet for me to hear.

Almost back to our seats, Liam finally managed to yank his attention away from Zoey and was now watching his sister with curiosity. His dark eyes were already filled with anxious worry due to the topic at hand, and it most certainly remained that way as he squinted at Cassie, mouthing:

'You okay?'

Her response was nonverbal, but it was clear from his reaction that she had, more or less, implied *no*. He traced her from foot to head as if he were searching for signs of injury, and then voiced aloud a concerned, questioning:

"Cas?"

She gently sat in her chair, and I followed. The gears visibly cranked in her mind as she stared at the tabletop, the conversation around us dwindling to nothing with Liam's call of her name. All eyes on her, Cassie took a deep breath through her nose, let it out in a sharp huff, and uttered:

"Well, don't stop for me. By all means, *continue.*"

I whispered, *"Cas."*

"I'll get to it," she replied.

"You're sheet-white," Zoey noted quietly, scanning her similarly to how Liam had moments ago.

"Circle back, Zo'," Cassie insisted.

"Kay," Zoey quickly spoke, placing a hand on the laptop before her. "I'm done with this, anyway—*I* am going to go at this thing with a goddamn baseball bat and burn it. Cas? You got news?"

"You're jumping ahead," Claire told her. "Yes, of course, *fucking burn it.* But take the time to look through it first to see if there's any more connection to him and the missing women near us."

"Everything with *him,"* Zoey leaned forward in her seat, flexing her fingers that laid on the computer, "is over!" She spoke to the entire room with an exhausted whine, "Let's *move on.* Why does it even matter if 2D was related to the missing women?"

Colton shook his head. "If that ain't the *worst* question I've ever heard—"

"*Zoey,*" Liam croaked, her inquiry seemingly hitting him like the crack of a whip. "I'm not going through this shit again."

Luke looked to both of them with buggish eyes while Claire cut in, "If it's *related,* there could be others."

Upon the last word, the void of the past loomed over the table, hanging low and holding a grim reaper's scythe. Even though Peter was gone—even though the laptop inside of 2D that could potentially have evidence on it aside from the rampant search of missing and murdered women was in our hands—if this were, indeed, part of something bigger, it could mean that there were others that knew of his death. Others that he worked with. Others who knew of Zoey and could inevitably return.

Others who may have gotten their eye on Cassie, and the remainder of our found family were none the wiser.

"'*There could be others,*'" Colton slowly repeated Claire's previous sentence, pausing to ensure that he had our attention, and then quoted Liam, "'*I'm not going through this shit again.*'" His icy gaze wandered to Zoey. "Something along the lines of, '*This shit is over and done wit h.'"* He deduced quietly, "You're makin' it sound like he stopped...that 2D went away." Colton looked to all of us carefully—anxiously—until he finally inquired, "He went away, then? He stopped?" The air hung heavy, we all nodded, and Colton hesitated before he bluntly asked, "Why?" Our collective attention was kept either on the table, the laptop, or each other. *"Okay,* well, he's obviously gone somewhere in a goddamn hurry if he left all of his shit and a computer behind. Where is he, then, if 2D's unoccupied?" I felt Cassie begin to fidget with her hands beneath the table again, and found them shaking when I reached for her. Colton threw his head back, groaning to the ceiling before eyeing us all again and pleading, *"Dammit,* guys, we need to fuckin' help each other here! If 2D is involved in this shit, gets back from a little *vacay,* and somehow figures out that I broke into his place and stole his computer with God-knows-what on it along with some of his drugs, fuck *jail,* he could find me, and I could be *dead."* He breathed in once, and then out. *"Very* dead. And you're right—there *could* be others, but we can't figure out if that's true if ya don't talk to me—"

Zoey exclaimed, "He's *gone,* okay?!"

None of us could argue the admission. Perhaps none of us *wanted* to argue the admission because it was clear that whatever knowledge Colton had on the situation that could be interwoven with our lives was desperately needed.

Our lines of sight all eventually made it to Colton to see that he had briefly frozen. Jaw slightly agape, Zoey's words appeared to sink in for him, and Colton pushed himself to sit on the edge of the stool, his back ramrod straight.

"From the look on your faces…he's dead?" We all took the sledgehammer to the chest of a question with grace, remaining silent until Colton pressed, "Yeah, I'm gonna need y'all to answer the question. Did you send me into a *dead. Man's. Apartment?*" The space between us turned stagnant and dirty with our further nonresponses, and Colton seemed to take our reactions as a *yes*. After covering his eyes with a single hand, he dragged it down his face, clutching his lower lip and chin for a moment while he stared off into space. When his gaze refocused, he dropped his arm back down and asked gravely, "How long?"

It was Liam who finally muttered, "Four months."

Colton's eyebrows shot up. *"Four months?* And his shit's still in 2D? Why'd you just now want in the apartment?" His head moved from side to side rapidly. "Not important. That's not important. What *is* important is if you think there's any loose ends."

He leaned forward slightly, anticipating our inevitable reply with an alarmed expression.

We all looked to the laptop and then back to him. I saw Zoey shake her head in the corner of my vision, and Colton sighed, his body sagging so heavily with relief that he almost melted into the bar behind him.

"Oh, thank fuck."

His reaction shouldn't have struck me as odd. It *was* a relief that Peter Milkovich was no longer. That the only discernable evidence of the cause of his death was now sitting on the tabletop before us. To that, I agreed. What prevailed over my recognition of his relief, however, was an anger that simmered in the depths of my diaphragm. The means in which everything had occurred—the horror that it left burned in the back of all of our minds—it was, at times, almost too much to bear, and I often wished that I could remove the memory altogether. That I could swipe at my brain like an eraser on a chalkboard, leaving the remaining smudges entirely unrecognizable—*gone.*

It wouldn't be gone, though. The residue from the white streaks would still prevail, and there was no metaphorical cleanser that I could dream of that would do the trick.

"Thank fuck," I whispered bitterly. *"Thank. Fuck?"*

Cassie squeezed my hand.

"Yeah," Colton returned, *"thank fuck.* Because it's been long enough that if he *was* involved in everything else, he's been considered collateral damage by now."

My chest twinged with an unrealistic hope, and while everyone else seemed to be processing the possibility, Luke uttered:

"You can't be so sure of that."

"I can," Colton told him.

Claire gritted out, "How?"

"This isn't..." Colton looked upward, seeming to be figuring how to phrase it all, "it isn't organized like a mob family or somethin'. They're not vengeful. They aren't operating under some Hammurabi eye-for-an-eye shit. They work up to one," he held up an index finger with purpose, "head honcho. They work separate—sometimes alone, sometimes about two or three people a piece. If they provide, they're rewarded. If they fuck up, they're *eliminated.* That's why they *work separate*—to allow room for error." He paused, then turned to Zoey. "Four months? If no one's come to find you within *four months,* my bet is that even if he was involved, he didn't talk you up the line yet, and he was *alone* in this. And if y'all don't think there are any other loose ends with evidence, then you're...fine."

The exhale that came out of Zoey was so long that I could hear it pull at her lungs, and she hoarsely questioned:

"What?"

"Even if he was involved, he's collateral damage by now," he repeated. "He was an error, Zoey. *I think you're safe.*"

We all stared at him in disbelief. To each other with the unspoken reminder that we should by no means take what Colton says as fact, though the large chunk of salt that we were consistently taking with his words felt as though it were beginning to disintegrate. The way Colton said it with an uncharacteristic sympathy was such a weight off of our collective shoulders that I could feel the tension in the room ease. Even *Luke's* guard seemed to have lowered with the way that his eyes fluttered closed and oxygen flowed through his nostrils.

There was little else to be said. We could go round and round until we were all blue in the face, devoid of air, but there was no use. Not with this, at least.

Zoey looked at the computer with a hardened stare as if she loathed its very presence, and I understood her itch to destroy it without a glance at the contents. For this to just be *over*. I knew that she wouldn't, though. Even if she wanted to, I could picture Claire's defensive, biting words—could see Liam holding her back with a single arm and gentle pleas spoken in her ear for we wanted *answers*. Regardless of the thought of Peter being *collateral dam-*

age, we wanted to know if there was any reason for us to be looking back.

"I'll, um, take this home and look through it," Zoey murmured. "Just to see."

Everyone nodded, and there was a semblance of relief that surrounded us. Unbeknownst to everyone else, though, there was very little of the emotion for me and Cassie...and the time to address that was now.

"Cassie."

I spoke to her with a heaping amount of compassion. She looked at me for the briefest of moments, recognized the purpose of my call of her name, and closed her eyes tightly as if she were biting a metaphorical bullet.

Cassie twisted on her sit bones rapidly to speak to Colton.

"I knew Delaney."

The short sentence fell out of her mouth as if the words were resting on the tip of her tongue, ripe and ready to tumble from her lips.

Quiet, somber mutterings were shared around the table, all blending together as Liam's voice rose above them with a more pointed:

"Delaney? Delaney *who?*"

Zoey whispered to him, "Delaney *stripper with no next of kin from the article she found earlier,* Delaney."

Liam sadly murmured, *"Oh."*

Cassie paid her brother's comments no mind. She was simply waiting for Colton to respond.

His surprise at the admission quickly gone, Colton was investigating her expression as if he could read it—as if the picture of her life's story were painted on her cheeks. He nodded slowly, and then asked:

"Knew her from where?"

Cassie timidly returned, "My work."

For Zoey, the realization was immediate. Though I wasn't looking at her, I felt her shoulders sag with her exhaled, *"Oh,* fuck." Her elbows hit the table with a thud as she rested her head in her hands, and Liam voiced:

"She worked at your accounting firm *and* a strip club?"

I pressed my lips together tightly at his immediate assumption, and no one answered him, for Colton was now leaning forward with his forearms on his thighs, questioning Cassie:

"Gas Lamp?"

Cassie's pitch raised to an uncharacteristic squeak. "Yuh huh."

Under his breath so quietly that I wondered who was able to hear it, Colton uttered, "Knew I recognized you from somewhere."

Luke and Claire simultaneously groaned, and Zoey muttered to me, "Is that why you've been so fucking weird lately?"

It was obvious that comprehension had dawned on all of them. The fact that I had gone to Gas Lamp. The fact that I was, as Zoey had phrased, *fucking weird* about it. The fact that Cassie had just admitted to her means of work. It was all clear for them. That side of the puzzle was built—Cassie was, very obviously, the dancer that I had alluded to. The other side, however—the one where Cassie and I were romantically involved—was yet to be assembled. I was grateful for the lack of additional drama in the moment, but at the notion that we could still maintain a *granule* of finesse while easing our relationship into the group, I attempted to halt any potential questioning with a hiss of a reply to Zoey:

"Is *now* the time for this?"

"I don't—I don't understand." Liam shook his head, face twisted in confusion as he finally looked at me and assumed, "Oh...*oh,* shit—Jay, did you see this Delaney chick when you went to Gas Lamp?"

I let out a quiet, uncomfortable noise, pinching the area between my eyes as Liam's lack of understanding yanked at my insides.

Zoey sympathetically muttered, "Oh, *Lee.*"

He murmured an altogether innocent, "What?"

There was a moment of silence in which we all looked at him. Cassie slowly turned in her chair to peek at her brother, and his head bobbled as he attempted to take us all in at once.

Colton bluntly said, "Your sister's a stripper, dude."

Claire yelled, *"Colton!"*

"What?" he returned with the slightest of smiles. "Didn't seem like y'all were gonna say it. Big guy needs to know."

Liam's mop of blonde hair cocked to the side, and he incredulously laughed out, "No-no...Cas, um..." He hesitated as he looked to his sister, saw that she had the face of someone who was bracing for an upcoming impact, and deflated as he groaned, "Are you fucking *kidding* me, Cassandra?"

Chapter 16

"I make a lot of money!"

"*Made* a lot of money," I corrected Cassie quietly. "You said you wouldn't even give two weeks if you were quitting."

Cassie quickly held an index finger so close to my face that she almost struck me with it.

As I flinched backward, she snapped at me, *"Not now."*

"You make a lot of money by *taking your clothes off*," Liam whined.

"It's just a *body*, Liam!" she exclaimed. "Who gives a shit?!"

"Just a body? *Cas—*"

"Stop!" Zoey exclaimed. "Cassie, no one gives a shit if you strip."

Liam chastised, "Zoey!" at the same time as Cassie began to say:

"Thank you, Zo—"

"But ya kept it a secret even when you heard through the goddamn grapevine that dancers are going missing, and now you're giving your brother a *fucking. Aneurysm,"* she trilled. "You two need to can it for now. There's a *lot* going on."

Liam sank low into his chair, arms crossed over his chest while he chewed on the inside of his cheeks, and Cassie mimicked him.

I muttered down to Cassie, "That went well."

Her dark eyes rapidly shifted up to me, holding the smallest of smiles, but her lips remained irritatingly puckered as Zoey admonished me with:

"Don't get me started with you. *Enabler."*

I retorted, "What was I supposed to do? *Out her?* I was sworn to secrecy."

Liam's face contorted as if he had just now realized that I had, in fact, seen his sister working. I found myself making the same expression while I shifted my line of sight to anywhere but him.

"So…" Colton spoke slowly, and Cassie rolled her head to view him as he noted, *"That was fun.* Delaney?"

Cassie sighed. "Yeah. Knew her when I first started working there. She stopped coming in…I dunno, two months back? Maybe?"

He gave her a mournful frown. "Sorry."

She shrugged. "'S'okay. Thanks."

"Did you two talk much?"

"No." Cassie shook her head. "But, um…there were other dancers that stopped coming in, too."

I heard Claire groan, "Oh, *God,*" but I kept my eyes on Colton as I watched his brows flicker up and then lower back down.

"Figured. Do you have their names?"

Cassie's head bobbed backward. *"All* of them?"

"Um…yeah. All of them," Colton replied, matter of fact.

"I don't—I don't remember all of them. There's probably a girl or two each month that no-call-no-shows. I—it's been like that since I moved here in the summer. It's not like I kept track," she rattled back.

"Okay, *okay.*" He held up a hand to stop her. "Anyone recent?"

"Yeah, um—Lacey Rhone? Harper Phillips. That's, ah…that's all I can remember for now."

"'Kay. What about them? Did you know them well?"

"Er…no."

Colton squinted. *"Okay.* What about…I dunno, rumors? Did they use?"

"No," she told him quickly.

"Spend a little *too* much time with clientele?"

"No."

"Ya sure about that?"

"Yeah!" she bit back. *"I'm sure.* Just because we're strippers doesn't mean we're prostitutes." Liam coughed loudly as she snapped, "The fuck kind of a question is that?"

"Easy," Colton replied. "That's not what I meant. Even if I did, I'm not gonna judge. Just asking if there was something common between them. Same people that come in to see them? Maybe those people are extra chatty? Maybe they frequent champagne rooms for privacy? Shit like that."

Cassie pondered that for a beat, appearing mildly downtrodden, until she said, "Not sure. Faces blend together, y'know? I normally just keep my head down and work."

Colton exhaled loudly. "Okay, let me make sure I have this straight. You moved here in the summer, so...you've been working there for upward of half a year?"

"Uh huh."

His face twisted. "And you don't know more? *Nothing* seemed off?"

"Look, I focus on my own shit at Gas Lamp," Cassie returned, exasperated. "You have some names. I can tell you what they look like, too. What—what exactly do you *want* from me?"

"What, do you think I have a magical database to search? Oh, *here,* let me pull this laptop outta my ass." Colton threw her vexed attitude right back and mimed reaching for his backside. Claire sighed heavily as he went through the motions of placing a very invisible computer on his lap and cracking it open. With either of his index fingers, he pretended to click on a keypad several times, mocking, *"Beep-boop-bahp.* Ah, yes. *Thank goodness* I had those dancers' names and absolutely nothing else! With my handy-dandy system here, I now know every person those women interacted with before they went missing, cross-checked them, and found the culprit!" He then gave us all an enthusiastic representation of *jazz hands.* *"Yaaay!"*

Claire whined, "Don't be an ass, Colt."

"I'm not—" Colton caught Claire's narrowed gaze, and he shifted his tone to one that was less grating. "I'm not trying to be. I just wanted more, that's all. I could'a gotten *that* from another quick trip to Gas Lamp myself."

She returned, "Didn't you *kinda* know who's responsible already? Friends of friends that you heard shit about?"

"First of all, none of them are *friends.* They were hardly even acquaintances, and they're nothing to me now. *Fuckers.*" Colton spoke the last word under his breath with disgust, and he added, "And no. I don't. Remember—I said that they work separately. I knew *one*. I don't know other names 'cause *he* didn't know other names. I know trends. Vague locations. Cause and effect."

Claire's eyebrows rose. "You *knew* one?"

Colton went quiet, his gaze locked with Claire's, and he calmly stated, "He and the guy he teamed up with turned on each other."

Her jaw went slack. "You say that as if it was convenient."

"It was," he told her. "They're both dead."

We all blinked several times in succession, absorbing his words. He didn't elaborate further, and none of us pressed him to do so. There was no question, to me, that he was involved in their inevitable demise. However, whether he simply planted the seed or performed the act himself was left a mystery, for the brief veering of conversation was one that we didn't need to venture down.

Cassie questioned, "Can't you do a lot with a description of the two women I gave you?"

"Do what? Go to the police?" he replied with disbelieving eyes. "My dirty-ass record will get pulled up in no time, and then they'll *really* have questions for me."

Claire suggested, "You could call them anonymously?"

He gave her a pointed stare. "Would *you* call them anonymously? There's a man that y'all have a *colorful* history with who could have been involved in all of this that's now dead. There are *still* sedatives in that closet—I only snagged the one bottle—and we all know what that room looked like. I've got no idea what the cops know, but if they're anywhere near this, they're gonna think that's *mighty* skeptical. Considering all this shit, do you feel comfortable fuckin' *breathing* in a cop's direction, anonymous or not?"

She crossed her arms and grumbled back, "No."

"Cue my point." Colton focused back on Cassie. "Just names and descriptions of the girls does jack shit for me. I'm guessing the answer is *no*, but do you know anyone who could know more?"

"Like I said," Cassie replied, "I normally just keep my head down and work. I'm not really tight with any of the dancers. That's more Sky—*oh.*" Realization dawned on her, and she murmured, *"Sky."*

"Sky?" Colton inquired.

"Friend from work," she replied. Colton shot her a pointed look, and she clarified, *"Friendly* friend from work. Social butterfly. If any of the dancers know anything, it's her."

"Good," he sighed. *"Good,* good-good." Reaching into the front of his jeans pocket, he pulled out a cell phone that one could only describe as a *burner*. It was similar to one I had used in the early 2000s—a flip phone that was designed long before touch screens were a standard. Colton flicked his wrist to open it, assumedly checking the time, and closed it with a satisfying *smack!* He asked Claire, "When does this place open?"

Claire looked to the table, tapping the screen of her own cell. It lit up her face in a blue-tinged light, and she replied:

"Ten minutes."

"Yeah, I should get outta here." He looked to Cassie. "What are the chances I can talk to your friend, like, *soon?* And not in a bar filled with people?"

Cassie shrugged. "I'll call her, then call you?"

He snapped his fingers, pointed at her, and smiled as he stated, *"That.* Claire?" Claire's tired eyes snapped to his, and he asked, "Be a peach. Text me her number?" She threw him a thumbs up with little enthusiasm as she picked up her phone. *"Cool."* His index finger moved to Zoey. "Zoey. Don't be dumb—"

Liam snapped, *"Hey—"*

Colton splayed his extended hand out wide. "Look through the damn laptop." Liam went quiet, and Colton continued, *"Then* burn it." Zoey gave him a short nod and an eye roll that said she already intended to do just that. He seemed to consider his thoughts before he stated, "And for the record, if you're thinking *actual* fire—I'll light the goddamn match."

He blurted the words out with a shocking amount of conviction.

Zoey's brows rose. "Are you into pyrotechnics now?"

A corner of his lip pulled up in the quickest of grins that was then gone in a flash. "For this, yeah. Later."

He hopped from his stool, and we all watched as he strolled across the bar to the entrance, unlocked the door, and left without a further word. The silence was heavy for only but a second, and Liam spoke again:

"You're quitting."

"I came to that conclusion myself, thank you," Cassie told him.

He nearly spat, "Good."

"Good?" she incredulously voiced. "Liam, I'm quitting my job, and I don't exactly have another one lined up. It's a necessity, but it's not *good.*"

Liam took in a long breath. "I know," he exhaled. *"I know,* I'm sorry. I'm still all..." He waved a hand in front of his forehead in a circular motion. "I can't think straight."

"Okay, um," Zoey spoke up, "Different subject—Cas, why don't you stay with us for a while? Considering everything?" She looked up to Liam, and he nodded emphatically.

Cassie squinted. "On the couch?"

Liam responded, "Yeah."

"I'd rather a bedroom," she grumbled.

"Well, I don't *have another bedroom!*" he quickly retorted. Liam reached up to pinch at the bridge of his nose and said, "Just—just—you can get a blow-up mattress or something if you *really* need it."

"Sure," she returned with a roll of her eyes, "with all the money I have from the job that I'm quitting."

"I'm sure you have plenty saved up from stripping," he snapped.

Zoey smacked his chest. *"Liam!"*

"Don't act all high-and-fucking-mighty," Cassie bit back. "You've joked about applying to work at strip clubs for *years.*"

"Joking doesn't mean I actually *did it,* Cas!" he exclaimed.

Interrupting their sibling bickering once more, Zoey stated, "Don't pretend like you have anything against stripping, Lee, *come on.*"

"I don't," he told her. "I have a problem with *my little sister* stripping."

"Yet you had no problem with it when I said I should apply at PT's," Zoey argued.

Liam replied through his teeth, "That's different."

"Oh, why?" Cassie asked innocently. "Because I shouldn't be seen as a sexual object? I'm not a *child*, Liam. Plenty of men—and women, for that matter..."

The latter half of her last sentence made me choke on my spit, and Liam interrupted with a grimace:

"*Ah*, no-no, we aren't talking about this."

Cassie smirked, crossing her arms as she said, "You're the one that started it."

Zoey sighed loudly. "Topic at hand. You live alone, and your house is in the middle of nowhere. Stay with us, yes?"

Cassie's face twisted at the thought of an extended stay in her brother's living room. "I've gotten used to privacy."

Claire spoke in a mousy tone, "Erm—*Jay?*"

I glanced at her to see her blue gaze expectant, and I voiced, "Hmm?"

Claire tipped her head toward Cassie, and there was no doubt in my mind what the intent was behind her quiet call of my name. She was implying that I should offer for Cassie to stay with me.

"*Oh,*" my voice went high as I quickly glanced at Cassie, and I looked back to Claire to find her gaze a silent, gentle plea to, '*Do the right thing.*'

Luke avoided making eye contact with anyone, as it was clear he didn't desire to insert himself in the middle.

Cassie cooed, "You *do* have an extra bedroom."

"I do," I replied succinctly, knowing full well that Claire's old bedroom would be thoroughly unoccupied if Cassie were to be staying with me.

Zoey obliviously shrugged. "Problem solved—"

"*Not* problem solved," Liam interrupted, throwing a hand toward Cassie. "She's gonna drive Jay insane."

"I'll be on my *best* behavior," Cassie assured him wryly.

Liam groaned, *"Cas."*

"It's fine," I interrupted Liam rapidly. "Really, it's fine. Cas, you can stay with me."

Cassie smiled wide at me, not a trace of guilt or our shared secret written on her face as she noted, "Problem solved."

I was idly chopping a red bell pepper in the kitchen when the front door creaked open, and Liam appeared. His freckled face was worn, the stress from, well, *everything* written across it as he lugged a large, black suitcase across the threshold. The wheels hit the hardwood with a *clack,* and he grumbled:

"You packed your entire goddamn closet."

Cassie strolled in with a single white pillow under her arm, remarking as she walked past her brother, "Well, I don't know how long I'll be here. I'm not about to go to the laundromat three times per week."

"Fine," Liam acquiesced, shutting the door behind him. "Fine. I get it." He pointed toward Claire's old room. "Go bring—"

Cassie daintily grabbed the top of her luggage, extended the handle, and quipped, "I know where to go. It's not like I've never been here." She beamed in my direction. "Hi, Jay."

I waved with my knife-laden hand. "Hi, Cas."

"Whatcha cookin'?" she asked as she walked her suitcase across the living area.

As per all things in my life, I typically would have that planned out before I went chopping away. However, with the knowledge that Cassie was soon to be arriving with her brother, who was none the wiser regarding our closeness, I was terribly on edge. I checked her phone's location several times while waiting, and when they were just down the street, I decided that busying my hands would be the smartest course of action. The red of the bell pepper caught my eye before anything else in my fridge, and I began to slice without a second thought to its purpose.

"Uh," I hesitated. "Stir fry."

"It's early for dinner," she noted with a smile, "but I haven't eaten."

Ambling past the kitchen table to me, Liam called out, "He's not cooking for you, Cas!"

All I heard was her soft laughter as she disappeared around the corner, and Liam stopped his steps when he reached the opposite end of the island. He looked to me apologetically, rubbing at his neck, and I set my knife down with purpose.

"I have no problem cooking for two, Liam."

His arm fell to his side. "I, ah, think I owe you on this one."

Guilt swarmed me. "Nah, you don't owe me a thing."

Liam murmured, "I know how Cas can be."

It was then, more than any other point, that I was tempted to come clean. To look Liam directly in his eyes, which were *so* like his sister's, and let the bomb drop. It may come with inevitable, metaphorical shrapnel...but it would be worth it. Our found family dynamic could shift, sure...but only slightly. I simply wouldn't allow the explosion of an admission to crumble everything that we all had to the ground, after all.

I couldn't do it, though.

His expression was so...so mentally tired that any prepared words that I had for him remained lodged in my throat. Concern over the potential peril regarding the two most important women in his life was so clearly shown on his face that it was palpable. It didn't seem fair for me to unload what was on my shoulders when I knew it would be directly transferred to his. And that's exactly where this confession would land—*heavily* on his shoulders because there was no chance in hell that he would immediately understand and be delighted at our seeing each other.

No matter how gently I worded it or how verbose I was about the care I had for Cassie, he was bound to twist the pertinent details into phrases such as:

I screwed your sister.
No, it wasn't just a one-time thing.
Yes, I'm going to happily continue sticking it to her.
Oh, and she fucking loves it.

No—I couldn't allow the burdensome, even betrayed thoughts that would come afterward to ruminate in his mind. Not now, when he was looking like a lost puppy—a rather large puppy who nearly looked down on me due to his stature, but a puppy nonetheless.

Instead, I made sure to catch his eye and truthfully said, "I'm glad she's here. This shit's messy." Liam gave me a smile that looked near-pained, and I rephrased, "More than messy—fuckin' nerve-wracking. *I'm glad she's here.*" I stated the last sentence with more gumption, Liam seemed to soften a bit, and I joked, "Even if she does eat all of my food."

I casually picked up my knife, continuing to slice vertical strips from the pepper and concentrating on the rocking motion of the blade. Liam's quiet chuckle brought a small smile to my lips, and he yelled to Cassie:

"You're goin' to buy groceries tomorrow!"

Her laughing, *"Yeah,* yeah," was muffled from beyond the walls of the bedroom.

Liam exhaled heavily, murmuring, "Thank you."

I slid the backside of the blade across the cutting board to move the cut pieces to the right-hand side, glanced up to see that his words were directed at me rather than his sister, and quickly shook my head.

"You don't need to thank me."

Liam hesitated as if he weren't quite sure what to say. I contemplated whether I wanted to dice the pepper strips before me, and he said:

"You're a good friend, Jay."

It was a shock that I didn't keel over—hands on my knees, gasping for breath as the gut punch of his gratefulness knocked the wind out of me. Instead, I swallowed, set my knife down with a *clack* against the granite, and steadied myself with both of my hands splayed out on the counter.

"I'm really not," I replied as casually as I could muster.

He rolled his eyes in return, clearly assuming that I was taking a stance of humility.

"Look, I'd stay, but I gotta get some studying in. I have an exam on Monday, and I'm *behind,*" he told me with an apology in his voice.

Of course he did. He didn't speak of them much, but his studies kept him rather busy…and his mention of them made me recall the stress of obtaining a college education. The worry of learning and maintaining the knowledge—of putting your skills to the test by placing pencil to paper—of just wanting to *be done* so the constant weight of it all could be over. My experience wasn't comparable to Liam's, though. Not in the least. Not only had I gone through my college years by the time that I was Cassie's age rather than his more mature twenty-six, but I had little else to concern myself over.

I didn't have to worry about employment; Liam hopped around working contract construction jobs to make ends meet. I didn't have to *pay rent*. I didn't have a girlfriend who murdered her stalker. I didn't have a friend who was fucking my little sister behind my back.

You know. *The little things.*

Liam mumbled, "This shit has me so fuckin' distracted."

"I'm sorry, man. Which class?"

"Oh, um," he hesitated as if he weren't anticipating the question and gave me a grin as he recited, *"The Youthful Mind and Children's Literature."*

I immediately pictured his large body squat on a stool made for someone a third his size, enthusiastically reading an illustrated book to a horde of small children.

Elementary education would suit him.

Willing the thoughts of *worry* away, I found a smirk pulling at my mouth as I remarked, "Yeah, I'd help you study, but I don't think I'd do any good there."

His grin grew, and he waved me away as he stated, "Zo' made me flashcards. I should be fine."

I chuckled. "Flashcards, huh?"

A dimple formed on his right cheek. "Uh huh. And a checklist for all my shit to finish before graduation."

Nodding, I asked, "Next month?"

"Yup," he replied happily, popping the *p*.

Cassie interrupted our oddly pleasant conversation with, "Ya gonna chop anything but that pepper, or what?"

We each turned our heads to see her having crept up on us—barefoot and comfortable, she was leaning a shoulder against the wall at the edge of the kitchen. She had tied her hair back—pulled away from her face in a perfectly messy knot at the base of her neck. Arms crossed, her eyebrows rose as she looked at me with her typical challenging expression.

Liam quipped to me, "If she drives ya nuts, send her across the hall." Her eyes shot to the ceiling, and I didn't get a chance to say so much as, *'I think I'll live,'* or, *'Ha. Okay,'* because he followed it up with, "I'm outta here, Cas."

"Flashcards?" she asked knowingly.

"Flashcards," he confirmed. "You call your friend?"

Cassie shook her head. "Texted. She's busy. Maintenance at her apartment—it's a whole thing. She'll get back to me. I'll let you know."

He gave her a curt nod, saying, "'Kay, good." Walking toward the front door, he lifted a hand to waggle his fingers at her over his shoulder. "Later."

"Byeeee," she sang, splitting the word into two syllables, and when the door shut behind him, she asked, "You want me to grab you an onion or something?"

"We need to tell him," I groaned.

"I was assuming that we both still thought that *now* was a bad time."

"I do," I agreed. *"I do.* It would be bad. Like, the poor man's fucking brain would explode from being overwhelmed *bad,* but...*God,* Cas, he called me a *good friend.*"

Her warm eyes showed me sympathy. "You *are* a good—"

"No, the fuck I'm not," I argued. "I've stuck my cock inside of his litter sister, and he has no idea. I am *not* a good friend."

"To be fair," she returned lightly, "I wanted your cock."

I pressed my hands to my eyes, whining, *"Cassie."*

She giggled. "What?"

Sharply pointing at the entrance, I demanded, "Go lock the door before your brother comes back and hears you talking about my cock."

"Yes, sir," she mocked as she spun on her heel. I watched her nearly skip around the couch, past the kitchen table, and to the door. She flicked the deadbolt, and I felt a relieved breath leave me. She asked, "Can we stop talking about my brother now?"

In what came across as a quiet plea, I returned, "Can we tell him about us once we feel like we're not in crisis mode?"

Cassie flashed me a megawatt smile—one that blinded me and caused her nose to scrunch in the way I had long begun to adore—and she cooed:

"Yes, baby."

She said it casually. *Offhandedly,* as she traipsed her way to the pantry that resided to my left, beside the refrigerator.

And though it had left her mouth in the most natural of ways, she had still said it as if she knew that the word would string me up by the ventricles. As if she knew that the endearment she had bestowed upon me would hang over me in a pink-tinged mist, run through my nostrils, flood my olfactory system with her trademark vanilla, and render me lovesick.

It did, of course, because the woman made me fucking weak.

And instead of mentally damning the way that she was so easily able to wipe the slate of my mind clean, I fell into it. Despite the horror of the reasoning for her being here and the entirety of my feelings surrounding her brother, which could simply be deemed as guilt-ridden and uncomfortable, I just found myself wanting her—cherishing the feeling to the point that I moved to meet her where she stood.

Eyeing the shelves, she inquired, *"Did* you want an onion? I like onion in a stir—"

It was clear that she had sensed my presence behind her, but it was when I reached for her face that she cut her sentence off mid-word. In one swift movement, she turned into my clasp of her jaw. I pulled to usher her lips to mine, and when Cassie began to close the distance between us, she caught my eye and froze. The altogether playful attitude that she had from the moment she walked through the door dissipated, and her brow furrowed as she placed a hand on the left side of my chest.

"You okay?"

Through all of her thought-clearing haze, I still knew that I wasn't. It was a fact that none of us were—we were simply putting on brave faces to muster through it all because there was no other viable option—and I didn't care to delve into that. Though I appreciated her ability to see through me, and her questioning of my well-being made warmth flood beneath where her palm laid, I knew that I would be a song set on repeat, replaying my anxious melody time and again.

There was no use for that.

I finished her previous motion for her, leaning forward to give her a soft kiss. She hummed into it, but when we separated, her eyes were still tinged with a gentle worry. I answered her question with another:

"Are *you*?"

"Touché."

"I'm as fine as I can be," I told her.

Cassie nodded. "Me too."

My thumb traced along her jawline. "I like you here."

Her lips quirked up. "Me too." She tightened her hand on my chest into a fist, grasped my shirt, and gave it a tug. Eyes darting to my lips, she whispered, "Come back."

I sealed my lips on hers with the quiet insistence that I had intended before. Our touches on each other were smooth and quiet, hers moving to my waist to beckon me closer and mine cradling her face, and our mouths remained closed—sweet and slow, yet burning with a forward motion.

Sweet and slow quickly turned hot and feverish. Tongues clashing, her nails beneath my shirt and digging into my lower back, and my hands gripping a shelf behind her, our bodies were flush—only separated by the thin layers of clothing between us. A rough flex of my hips pinned her to the shelving, and Cassie's breath hitched as the canned goods clunked and clattered.

And it wasn't that I was a caveman who simply wanted her here and now.

I mean...I was. But that wasn't the entirety of it.

There was just something about the way that we melded together. Something about the way that she grabbed me just as tightly as I did her. Something about the way that our respective movements carried the fluidity of water—no matter whether I was gentle and patient or progressing to rough and ragged, Cassie was there to meet me halfway. She mirrored me with enthusiasm. With a well-read return of my emotions in her eyes.

It drove me manic.

I kissed her neck; she kissed mine. I bit, sucked, and licked; so did she. I moaned quietly in her ear; her soft noises brought me to insanity. She led me to unabashed hedonism—and though it truly was so much more than seeking pleasure with Cassie, it didn't matter that we weren't whispering sweet nothings to each other to profess our adoration in this exact moment. We could see it. *Feel* it around us without having to utter the words, and I think it was because of *that* that we were able to progress rapidly into the comfort of absolute filth.

She wrapped a leg around my backside, squeezed her hand that had wound its way into my hair, and we gyrated in time together.

"I can feel your cock through your jeans," she nearly purred.

I dragged my tongue over her pulse point. "See what you do to me?"

"Mmm."

Her touch left me only to pull her top off, returning to yank mine overhead, and I assisted her with greedy hands. The bralette she wore was baby blue, the lace sheer to the point that I could make out the outline of her areolas, and the sight alone made me let out a quiet:

"Jesus, Cas."

The material scratched at my fingertips, her breast filling my palm as I kneaded her through the fabric.

She exhaled, "Ah," and I swallowed the noise by crashing my mouth to hers.

I tugged the thin straps down her arms, letting them hang loose by her biceps, and I broke our kiss to shift my lips back to her neck. Her shoulder. Down her chest that had begun to heave and over the lace. I nudged it with my nose to reach her nipple, taking it into my mouth. She let out a whimpering, *"Jay,"* as I ran my tongue where I so pleased, and my vocal cords rumbled as I eagerly shifted to repeat the actions on the right side of her. Her fingers had tangled in my hair once more, but I felt one of them leave me—tracing its way down my abdomen to reach the waistband of my jeans.

With much self-control—self-control that I didn't think I had when it came to Cassie—I shifted my hips away.

"Mmm-mm," I hummed in disapproval against her chest, "my turn."

She let out a pleased sigh, bringing her hand back to my scalp, and she yanked my face to hers to kiss me with purpose. Our tongues touched twice, our hips ground together once more, and she pulled away from me to breathe:

"Take me to bed?"

I wanted to. *Shit,* I wanted to. I wanted to abandon the menial task of preparing our early dinner, throw her flat on her back, and get lost in her until we were forced to take pause for food or water. *And I would.* My thoughts had flashed back to our previous intimate acts, though—her nearly collapsing on me in front of her fireplace and the way her thighs shook in her shower—and there was a different desire that was ripe in my mind.

"Not yet. I want you standing." Before she could so much as respond, I told her, "I have a feeling that your legs always go weak when you come."

A devilish smile came to her lips, her tone even huskier than normal as she replied, "Only when it's good."

"Good," I rasped, reaching for her leg that had wound its way around my right hip and ushering it to the floor. I grabbed her face—roughly, just on the edge of her jawline—and ensured that her eyes were on me. Her gaze was hooded with lust as I whispered, "I'm gonna eat you until your fucking knees buckle."

Her head fell back to the shelves, and she moaned a delighted, *"Shit,* Jay."

I planted a kiss on the center of her throat and felt her inhale on my lips.

"Shhh," I shushed her between peppered kisses as I worked my way down the center of her body. "The walls are thin in this place, Darlin'."

I sank to my knees, holding her waist in both of my hands, and the silver jewelry in her navel came into my line of sight. I dragged my tongue across it, the balls' cold, erotic sensory on my tastebuds, and the metal clacked against my teeth in a way that made my eyes briefly roll to the back of my head.

Though her skin jumped beneath my touch, Cassie quieted herself, her *ahs* and *mmms* turning to sensual murmurs that pleasantly tickled my eardrums.

I smiled as I hooked my fingers into the waistband of her black leggings, my dick straining against the zipper of my jeans at the reminder that she was sexually obedient. Our eyes locked as I tugged at the fabric, her gaze remained slow-blinking while she leaned on my shoulders, and I disrobed her from the waist down. I sat on my heels, Cassie's breath shaking as I made my way to the space between her thighs, and I licked along the crevasse that led me from her leg to her hip. Her back arched, her hands that always found their way into my hair squeezing at the roots; her head rested back against the shelving again as she panted to the ceiling, and I gently placed my mouth over her clit.

I won't distort reality and say that she was like the essence of honey or the scent of a rare flower. There was a slight salty twang from sweat in the crease of her thighs, and she tasted how a woman should taste. She tasted like pussy. *Really fucking good pussy.* I made no attempt to stifle my moans, but thankfully, I was so buried in her that my noises were muffled. I dug my fingers into the sides of her pelvis, matching the rhythm of her rocking with insistent squeezes, and encouraged her to ride my face to her heart's content.

Her movement against me had begun slow—all soft flexes of her hips, smooth brushes of her pussy on my tongue, and little calls of my name and the occasional *baby* between gasps of air. I watched the rise and fall of her breasts increase in speed as she quickened her motions to a more furious pace, and she looked down to view me—jaw slack and brow furrowed. Her shoulders hunched. The muscles in her abdomen flexed. I hummed against her, and when her legs began to vibrate, I wrapped my arms around her ass and thighs.

Cassie whispered a strained, "Fuck." I breathed her in, though I was nearly suffocating, and she mewled, *"Yes."* Her pleading affirmative was a hoarse chant with every exhale, turning louder as she approached her release, and she inevitably brought one of her own hands to her mouth to quiet herself.

Cries of ecstasy were subdued by her palm. Her torso curled over me. The gentle shaking of her thighs turned near violent, I tightened my grip to support her weight, and her knees gave out. I felt her repetitive spasms on my mouth as she rode through her orgasm, and when her body finally went entirely weak, she murmured:

"Let me down."

I kissed between her thighs softly as I loosened my hold around her. She sank to my lap, and her sated eyes met mine for only a second before her mouth was on me. Arms thrown around my neck, her skin burned into my naked chest, and I returned her kiss with enthusiasm—embracing her with a squeeze around her back and shoulders. Cassie snaked a hand between us, reaching to palm my cock through my jeans, and I cursed on an exhale:

"Shit."

Her teeth at my neck, nipping in areas that she knew I loved, she asked, "My turn?"

"Bed," I insisted.

She returned to my lips, nodding in response, and spoke against me:

"Lead the way."

I obeyed, standing with her but ensuring that we stayed connected at the mouth. There was no stumbling. There was no *rush*. Though I felt like I needed her on a very real, physical level, there was no itch to race to the finish line. Desperation was present, certainly, but the remainder of my clothing was stripped before her with slow purpose. Her dainty bra that was hanging loose below her breasts was unclasped and fell to the floor, and after taking in her naked body as if I hadn't just worshipped her on my knees, I closed the distance between us, and we fell to the mattress.

Chapter 17

She's a fucking dream.

That's all that I could think of while I drank my coffee at the kitchen table. That Cassie Cohen was a fucking dream. I reminisced of the night prior as the bitter tannins of black coffee pulled at the sides of my mouth.

We had moved in a fashion that blended the lines between sexual passion and aftercare. Stretched underneath me on her back, Cassie cradled the sides of my face, quietly demanding my attention while I pushed inside of her with utmost patience. Her legs had turned pliant, spread wide and gently bouncing with each flex of my hips, and I massaged the insides of her thighs with soft squeezes of my hands. Our foreheads touched. We whimpered in each other's ears. She kissed me deeply, eventually wrapping all of her limbs around me in a full-body embrace, and we were simply connected motion. A beautiful rocking that evoked a high that enveloped us in the color of a sunset until she plead for us to roll, and then she was situated above me. I watched her come apart at the seams as she rode me, and she took me with her.

I could have stayed in that bed, stomach starved yet sated by her touch, until I wasted away. Nothing but skin and bone, I would still reach to her and smile as we begged each other for more.

We didn't, of course. Instead, we rose. We dressed. I adoringly ordered her to, *'Get out of my kitchen and sit,'* while I prepared our dinner, and she obliged—watching me with a slight grin from the dining table. She jokingly refused to sing my praises while we ate, yet she cleared her plate and helped herself to seconds. We had the chance to *relax*. My arm had casually draped over her shoulder while we watched television. I offered her a nightcap, and she accepted the glass of whiskey with joy. It was inevitable that we would eventually wander to bed, but we fought sleep as we lounged on the couch together, for sleeping meant a fast-forward to the next day. And among our blissful relaxation that I considered to be heaven rather than purgatory, Cassie had spoken to both Skylar and Colton.

They were slated to arrive at my apartment by ten o'clock in the morning—which meant that Luke, Claire, Liam, and Zoey would be joining us, as well—and with one peek over my shoulder at the oven's clock, I noted that it was 9:30. I breathed in, let it out in a long exhale, and allowed myself to continually relive the night past rather than focusing on the present. My vision was unfocused as I stared ahead at nothing, and I felt my eyes go hooded and my lips stretch into a lopsided smirk as I blindly lifted my mug to my mouth.

"Hmm...you look lost in space."

I glanced to the right to see Cassie having just stepped out of the bathroom. A dark grey towel wrapped around her chest and hanging down to her upper thighs, her hair sopping and slicked back, she was freshly showered and wearing a wry smile.

I finished giving her a thorough once over and returned, "Maybe I am."

"But a *good* lost in space." She walked toward me, halting when she was close enough for me to reach her. I brushed along the skin of her damp thighs with my right hand as I looked up to her, and she touched a single finger to the space between my eyebrows. She traced over the spots on my forehead that she had once told me contained *worry wrinkles* and ended where my hair was tucked behind my ear. "Is it pleasant up there?"

I smiled. "Mhm."

Cassie hummed happily and looked down at my mug. "You made coffee?"

I nodded. Though I knew that Claire and Liam, the two more avid coffee aficionados, would bring their own fresh brew—they usually did whenever we met as a group at one another's apartments for morning coffee—I had made my own. The pot was a simple drip, tucked away in a corner on the countertop in the kitchen, and I gestured to it with a tip of my head behind me.

"I did," I told her.

Her brow furrowed at my cup. "You don't normally drink it black."

She was right. I didn't. However, my headspace this morning had rendered me only able to pour and sit, and I truthfully didn't mind the taste without my usual dash of milk and sugar.

I shrugged. "You remember how I like my coffee?"

Cassie chuckled back, "I'm observant."

"Or ya like me and you took note."

"Or I like you and I took note," she said with a grin as she leaned down.

I twisted to face her fully, the drenched strands of her hair brushing my hand that had long abandoned my mug and now lay free on the tabletop. I grasped at a piece that left cold droplets in my palm and gave it a tug.

"I like you wet," I murmured against her lips. "You're pretty when you're wet."

I felt rather than saw her smile. "I like you dirty."

"You're even prettier when I'm inside of you, though," I unabashedly spoke my recollections of our actions aloud. "You're *so* fuckin' pretty when I'm inside of you."

Cassie let out a giggle, and then simpered, *"Filthy boy."*

Our soft laughter turned to hums of appreciation as she pressed her lips against mine. The audible smacks of our mouths, though rather quiet, rang in my ears and fueled the fire that was already raging for her. The moment our tongues touched, I was considering the amount of time we had until company was to arrive—debating telling her to lock the door that I had pointedly unlocked mere minutes ago—dreaming of reaching for her towel and letting it fall to the floor—perhaps carrying her back to bed or taking her right on the kitchen table.

None of that could happen, though, because someone was early.

The entrance swung open, my heart struck my sternum, Cassie let out a high pitch that was so unlike the one that I wished to be hearing, and Colton stood in the doorway. It was clear that he had witnessed Cassie rapidly pulling away from me, for his light eyes bounced between the two of us twice...but he was far less than taken aback. The door shut behind him, his expression maintained a casual flair, and he gave us both an uptick of his head.

"Hey." Colton walked to the chair closest to him, which just so happened to be at the opposite head of the table from me. He glanced at Cassie. "You wanna get dressed, or…"

Naturally, she didn't.

"What are you doing here so early?!" she whisper-hissed the chastise to Colton.

His brow pinched together as he sat. "Seriously?"

"Cas—"

"Your brother," Colton pointed at me, "fuckin' bit my head off for being late yesterday. Now I'm early, and your girl's yellin' at me."

"A *half hour* early," she bit back.

"Y'all said—and I quote," he held up fingers to use as quotation marks, "get here around ten. Door will be unlocked. Just let yourself in." Colton's hands fell back to the table. "Door was unlocked, guys. I'm early. Who gives a shit."

"I give a shit—"

"Cassie, just go get dressed, please," I begged as I rubbed at my eyes. Her response, which I knew would crack like a whip, wasn't spoken. She wasn't able to because the door was opening *again*. My hands dropped from my face, and before I could even see who else had arrived, I was grumbling, "For the love of *God.*"

It was Claire who was waltzing through the foyer first, holding a French press that was filled to the brim with coffee. She stopped so quickly at the scene before her that Luke had to balance on the balls of his feet to avoid running into her from behind, and she was forced to extend her arms to steady the liquid and prevent a spillage of massive proportion.

Luke murmured, *"Jesus,* Claire, careful," as he grabbed her on either of her upper arms. "Could've burned yourse—"

He stopped when he followed her eyes to see Colton looking at them both, to Cassie, who was still standing only a step or two from me and clothed in only a towel, and to me—and I was positive that I looked as though I wished time could be reversed.

They both crossed the threshold, closed the door, and while Claire remained silent, glancing to me and Cassie with a narrowed gaze that made me squirm, Luke spoke to Colton in an altogether irritated tone:

"You're early."

Colton waved grandly at Luke while keeping his focus on me. "And he says it like it's a bad thing. Do ya see what I'm talkin' about? Do I have to be a fuckin' pariah here?"

Luke let out a dramatic exhale, and Claire ignored Colton's words, instead asking Cassie, "Why aren't you dressed?"

"Well," she crossed her arms, "you *all* know that I'm staying here. You *all* know that there's only one bathroom in this place. And you *all* know that it's right," Cassie pointed behind herself, toward the bathroom door that was left ajar, "over there. We said ten o'clock. *It is 9:30.* I'm not ready yet! Sue me! Why is everyone barging in here so goddamn early?"

"I was trying to get in your good graces," Colton quipped with a smile to all of us. His focus inevitably landed on Luke and stayed there. "How am I doin'?"

Luke walked to the table, choosing the chair directly to my right, and slumped down onto it as he replied, "It's probably best if we don't talk."

Colton nodded as if it were the reaction that he was expecting while Claire continued to eye Cassie skeptically.

"I was anxious," Claire remarked slowly in response to Cassie's questioning of their arrival time. "Figured I'd come by and bring coffee while we wait..."

Claire moved to stand between Luke and Colton, set the stainless-steel contraption on the table before them all, and began to make her way to the kitchen to grab several mugs.

As she reached into the appropriate cabinet, Colton asked her:

"Can you grab me one?"

Luke muttered, "Can't you get your own?"

Claire's body sagged, one hand on the handle of the cupboard as she looked back to Luke and gently spoke, *"Baby, can you not do this?"*

He blew an annoyed breath through his nostrils in response, and she finished her task at hand, grabbing three mugs—all the same design as the small, white one that I was currently drinking from. She bustled about behind the island expertly while holding them all deftly by the handles with a grip of her left hand. Packets of sweetener from the countertop and a small container of cinnamon from the lazy susan cupboard were placed in the mugs, the quart of milk that sat in the fridge was snagged by her free hand, and she closed the refrigerator door with a sharp bump of her hip.

Sitting at Luke's right, she set everything down. He quietly thanked her for the cinnamon, as it was a typical addition to his morning beverage, and she gave him a small grin in return. Colton waited silently while they both prepared their drinks.

Cassie cleared her throat. "I'm, ah, gonna go get dressed." She took two steps. Two small, quiet steps. And the creak of the front door sounded once more. Cassie groaned, "Please, God—*no.*"

Her plea to a deity was unanswered as her brother strolled inside with his own French press in hand.

"I *thought* I heard—" Liam's attention was immediately drawn to his sister, and he grimaced as he admonished, "The hell are you doing? Get some clothes on!"

"Oh. *My God!*" Cassie whined. "Ten o'clock! We said *fucking. Ten.* I just got out of the goddamn shower!"

Zoey, who was momentarily hidden behind Liam's large body and holding a container of sugar cookie-flavored creamer, walked past him and toward the kitchen table.

Less than concerned about Cassie's appearance, she greeted Colton with a murmured, "Morning," moving to sit on my left and setting her creamer down in front of her.

He pointed at her enthusiastically. *"That's* how you say hello," he told both Cassie and Luke as he looked between the two of them.

"Cas," Liam exhaled her name in exasperation as he closed the door behind him, "I know you're staying here, but ya can't walk around like you *own* the damn place."

Now filling his own mug halfway with coffee from Claire's French press, Colton squinted at Liam. He set the contraption down, replacing it with the milk, and cocked his head a near ninety degrees to the side. Filling the mug until I knew his coffee would be colored a light beige, he looked from him, to me, to Cassie, and then back to Liam. He appeared to be reading the room and absorbing the vibes as if they were moisture and he a wrung-out sponge; however, as he reached for the sweetener and grabbed three packets, he said nothing.

Luke's nose scrunched as he watched Colton tear the tops off of all three of the green packets and empty them into his cup in one fell swoop. Mild disgust at Colton's obvious preference for overly sweet, milky coffee was clear in his contorted grimace.

"I was just. Going. To get. *Dressed,*" Cassie stressed to her brother. "And I was *considering* getting a coffee before I did, but then you guys all showed up at once."

"You can put on clothes before you go walkin' through Jay's kitchen," he argued. "You're giving everyone a free show."

Zoey scoffed. "It's just a *towel,* Lee."

Cassie bitterly retorted, "Well, I can't ask for payment for my *shows* anymore since I had to quit my job! So, it's *all* fuckin' free now."

Mug half-lifted to his lips, Colton barked out a laugh. Everyone simultaneously turned their heads to look at him, and he quipped:

"What? That was funny. She's funny. So...you quit?"

Cassie said, "Over a voicemail. No notice...not exactly ideal, but—" She paused as she noticed Liam's eyes narrowed in Colton's direction and exclaimed, "Oh, for the love of—Liam, he said I was funny. He didn't say he wanted to fuck me!"

Colton rapidly finished a sip from his drink and then set it down to tell Cassie, "For the record, I don't. No offense, but you're not my type." He casually spoke to Liam, "Ya got nothing to worry about there," and then shot me the quickest of side-eyes as if he were silently telling me the same. No one else had caught it, but his quiet recognition of my closeness with Cassie made me cough into my coffee mug. I cleared my throat loudly, setting the ceramic to the table, and Colton voiced, "Ya left a message and quit. Got it. Probably a good call. When's your friend gettin' here, anyway?"

Cassie's jaw dropped open. *"TEN!"*

She then abandoned all thought of getting coffee, turned on her heel, and stormed into Claire's bedroom where she had left her suitcase.

There was little conversation to be had while we all waited for Skylar.

Liam had eventually sat between Zoey and Colton with two more procured mugs from my cupboard. He poured from his French press into his mug and added nothing else; Zoey drank mostly creamer with a splash of coffee. Colton asked if he could have some of her flavored creamer, and she gave it to him without a verbal response. Luke and Liam both watched in horror as he added even more sweetness to his cup.

Cassie returned to the common area, having quickly thrown her damp hair in a bun and donned jeans and a long-sleeved white shirt. Because the seats were all otherwise full at the dining table, she had taken it upon herself to sit atop the granite on the kitchen island behind me. Legs dangling over the edge, I could see her in the peripheral vision of my right-hand side as she casually drank her coffee, which was prepared exactly like her brother's.

It was odd to say, but despite what I knew was coming upon Skylar's arrival, it felt...*normal*. Well, normal in the manner of an awkward breakfast in which no one desired to speak general pleasantries, but normal, nonetheless.

The casual feeling of morning coffee with friends and acquaintances alike lasted until approximately 10:05. Claire checked the time on her phone. Cassie's right foot began to bounce from side to side. Liam questioned her hesitantly:

"You said ten?"

I answered for her, "I think we *all* know she was supposed to get here at ten, man."

"Y'all need patience," Colton noted before draining the last dredges of his mug.

"Didn't you tell me her car's in the shop or something?" I twisted in my chair to look at Cassie and found her looking particularly worried. I assured her, "She probably had to catch an Uber to get here. So she's a few minutes late. That's not weird, Cas."

Cassie shook her head. "Sky's *punctual*. This isn't like her."

"It's only five minutes after ten," Claire gently spoke.

"The girl shows up to work fifteen minutes early—without fail," Cassie stated. "She sits in her car in the parking lot so she's not a bother until she's *perfectly* on time. Checks out the parking situation before we ever meet up for lunch or dinner so she knows exactly where to go and doesn't get lost."

Colton sarcastically muttered, "She sounds super laid back."

"I'm telling you," Cassie insisted, "this is weird." She picked up her phone that was resting on the countertop beside her, and glanced at the screen. "No text, no call, no nothing."

Zoey asked, "Well, when did you talk to her last?"

"Last night?" Cassie replied with an upward inflection. "Called her and chatted for a bit. Texted her the address after."

"You just called her up to tell her about her dead friend?" Colton inquired with raised eyebrows.

Cassie sighed heavily. "We knew Delaney, but neither of us were *friends* with her—and I kept it brief."

"How brief?" he pressed. "Like...*Hey, girl! Quick thing. Remember Delaney? She's dead and I'm a skosh worried about other dancers that didn't make their shifts. Long story. Wanna come over tomorrow and chat?*"

She rolled her eyes at the insinuation. "No. *Of course* not."

I recalled the short amount of time that Cassie took to speak with Skylar on the phone and there was no doubt that it was, as she had described, brief. She had emerged from Claire's bedroom afterward, appearing slightly shaken, noting that while Skylar wasn't privy to *all* the details, she did tell her about Delaney. Aside from mentioning that Skylar wasn't entirely alone—her bathroom still needed work, and she was staying with her parents—Cassie had little desire to speak of it all. I understood entirely, for we knew that the subject would soon be revisited.

"What *did* you tell her?" Zoey spoke my thoughts, a hint of anxiety in her vibrant eyes.

Cassie immediately replied, "Just that I found that article about Delaney...broke that to her as gently as I could. Didn't even mention the other dancers, yet—nothing about the laptop, nothing about 2D."

Zoey gave her a curt nod, and I asked:

"What does she think she's coming over here for?"

Cassie shrugged. "Coffee?"

"*Coffee?* You didn't tell me *that*. That doesn't seem like enough detail...what happened to being concerned for her safety?"

She returned my rapid tone, "She wasn't on the schedule for work last night, and I *told* you that she stayed at her parents' house because her bathroom's still messed up. She wasn't alone."

"Oh, how convenient about her bathroom," I sardonically stated. "I didn't realize we were dropping fucking *bombs* on this poor woman today."

"It's a bomb no matter when I tell her, James," she hissed.

"So, you decided to invite her over for *breakfast?*"

"Jay," Luke cut in. My head whipped to his, and he quietly demanded, *"Ease up."*

Cassie said, "If I told her everything at once, she's bound to ask why we haven't gone to the police yet." The reminder was apt, and I sighed loudly as she told the entire group, "I didn't exactly have an answer for that."

"Yeah," Colton remarked slowly, "just...I dunno...tell her we're tryin' to get all our ducks in a row before talking with the cops."

"That's a lie," Claire unnecessarily pointed out.

"Uh huh." He shot her a wry grin. "Would you rather the truth?"

"You know we wouldn't," she griped.

Liam voiced to his sister, "If you think your friend knows anything about these missing women, why don't you just tell her it'd be best for *her* to go to the police?"

Colton pointed at him. "Ooh. *That.* So simple, we won't even have to go into much detail, and then the cops are involved without any of us being questioned."

"Well, *you're* gonna question her, though," I said. "She'll probably ask why you're so damn interested."

"Maybe I'm dating a stripper who works at another club." Colton looked to me with a secretly mocking smile, and Cassie grumbled something unintelligible from behind me as he continued, "Call her Peyton...Peyton's a good name." He murmured the latter half softly to himself, and then powered on with, "That'd make me emotionally invested enough, right?"

Cassie exhaled a bitter, succinct, *"Sure."*

Without even a pause, Colton abruptly swung the subject. "But I'll cross that bridge when we get to it. Since she's not here yet..." He glanced at Zoey. "You look through that laptop?"

"Mhm," she replied. "Nothing else that I could see."

"Nothing else that you could see?" he repeated back to her with a narrowing of his eyes. "Saved pictures?"

"Nope," she muttered.

"Emails?"

"No saved passwords."

"Messages?"

Her expression pinched. *"Messages?"*

"Texts," Colton clarified with purpose. "Text messages."

"How the hell am I supposed to check his text messages?"

He stared at her for all of two seconds before stating bluntly, "It's a Mac."

Zoey hesitated. "Uh huh...and?"

"And those have the ability to sync up with an iPhone." His head cocked to the side as he looked to us all. "Did y'all not know that?"

Zoey said nothing in return while Liam blinked rapidly, murmuring, "Don't look at me. I'm not rich enough for that shit."

Claire mumbled, "I don't have a computer," and Cassie agreed.

Luke shook his head as expected, showing off his technological ineptitude.

I, however, was well aware of the feature...I had just been far too distracted to think of mentioning it.

I groaned, "I do. I didn't even *think* about that."

"'Kay...hoping ya didn't burn it yet," Colton told Zoey.

"No, no," she replied.

He began to say, "You should probably—"

"I'll check it again," she cut him off sharply. *"I got it."*

"Okay." He held up his hands in mock defense at her tone, let them fall back to the table, and set his eyes back on Cassie. "So...thoughts on time here?"

She shrugged, lifting her phone to peek at the time once again, and immediately began to tap across the screen. Raising the phone to her ear, she waited for a beat before letting out a gritty, frustrated noise, and she dropped her cell to the counter with a loud *clack*.

"One ring. Silenced to voicemail," she griped, pressing her hands to her eyes. "God *dammit*, Sky. For all we know, she's tied up in some dude's basement somewhere—"

"Okay," the panic in her voice forced me to speak up. "Cas...it's only fifteen after the hour."

"I know what fucking *time it is,* Jay!"

Zoey interjected, "The last thing we need right now is you two bickering."

I retorted over my shoulder at her, "We aren't *bickering!*" before turning back to Cassie. "I'm sure Sky's fine. She was at her parents' house last night?"

"In Roanoke." Her casual, following, "Uh huh," was nearly drowned out by the audible buzz her phone made as it vibrated beside her. All heads whipped to the source of the noise; it was in her hand in the blink of an eye, and her shoulders sagged as she let out an exhale.

Weighted silence filled the room, for Cassie's expression seemed torn...and it wasn't clear whether her reaction was one of relief or further worry.

Liam questioned, "Well, was it her?"

"Sky," she grumbled. "Yes, it was her." Cassie's voice turned to a higher, sweeter pitch as she read from her phone, emulating Skylar, *"'Sorry...family drama, long story.'"*

"Family drama?" Colton repeated, *"Family. Drama?"*

"That *is* what she said," Cassie sardonically remarked.

He scoffed. "People are dying. This isn't exactly the time to prioritize a fight with Mommy."

Cassie typed while sneering, "It's probably not just a *fight with Mommy.*" She looked up to him and mentioned, "It's not like her to bail."

"Is she bailing?" he asked. "Or is she just late?"

She bit back, "What do you think I just asked? I'm not just..." It was clear her phone had vibrated as she stopped herself mid-sentence to look at her palm, huffed out a breath, and said, "She's not coming."

"Perfect," Colton complained quietly. "As much as I'd *love* to stay for breakfast, I'm gonna go." His chair scraped the flooring below as he stood, and he gently suggested, "Maybe give her some more incentive to *actually* show next time?"

"I *did* think—"

"I know, I know." He waved her away as he strode toward the door. "Another time."

The door closed, and all that lingered was a sense of hopelessness. Not fear, nor the loss of control as life rapidly careens off of an expected path—just hopelessness. Hopelessness and the sensation of a ticking clock continually counting down with no knowledge of the time remaining, and no way to figure out if disaster would strike upon *zero.* There was no use in pondering it—no use to fall into the hole of unease that seemed to stretch on to eternity.

Feigned braveness abound, the clock ticked on.

Chapter 18

I cherished the moments when Cassie and I were left alone. The ones in which we felt that we could abandon the chaos of the surrounding world and just sink into each other. I think we both knew that the privacy we were granted from whatever deity above was fleeting, and while I so wished that I could abandon all responsibility only to relish in our personal lives that had entwined with such beauty within darkness, I couldn't.

I told myself that, anyway, as we went about the day as normally as we could.

Grocery shopping.

Her accompanying me to the laundromat.

Finding a restaurant to eat lunch at while we were out.

Returning home and simply living.

It all passed far too quickly, and though we both relished in the occasional brush of our hands—a stolen kiss—an embrace that left us wanting to consume one another—I could see in Cassie's eyes that she was on edge. Every glance at her phone was with the intention of checking on Skylar. Brief texts were sent, read receipts were received, and her responses were quick and succinct, but Cassie continued to watch her screen with a narrow-eyed skepticism.

My questioning of it all was waved away, her muttered, "It's nothing," was continually repeated, and it lasted through the night—returning after ever-brief shared moments of peace until we eventually drifted off to sleep.

It was early. I *knew* it was early. The familiar feeling of being torn between reality and what occurs in the depths of my mind kept me in half of a trance. Physically, I was comfortable. Warm. I was well aware that Cassie was beside me in my bed, but for whatever reason, I was filled with dread.

My recurring nightmare attempted to cling to me, settling on my brain like a cloud of cigar smoke. *Stale* cigar smoke that lingers in your throat, burrows into your clothing, and coats your hair in such a way that it's damn near impossible to clean. The usual visions that I was familiar with were unable to be entirely recalled, and for that, I was thankful.

What did remain was water.

Water.

Covering me. Choking me. Drowning me.

It was new. It was terrifying. And I had no idea why.

"James?!" Cassie's alarmed voice rang through the haze, and I felt my body flinch in response, but my mind was not yet willing. "Wake up!"

I attempted to speak, but it came out garbled. I only managed to groan a nasty, guttural noise as I remained caught between two worlds. Oxygen ran through my lungs, but it seemingly did no good as I was starved for air, and I gasped desperately for its relief.

"Jay? *Fuck...James!*" Cassie's tone turned raspy. *"Baby, please."*

It was on her plea that my eyes were able to snap open. The ceiling of my room came into view. My breathing slowed to a normal rate. I slowly removed my right hand from my chest, finding my palm sticky with cold sweat, flexed my fingers into a fist and then released them, and rolled my head on my pillow to see her.

The moment that I was able to register her appearance through the dark, I inhaled sharply, sitting up so quickly that it dizzied me. The lamp on my side table was on in a flash, and the room lit up in an ambient glow.

Dark eyes red-rimmed, face damp, her tears were hot on my palms and continuing to fall down her cheeks as I rapidly swiped them away.

"Shhh-shh, what is it?"

She scanned me up and down, looking as if she had deduced that I was fully awake before hesitantly touching my upper arms. Cassie's breath caught in a quiet sob that eviscerated me, and she rushed out:

"Are you okay?"

"Am *I* okay? *Cassie...*"

I was certain that my expression was telling. That my nightmares had caused my heart to race—my skin to perspire in panic—my muscles to clench as if I were prepared to scream. I had woken immersed in them. Drenched in them. Yet the moment that I saw her, I attempted to whisk away the thought of being lost in my mind. The feeling wasn't *gone,* of course. The tremor of anxiety that followed my typical waking at two in the morning remained deep in my muscle tissue, but it didn't matter.

Well...it *did* matter.

But I was trying with all my might to push it to the back of my brain because the visions weren't real. Not at this exact moment of my life, anyway. And seeing Cassie with tears streaming down her face—whether or not she was trying to stem the flow of them with sniffles and rapid blinking—was nothing less than startling.

I had never seen her *really* cry. A tightening of her throat here or there, I had heard, sure. But crying—actual tears paired with a single sob—*no.*

"What is it?" I asked her again in a whisper. "Is—" My head whipped away from her and to the side table behind her where her cell was charging. *"Shit,* did something happen?" I looked back to her, assuming aloud, "Sky? *Fuck*—Liam? What's wro—"

"Jesus—no, nothing. Nothing happened." Cassie moved one of her hands to the left side of my chest as I sighed in relief, settling it in the exact spot that she does when she's seemingly trying to sense my anxiety level through her palm. More calmly this time, she inquired, "Are you good?"

"Nightmare. I'm *fine,* Cas. Are *you?"*

My thumbs brushed at the areas that had begun to dry, and she murmured, "Fine."

I shook my head. "Why are you crying?"

Cassie released me, reaching to usher my touch away from her cheeks. I let my hands fall to the little mattress space between us while she rubbed at her eyes.

"This is fuckin' backwards," she grumbled. "I'm good."

"Cassie."

"You just scared me, okay?" she blurted as she removed her palms from her face. "You looked like you were in pain, and I just..." Cassie looked to the left and right before landing on me and exhaling softly through her nose. "I didn't like that."

I nodded, gently replying, "Okay, okay." Shimmying back down into bed, she followed me, and I muttered, "Come here."

Despite my cool sheen of sweat, she obliged, tightly holding me around my waist as she rested her head on me. It took quite some time for her grasp to soften—so long that my unease from my dreams had fully passed—so long that she could have gone back to sleep, though I knew that she hadn't.

Cassie eventually spoke into my pectorals, "What were they about?"

I understood the question without further elaboration. "Just bad memories. You know."

"Right...I do," she replied. Silence stretched between us, and I felt Cassie take a quick breath before stating, "I never really had nightmares."

"No?"

"No," she replied somberly, "but Liam did."

I found my hand stroking aimlessly up and down her back. "Oh?"

"Mhm," she hummed. "Teenage years weren't exactly the best."

I whispered, "Right...I know."

"Always felt like he got the brunt of it," Cassie admitted. "After she left, we shared a room for a while. Sometimes he'd wake up screaming."

My insides coiled uncomfortably at the obvious, casual mention of her mother along with the confession of Liam's grief, and her reasoning for speaking of it sat heavy in my gut.

"Is that what you thought I was going to do?" I asked. "Wake up screaming?"

She shrugged. "Maybe."

The realization of the memories I had brought forth for her struck me deep, and I gave her a squeeze as I murmured, "I'm sorry you went through that."

Her shoulder bobbed once more. "It didn't last long. That was when he moved away."

The enigma that was her rough upbringing had consistently lingered in the back of my mind from the day that we had built the bench on her front porch. As much as I wanted to know her on a deeper level, it didn't feel *right* to ask about her formative years—more specifically, the time after her mother had died. I assumed we would speak of it eventually, and considering the depth of my feelings for her, I knew that it would hit me hard.

I simply hadn't expected that time to be now...and her words regarding Liam moving here to Salem caught me entirely off guard, for I had never considered the timing of it all.

I had automatically assumed differently before. That Liam had already left to start his life as an adult away from the town he had grown up in. That, maybe, he didn't have the financial means to return upon his mother's death...but that wasn't the case.

"Liam...left you?"

"Hmm?"

"You were fourteen," I recalled the information aloud. "Your mother died...and your brother thought it was a good time to up and pack his bags?"

"Oh." Cassie recognized my accusation and, as casually as she could, replied, "No, it wasn't like that."

"He left you alone with your *abusive father,*" I noted, near-horrified. "I don't—Liam's so protective of you. I don't—I don't understand."

It exited me in a disbelieving tone, for it didn't sound like something Liam would do in the least. There were times that his overprotection of her resembled that of a guardian rather than a sibling, and try as I might to imagine the scenario, I simply couldn't.

She angled her head to look at me, sadness in her gaze as she audibly swallowed.

"This is a, um...bit of a band-aid rip conversation," she admitted. "There's no use easing into it. It just makes it...harder, I dunno. Are you sure you want to jump on this train?"

There was nothing but steadfast trust in her somber eyes, and my heart fluttered at the notion as I truthfully returned:

"I'm already on the train, Darlin'." Flexing my fingers where they had stopped on her waist, I said, "Just rip."

And rip, she did.

"She shot herself." My pulse slammed my ribcage. "In our home." My lungs burned. "Liam was the only one there, and he saw it happen."

My breath left me to the point that my, "Oh. *God,*" was practically silent.

Voice a mere rasp, she said, "He didn't *leave* me. He stayed for months." Cassie rephrased, "He stayed in *that house* with me for months, but he wasn't...well. Begged me to go with him when he said he needed to go. We fought for weeks 'cause I knew he needed to leave for his own good, but he kept refusing to go without me. I just," she paused, "there was too much change at once for me, I think. I stayed 'cause I was young, y'know?"

"You were only fourteen," I whispered, perhaps more to myself than to her.

She just nodded, continuing somberly, "I don't think he'd be here if he stayed. After mom died, he spent more time bleeding than not. Carter was...he just didn't stop. He wouldn't have stopped."

The knowledge was gut-wrenching, and she watched me carefully as her words sank in. There was no misunderstanding them—she truthfully believed that their father, Carter, would have eventually beaten Liam to the point of no return. And while I knew through context clues within memories of months past that he was abusive—and it was clear that Cassie knew that I knew that—I hadn't fathomed the extent of it.

I don't think I could have without the explicit explanation.

For the second time in the last week, I thought back to the moment Cassie and I had met over the summer—when I had arrived at her home with the remainder of the group in tow. Liam's blond head was matted with red, a result of a car accident. She hadn't known—no one had explained the turn of events—and I recalled how she stormed across her front lawn. How her long, tan legs had marched up to her brother. How anger had contorted her pretty face as she roughly examined the injuries on his scalp.

She had thought that Carter had done the damage, then.

And it wasn't until now that I realized that it wasn't a stretch of her imagination in the least. There was no doubt in my mind that she had seen her brother in a similarly beaten state at the hands of their father, and I felt my stomach churn at the thought. Liam's face flashed in my mind: his smile lopsided and typically carefree, and an old, thin, white scar stretching over the left side of his lips.

I had seen it before, sure. It was just that I never considered it to be a trait that identified him. I considered what could have caused it—*who* could have caused it—and I knew there was no possibility that it would go unnoticed for me from here on out.

Cassie spoke once more, "He wasn't really *gone* when he moved, either. He drove back to check on me constantly...once a week, for the longest time until I was older. No idea how the fuck he afforded the gas for that."

She said the last sentence with a bittersweet chuckle, and try as I might to allow the sound to comfort me, it didn't. My throat was tight to the point that I wondered if the anguish would spread and I would cry on her behalf—on *Liam's* behalf. I didn't. I simply blinked as I let the reality of her past wash over me, and I debated my response for a beat before hoarsely questioning:

"Where did you live?"

As if she were unsure why I would ask that, she returned, "Hmm?"

"I mean…you didn't live with your father," I rephrased. "Right?"

"Oh…no, I did," she told me.

"Did he ever—"

"Hit me?" She bitterly hummed, "Mhm," but didn't elaborate any further. My teeth were clenched as she noted, "I steered clear of Carter if he was in a mood. It never really got *bad* for me. Got a lock for my door. I was fine, Jay."

I nodded, forcing myself to swallow any further remarks because she didn't need my sorries or my anger. I had plenty of it to give, but I knew that it was unnecessary. She also, remarkably, didn't seem to need my comfort. The story, even when coming straight from her own mouth, didn't cause her to crumble as it should have. Her tears from earlier were long gone, and it was just…her past. Lived so long ago that it was a simple fact rather than a sordid tale. I brushed her cheek with my thumb, she leaned into it, and I noted:

"You're such a strong woman, Cassie."

She smiled ever so slightly. "And yet…I feel like you could break me so easily."

The acknowledgment of whatever soft spot she had for me warmed me through.

I moved my head softly from side to side, murmuring, "Not a chance, Darlin'," because she was anything but breakable.

However, the walls that she naturally piled high for those who weren't close to her weren't symbolic of her strength. They were her defense...and that wasn't to say that her metaphorical walls were constructed of a sturdy brick that had inevitably crumbled to the ground. I hadn't chipped away at her, and she hadn't been bent so roughly that rock laid in a pile at our feet. No, instead, it was clear that she had willingly lowered them for me. Any vulnerability that she shared with me wasn't a slip-up or a crack in her armor...it was a gift. Something to be *earned*.

I knew this already, but the reminder made my chest ache, and I silently vowed to wear that badge with honor as I traced the edges of her cheek with my fingertips. She had broken me long, long ago...and truthfully, my body had begged for it. I *needed* to be disintegrated—splintered—shattered into glass pieces so tiny that I was turned to dust. I was a crystalline powder, and all of our hardships aside, it felt *so goddamn good* to be able to blow in the wind with her.

Cassie wouldn't break, though. I wouldn't allow it because she needed the control. She may have lowered her walls, but she was trusting me to keep her whole, and I would do just that.

I would keep her whole.

I pondered the thought while I should have slept. Kept the promise that I made to myself ripe in my mind as I laid beside her. Attempted to silently communicate the feeling through gently peppered kisses across her face to wake her when it was time for me to leave for work. Cassie had laid under the plush green comforter, the material pulled all the way to her cheeks. Her hair was splayed out on the pillows, tangles galore, and despite the fact that her eyes had fluttered open when I forced myself out of bed—despite the fact that she had given me a wistful smile when I kissed her good morning—despite the fact that I had murmured in her ear that I was leaving for work in approximately thirty minutes, and I had reminded her that she needed to go across the hall to her brother's apartment so she wasn't alone—she looked to have fallen back asleep.

"Cas," I whispered, but she didn't budge. I gently brushed the side of her face, and she nuzzled into my palm. I called to her again, "Cassie," and her only reply was a sleep-filled groan. A smile pulled at my lips. "Darlin', you gotta get up to go to Liam's. I have to get to work."

Eyes remaining closed, she nearly slurred, "Get back under the covers and call me *Darlin'* again."

"I would, but I have to go," I laughed. "Up. Dressed. Across the hall."

With a hefty grumble, she obeyed. Through heavy-lidded eyes, she haphazardly pulled on the comfortable clothing I had inevitably stripped from her the night before. I stole a last kiss from her before we opened my front door, we shared appealingly domestic adieus, and Cassie murmured that she would see me when I got home. She let herself into the apartment across the hall with the key Liam had given her long ago, I made a move for my car, and we went our separate ways.

It was unsettling being away from her. The daunting unknown that surrounded us—the mystery of whether Cassie was someone who could still be in danger—was an unfortunate constant...and the feeling of separation after deeming her presence a necessity squeezed my heart in a vice grip while I drove. But because it was, in fact, a *constant*—because there was no definitive yes or no to the question of her safety—because all we could do was stick together as a group, as we always did—normal life just...had to go on.

I listened to nothing but the sound of tires roaring against the highway pavement, and my attempt to will away my nervous meanderings was naught.

That is, until my phone lit up with a notification. Propped in its usual position in the mount to the right of the steering wheel, my eyes were off of the road for only a moment to glance at the screen.

Cassie Cohen

Today 7:43 A.M.

> Have a good day. Analyze the fuck out of those spreadsheets. x.

The grip in my chest loosened as I let out a hearty chuckle; my cheeks heated as I quickly read it for a second time, and it was all I could do to unlock the screen with a swipe of my finger. I tapped on the glass face twice—first to access my call log and again to hit her name—and the ring only sounded through my car speaker twice before she answered.

"Long time no talk," she cooed.

"Just assuring you that my spreadsheets will be thoroughly analyzed," I said. "Vlookups and pivot tables are sexy, right?"

She laughed softly. "You don't use index match? Or Xlookup? *We should see other people.*"

The only way I could describe the noise that erupted from me was a *giggle*.

"*God,* I like you."

Cassie hummed happily. "The feeling is very mutual."

My cheeks began to ache. "You're speaking pretty damn freely. I take it that no one else is awake yet?"

"Nope," she replied wistfully. "All by my lonesome. Lying on the couch. Wishing it was your bed."

"You know…it's dangerous to give a man an erection while he's driving," I remarked in a sultry tone. "Blood flow away from the brain impairs reaction time."

"Does it, now?" I could hear her smile.

"Mhm."

"That's too bad," she simpered.

"Thankfully, I'm a different breed of man," I confidently quipped.

"Are you *really* that exceptional of a driver?"

I was intending to respond with a joke referencing my ability to maintain a level head while my cock was hard. She would have disagreed because she knew as well as I did that *that* was a bald-faced lie. Our newfound filthy banter would have been a delight that yanked my head further out of the darkness that hung over me, and perhaps it would have even stretched on until I was pulling into the parking lot at work. I could see myself remaining in the warmth of my vehicle, minutes passing as we continued to chat away, and I would eventually stroll into work—guiltlessly several minutes late.

The red and blue flashing lights that illuminated behind me rendered all of that null and void, and all I could do was groan:

"I'm getting pulled over."

"So...no, you *aren't* that exceptional of a driver, then," she mocked.

I eyed a shoulder further up the highway in which I could pull over and flicked on my blinker to change lanes.

"Come on, Cas."

"Were you speeding?" she asked, gentler.

"I don't know," I checked my blind spot over my right shoulder. "Maybe."

"Not the best start to a Monday," she sympathetically noted.

I slowly braked. "It was going so well for a minute, there."

Cassie whispered, "Sorry, baby."

Shifting into park, the policeman filed behind me; the reminder that I had been pointedly avoiding people of authority for a reason flared my anxiety, and I was forced to mentally assure myself that I had no visible criminal record as I saw his door crack open.

I sighed, "I gotta go."

"Let me know when you get to work?"

I watched the man step my way in the rear-view mirror and muttered back, "Uh huh. 'Course. Bye, Cas," and rapidly ended the call.

Cold air hit my face as I rolled my window down. I reached for my wallet that was resting in my center console, and popped the glove compartment open to locate my car's registration. The policeman's steps were audible as he approached. I took a deep breath and righted myself in my seat as I let it out.

The first thing I noticed—aside from the gun holstered at his hip—was his lanky frame. He made no attempt to ease my strain to meet his eye, standing tall with his thumbs hooked into his belt loops, and I had to crane my neck to the point that it slightly ached. Sunlight reflected off the mirrored frames on his face, he cracked a small bubble in the gum he was chewing, and he ordered:

"License and registration."

I nodded, opening my wallet to fish out my driver's license. "Can I ask why you pulled me over?"

The man's head cocked to the side, and the light glinted off of his sunglasses once more, flashing in my eyes and causing me to wince.

After a brief hesitation, he replied, "You were swerving."

"Swerving, really?" I returned. "When?"

His head moved once more. I flinched when the bright reflection caught me for a second time, and he asked, "You alright there, son?"

I was unsure as to why he was calling me *son,* as he only looked to be around forty years old, but I said nothing on that line of thought.

"Fine," I returned, pointing at his face. "Your glasses are catching the light." I extended a hand with what he had requested. "Here."

He took them from me but remained where he was, lifting his glasses away from his eyes. They sat atop his dark hair, the visible crispness of the gel in his short cut holding them upright. His gaze was skeptical as he squinted at me.

"You have anything to drink this morning?"

I was unable to hold back my disbelieving scoff. "As in alcohol?"

"Yes."

"It's not even eight in the morning, and I'm on my way to work," I noted.

"I'd appreciate it if you answered the question."

"No," I stated as quickly as I could. "Not at all."

His jaw worked on his gum. "Step out of the vehicle for me."

I blinked several times in succession. "Why?"

"Quick field sobriety test."

I've always been staunchly under the impression that field sobriety tests can easily be failed. Trip on a rock while walking heel-to-toe? *Fail.* Wobble while trying to balance on one leg? *Fail.* The policeman thinks you could be under the influence regardless of the fact that you've passed everything they've thrown your way? *Remarkably, fail.*

"Respectfully," I nearly cut him off, "no."

"No?" he asked.

"I'd like to not be subjected to a field test," I stated. "Breathalyze me. I'll blow zeros."

He exhaled loudly. "Big guy, I don't have a breathalyzer. My portable one's on the fritz. If you're telling me that you'd like to deny a field test, I'm bringing you in under the suspicion that you're intoxicated."

The officer handed my items back to me, and I quickly stowed them in the center console.

Despite my nervousness at his presence, I shook my head and immediately unbuckled my seatbelt. "Then bring me in. Test me there. I'm telling you, I'm not drunk."

Snagging my phone from the holder on the dash, I placed it in my pocket along with my wallet that I had left in my lap. I turned my car off, pocketing the keys as well, and when I reached for the door handle, the policeman chastised:

"Slowly."

I mumbled, "Okay, slowly, got it," as I stepped out.

"Face away from me, hands on the vehicle."

My eyebrows shot up. "For what? Are you patting me down?"

"Protocol, son, turn around."

The man then held up an index finger, twirling it in a circular motion.

I obeyed his request, but as I placed my palms on my car's roof, I quietly noted, "This doesn't feel like protocol."

His hands tapped along my ribcage and down to my waist.

"I'm assuring you aren't armed."

"I'm not," I replied insistently. A sharp pinching sensation on my right glute where his hand met my slacks made me whisper, *"Ow."*

"Apologies," he muttered, though it wasn't sincere in the least. "Spread your legs."

I did as I was told. He continued down either one of my legs, and once he seemed to be finished, I asked, "All good?"

"Set," he replied. "Hands behind your back."

"Hands behind my—why?" The clinking of metal sounded behind me, and realization snapped into place. *"Am I being arrested?"*

He reached for my right wrist, pinned it behind me, and made for my left. Either out of shock or compliance, I allowed him to do so.

"Yes," he said. "You're being arrested for being under the influence while operating a vehic—"

"You haven't tested me at *all*," I argued.

The handcuffs encompassed my wrists with a series of metallic *clacks*.

"You refused the field sobriety," he reminded me.

"Isn't that voluntary by law?"

He guided me by the upper arm toward his car. "It is. However, you were swerving before I pulled you over, you appeared impaired when I approached, and I can smell alcohol on your breath."

"I—*Jesus*, okay—one, I don't know when I could've been swerving. I was just talking on the phone. *On Bluetooth*, on my phone. My eyes were on the road. I didn't swerve."

The man tugged me along, and my steps faltered as my shoes scuffed a rock that was frozen to the ground.

"Watch your step."

"Two," I continued to plead my case, "I don't know how I seemed *impaired*, but the only thing bothering me was your sunglasses blinding me, and three," I powered on as he opened the rear driver's side door, "there's no way you can smell liquor on me. I haven't had a drop today."

He ignored me, placing a hand on the back of my head and saying, "Mind the door," as he ushered me to my seat.

I did nothing to fight him as I sat. The door was shut for me, I grumbled as I recognized a dull ache in my right leg, and I stretched it as much as I could to no avail. The moment the police officer returned to his own seat, I asked:

"What's your name?"

"Officer Dowler."

"First name?" I clarified.

"Randy."

We began to move after he fastened his seat belt.

"Officer Randy Dowler," I repeated his full name to myself in an attempt to sear it in my memory, "Is this when I'm told I have the right to an attorney?"

His eyes flashed to the rear-view mirror. "You're not getting brought in for questioning."

"But I do have the right?"

He watched me carefully, as if he were biding his time. "Yes."

It was then that I stopped talking. I assumed that we would arrive at the station, my belongings would be held for safekeeping, I would be offered a phone call or two, get tested for drugs or alcohol, and be subsequently released.

I'd be late for work and cite having car trouble rather than going into the full story. I'd spend my free time during the day researching knowledgeable lawyers to seek legal action and report the fuck out of *Randy Dowler* because this felt like a massive abuse of power.

I pondered who I would call—whose phone number I had memorized. How long it would potentially take for me to get through this so I could return back to my car and go on with my day.

Officer Dowler performed a U-turn.

My feet began to tingle, and I internally cursed the hard seats and lack of space.

He peeked at me through his mirror.

Other thoughts in my mind muddled together, and eventually faded away when I realized that we were now headed away from the city.

He peeked at me through his mirror.

The tingle spread up my legs and to my hands.

He peeked at me through his mirror.

My limbs went heavy.

He peeked at me through his mirror.

My head nodded down to my chest.

Darkness took me.

Chapter 19

Cassie

Zoey sat across from me at the circular kitchen table in my brother's apartment, having woken so recently that she hadn't even tamed her hair. The short strands were sticking every which way, signifying that she had either had restless sleep, reckless sex, or both…and because I didn't care to vomit first thing in the morning, I assumed the former. Her green eyes were trained on a laptop before her, the screen reflecting through the thick-framed glasses that she always wore when she had yet to put in her contacts. The image was indiscernible in her lenses, but her unbothered expression showed that she was far from worried.

Ready to bustle out the door, Liam strode his way over to her with a large, black mug in hand. He set it to the right of the computer, and Zoey glanced to it, up to him, and back to the mug, stretching her neck to inspect its contents.

Clearly realizing that it was intended for her, she gave him a small smile. "Thank you."

He smiled back. "Mhm."

"You have to go?" she asked.

Liam nodded, taking two steps away from us toward his couch. His over-the-shoulder bag was resting on the floor, packed and ready, and he lugged the strap over his head. It appeared to be heavy, biting into his grey hoodie and bunching the fabric, and I wondered if he had managed to fit in a textbook or two so he could do some last-minute cramming for his exam.

He looked between the two of us with a crease between his thick brows, and he pursed his lips before he hesitantly remarked:

"You two are staying here?"

I spoke to Zoey, "We went over this, yes?"

She glanced to me with the slightest of amusement in her eyes. "That we did."

Liam sighed heavily. "Fuck me for being worried, right?"

Zoey's gaze softened as she took in his obvious concern. "We'll be here. The door will be locked. The chain that we added," she gestured toward the door, which had a shiny, new, gold chain lock affixed, "will be slid closed."

"You have work, right?" he pressed.

Zoey was employed at a local boutique, *Zest*. Her schedules were irregular, varying in day and time depending on the remainder of the staff, and it never seemed like she minded...she was only thankful for a decently paying job. On top of that, it was located only a short walk down the street, and considering that she no longer owned a car—hers was totaled in a car crash several months back, and she never shopped for a replacement—her lack of a commute most likely far out-weighed the con of an abnormal schedule.

"At noon," she confirmed.

"'Kay." He focused on the ceiling as he mumbled to himself, "Ten o'clock test—an hour...hour and a half for time—fifteen minutes to drive back—"

"Lee," she assuaged, "just go take your test. We'll be fine."

"What if," he replied slowly, "I have the flu."

"Liam."

He held up an index finger. "Hear me out."

"How long are you gonna *have the flu* for?" she retorted.

"I dunno! A—a few days? A week?"

"And what good will that do?" Zoey questioned, lifting her mug to her mouth.

I replicated her motions, reaching for my own. It was nearly empty by now, as I was the one who made the coffee and I had poured myself a cup the moment it was brewed. I had to tilt it significantly to take a sip.

"I just..." His shoulders sagged as his eyes bounced between us. "I'd feel better if I were here."

The way he said it swung my mind to James, for he had echoed the sentiment to me several times when we addressed going back to reality. Well...truthfully, my mind didn't need to be *swung* to him—he had been there for a while, and there was no getting him out. Not when all I could imagine was him on his knees. His beard scratching the insides of my thighs. Him holding me upright as I crashed down to Earth. Me drinking in the haze of pleasure on his face while I rode him in his bed.

There were plenty of our sexual encounters that permanently resided in my thoughts, but naturally, it wasn't all that I envisioned when it came to James. I pictured his smile. His genuine care for those he was close with that radiated beyond his sarcasm and sass. Him telling me that I was *strong*, and the conversation that led to it. The way his hair was *just* long enough to escape the space behind his ears, how he always tucks away the left side before the right, and the smattering of grey that I've been debating teasing him about. I see his eyelids fluttering shut momentarily whenever I place my hand on his chest, feel his pulse tickle my palm, and recognize that mine replicates it.

My heart flickered as I thought of him, and I pondered the possibility of his doing the same at this exact moment. As if we were tied together. It felt that way, anyway, and there were moments when the tether would tug. It yanked at me now, and instead of resisting the pull, I was leaning into it—seeking out the intimacy between us that I rapidly deemed of paramount importance—*happily falling*.

I swallowed my coffee, pressed my lips together to hide the inappropriate smile that fought to escape me, set the ceramic to the counter, and pulled myself back to the conversation at hand.

"We're not in..." Zoey considered her words. "In imminent danger or anything here, Lee."

"Sure as hell feels like it," he muttered with his hands on his hips as he looked to the floor.

"I know," she said. "I get it."

"I'd be more comfortable if we knew more," he explained as he glanced to her. "That's all."

"Well, we don't," Zoey replied bluntly, but she softened it with an uncharacteristically gentle tone. "There's nothing on this computer. A few texts from Mister Milkovich asking for rent...some from an unknown contact saying to call them back..." She squinted at the screen as she appeared to scroll downward. "A handful from someone labeled as *R* who seemed..." she slowly scrolled once more. "Sick of his shit. Lots of *stop being stupid* and *what is wrong with you* with vague responses back. Ended up with him just asking where the hell he is once or twice per day, and then the messages stopped." She huffed out a breath. "I'm assuming loads of messages were deleted...I can't follow anything. My eyes are bleeding from staring at this goddamn screen." Zoey touched a dainty finger to the top of the laptop and flicked it shut. "You *do* realize that this may not be something that's able to be figured out...right? Shit goes unsolved all the time in life. Sometimes things just...*happen.*"

"I don't wanna believe that, Zo'," he muttered in a grave tone. "What about your friend?" he asked me. "Tell her more and get her down here so she can talk to Colt, and we can connect some dots. Let's fuckin' bury this shit—I'm goin' insane here."

My chest twisted at the desperate look on his face.

"That was the plan," I admitted. "Tell her a little more. Tell her we're getting our ducks in a row, and she can talk to the police since she knew the other dancers more than I did. *All that.* She won't answer her phone. Texts are few and far between. It's—" I paused. "This isn't a conversation I can just shoot over via text. Imagine if, *God forbid,* her phone gets in the wrong hands. I'm trying. *Trust me,* I am."

He rubbed at his eyes, groaning, "I know you are."

"You're going to be late," Zoey told him.

"Okay," Liam sighed and looked to me. "If I'm not back by the time Zo' leaves for work, go hang out with Luke and Claire upstairs."

"I know the drill," I replied. *"Go."*

He nodded, seemingly appeased though still far from thrilled, and walked to stand before Zoey. She angled her head up to him, giving him an altogether casual smile.

"Good luck on your test, Sweets."

The endearment that they used for each other that was so rarely publicly spoken seemed to soften him, if only slightly. Reaching for her face, he gently pushed her glasses to sit atop her head and leaned down to kiss her. Closed-mouthed and sweet, the first was less than brief, and I trained my eyes on my mug in an attempt to offer them a semblance of privacy. Their lips smacked not once—not twice—but three times, and I easily ignored the sounds because they were rather quiet. What I couldn't allow to bypass, however, was my brother's deep, *"Mmm."*

I felt my mouth contort into a grimace at the noise.

"You're going to be la-ate," Zoey said again, singing the last word softly.

He replied in a husky, *"I could be later."*

She began to chuckle, and I deadpanned:

"Y'know, this is why I'm staying with Jay rather than you guys, right?"

I looked up once again to see them slowly separating, Zoey with a smile that lacked a granule of regret and Liam with the mildly perturbed look of a man interrupted.

"I thought you said you wanted to make sure you had *privacy?*" he asked.

"I didn't say there was only one reason I'm staying across the hall," I retorted.

2A also offered freshly cooked meals, plentiful orgasms, and grey eyes that made my brain seize forward motion.

With a heavy roll of his eyes, he grumbled, *"Yeah, yeah-yeah."* Liam didn't question my reasoning any further. He looked down to Zoey, let the hand that had lingered on the nape of her neck fall away, and murmured, "Later, Sweets."

I watched her watch him leave. Watched her smile softly to herself as the deadbolt locked from the outside. Zoey then took a long sip from her coffee, set it down on the table with care, and looked to be savoring the taste before she grinned at me.

"So," she spoke, "are we gonna talk about it?"

There were several things that I loved about Zoey—one of them was her bluntness.

"*Ah.* There are several *its*. Which one are you referring to?" I lightheartedly asked. "My previous employment, the reasoning for my leaving said employment, my brother's reaction to both, or the whole clusterfuck?"

She laughed, her glasses slid down her nose, and she pushed them up with an index finger.

"Well, I figured you've had enough of that," she quipped. "But since you mentioned it, you're...*good*...right?"

Her brow furrowed as she questioned me, and I saw the concern flaring in her eyes as she waited for my response.

"*Good* is a weird way to put it," I offhandedly replied.

"You know what I mean," she mumbled, "and you know that I'm never all," Zoey's naturally high voice hitched even higher, "'*Ooo, girlfriend, tell me all the feels.*'"

I snorted at the insinuation. Anyone of reasonably sound mind would realize that Zoey was, if anything, quietly empathetic. While it was clear that she felt deeply for the ones she cared for, she wasn't one to scream her feelings from a rooftop...nor was she regularly offering to be a shoulder to cry on. She simply cared—and she only spoke of it when she felt it was needed, which weighted her words all the more.

"I'm well aware of that," I said softly.

She gave me the smallest of smiles. "Just making sure you're not...I don't know...having a silent mental breakdown? This has been *really* heavy."

I assured her, "I'm alright, Zo'. We don't need to talk about it, really."

Zoey's head bobbed up and down, she hesitated for but a second, and her smile grew into a wry, wide one.

"Are you saying that because of whoever was on the phone earlier? *Baby?*"

Now, I'm never caught off guard. I swear, I'm not. But her oh-so-casual mention of the term that I've started using for James threw me for a goddamn loop—I had no idea that she would be able to hear me while I spoke with him on the phone earlier, even if she were awake.

I sucked in a sharp breath. Air stung the whites of my eyes. I was entirely unable to pull my gaze from hers as I rapidly inquired:

"Come again?"

Zoey brought her mug to her mouth, her eyes dancing above the lip as she drank, and she was barely able to swallow before she asked:

"Is that what *baby* tells you to do? *Come again?*"

Words left me. I could have said *anything*. Potential answers rushed me in a flurry—*yes, no,* or *it's none of your business* seemed too little of a response. *I'm abstinent* was too much of a lie, and would have caused her to burst into laughter. *Uh huh, and it's James' hands, face, and cock that I've come on—repeatedly* was just...too much of a slap in the face of unknown information. So, unfortunately, all that I could manage was a near-vibrating:

"*Um...*"

Zoey gave me a knowing look. "You used to strip, Cassie—*this* you get flustered over?"

I cleared my throat. "Liam didn't, ah...he didn't hear anything, did he?"

"*Oh...*no-no, he was asleep," she muttered, clearly thinking that my concern was only regarding my brother overhearing me. "But...for the record, I'm a *very* good secret keeper." I let out an incredulous laugh, and she retorted, "What? I am. I'm actually the best one in this whole damn town—*don't tell your secrets to Claire.*" She pointed at me with purpose from across the table. "Her and Luke practically share a brain. Love her, but she's a gossip."

It wasn't that I was uncomfortable speaking with Zoey about my romantic life. On the contrary, it would be a sisterly bonding that I believed I would enjoy. The subject of my romantic endeavors, however, caused unease to wriggle under my skin because...well...she had dated him. It was months ago, I wasn't there to witness it, and from what I had heard, it was over quite quickly...but she still had dated James. And fact aside that I knew she was in love with my brother—fact aside that I had never seen her so much as glance in James' direction in a suggestive manner—I still questioned how she would react about us.

"Ah," I hesitated. "It's new."

While true, it didn't *feel* new. It was unfathomable to me that the first time the energy had significantly shifted between me and James—when I had started to give him a dance at Gas Lamp—was only just over a week ago. Our first kiss was this past Thursday, along with the fighting concepts of forgetting our feelings and irrelevancy. Irrelevancy quickly won. We slept in each other's beds two times each. And, now, it was Monday.

It was a shockingly small amount of time considering the intensity of our relationship. And, *sure,* James was no stranger to me before. He was far from it, but that didn't mean that what had grown between us hadn't gone off like a goddamn bomb.

"New, huh?" Zoey waggled her perfectly manicured brows, and then dramatically whispered, *"Is the sex good?"*

It would have been hilarious otherwise. If she weren't unknowingly asking about James, I would have laughed loudly—perhaps I even would have proudly replied *yes*. But because of the hidden nature of the circumstances, my face went hot, and I found myself tearing my eyes from hers to look at the large clock on my right that hung on the wall. The vintage blue, almost rustic design of the analog had two arms pointing nearly in the same direction—one approaching *9* and the other approaching *10*. And I had known that it was around 9:45 in the morning...but there was something about the combination of the visible reminder, Zoey's asking who *baby* was, and the realization that my phone hadn't made a peep in over two hours that made me question the time.

"Sorry, sorry," Zoey trilled. "I'm a sucker for details...but I *will* say that you're blushing."

Her mention of my flushed cheeks was barely even heard. My eyes narrowed at the wall as the gears cranked in my mind, and I picked up my phone, which had been purposefully resting face down on the table beside me.

There were no new notifications.

"Which either means yes...or you haven't done it yet." She continued her interrogation. "And you've definitely done it."

I knew what she said—*I did*—but my brain had yet to register it. I rapidly typed to James:

Today 9:42 A.M.

> You make it to work? x.

I watched it send, set it down, and then looked back to Zoey. "Huh?"

She squinted, halting only God knows what her next words were, and her tone deepened as she asked, "What's wrong?"

"Nothing, I—"

My phone buzzed, and I let out a sigh as I read:

Yes.

Blinking several times in succession as foolish relief flooded me, I mumbled to Zoey, "Sorry, one sec," as I messaged back:

> Did you get a ticket when you got pulled over?

An ellipsis insinuating that he was typing appeared below my message immediately, and it was replaced with:

No.

My fingers danced across the screen.

> Good. Have a good day. x.

Zoey's inquiries from before suddenly came forth in my mind, and with my phone still secured in my hand, I looked back to her and scoffed.

"Wait...were you asking me if I'm currently sexually active?"

Zoey shrugged. "Before you looked like someone kicked your puppy, I was—you good?"

"Fine," I replied. "Was just expecting someone."

"Baby?" she asked with a large smile, and I sucked on the inside of my cheek to withhold my smirk. Her green eyes glowed. "So, it's a secret, then?"

"Maybe."

Zoey chipperly replied, "I won't make ya tell me, I won't...*wait, is it Garrett?"*

I chortled at her reference to the bartender. *"No,* it's not Garrett. The poor guy smiles at me one time, and you all think that he's ready to jump my bones. I wasn't into him anyway."

She laughed. "Ah, you were into *baby,* instead?"

"Something like that," I uttered.

My phone vibrated in my hand, and I looked to it to see the preview of his message:

A single thumbs up emoji.

I unlocked my phone once more to see our text message exchange, and once I truly took in his responses, I felt my insides twist because it just felt...off. I reminded myself that I really didn't *know* his style of text communication. In fact, it seemed more likely for him to respond to a text message with a quickly returned phone call...and I assumed that this was the case because of how verbose the man is.

Therefore, he could simply be a bad texter.

I won't lie, it was amusing to liken him to an older individual who didn't understand how to appropriately respond to someone via text. Hilarious to place the future joke of me calling him a *boomer* in my back pocket. However, the more that I read over the messages, the more I felt an intuitive nervousness.

There was no text or call after he was sent on his way by the cop.

No returned *x* in his replies.

No further explanation.

Just blunt, to-the-point information.

And that was *fine.* That aside, the urge to confirm what I already knew was biting at my heels.

> You're leaving work around 5?

I followed it up quickly with:

> Should I cook for you tonight, instead?

> I hate to brag, but I'm great at following the instructions to boxed mac and cheese…and there's a brand new box sitting in your pantry.

The ellipsis that I had anticipated was flashing the moment that I had sent the first message, and by the time the last was sent, his responses came through:

> Have to work late. Sorry.

> Come over another night.

Come over another night.

Come over another night?

I rotated my shoulders back as my spine straightened, but they did nothing to aid the tension that gathered in my muscles as I read it time and again.

Come. Over. Another. Night.

Not *I'll let you know when I'm on my way.* Not even a perturbed *I'm busy, Cas. See you at home tonight.* The message insinuated that we weren't currently sharing a living space…and I can't say *why*—perhaps it was the strange, instinctual thrum in my veins—but I found myself focusing on the icon of his contact located just above our messages. My attention on the grey circle that had defaulted to his initials, *JT,* made me think back to James' instructive explanation that he had given me. After tentatively using phrases such as, *'I have a...request,'* along with, *'I'm not saying I'd like it if you did, but you can say no,'* and, *'This doesn't mean that I don't think you can take care of yourself,'* he had asked if I would share my phone's location with him.

His light eyes were pleading, and upon considering the positives that would go along with him being able to see where I was at a moment's notice, I obliged. Because I had never used the feature before, James had happily showed me the process by sharing his own cell's location with me, simpering with a large grin that it was, *'tit for tat,'* and I could now, *'watch his every move,'* if I so desired.

I did the same now as I did then, tapping on the *JT*. Days ago, I had seen his contact information listed above a map, and the grey icon that signified James himself appeared as a single dot on the picture—exactly where I knew my house was located.

I didn't see that now.

I didn't see a map at all.

The contact information that I had anticipated was shown, but the rest of the page was blank—as if I had never been able to see his location in the first place.

I muttered, "What the fuck?"

"Okay, seriously," Zoey pressed. "What's up?"

My unease rapidly progressed from foolish to anticipatory anxiety, and I assumed that it was audible within my voice as I said:

"I—I'm ignoring you. I know. I'm sorry—just give me a—"

Zoey cut me off, rambling, "Yeah, that's my point. You're not the type to ignore, and not once have I seen you focus more on your phone than the people around you. I'm not *offended*. You look jittery as fuck, and considering everything, it's making *me* jittery as fuck." She leaned forward with purpose. *"What's up, Cassie?"*

I took exactly two cleansing breaths, attempting to mentally assure myself that I was overreacting because...people get distracted. Texts can be misconstrued. Technology can be unreliable—and certainly *that* was why the little map with a grey *JT* was no longer appearing. The half of my internal monologue that was demanding me to be *reasonable* repeated those three sentences over and again.

But the dreadful sensation was nagging at me. The reality that we were living in where we were unsure of our collective safety—where we didn't know answers—where we didn't know who was a potential threat—had already fried my nerves. Anything outside of the usual status quo was beginning to make my hair stand on end. The nape of my neck prickled in such a way that I shivered, and Zoey ushered me:

"Cassie!"

"It's...dumb," I told her. "I'm just on edge."

Her head cocked to the side in confusion. "Is it your friend?"

"Hmm?"

"Skylar?" she clarified.

"Oh," I replied. "No, she said she's still dealing with her family stuff—not even going to work."

My words went quieter as I spoke. Zoey nodded though her concerned, questioning gaze remained, and a jolt ran through me as the mention of Skylar's name reminded me of something I had said mere minutes ago:

Imagine if, God forbid, her phone gets in the wrong hands.

Without a further thought, I quickly refocused on my phone and typed:

> I'll stay at my place tonight, then?

James' response would be telling. If he were perfectly fine and simply distracted, his typical anxiety would rear its head, and there could only be a few expected replies. One anticipated reaction would be an immediate phone call reminding me to stay at 2B or upstairs with Luke and

Claire. The others were a variation of text messages along the lines of:

What? No.

Are you insane?

Stay the fuck put.

His brief aggravation, which always ran parallel with his protectiveness, would calm me. I would explain my last message away with all the honesty I had, saying that his uncharacteristic curtness had made me nervous. That his responses truthfully didn't seem like him. That the wild skyrocketing of my anxiety had caused me to jump to conclusions, and I truthfully considered if it wasn't him on the other end of the line. That I didn't know who that someone would be…and that their reasonings for hiding his location and responding on his behalf were of ill intentions.

James would find my concern endearing, of course. When he would return home tonight, he'd look at me how he always does when I speak or show my affection for him—with hearts in his eyes that made mine skip a beat. That was what I told myself while I was waiting for the message in reply to my testing one, anyway.

The wait had me nearly hovering in my seat, and the moment that I felt the buzz in my hand, I read:

> Yeah, I'll be beat tonight. I'll hit you up later.

The only thing that came to my mind was the indisputable fact that whoever *this* was...was *not* James. And if we were under normal circumstances, the notion wouldn't have caused my skin to crawl, my pulse to rise, and my hand to drop my phone to the table with a dull clatter.

I stood quickly enough for Zoey to alarmingly exclaim, *"Whoa!"* Her vibrant eyes were on me, wider and more inquisitive than ever, and she shot to her feet with me. She watched as I raced to the left—to the kitchen island. I snagged my keys off the marble, and they clinked together madly as Zoey asked, "What's going on?!"

I rapidly told her, "I'm going for a drive."

If I were being honest, I assumed that she would argue my announcement—that she would try to stop me or demand answers to her questions. My assumption was proved wrong when I looked at her, she saw whatever damning expression was on my face, and she immediately responded in an act of ardent solidarity:

"I'm going with you. *Where are we going?*"

Chapter 20

Cassie

Zoey followed me expeditiously. There was no hesitation in her quick steps as she grabbed whatever she could to protect herself from the cold. She sat beside me now in the passenger seat of my vehicle—silent, alert eyes behind her glasses peering every which way as I pulled out of my parking spot on the street. One of Liam's sweatshirts haphazardly pulled over her head and draping down to her mid-thigh, the black fabric offset with the winter pallor of her skin, and at first glance, she looked small—pale—meek.

However, on par with all things Zoey, she was anything but, for her presence was large.

All I had managed to say before she rushed out the door with me was, "Talk about it in my car?" and because we had said nothing since, she had close to no details on the source of my nervousness. Not knowing where we were going or why and racing alongside me, her appearance of meekness was a falsity. Her silence was a choice. A bold one that solidified what I already knew about Zoey and encapsulated the definition of *ride or die.*

I glanced her way as I turned onto the main road and headed for the highway, her focus locked on me, and though I knew that *now* was the time to explain my panic away, the words were caught in my throat. One would imagine that my inability to speak on the subject was due to my hesitance to admit my relationship with James, but that concern was long gone. I just...didn't know where to start. *How* to start. And when I had realized that Zoey was adamantly sticking with me, I knew that I would have to confess it all. It was...unideal, to say the least, but I had thought that if it were up to me, I could manage to do so delicately.

The thought of anything *delicate* was impossible now, and all I could do was cut to the chase.

"I'm gonna tell you something that's gonna feel like the main part of this story," I admitted rapidly. "I mean, I fucking *wish* that it were the main part of this story, but it's not—it's background information that you'd end up getting anyway with all the bullshit that's happening, and I..." My words began to meld together. "I want to be-straight-with-you, and it feels weird to have you grasping at straws about why I'm so goddamn nervous, how-I-know-certain-things, and where-we're-going-and-why—"

"Cassie, whatever it is, *I'm fine,*" Zoey interjected sharply. "Stop being so considerate of my feelings and just spit it out."

"Try not to react or—or focus on it 'cause it's not important." I rephrased, "I mean, it's important—*it is.* It's just not important *right now*—"

Zoey exclaimed, "For the love of—*spit,* Cas!"

"Me and Jay have been seeing each other."

Her eyebrows shot up above the rim of her glasses. "Seeing each other as in..." My hesitation to answer made her squeak an alarmingly high-pitched, *"Oh* my GOD!"

"Zoey."

She smacked a hand over her mouth. "Not reacting—totally not reacting."

Due to the circumstances of the anxious undercurrent surrounding us, I would have thought that her tone being downright muffled glee would have been impossible. She let her fingers fall away from her face, delicately placing them in her lap, and I realized I was wrong as she seemed to be struggling to contain a large smile.

And, yes, I did feel as though we were on the precipice of...*something*. But because I couldn't tell what exactly that *something* was and there was no tangible proof for the reason of my nervousness, I allowed myself to ask:

"I'm sorry, are you...*happy?*"

Zoey looked at me hesitantly. "I'm allowed to react?"

I shrugged. "For a second, I guess. 'Cause I don't want this to be weird and—"

"Not weird," she immediately replied with a rapid shake of her head. "Not even a little weird. I—*yes,* happy, good, great. This is a secret at the moment?"

I nodded, letting out a sigh that conveyed the weight of her approval leaving my shoulders. *"Liam,"* I spoke my brother's name with no other explanation for I didn't think it was needed.

"Oh, *him,"* she remarked. "Yeah, I'll have to buy *him* a casket once you tell him, but I'll cross that bridge when I get to it. *I'm* great. I...have about forty thousand questions for you, and we *will* circle back to those when it feels like shit isn't in the process of hitting the fan." She paused to blow out a quick breath through her mouth, and asked more seriously, "Main part of the story?"

I exhaled, "Thank you."

She waved a hand in the air as if to say, *'Nothing of it—go on.'*

I told her, "Something's up with James."

"How so?"

"Well," I began, "we talked on the phone this morning after he left, right?"

Zoey appeared to be biting the inside of her lower lip. "I have connected that puzzle piece, yes."

"And he was fine." I eyed the road ahead, knowing it would be the start of James' commute to work, and got in the right-hand lane in preparation to turn. My blinker clicked away as I reiterated, "Totally fine." I turned the wheel, and the clicking ceased. *"Happy."*

"You're making me want to ask all those questions that I said I wouldn't, Cas," Zoey said. "What's the gist?"

"He got pulled over driving into work."

"Señor-rule-follower got pulled over?" she returned with a smirk. "Why?"

I shook my head. "I have no idea 'cause he didn't call me back."

Zoey squinted. *"Kay."*

"So, I texted him, I dunno, two hours later." I grabbed my phone that rested in the cup holder between us and blindly handed it to her. *"Five-two-nine-seven,"* I spoke my password without hesitation. "Look at our messages."

She tapped on the screen several times, swiped down, and chuckled, *"Ha—*when did he *'ducking ditch you,'* exactly? You sound *pissed."*

"That one's old, Zo'," I admonished her referencing my first texts to James when he had rushed out of Henry's with his friend, Brooks. "Scroll to today."

"Not exactly hard. Y'all don't text much," she murmured.

"Don't think Jay's much of a texter," I replied.

Zoey snorted. "Old fart."

I rolled my eyes. "And we've been basically living in the same place since Colt showed up, anyway...there's not much of a point to messagi—"

"I'm sorry, you've been *what?!"*

I snapped, *"Messages, Zoey."*

"Fine, fine." Reading quickly, she scoffed and muttered, "Grumpy old man—*oop*—come over another time?"

"Yuh huh."

"Weird phrasing."

"Exactly," I returned. "That with his short-ass responses...I dunno, it made me nervous, so I checked his location."

Zoey shot me a side-eye. "You have his location?"

"He asked for mine and gave me his."

She clicked her tongue several times. *"Possessive,* Jay."

"He was worried about me," I retorted with more bite than I intended.

Zoey smiled wide. *"Defensive, Cas."*

"Point," I reminded her in a stern tone, "is that I had his location. *Had.* It's gone now. It's not showing up anymore."

Her expression pinched together. "You think he turned it off? Unshared or something?"

"He wouldn't do that," I said confidently. "And no *way* any of those new messages are James. They're too short, they don't make sense considering I'm *living* with him for the time being, and if I told Jay this morning that I was planning on going back to my place instead of his," I let out a sharp, bitter laugh, "he would have *freaked.* I mean, the man's been anxious as *fuck.* All," my voice lowered to imitate him, *"'I need to be around you. I need to know you're okay—'"*

"Stop, *stop!* Specifics later. And I really mean that—if you don't give me details, I will *perish,* Cassie." She paused and then clarified, "Your point is that he wouldn't be like, *'Oh, sure, stay at your place! Deuces.'"*

"Well, I don't think Jay would ever say *deuces* in place of *goodbye,* but yes." I sighed loudly. "That was my point."

Zoey questioned slowly, "Maybe...a friend from work got ahold of his phone?"

"And decided to turn off his GPS, text me to say that I shouldn't come over tonight, and that I should just stay at my house?" I frustratedly threw a hand up only for it to fall back to the wheel. *"Why?* Why would *anyone* do that?"

"Okay, ah...what are you getting at, here?" Zoey asked hesitantly.

"I don't know," I whispered. "Just have a bad feeling."

"Well, where are we going?"

"I don't—I—I'm retracing steps, I guess? He was on his way to work, obviously."

"Right...one sec."

Zoey placed my cell back in the cup holder and retrieved her own from the front pocket of Liam's black hoodie. Her fingers tapped away, and just as she was lifting the phone to her ear, I asked:

"What are you doing?"

"Covering all bases," she said quickly before she spoke into her phone, "Hey, Claire. Quick question. No context. Have you heard from Jay this morning?" I caught her eye as she admonished, "I said *no context*—'kay. What about Luke?" She listened to Claire's response, and then abruptly trilled, "Mmkay, cool, thanks, bye!"

Claire yelled through the speaker, "Zoey, *wait!* Why—" but it was cut off by Zoey immediately ending the call.

"You hung up on her," I noted.

"She'll forgive me," Zoey returned. "No one needs her digging for details right now—she said no, by the way."

I had already assumed that was the case. I mumbled back, "Thanks for that."

"Mhm," she offhandedly hummed. "What are your thoughts, exactly?"

"Best case scenario...I guess I find him safe at his work because a fuckin' class clown of a coworker took his phone?" I murmured, "As much as I want that outcome and know that I shouldn't cause an act of violence at his work, I swear to *God,* I'll punch whatever fucker thought this was funny."

"Atta girl," Zoey mumbled.

"Hold me back, for Jay's sake?" I asked.

She chortled, "I can *try,* but that may be on him."

I looked over to give her the smallest of bitter smiles, she returned it, and I continued, *"Worst* case scenario..."

My words were cut short when I focused ahead once more, and I saw James' grey sedan on the side of the road. There was nothing peculiar about it—no trails of spinning tire tracks or skidding steps through the muddy snow that had almost completely melted. Only his car, and nothing else.

My thoughts just...stopped.

I heard Zoey call to me as I let off the gas. Recognized the profanity that fell from her mouth as I firmly depressed the brake. I didn't have the headspace to respond while I quickly turned the wheel to pull up behind his vehicle, though. I barely had the chance to shift into park before my seatbelt was off, I swung my door open so hard that I heard the hinges complain and rattle, and I was running.

There was nowhere to go, really.

It was seven frantic steps until I reached James' car, parked neatly on the shoulder. I stood beside it, my breath running through me heavy as I saw all there was to see—an abandoned vehicle on the side of the highway. I vaguely heard myself muttering, *"No, no, no,"* as I peered into the driver's side window that had been left open.

It was clean on the inside, as I already knew it was. A holster for his phone that was affixed to his dash was empty. The back seat was barren. The front seat held only his work briefcase. There were no clues. No tells. Just a horrid realization that I may have been right.

"Cassie?" Zoey nervously spoke my name as she approached.

My breaths went shallow. "I...um...I don't...I don't understand."

"Maybe he had car trouble?" she offered gently. "After he got pulled over by the cop, I mean." Zoey squatted down. "Are the tires fine? They seem fine."

My head whipped left and right, and I pointed toward the ground behind his car. Though it hadn't appeared that his pulling over into the mud was out of emergency and there was indeed no sign of what one would deem a struggle, there were other indentations in the earth.

"Tire tracks."

Zoey followed where my hand gestured with her eyes—over the impressions that the thread's groove made—and there was no arguing where the vehicle had gone. It appeared that it had pulled up behind James' car just as mine had and then drove back onto the road. What may have been footprints were scattered about, but because neither of us were detectives by any means, there was no telling who they belonged to, which occurred first, or where they were going and why.

"Um," Zoey thought aloud, "the tracks could be old? Or—or from an Uber or something, if he had to catch a ride to get to work?"

I shook my head, for there was just...no way. There was no. Goddamn. *Way.* That the outcome of all of this was that simple—that he was pulled over, had car trouble shortly thereafter, just so happened to forego contacting me while we felt like we were on the precipice of a crisis, and then had his phone confiscated by God knows who...who was sending me messages that were so unlike James.

Yeah—*no goddamn way* was an understatement at this point, and it was all I could do to grunt some sort of dissatisfied noise in Zoey's direction before I spun and began to stomp back to my Jeep.

"Cassie!" Zoey exclaimed. "What are you—"

"Car!" I yelled over my shoulder. *"Now!"*

Her steps scurried behind me, and we were both barely planted into our seats when I hit the gas. Zoey's hands splayed on the window and center console to secure herself as we returned to the highway, and once we were free of the mud, gravel, and rock from the side of the road, she reached for her seatbelt. I did the same, and without any provocation, I spoke my thoughts aloud regarding her assumption that the tire tracks could have been from a ride service:

"He could have called me—I could have driven him to work."

"And pull you away from the apartment?" she countered. "We'd ask why. Lee would've been weird about you leaving alone—"

"Yeah, yeah, right—Jay, too…but if not me, then Luke, right?" I added, "And Claire hasn't heard from him. *Luke* hasn't heard from him. None of this makes any fucking *sense!* And…and he would have *told* me. He—he would have called me again. Been like, *'You're not gonna believe this,'* or—or-or, *'M-my morning's gone to shit, Darlin'.'*"

My argument began firm but turned frantic, my vocal cords shaking while I stammered back to her.

"*Okay,* okay, *shhhh,*" Zoey consoled from my right. "Where's your brain goin' here, Cas?"

"I don't—I don't know, but dancers have been disappearing, right? I—he's been to Gas Lamp. He's associated with me…"

I couldn't finish the thought.

"What, you think he's been…like…*taken?*" Zoey disbelievingly replied. I said nothing in response, and she returned with a sigh, "Look, I get that you're worried—I *do.* And I'm with you, this is weird, but…why would that happen?"

I shook my head. "I have no idea, but it—it all feels *wrong.*"

"We…we can't jump to conclusions."

It was said in an assuring manner—as if hearing it would calm me—and while I knew I appreciated the sentiment, I didn't have the ability to absorb the gesture.

I shrieked, "Jump to conclusions?!"

Zoey flinched. *"Easy,* Cas—breathe—"

"All I'm *doing* is jumping to conclusions, Zoey! How the hell can I *not?!*"

"I'm just saying that he could still be at work," she clarified.

"And even though his *goddamn briefcase is in his car,* I'm driving there on the off-fucking-chance that he is," I snapped, "but I'm a *tad bit* concerned about whatever the hell we're supposed to do if he's *not.* Go to the police? Report him missing? Give them almost none of the information we have because otherwise, we may be incriminating ourselves with *fucking murder* since this shit all seems tied together? And then, guess what?" I looked at her with what was most likely a crazed glare, and she appeared to be holding her breath as I remarked, "It's not like they're gonna send out a goddamn search team right away without probable cause of him being in danger!"

Her arms outstretched toward me as if she had the intention to soothe me, but her expression twisted as she appeared torn on what to do, and her limbs hung in the air.

"I know, *I know,"* she spoke, "I—I'm sorry, Cas, I'm freaking out, too, but let's just...stay calm and take this one step at a time."

The suggestion was valid. Reasonable. *Level-headed.*

Unfortunately for Zoey, though, I was not. My lungs were burning. Tears were flooding my vision. My heart was thrumming wildly as if it were trying to escape my chest and pounding in my ears, and my response ripped through my lips in an angry, shrill:

"He could be GONE, Zoey! *Missing!* I don't know what to *do*—I don't know how to *fucking BREATHE* right now!"

Zoey's lips pressed together tightly as she silenced herself. I saw her watching me in my peripheral vision as I rapidly wiped away the evidence of my crying from my cheeks, and she finally offered:

"Do you want me to drive?"

"No." I sniffled, as my nose had gone runny. "Thanks."

"You know where you're going?" she asked.

Though I had never visited James' workplace, I nodded. In a pleasant conversation so recently had on his couch, we had casually discussed his job. I thought back to it now, wishing I could smile as I remembered his hearty chuckle when I joked that the name of the establishment was a mouthful, and I had accused him of making up the title on his own in jest. He hadn't, and he had proven as such by showing the name on a map app in his cell. Identified with an icon of a small briefcase, the text was displayed in its entirety between two parentheses after the label of *Work,* and he had pointed at it with a playful, enthusiastic, *'See?'*

I swallowed through the lump in my throat. "Analytic Integrative Solutions, International LLC. Not far from Gas Lamp...it's off Third Street and Pine, but I've never been. You mind looking it up, just in case?"

She obliged, and there was no further inquisition. No additional attempts to assuage me. It was silent as we drove save for the occasional clearing of my throat, directional instruction from Zoey, or clicking of my turn signal, and after what I knew was ten minutes but felt like far longer, I was pulling into the parking lot outside of his work.

James and I had once spoken about the feeling of existing within a living hell...and I had thought that I was already there. When I had rapidly left 2B with Zoey, my odd, keen sense of anxiety was reminiscent of a premonition—a forewarning that I was desperately trying to shake. But it wasn't then that I considered my presence within a realistic hellscape. It was when I had seen his car, abandoned with no sense of where he had gone, that I had considered, or, rather, *realized,* that I was stuck in the flames.

The visit to his workplace had lasted all of five minutes.

The building was small, grey, and no doubt created for an office space. Windows lined the walls of the single story, darkened with a tint so passersby couldn't see within, and the entrance was clearly visible. The glass door had white lettering on it, but it was illegible from where we were parked.

Zoey and I had marched through the front door, and I found myself taking in the space with an eye of scrutiny.

A white desk was situated directly in front of the door, a large computer monitor resting atop it. To the left was nothing but two doors—one for a women's bathroom and the other for the men's—and on the right, a glass dividing wall that lacked any opacity whatsoever. What appeared to be an area to scan a key fob for entry was directly next to the door handle, and beyond that, I could see straight into what I assumed was a break room. There were two individuals chatting while pouring coffee, and I recognized neither of them.

"How can I help you two?" the woman from behind the desk had asked us.

I didn't recall any of her features—only that she was dressed in a blouse that was colored a vibrant blue. I also couldn't remember our exact response. I knew that I had asked if James Turner was in the office, and Zoey had interjected to state that we were planning to meet him for an early lunch. The woman had squinted at us curiously, and I assumed the reason for that was twofold:

Firstly, it was only just approaching 10:30, and the notion of *lunch* seemed far off.

And secondly, our collective appearance didn't exactly depict that we were ready to publicly sit down for a meal.

Despite that, she had still replied in a chipper tone, "Oh, sorry—James is out today."

Her casual mention of there being a *nasty flu going around* and questioning of whether or not she should *leave a message for him from us* hung in the air until Zoey inevitably responded for me. Her tone was light and offhanded, not a word of her reply was heard by me, and she ushered me back out the door with a hand on my lower back.

As if I had just left an active warzone, I was riddled with tinnitus. I stared forward from the passenger seat while Zoey took the wheel. My cheeks were salt-streaked and wet, and I made no attempt to remedy that. For there was nowhere to run and no clue of direction, the sensation of being trapped swarmed me—buzzing in my ears until my phone began to vibrate loudly within the cup holder between us.

I grabbed it, my limbs moving in slow motion, and squinted curiously at the contact before swiping across the screen and setting it to speaker.

My voice was quiet as I answered, "Colton?"

Zoey's focus snapped to my cell.

"Yes, hello, hi." He replied in what I've learned is his usual sarcastic tone, but it carried an apparent angst. "Are we past the pleasantries?" He didn't wait for me to respond. *"Cool.* We need to talk. Are ya free?"

His obvious urgency woke me from my despondence. "If you know anything about James, then yes."

"James?" he questioned. "What am I supposed to know about James?"

He sounded altogether confused at the mention of his name, and my stomach dropped even further.

"God *dammit,* Colton!" I hissed. "And I thought for a *single second* that you'd be a lifeline—"

Colton pressed again, "What am I supposed to know about James?"

"He's. Fucking. *Missing!"* I yelled. "That's what!"

"What?!" He returned my alarmed decibel. "The fuck do you mean he's *missing?"*

"I mean that I cannot find him," I retorted. "What the hell do you think I mean?"

"Jesus—this isn't productive," Zoey interjected. "Hi, Colt. Long story short, Cas had reasons to believe Jay wasn't at work even though he had texted saying he was. *And* he's not at work. We checked. Found his car on the side of the road—no crash, no *nothing,* just pulled over."

"Oh," he replied. *"Fuck."* Colton hesitated for a moment, and then slowly asked, "I...take it that you haven't been to your previous place of employment to pick up your check?"

I bit back, "Does it sound like that's on the forefront of my mind?"

"No," he quickly responded in a high pitch. "Nope. Not at all, but, ah, *coincidentally*, I was there this morning," he quickly explained, "less crowds, easier to talk, yadda yadda—and *get this*...it's a goddamn ghost town."

I blinked several times over. *"What?"*

"Apparently, there's been somewhat of an exodus."

Zoey and I glanced at each other with wide eyes, and I inquired, "What kind of exodus?"

"Er—of the *mass* variety?" He rephrased with purpose, "A mass. Fucking. Exodus."

"Okay, um—wait," I spoke, "what do you mean?"

"I mean that if ya think the place was understaffed before—which, we *both* know that it was—then you should see it now. Like I said. *Ghosty."* He clarified, "Talked with some staff there—casual shit, right? Dancers are flying out the door since this past weekend...not disappearing—*quitting."* Colton waited for a beat that held a substantial purpose. "I don't...I don't want to say this is related to Jay, but—"

Zoey interjected, "Why do you think shit from Cassie's work would be related to *Jay?*" She narrowed her eyes skeptically. "The hell do you know that we don't?"

Colton groaned as if we were acting oblivious. "I was calling in the first place 'cause the timing of me talking with you guys about all this shit before, combined with a bunch of dancers cutting and running from a place that *pays them to be there,* was coincidental as *fuck.*"

It was my turn to squint, then, and I asked, "What are you saying?"

"I'm saying that it makes me feel like word could have spread...and typically in *big bag guy land,*" he began sardonically, "when news about *big bad guy shit* is spreading around like wildfire, those *big bad guys* aren't terribly appreciative of that." Zoey rolled her eyes at his tone, and my gut twisted as his pitch dropped to one that was grave. "Which, again, is why I called. 'Cause if rumors are being spread or something, this could be—to put it mildly—*very* bad if it gets back to any of us. To me—to you—*to Jay*. Did you—"

"Start rumors?" I cut off his insinuation. "Of course not."

"Even if she did," Zoey remarked, "how would that get back to James?"

A burning sensation similar to acid reflux crept up my throat.

"Jay said he went to Gas Lamp?" Colton inquired.

"Yeah, him and a million other dudes, I'm sure," Zoey noted. "So, he's been to your work—*so what?*"

Colton hummed. "Did he make it obvious that you're together?"

Zoey's focus moved from the road to my phone. "*You* know that they're together?"

My head fell back to the headrest as I griped, "Is that relevant?"

He dismissively answered, "I walked in on them sucking face."

She immediately diverted her attention back to the highway, pressing her lips together tightly as if she were forcing herself to remain silent on the matter.

"And *yes*," Colton said, "it's relevant. If someone thinks you know anything or are spreading word around and *he's* close to *you*..."

"If that were the case, why wouldn't they just take *me?*"

I heard Zoey blow a rough breath through her nostrils, and we all went quiet for a beat.

"Maybe he was just an easier target?" Colton pondered aloud.

As I considered the thought, I forced myself to swallow through the burn. With me being passed around like precious cargo, James had been the only one of us who was isolated...and he most certainly would have been an easier target.

I murmured, "Maybe."

Colton grumbled something unintelligible before saying, "I just...I dunno. I don't know what we're missing, but it's something."

The leather creaked beneath us as both Zoey and I shifted in our seats uncomfortably.

"I can agree with you there," I replied.

"What, um...what are y'all planning on doing? Talk to the cops?"

I sighed heavily, looking to Zoey for a moment as we exchanged expressions that said, *'What the hell else are we supposed to do?'*

"Yeah?" I returned with an upward inflection. "I mean—*yes.* Yes, definitely, I just—Luke doesn't even know yet. I don't know what to tell the police or where to start."

Speaking to me rather than Colton, Zoey reminded me, "From an outsider's perspective, without admitting to a *hell* of a lot, you're, erm—"

"A confused, paranoid girlfriend," Colton cut in. "They're not exactly gonna send out the SWAT team for that. Ya need your ducks organized. I got it." I nodded in agreement, though I knew he couldn't see me, and rather than wait for my response, he asked, "Meet you at 2A or 2B?"

Zoey's brow furrowed. *"What?* Why?"

"Heads together for the ducks, right?" he replied, matter of fact. "I already told y'all—in for a penny, in for a pound. And if my gut's right on this, you may be pointing me in a direction that I *really* want to go. *2A or 2B?"*

"B," I spoke.

"On my way. See you in a bit."

Without an ounce of hesitation, the line cut off.

Chapter 21

James

The skin-on-skin noise of a palm hitting my cheek reached my ears in a quick *tap-tap-tap-tap*. My sight was blurry as I woke, the man before me having no significant features as he continued to usher me awake. My head lolled to the side, and I made no effort to right it in the moment, for my brain was...*heavy.*

Smacking continued on my face in a repetitive sequence of four, and I couldn't have been sure if the man had increased the gumption of his slaps or if I had finally begun to feel them as I came to. The left side of my face stung every time his hand met me. I groaned, and as I tried to cringe away from him, I realized that I was sitting in the corner of a small room.

There was little lighting to speak of—only a single overhead that lacked a fixture. The wiring was exposed behind it, and the bulb burned at my eyes. I swallowed through the dryness in my throat. The man's face was finally in focus as he squatted before me, and I instinctually leaned away from him. I was going to ask where I was—what was going on—what he *wanted* with me—but I didn't get a chance to gather my voice before he gritted out:

"Finally." He stood to his full, lanky stature, and the only thing that I could note about him was that he was dressed in policeman's garb as he stated, "Stay put."

There was no need for him to tell me to remain where I was. My attempt to shift my seat by pushing myself up with my hands was hindered, for I was shackled at the wrist, and the cuffs seemed to be attached to something hard and resistant.

The man turned on his heels to leave, his footsteps a noise that I could only describe as an odd, airy *squish*. I could feel beneath me that the flooring was padded—realized as I tried to sit up straight that the material under my sit-bones had eased the strain on my joints unlike a typical carpet or hardwood—and the slow-cranking gears in my mind struggled to catch up. I grunted, twisting to look at my wrists secured behind my back, and managed to catch a glimpse of the chain links—they were looped through a metal fastening that was screwed into the wall. Metal-on-metal clinked as I observed it, and one would think that *that* was what made profanities leave my mouth in a horrified exhale.

It wasn't—it was the sight of the room as a whole that shook me.

I was situated in the corner of a repurposed closet. Or, at least, that's what I assumed it to be due to the size of the room. My eyes scanned from floor to ceiling, and I saw that the same material that I sat upon spanned along the walls. It was a grey padding. A grey, textured, soundproofing padding that was all too familiar for I had seen it before—only through a camera's lens, but I had seen it nonetheless—and I knew that it was what had covered the ominous room in 2D.

The sight was chilling…and while my breath rattled with quiet curses, my mouth dried even further, and my hands shook within the cuffs, that reaction was nothing compared to when the man returned.

He stood in the doorway, tall, and seeing him jogged my memory to the point that I remembered it all. I recalled him pulling me over, his reasoning for doing so lacking substantiation, the pat down, the pinching in my glute and ache in my thigh, the feeling of handcuffs biting into my skin, and my inevitable drop into unconsciousness in the back of his car. Officer Dowler had sedated me—there was no doubt about that—and now that I had come to, he was eyeing me with purpose...and he wasn't alone.

Like anyone else, I'd experienced déjà vu before, and typically, it's a mildly unsettling sensation—one that makes me slightly shiver and wonder why the moment I was in was so damn familiar. The room alone didn't spring the feeling on me, but seeing her hit me like a freight train. She was the sight that I had seen in my dreams over and again—the one that had rendered me confused and attempting to piece the puzzle of premonition together. The blonde woman had bruises along her left cheek—from the tip of her eye to the bottom of her jaw—and her eyebrow and lip were both split. The injuries were no longer fresh, the blood appearing to have fully dried as it dripped down her face, and the discoloration along the swelling was a nasty purple.

In my dreams, I didn't know her. Of course, I didn't. Otherwise, I wouldn't have questioned her place within them. But the extension of the reality beyond the vision of her face snapped me into quick recognition, and I was choked.

"Skylar?" My voice was hoarse, as I had anticipated it to be.

There was no question that it was her. With slim and sharp features, skin akin to ivory, and dressed head-to-toe in black, she looked just as I remembered her aside from the wounds on her face.

Cringing away from the man as he held her by the upper arm, she spoke in a plea, "What do you *want?* I don't understand, I—"

"I explained this to her," Officer Dowler noted casually, shaking his grip on her. *"Many* times. You know this woman, yes?"

I stammered, "I—um—what—"

"You know her?!" he raised his voice, and Skylar flinched.

It ran through my mind to ask if he was the one that had hurt her—to yell regarding why he would do such a thing—but there was no room for questioning here. The situation that I was thrust into was one in which I was expected to be obedient...and I considered the need to toe the line of obediency and wit. Because I had already spoken her name, I replied:

"Yes. I know her."

"How do you know her?" he asked. I looked at Skylar rather than him. She avoided my gaze, and he admonished, "Don't look at her, *look at me.*"

"Friend," I hesitated. "Friend of a friend."

Officer Dowler appeared to suck on the inside of his cheek. "Right."

Skylar whined, "He doesn't know anything! *I* don't know anything—"

He looked down at her as if he were mildly frustrated. "If you don't know anything, then why the *fuck* are you spreading word about my shit?"

"I don't even know what your stuff *is!*" she cried.

"No." He sardonically spoke, "Of course you don't. You just...*happened* to say enough to scare your little stripper friends into up and quitting." His fingers tightened on her bicep as he pulled her closer, and she shrank downward as he towered above. "And I don't give a shit about that, but do you know how many calls I got about missing women? *Ten.*" His narrowed eyes turned to me. "Ten. All of 'em crying about shit that they heard from a friend named Skylar. That's ten too many, and I don't need other officers questioning my authority and butting in on *my shit.*"

"All I told my friends was that Delaney was gone," Skylar said, her voice strained. "I saw the article, that's all I know—"

"And then *they* saw the one for Taylor," he finished for her as if he had heard the story already. "And Casey. And Melanie. And they were *all* said to have overdosed, and it seemed *so strange.*" Randy's tone warped into an odd, menacing coo upon the last two words, and a shiver rolled down my spine. "Strange because you have such a little *fucking* community, and you knew that *no*—none of them used *drugs.*" He mockingly gasped. "They would *never.* And that made you *nervous.* And *jumpy.* And since ya make so much goddamn money ripping your clothes off, you quit. Seems like your friends quit, too. And *then*...I saw in your phone that someone had sent you that article about Delaney around about the same time as a phone call to the same contact...after that, you spam-called about fifteen different numbers—some picked up, some didn't...and the contact that had sent you the article said to plan on meeting the next morning at..." Randy turned to me, smiled, and said, *"Your* place."

"For coffee," Skylar interjected in a panic. *"Just for coffee—"*

"At *your* apartment," he continued. "Now, why in the *world* would she be running to your place to meet up after she gathers up all this lovely information?"

"Coffee," I agreed with Skylar. "Swear—swear to God, just coffee—"

"What do you know?" Randy asked me casually. "And *who told you?*"

"Nothing, I—"

I silenced myself when he roughly grabbed Skylar by the jaw, angling her face and all of the damage done directly toward me.

"*Ah!*" she yelped in a mixture of surprise and pain.

"Do you see her face, James?"

He squeezed his grip, and Skylar winced.

I exclaimed, "Stop! You're hurting her—"

"I asked if you saw her face," Randy repeated. "It's simple—you can either talk to me, or you're about to look *very* similar to Skylar here."

The options were laid out before me, and they were obvious.

I could lie. Tell him that I had no idea what he was talking about and I had only seen the article that Skylar had referenced.

I could say that it didn't matter how much he beat me. That he was scum. That I wouldn't tell him a goddamn word.

*Or...*I could obey his every command. Admit that I was acquainted with a man named Colton who knew of a trafficking situation, and he had spoken with us in an attempt to obtain more information. That it had outright terrified us all to hear the news. Cassie had alerted Skylar only about Delaney, and it was clear that the women had pieced together other information and *that* was what had caused the domino effect he had mentioned. Maybe he would appreciate the transparency. *Maybe he would let me go.*

I would be kidding myself if I didn't say that the last thought gave me a glimmer of hope...but *would he?* Would he let me go? The single sparkle faded away as I deduced otherwise—surely with the knowledge of who he was and the insinuation of crimes he's committed, I wouldn't be allowed to see the light of day. Not now and not ever...and my stomach sank slowly as I came to the conclusion that there was a large possibility that I would die here.

And if I were to confess all I knew...it was most certain that he would find Colton and end him, too.

The slim chance of survival aside, it felt like a coward's way out. In fact, even if I were to come out of the other side of this alive, by stooping so low to give him the information he craved, he could go on happily committing atrocities...and it was with that realization that I began to shake my head.

"Why...in the *fuck*...would I tell you anything?" I incredulously questioned. Randy's eyebrows rose, and I added, "Even if I *did* have exactly what you were looking for..." I scoffed, "You're a fucking monster."

He seemed to be assessing my sincerity for a moment, and then he nodded.

"*Bold,* James," he murmured. "Very bold."

Randy then turned quickly to stalk away, dragging Skylar by the arm, and she yelped in surprise, meeting my eyes only briefly before they both disappeared from view.

"Where are you taking her?!"

It was clear that Skylar was fighting against him as he moved her, anxious calls of, "No!" and, *"Please,* no!" falling fainter and fainter on my ears until a thud from afar vibrated the air around me, and her pleas turned into a shrill scream that could have curdled blood.

"Hey!" I yelled, "She's innocent in this—*let her go!"*

There was no point to my movements, but I still yanked against the chains. They bit into my wrists harshly, and I frantically looked around the room for...something. *Anything.* I knew that now wouldn't be the time to attempt escape, but perhaps I could stow away the idea for later...fabricate a plan to get myself out of the cuffs and onto my feet.

There was nothing, though. Nothing but grey padding, a light above that continued to burn my retinas, and unyielding metal behind me that I knew would inevitably cut into my skin.

The sound of Skylar was abruptly cut off with the closing of a door in the distance and from then, I could only hear footsteps. By the time Randy returned, the air around me was thin, and though it ran through me rapidly, it seemed to do little good because I felt oxygen-starved. He watched me for a moment as he stood in the doorway, a small, wooden stool held in one hand and what looked to be a wash rag and a water bottle held in the other.

"Time to chat." He sauntered up to me, set the items down with care, and took a seat. Officer Dowler took a large breath in, letting it out as if it thoroughly relaxed him. "Where should we start?"

I had the urge to ask, *'Haven't we already?'* but instead, it just came out as:

"Start?"

"We can recap," he remarked. "Let's circle back to the beginning here, just to get the record straight. Here's the deal—my partner was an idiot."

I felt my expression pinch in confusion, for the word *partner* could mean several things—work accomplice, lover, and partner in crime all among them.

"Partner?"

"Mhm." He moved on without clarifying my internal thoughts. "Reckless. Obsessed. Balls-to-the-wall at a moment's notice. Had this crazy look in his eyes when he got an idea ingrained in him. And I thought...hell, he'd be an asset because I'm careful. I'm a strategic man. I needed a little...*fire.*" Randy shrugged as he let out a sigh. "But *fuck*, his fire was too much. Started pin-pointing the wrong targets—went off of his own interests rather than ours as a team—I had to start covering his tracks because he was *obvious*. He acted like...like this shit was his own personal sex service. I mean, he was *dramatic*. Obviously dramatic. To the point that he went AWOL." Randy paused. "Fucking. *AWOL.* Swear to God, he had to have been high because he was *running*. Chasing after women to get his goddamn rocks off. The kid was a nut and a half, and that's my fuckin' bad, but my point," he locked eyes with me, "is that he was too close to making himself known—making all of our shit known, whether I was looped in on it or not. And it was clear that who I report to took him out...which was for the best. I didn't have to get my hands dirty." Bile rose in my throat, and as my eyes widened, he took the sight of me in with a tilt of his head. "Do you know what he did to him, James? He beat him in the middle of the woods *so badly* that when his body was found, you could *see brain.*"

The mention of *woods* and *brain* made the image of Peter Milkovich flash in my mind. He laid face down in the grass, only steps away from where Zoey was cradled in Liam's lap after just having cracked his skull in with a rock.

I was unable to hold back my sickened, *"Oh, fuck."*

"Now, the boss didn't come to me and admit that he offed Peter." Randy's mention of his name hit me square in the diaphragm, and the noise I let out sounded as if the wind had been knocked out of me. "He doesn't tend to...*admit* to things because he's an under-the-radar type of man. *But* I know blunt force trauma when I see it. Peter was a threat, and it was *far* too easy for the rest of the PD to agree that the rocks in the river banged him up."

The connection was dizzying. Somehow, Peter met Randy and partnered with him in all of this. Peter targeted Zoey in his own manic way due to his tendencies that Randy had described as *reckless and obsessed.* The officer didn't know of Peter's actual demise. He thoroughly believed that because of Peter's recklessness, he had been killed by the man at the head of the whole organization—the *head honcho,* as Colton had once called him—and not only that, Randy had convinced the rest of the police department that Peter's death was an accidental drowning.

He had no idea. And it was all I could do to ask:

"Why are you telling me all of this?"

"Because if you tell me what you know, I won't do what he did to Peter. I'll make your death pleasant." Randy smiled. "I think we both know that you're not leaving here alive...but this doesn't have to be difficult."

My body trembled as he confirmed what I had suspected—he had no intention of ever releasing me.

I whispered, "Why do you think I know anything? Just—just because Skylar said she was coming to my apartment after she talked to all the other dancers?"

Wrinkles formed in his forehead...as if he were confused as to how I hadn't put the remainder of the puzzle together.

"I...know where you live, James. I've been there before. I met the previous tenant. Little blonde thing?" I attempted to keep my expression neutral, even with the mention of Zoey—I knew that I had done a piss poor job of it as my breath continued to rattle and it sounded like my heartbeat was audible, but I attempted, nonetheless. Randy pressed on, "I made sure I was the one to arrive at the scene because I was *so damn sure* that it was Peter with the detail she gave about a *stalker* on the call in, and I had to cover his damn tracks. I *know* you know her...and it wasn't hard to figure out you had moved in after I paid the place a visit." He paused, ensuring to hold my attention. *"I let her go.* She didn't fit the bill, she had too many personal connections, and Peter didn't get far enough for her to be a threat before he was done for. She never reported anything after that. She *knew nothing.* She moved on with life. *I* moved on with life. But now...you're a common denominator. Now, Peter's front door got busted in, the main course of action was directly for his room like this one, and I had to shut down his damn family questioning it. *Now...*you seem like you know more than you're leading on."

"I don't." I stated over and again, "I don't-*I don't-I-don't—*"

My panicked repetition was cut off quickly as something made contact with my cheek. Because I had squeezed my eyes shut as I began to rattle off the same words, I hadn't seen him move. I had only felt the quick, sharp impact of a solid material followed by radiating pain that made my ears ring. I grunted as my head swam, and once I stopped spinning from the force of the hit, I looked to see him standing above me. Officer Dowler had a gun—one I could only assume was police-issued—in his right hand. He held it by the handle like a club, and there was no question that it was the barrel of the weapon that had hit me.

The moment I had absorbed his appearance, he moved again. He swung his arm, finding the same position on my cheek, and try as I might to push myself away with scrambling legs, there was nowhere for me to go. I was stuck, backed into the same corner, and Randy was still there.

"You want to reconsider your answer?"

His question was forcedly calm, and I replied:

"Fuck you."

There was no hesitation as he struck me again—and again—*and again*—and each instance that he stopped to speak was similar to the first. The pistol whipping rendered the left side of my face wet and bruised, my skin swollen and tangibly stretching across my cheekbone, and throbbing shot through to my skull in white-hot waves.

It would end, eventually.

I knew it would.

What I didn't anticipate was for Randy to squat down to my eye level, grab my jaw to force me to meet his eyes, and ask:

"What are you trying to do? Protect your girl?"

My chest panged as my heart attempted to escape its confines, and I exhaled, "What?"

Randy squinted. "What does *Cassie* know?"

Her name on his lips nearly made me vomit, and my response came from my gut in a visceral snarl:

"Leave her out of this."

"Ooo." His eyes brightened. "Now we're getting somewhere."

He was so close to my face that I could see his in high-definition, and I knew that the vivid image of him would be marked into my memory for as long as blood still coursed through my veins. The lines on his forehead and between his eyebrows were more prominent than his crow's feet—the mark of a man who rarely smiled genuinely. Though his gaze into me was now glowing with anticipation, I could still note his sleeplessness behind the dark circles and bloodshot red that surrounded the green and brown of his irises.

The thought that I would be cursed to see his face for the rest of my days made anger roar in my ears as if a plane were flying overhead, and as soon as I felt the urge, I spat.

He flinched as it hit him, and I watched with pleasure as the blood in my saliva dripped down the sharp angles of his nose and lingered in his stubble.

Face contorted into a grimace, Officer Dowler said nothing. He shoved me away with disgust, reached to where his stool was behind him, and snatched the towel on the floor beside it. Wiping my spit away with a frustrated grumble, he then threw it at me. It landed across my eyes, taking my sight from me, and despite my efforts to turn my head from left to right, it stuck like glue, for it was heavy and damp. I heard a single *squish* as he moved. He adjusted the towel to cover my entire face with rough tugs coupled with rage-filled grunts, he briefly shoved his hand in my mouth, and I tasted the material on my tongue.

"Ah! Wha—"

Any sound I made was muffled by the cold, wet fabric, and my breath, which had turned to a staccato rhythm, quickened further. Droplets from the towel dripped into my mouth—down my throat with every inhale—pulling air through my nose instead offered no escape, and the horror of oxygen being stolen from me made my chest heave to no avail. I screamed through the material. I tried to plead *no.*

Randy still remained silent, though, and all that reached my ears was the quiet cracking of plastic before the water hit me.

And I was drowning.

Chapter 22

Cassie

In my humble opinion, hysterics would have been appropriate.

And I wanted to be hysterical. I *wanted* to yell—to scream—to cry out in the act of a woman scorned because it felt as though he were forcibly taken from me. As if he were ripped from my hands. It was an asinine notion, and I knew that it was unreasonable...but it was *James*. Through anything chaotic that had happened as of late, there was no question as to whether he would inevitably run to my side because he was my constant. And not knowing where he was—realizing that he was not, in fact, on his way to bound right through the front door and yank me into his arms—had left my chest slashed open. With my heart somehow still beating despite being exposed to the elements, each passing second was sheer agony.

I couldn't fall into hysterics, though. Not when it seemed like he was *just* out of my reach.

Zoey had rushed to 3C to pound on Luke and Claire's door. According to her, she had given them no hint as to why they were needed with us in 2B, but with the perpetually alarmed expression she was wearing and the cryptic call she had earlier with Claire, I was certain that they had managed to connect a few dots. They arrived with her, looking expectant and carrying themselves carefully—similarly to one preparing for an upcoming storm to meet them head-on.

Though I hadn't gone into the background detail that I had with Zoey regarding my relationship with James because it now felt...*pointless,* I had explained our concern away quickly.

Luke was quiet—absorbing it all as if the information had stripped his lungs of air. His jaw eventually went slack, and he whispered a sharp, *"God fucking dammit,"* before spinning one-hundred and eighty degrees from where he stood and walking wherever his feet would take him within the kitchen.

While Claire had also looked to us, aghast, she still managed to narrow her eyes and question details with a lightly asked, *"How..."* or *"Why..."* but Zoey was there, rapidly butting into the conversation with quiet hisses of her name accompanied with a curt shake of her head. Claire's inquisition ceased rather quickly, then. Whether she put two and two together regarding my relationship with Jay or not, I wasn't sure. All I knew was that after she had clearly assessed Luke's well-being and determined that he thoroughly needed to be left to his own thoughts and rapid footwork, she had eyed me up and down. Obviously recognizing my panic regarding the situation at hand, she coaxed me into sitting with her on the couch.

I had obliged, if only for a moment, and she had sat with me while comfortingly stroking a hand up and down my back. She spoke nervous reassurances that she was sure James was fine to the entire room. Luke vehemently disagreed, and Zoey remained silent as she returned to her spot at the kitchen table to open the laptop. I could only manage to rest for so long, and it wasn't that I didn't welcome her comfort—I did, *truly,* and she had given me a tight-lipped smile that had shown she knew my appreciation without having to speak it—it was simply that I was far more than restless. Far more than anxious. Far more than panicked, believe it or not. My heart had ceased its pounding, and I had grown accustomed to the horrid sensation of dread that was steadily poisoning me. It wasn't long until I stood and mimicked Luke. With shaking fingers and paces that stomped back and forth along the coffee table by the couch, I just...started to walk.

Claire remained on the couch with her spine straight and her eyes wide as she rapidly offered explanations as to where James could be. I consistently batted them away with various reasonings, and Luke would respond with a grunt and an agreeing stab of his index finger in my direction. In the short minutes that had passed, my line of sight was not on either of them, though. Nor was it on Zoey, who was still squinting at the computer screen as if it would provide us with more information. All I could see was the clock beyond the table at which Zoey sat.

It was approaching eleven o'clock now, and the only thing repeating in my mind was that it had been three hours since I spoke with James last.

He had been missing for three hours.

"Okay...one more time, Cas?" Luke spoke while still maintaining his quick strides.

He looked so *very* like his brother in this moment with his alarmed, light eyes darting around the room—the same grey as James' and tinged with a familiar anxiety. His hair entirely free of its usual product and hanging loose down to his cheekbones. A smattering of stubble that he had yet to shave. The thought made a metaphorical knife lodge in my gut and stay there.

I looked to the ceiling as I replied to him, "He left for work. I called him while he drove. He was totally fine." I rubbed at my eyes, for they had begun to burn again. I noted that my face had consistently remained damp, though I had little headspace to give a damn. "He said he'd let me know when he got to work—he didn't. I texted him. The messages I've gotten from him in the meantime are *clearly* not him. His location's turned off, his car's on the side of the fucking highway, and he's not at work." I hesitated for a moment, let my hands fall away from my face, and murmured to myself more than anyone else, "He's just...gone."

Luke exhaled heavily, halting his steps, and I followed suit as our eyes locked.

He and I always had an interesting relationship. Naturally, I had spent time with Claire and Zoey over the past few months—an occasional dinner here or there was altogether *nice,* and I found that I fit right in. Luke, though...he had more or less lingered in the background of my life. We had shared many conversations to the point that I felt like I knew him—his likes and dislikes, how he would react when placed in certain situations, and so on—but we weren't tied at the hip by any means. That aside, he looked at me now as if he could see right through me. As if, without a single question about my closeness with James, he fully understood, well, *everything*.

I didn't know why. Perhaps it was a Turner thing, but I didn't mind that in the least.

I could go on about how I *did* mind—well, *truly hated* is a better term—that it seemed as though my and James' privacy bubble had been forcefully popped. That it wasn't by the inquisitive nature of our friends nor the concern that James had over my brother's reaction, both of which I had happily anticipated at this point. But *no*...the horror that we knew had been hiding in the background had done it for us. And despite the fact that I truthfully had no idea if Claire or Luke really knew about us, it still felt like our bubble was no longer because there was no room to speak of it. Our collective anxiety rendered the mention of it moot.

And none of that mattered. I quickly buried the split-second of a thought that was spurred by Luke's familiar grey eyes because he looked to be priming himself to speak again.

"There's got to be some...some sort of trail," Luke said with what seemed like an attempt at conviction. *"Something* we can give the cops to find him without—without outing all the other shit—and you're saying Colton called you *right after?* Is no one else thinking that's *really* fuckin' coincidental?"

Claire griped, *"Luke."*

"Nuh uh." He waggled a finger in her direction. "You're a forgiving person, Claire—*I get it*. And I love that about you. *I do.* But—"

"But Colt was a manipulative shithead at the tail-end of me dating him?" she finished for him with an eyebrow cocked up high. Luke sighed as he looked to her, and she continued, *"Yeah.* He was. He did whatever he had to do to make more and more money—"

Luke cut in, "At the expense of those he claimed that he cared for."

"Out of necessity—and don't give me that look where ya scrunch up your nose like what I'm saying is insane." Luke's expression immediately shifted, and Claire stated, "I'm not defending him or saying he's a goddamn angel in disguise, but he's never intentionally hurt anyone."

Without looking away from the laptop, Zoey noted, "He blackmailed you, sweetie—that's a certain level of *hurt.*"

"Okay, *yes,* he blackmailed me to force me to help him because of what he was tangled up in, I'm aware—*we all lived it.* That doesn't mean he'd have a hand in *James disappearing,"* Claire retorted.

"I'm with you, I'm with you," Zoey replied with a wave of her hand. "Just sayin'."

"And *I'm* saying," Claire insisted, "I'm just as leery as you guys, but...look, he's done shitty things to save his own ass, but even you guys know that would be a huge stretch. I'm—I'm still leery...and I don't *get it*. But it's a stretch."

Zoey nodded.

I said, "Listen, I don't know the guy, but he *did* steal literal evidence for us." Luke clenched his jaw, and I added, "Ran from the cops. Brought said evidence back. I'm not sayin' he's an angel either 'cause I don't know him from Adam, but—"

As if we had willed him into existence, the front door opened, and Colton arrived.

Everyone glanced his way, and he peered around the room. Hair dark as onyx, parted down the middle and hanging loose around his face; stubble that had grown to the point that it was *just* noticeable from a distance; a hooded sweatshirt that matched the color of his hair and had a small emblem of a skull on the left side of his chest—he looked similar enough to how he had at each one of our meetings. What was different about him now was how he was holding himself.

Colton seemed to be a confident individual when I had seen him previously. Every time I had witnessed him stride through a door, he was doing so boldly—with purpose and perhaps charisma. Now as he stood, though, his gaze turned more and more concerned as it dragged over us all. Locking eyes with Claire first, a crease formed between his brows. Luke was next in his line of sight, and his Adam's apple bobbed as he swallowed. Then, his lips pursed together as he took in Zoey, who was still squinting behind her glasses at the computer screen. Finally, me—his shoulders sagged in a rough exhale, and his icy eyes went soft as they bounced across my face.

He shut the door behind him, quietly commenting on our appearances with a grimly muttered, "Yeah...that's about right." I assumed that it was because we had so recently spoken that there were no general pleasantries—only rapid strides as he pointedly powerwalked his way to Zoey. Seemingly in the same thought process as we were in attempting to find the impossible connection between 2D, missing dancers, and James' disappearance, he asked her, "You find anything on that computer yet?"

She exhaled loudly, glancing his way while he grabbed the other chair that was situated at the dining table. He dragged it to her left and sank onto it.

"*No,* otherwise you'd be sure as hell that we wouldn't be sitting here on our asses."

"Don't think any of us are *sitting on our asses.* Time is of the essence here," he grumbled nodding his head in gesture to the screen. "Text messages?"

"Mhm."

"That's it?"

"Mhm."

Colton muttered, "Not that much, is there?"

"No," Zoey returned with a sardonic chuckle. "Doesn't help that most of these numbers aren't even labeled as a full contact name. I mean...*this one?* Unlabeled, but clearly his landlord," she clicked the trackpad purposefully, mentioning Mister Milkovich without speaking his name. "Asking for rent, barely any responses back. This one?" *Click.* "Nothing telling, just someone named *R* being pissy with him and, *again,* not many responses back." *Click.* "This one just says different variations of *call me* over and over—"

"Have ya tried Googling them?"

She had begun to rapidly tap on the keyboard mid-way through Colton's sentence.

"Already on it."

Without a pause between us all and with a hefty cock of his head, Luke spoke up:

"Why are you so goddamn eager to find this guy?"

Eyes still on the laptop, Colton murmured, "We've been over this, I think."

"Right...the vigilante shit," Luke returned.

"Mhm." He pointed at the screen. "You're doing *that* one first?"

Zoey hummed in acknowledgment.

"Just seems like a far cry from what you were doing in North Carolina," Luke noted.

"Time passes," Colton said offhandedly. "Shit happens and makes you think. It ain't that deep."

"Shit happens," Luke said under his breath. *"Right."*

"What...what *kind* of shit?"

Claire had spoken it, and when I followed Luke's shocked glance to her, I found that she was looking to Colton with a morbid curiosity. Her blue eyes showed a quiet nervousness unlike what I had seen in them previously—one that was expectant—and when Colton met her gaze, he sighed loudly.

It appeared entirely genuine when he replied, "I don't exactly want to get into that right now."

She immediately countered, "Why?"

His head bobbed backward in surprise at her quick insistence. "Because there are some things going on that are a bit more pressing than me chatting about what I've done in the last year?"

I saw the muscles work in her jaw. *"Colton."*

He whined, "Why does this have to be a thing?"

It was then that I was tempted to interject. To needlessly remind the room that we have no idea where James is, what we can tell authorities, and where we go from here. That we needed to *focus*. However, Claire had already begun to speak along a similar line of thought...and her point was astute.

"Because someone that's a part of our family is *missing!*" she hissed, and his mouth snapped shut. My exposed heart painfully lurched, the air in the room turned tense with her verbal acknowledgment of it, and I was fairly certain that I saw Claire's nostrils flare as she pressed on, "I want to trust you, Colt. We all *need* to trust you. Do you have any idea how fucking backwards that feels? The fact that I want and *need* to trust you in this situation? It's...it's asinine." She laughed bitterly to herself. "That's exactly what it is—it's fucking *asinine*. Did you know that I still walk with a goddamn limp?"

I hadn't fully noticed that. Sure, over dinners that I had attended, Zoey would occasionally mutter to Claire, 'How's the leg?' It was a private question—I always knew it was—and that was why I had never butted in or asked about it further. I had only witnessed Claire's ever-consistent shrug of a shoulder and Zoey's quick nod in response.

And furthermore, if Luke were sat next to her and they were primed to move, he would always be ready at a moment's notice to spring up and assist her as she stood. With his hand extended and a gracious look in her eyes, he would smile as he pulled her to her feet.

It wasn't until now that the reason for instances like those clicked in my mind, and I realized that it was abundantly true. Claire always favored her right side over her left.

Colton miserably groaned, "From Travis?"

"Yes, from fucking Travis!" Claire yelled.

I didn't know who Travis was—naturally, I didn't, as I assumed this conversation was regarding Claire's history, in which I only knew the bare minimum. I did, however, recall that upon Colton's arrival in Salem, Luke had mentioned that Claire had been stabbed in the past. I now figured that it was in her left leg and that this *Travis* had done the damage. I didn't ask, of course…and I didn't question the quick deviation of topic, for I knew she was rapidly circling back.

Colton had closed his eyes while Claire's voice rose in her angry reply, as if he anticipated it—absorbing the impact rather than deflecting it—and when he opened them, he appeared to be waiting for her to continue.

"My point," Claire lowered her decibel, but her scathing tone remained, "is that I've been telling everyone that you wouldn't blindly fuck us all over for no reason, and the more I say it, the more it feels like I'm trying to convince *myself* of that."

"*Blindly fuck you over?*" he returned with a narrowed glare. "First off, I've never done anything *blind* in my entire life, and I," Colton whispered, "busted into the place next door for you guys—"

"Because you needed something in return," Luke grumbled.

"The fuck is going to make this better for you?" Colton snapped at them both. "You want me to get on my fucking knees? *Beg?* Plead for forgiveness? Hell, I was ready to do that a year ago when I tried to show up after everything went down with Travis." He threw his head back, speaking to the ceiling, "Swear to God, I would have dropped to the floor and scraped. My. Shit. *Up*. Apologizing for that shitshow, but I don't think you want it."

"I *don't* want it," Claire retorted. "I don't *need* it! I just need to know *why!*"

"Why?"

"Yes, Colt," she reiterated. *"Why?* Why are you doing this? Why are you *helping?* Why are you so hellbent over this?"

It seemed that the weight of the conversation had finally cracked something within him because at the moment of her repeated *why,* his shoulders straightened, and the light that was always present in his gaze flared. Not with what seemed to be his usual mocking sarcasm, but with hurt—with anger that flooded his face as if a constantly worn mask had been rapidly dropped.

Colton screamed back, "Because I've *BEEN HERE BEFORE!*" We all flinched at the volume of it. His jaw flexed, and he collected himself for exactly one inhale. Upon his exhale, he said, "You need to know details? *Fine.* I met a girl."

He spoke it quickly, but despite that, it was anything but lacking emotion. On the contrary, the words seemed as though they were forced from him. As if demanding that they leave his mouth coated his tongue in acid, and caused him physical harm.

Luke had tilted his head even further to the side in curiosity.

Even Zoey looked up from the laptop to evaluate his expression, which had turned downright gaunt.

"Oh?" Claire returned with raised eyebrows.

Colton went on, "She was wrapped up *deep* with the wrong people, tryin' to get out."

"So, like Claire," Luke questioned in a harsh tone.

"No," he replied, gritty. "Not like Claire."

Luke countered, "Oh, you *didn't* blackmail this girl, then?"

I could have sworn that I heard Claire swallow while Colton looked at him in horror.

"Do you think I didn't learn my lesson?" he asked in a murmur, not waiting for Luke to respond before saying, *"I did.* I did the second that shit started going downhill with Claire and Travis—"

Luke began to interrupt, "I'm *sure*—"

"I'm not *done yet!"* Colton snapped, and Luke let out a shaking breath as he crossed his arms. "I'm not gonna get into my *fucking feelings,"* he touched his chest briefly, "but I can *promise you* that I did. And no—I didn't blackmail her. *They took her."* We all remained quiet while Colton's voice trembled, "Not because of me. Just the luck of the goddamn draw. But they took her. I looked for her for months...I wound up finding her in the obituaries. She's fucking dead."

The gravity—the *finality* of his last choked word was heavy to the point that it weighed down the room.

Claire's expression was pained as she consolingly spoke, "Colton, I—"

"Don't make me talk about her," he begged. "You wanna know why I'm hellbent? It's because of her. You wanna know why you can trust me and believe that I'm one *million* percent in with this? It's. Because. Of. Her. *Please* don't make me talk about Peyton."

Claire nodded, whispering, "Okay."

While Luke appeared to glance at him with a shocked, begrudging, silent apology, Colton looked down to his right, meeting Zoey's somber face, and he gestured to the screen once more:

"You, ah," he cleared his throat roughly, "you Google that last number? Any idea who it was?"

It was a rapid deviation back to the topic that I had been itching to return to, but couldn't because the need for trust in whatever we were continuing to do with Colton was paramount.

And I couldn't be sure if *trust* was present...but any hostility toward him had rapidly dissipated because it was abundantly clear that he was telling the truth. That his quick, previous explanation of his behavior being related to the work of a vigilante was true, despite the group's skepticism...but his determination to seek justice was not solely driven by his desire to turn his life around. I didn't really know Colton as a person, and though he was quickly side-stepping his emotional outburst because there was no more to be said, I could still see it in him—*feel* it in the room amongst us. There was no arguing it:

This woman's death had broken him, and he was doing it all for her.

Yes, his shift back to questioning Zoey about the phone numbers on the laptop was a sharp left turn—and we all went with it.

"Oh." Zoey shook her head as if to clear it, her glasses slid down her nose, she pushed them up with an index finger, and she responded to him, "Yeah, um—family member, I think," she replied quietly. "This website came up—rapid people search dot net? You can put in a phone number or someone's name, whatever credentials, right? Basically pulls up public records."

He nodded. "Does it seem accurate?"

"Well, I checked mine," Zoey remarked. "Has all the addresses I've lived at since I was eighteen, my full name, my age...all that."

"Jesus," Claire muttered. "It *cannot* be that easy to find out where people live."

Colton shrugged. "Public record—it's not like it's a secret."

Zoey typed once again, loudly tapping the last key, and told her, "Yours checks out, too."

Luke's eyes bugged as he looked Zoey's way. *"Seriously?"*

"I mean, it still shows 2A as our current address," she clarified. "Not like any of us signed papers when we started subletting to Jay, but...current public record. Yeah."

It was the first time I had spoken in a while when I ushered her, "Well, *check more*. Who knows who else 2D was talking to."

"Try the guy that was getting pissed at him," Colton suggested with another point of his finger to the screen.

"Yeah, yeah-yeah," Zoey mumbled, and a rapid mess of clicks later, she narrowed her eyes at the computer.

Her skepticism made my stomach roll, and I pressed, *"What?"*

My questioning came out in a croak, and Zoey's eyes snapped to mine.

"Nothing," she assured me, and then blinked several times before her well-manicured brows pinched together. "One second."

Colton began, "Google his na—"

Her typing had already commenced when she interjected, "That's what I'm *doing.*"

We all looked at each other as the keyboard clacked, waiting for her requested *second* to end, and when her gaze widened substantially, Colton asked:

"Is that a fucking cop?"

"He was talking to a cop?" Luke asked. "Maybe...maybe he was onto him?"

"And texted him personally?" Claire announced. "No, that doesn't make sense at all."

"Well, maybe *that's* the guy we talk to? If these things *are* connected, then maybe he'll be able to figure it out without us going into detail."

"We can't talk to a cop that *knew 2D personally.*" Claire's face twisted at Luke's notion. "If we do that, other shit could get found out, and we're all at a higher risk of getting thrown in prison—no way would that work in our favor."

"Well, what are we *supposed* to do?" I questioned the entire room disbelievingly. "Let Jay stay missing?"

Luke started to pace again. "Fuck—*no,* obviously not."

"Okay, we're not gonna just *leave him missing.* There's gotta be something here." Colton looked down at Zoey. "Go back to the text—what's up with you? What's wrong?"

Lost in the back and forth, none of us had witnessed her expression after she had mentioned the contact being a police officer. Her focus seemed disassociated into the space in front of her—neither on the computer nor anything around it, lost in thought—and she didn't respond to him.

"Zoey!" Claire called to her, and Zoey jerked back to reality.

"I recognize this guy," she admitted to us all.

I felt my eyebrows raise. "The cop?"

"Uh huh."

Claire confusingly asked, "From what? When?"

She breathlessly replied, "The break-in."

"The break-in?" Luke repeated her words. "Like—like from—"

"Peter," she clarified. "2D. *Yes.*"

"Are you sure?" Claire asked. "Maybe he just looks familiar or something."

"No, no, no-no," Zoey stammered. "This is the guy. *Randy Dowler.* Officer Randy. I remember his name 'cause he was incompetent and drove Liam insane—every time we mentioned him, it was," she briefly imitated him with a deep voice, *"'Fucking Randy.'"*

"He was incompetent?" Colton questioned.

"Incompetent or just didn't give a shit," she said. "Everything that I told him got me, *'Oh, we can't be sure those are related,'* or, *'That's too little information to put out an all-points bulletin.'* It was—it was pointless, honestly, and we were planning on talking with the police again, but..."

She didn't have to finish the sentence that she let run off. That was when chaos had erupted, and we all knew it.

"So...you're saying that this *Randy* came to your place after 2D busted in," Colton hesitantly reiterated her telling of it, and we all nodded. "Basically blew off your complaints about a stalker." More nodding. "And—wait, he refused to put out an APB?"

"Said we had too little of a description," she stated.

He scoffed. "Bullshit—I've seen those announcements on the news before. *White male, approximately five-foot-ten, medium build, and wearing dark clothes* isn't terribly descriptive, but they fuckin' list it anyway."

"Did you just..." Claire paused. "Did you just describe *yourself?*"

"They didn't include *piercing eyes* or *devilishly handsome,*" Colton told her with a smirk, and she rolled her eyes in return, "but yes. *Point is,* I've even seen some of those listings say *suspicious male* or some other vague shit. The fact that this dude didn't put word out that you had someone violent on your tail sounds sketchy as shit...and *now* we find out that he knew the guy personally? Feels dirty."

The more he spoke, the more I felt my brain buzz. I tried to absorb what he said, but it was as if the words were water, and I were hydrophobic. They were rolling off of me in beads—dripping on the floor and leaving me standing in a puddle that I wanted to drown into to silence the noise—to stop the gnawing pain of the unknown.

But then, something clicked.

I had no idea if the thought was insanity over the reality of someone I loved becoming intangible.

That could have been it. I was well aware that I was in love with James...and I didn't mind in the least that I had quickly toppled head over feet for him. Instead, I felt that, somehow, he had as well. That when we had finally thrown caution to the wind and succumbed to each other, we had both just...fallen...but the sensation of it wasn't akin to smashing into concrete. No, it was more like being laid to rest on a soft pillow. Being swathed in a warm blanket. Sinking into a deep sleep that's full of pleasant dreams and gently waking with the sunrise, rested and refreshed.

Yes, I loved him.

And my certainty of that was what made me wonder if what had *clicked* in my mind regarding his disappearance was unreasonable. Perhaps I was simply grasping at straws, frantically attempting to find an explanation—*any* explanation—whether it was insane to think it or not. I spoke it, anyway:

"Jay got pulled over earlier today."

Colton's eyes brightened. "Oh...you *did* tell me that, didn't you?"

"Wait, wait," Luke held up a hand, "when did he get pulled over?"

"When we were talking on the phone this morning," I said. "He wasn't sure why...thought maybe he was speeding or something—"

"Jay, speeding," Luke sardonically grumbled as he walked back and forth. *"Sure."*

"But that was the last time I talked with him," I stated. "I—this is fucking crazy, but I feel like something happened with this cop."

Colton pointed at me enthusiastically. "I *knew* we were on the same page."

Without saying a word, Zoey seemed to entirely understand our viewpoint as she bobbed her head up and down vehemently.

Claire and Luke, however, were more hesitant.

"I—okay, no-no," Claire stammered, "Cassie, you're—you're trying to say that Jay's with this policeman?"

Luke added, "If he was arrested or something, it makes sense that his car's on the side of the road, but wouldn't his phone have been seized and stored? I don't think anyone would be able to message from it."

"Not arrested," I clarified.

"Dirty cops," Colton nearly sang. *"Dirty. Fucking. Cops."*

"Taken—and I don't know if he—if he thinks that Jay knows something about all of this or about," I groaned quietly to myself, "about all the dancers that up and quit from Gas Lamp because he's close to me, or what."

Luke stopped pacing, then, and his wide eyes snapped to me. "Dancers were quitting like you did?"

I nodded, waving a hand at Colton. "He told me."

Colton noted, "Felt weird. Thought there could be a rumor floating around about the ones that went missing."

Claire asked me, "But...*you* didn't..." I shook my head, and she then directed to Colton, "And you didn't..."

"Telling people shit I know doesn't exactly work in my favor 'cause of reasons like this," he remarked. "Y'all were an exception. I'm normally Fort Knox."

"The *why* doesn't matter at this point," I said.

"What matters is that if Randy," Zoey pointed at the laptop, "is dirty and fucking *took James* for whatever reason, then we have no idea if we can trust the police at all at this point."

Claire whispered, *"Fuck,* you're right."

Luke's attention bounced between us all. "So...we can't talk to the authorities."

We all simultaneously replied, "No."

"Then where the *hell* is this Randy?" he sneered.

I locked eyes with Zoey. *"Address."*

"Uh huh, yup, figuring that out." She typed quickly, paused for a moment, and then stated, "Neighborhood about fifteen minutes from here."

Colton muttered, "Is this guy in the goddamn *suburbs?*"

"Wait," Claire interjected, "what are we planning on doing here?"

Before any of us could answer her—before we could even speak a plan into existence—the front door began to open. The hinges creaked, and we all looked to the noise as my brother's voice chastised:

"Zo'! I told you to keep the door lock—"

Liam saw me first, and his sentence cut off as he thoroughly evaluated my expression. There was no hiding it—the tenseness of my shoulders, the tear stains on my face, the burning in my eyes, the pounding of my bleeding heart—I was sure that it was all apparent to him. And the way that his body froze in the entryway was all the confirmation I needed...but naturally, there was more. The color was sucked from his face. His breathing looked like it increased in speed. His jaw was slack.

And *then,* he looked to Zoey.

"Hi," she whispered sympathetically.

"What—" It seemed that he finally registered Colton sitting next to her. "Oh, God, *why are you here?*" His dark eyes scanned the room, taking in everyone's presence, and they landed on me once more. "What—Jesus, Cas, *what happened?!*"

Chapter 23

Cassie

Days ago, when James had arrived at my home during a blizzard and dramatically spoke of his care for me among the chaos that surrounded us, I had wondered if I would always be partial to the snow. The dawn that had extended behind him then was muted to a stormy grey, the snow clouds above blocking out the vibrancy of a new day's sun, but it was anything but dull, for the ferocity of the storm was reflected in his similarly colored eyes. The cold was near painful while the frigid gusts of wind and icy flakes in the air had bitten through our clothing as he stood on my porch and I in the threshold. I still saw it as a thing of beauty, though, for the winter storm was James' parallel.

The snow on the ground had almost melted since that day, but the flakes were falling again. It looked like they had been doing so for the entirety of the time we were all conversing in the apartment, and their soft fluttering through the air, along with the inch-deep covering on the ground, evoked a pensive melancholy within me. It layered much like the snow did in a blanket over my panic, and I truthfully wasn't sure which emotion was worse.

I pulled my car door shut, settling into my seat and fastening my seat belt as rapidly as I could. The sound of a closing door repeated twice—once from the passenger seat and once from behind me.

Zoey said, "Got the address on my phone. Hop onto main, get on the highway, and I'll tell you where to go from there."

I murmured, "Thank you."

"Cassie?" Liam tentatively spoke to me as I shifted my car into drive.

There was little inquiry from Liam as we had all taken turns rattling off our explanations of the morning some five minutes ago. He occasionally looked at me, perplexed, as Zoey or I would state something regarding text messages or GPS location, and his anger was far too apparent when he learned that we had left the apartment, but it was rapidly side-stepped as the reasoning for our collective frantic anxiety became ever-clear.

We left quickly to follow whatever trail of clues that would be bestowed upon us—Liam, Zoey, and I in my Jeep, and Claire, Luke, and Colton in Luke's car—and driving to Randy Dowler's current address was the only thing on our current agenda.

It wasn't confusion in my brother's questioning call of my name, for I knew that he was well aware of the scenario and the gravity that pulled us all down with it—it was concern.

Concern for *me*.

Something about his tone immediately made my voice crack on my replied, "What?" and I pointedly avoided his inquisitive stare.

"Don't take this the wrong way," he told me gently, "but ya look like you've been crying, and you normally...*don't*."

I exhaled, "I'm aware."

He huffed out a loud breath. "Are you okay?"

Zoey murmured from the back seat, "None of us are *okay*, Lee."

Liam twisted his body to look back at her, saying, "I know," but his questioning eyes still landed back on me.

When I finally brought myself to meet them, I swallowed through the lump in my throat and gave him a curt shake of my head *no*.

Seeing his face twist in worry that was clearly directed toward me made the vision of him blur, and I rapidly diverted my attention back to the road, sniffling to keep the tears at bay.

The silence that followed was thick, permeating the air in a weighted humidity that sat in my lungs like lead.

I changed lanes.

I got on the highway.

I wiped my face once, quickly, and then my phone began to ring through my car's speaker. Clicking the button on the steering wheel to answer it via Bluetooth without even registering the name on the incoming call, I spoke:

"Hey."

"*Fuck*, are you okay?"

It was Claire, and, yes, I had anticipated the person on the other end of the line to be the entirety of the three in Luke's vehicle, hence my expectant greeting. I would have said that her question about my current mental state was astute, but because of my tortured tone, it was more coming across as...*obvious*. While it would have been far nicer for me to thank her for her inquiry into my well-being and say something along the lines of, *'No, but let's focus on the matter at hand,'* the idea of doing such was far, *far* from my mind.

"*No*, Claire," I admitted in a whine. "I'm not!"

She stammered, "I—sorry, Cas, I—"

"Not trying to be a dick here, guys," Colton cut in through the speaker, "but we don't have much time until we're getting to this place. I don't think we can spend it debating who's okay and who's not." He rapidly went on before anyone could argue, "It's lookin' like we're going to a little neighborhood here, and if y'all haven't noticed, it's the middle of the day. We need to check out the area before we decide what the plan is."

"Wait...*no,* that's not what I thought..." Luke asked incredulously, "Are you seriously saying that we're getting to this guy's place and *staying put?*"

Colton replied, "The last thing we need is a neighbor poking around wondering what-in-the-*Scooby Doo* our group is doing—observe first. Act later."

The last word wriggled under my skin.

"Later?" I scoffed. *"Later?* Didn't you say that time is of the essence earlier?"

"Which is why we're dropping everything and going to check out this place *now,*" he assured me, "and we can figure the best time to get in there once we get our eyes on it. Normally, with something like this, ya gotta scope a place out for days. *Weeks.* Figure out a pattern, yadda, right? *We aren't doing that,* so let's just...breathe, okay?"

While I heard Luke anxiously murmur, "We're breaking into *another* place. This is fine. Everything's fine," Colton told him:

"Technically...*I'm* breaking into another place. Y'all are just...*accomplices*...aren't ya glad I'm here with my special skillset?"

Luke grumbled, "If I say *yes,* I fear for the size of your ego."

I announced, "Look, I'm glad we aren't waiting days or—or weeks, but I'm not waiting until fucking nightfall or some shit to see if we can find more clues from the *one* thing we've got right now."

Luke said something unintelligible on the other end of the phone, but it sounded like agreement.

"Off the highway at the next exit, Cas," Zoey spoke up, and I steered accordingly.

"I don't think nightfall's in the cards, anyway," Colton remarked.

"No?" Claire questioned him. "Bit more cover to get into a house, right?"

"Claire, we cannot wait *hours* until we're making moves to figure more shit out," Luke rasped.

"I know, *I know,*" she replied, her tone shaking with jitters, "and I agree, but if a neighbor sees and calls the police—"

A quiet thump emitted through the speaker, and I could practically see Luke's head falling back to the headrest in exasperation.

"God *dammit,*" he uttered.

"Left at the light," Zoey instructed, "then right on Quinton Street."

I drove blindly, and Colton sighed loud enough for us all to hear it.

"I get it," he said sympathetically, "but none of us are a help to James if we start getting questioned by the cops, *not to mention* if there are more police involved with this...I really do think waiting until dark is a no-go, though."

Claire asked, "Why?"

"'Cause he'd be home, right?" he replied. "Sure, it's the middle of the day right now, but as far as we know, this guy usually works a nine-to-five."

"When he showed up after 2D broke into Zoey and Claire's, it was late," Liam stated. "Not nine-to-five timing."

I countered, "If he's the one that pulled Jay over, it *would* be nine-to-five timing."

"We have no idea if he was actually on the clock for either of those things," Zoey noted. "We can all try to figure out his schedule, but there are too many variables with that." She paused. "Left here, immediate right, third house on the left."

I nodded as I stopped briefly at a stop sign and turned the wheel.

"Zoey's right," Colton said. "If it looks like no one's home, I'll go in. If not, we've gotta tail the place for a bit."

"And what about being seen if you're going in now?" Claire inquired.

"Snow's coming down a little harder," he said. "I'll pull my hood up—it's not like I'm robbing the place. Just looking for papers...shit behind locked doors...clues, yeah? If I just get in, get out, and get on my way, we should be fine."

I whispered more to myself than anyone else, "Yeah."

Turning once more, I eyed the road ahead, and it was the first time that I had absorbed the scenery around me while we were all speaking. The neighborhood was oddly nice considering our circumstances for visiting and the potential monster that lived within. Not overly-rich. Just...*nice*...and the picture of suburbia. Colored in what was most certainly home-owner's-association-approved muted palettes, the houses were all similarly shaped—as if the head designer had created the blueprint and simply hit *copy, paste.*

A children's play area was visible over Liam's shoulder, the swings moving slightly in the wind, though no one was present, most likely due to the snow. In fact, all seemed quiet. Any neighbors were out of sight—assumedly either in their homes and away from the blustery weather, or out and about.

Noting that the streets were wide enough to allow visitors ample room to park, I helped myself to a space on the right-hand side of the road, slowed to a crawl, and put the car in park. Luke did the same as I watched him pull up behind me in my rear-view mirror, and I looked to the house—the third one on the left.

The two-story home was painted a dusty, greyish pink. An attached garage that could store two cars side-by-side was closed. Snow in the driveway was a pristine, untouched layer, and the same could be said for what covered the walkway that led to the small eave of the front porch. The windows on the upper floor all had blinds drawn; however, there was one to the left of the front door that left our view into the house entirely unobstructed.

"Lights are off," Colton spoke my observation.

"Driveway's empty," Luke noted. "Think a car's in the garage?"

Claire stated, "No one's driven on that snow."

"No one's home?" I voiced my hopeful thoughts aloud.

"Doesn't look like it," Liam said. "Unless they've been home for a while?"

"Give it a few minutes," Colton murmured. "Eyes on the window—looks clear, but you never know."

I didn't look at anyone else, but the pause in our conversation gave me the feeling that everyone had collectively narrowed their gaze toward the same space, searching for any movement within.

There wasn't any. In fact, the small window allowed us to see directly into what appeared to be a living room...and all looked quiet. Undisturbed. *Empty*.

Still, I examined it as if that would change, as did everyone else.

Claire asked, "Colt, do you have your headphones on you?"

"Mhm," he hummed. "Y'all gonna look out for me?"

"Someone's gotta do it," she quipped.

"I'm going in with you," I nearly cut her off mid-sentence.

No one questioned why, nor did they argue that it was too risky to go along with him in the hopes of finding further evidence of where James could be. Instead, because all of us were jumpy with anxiety due to his disappearance, everyone was silent as Colton slowly replied:

"Tagalongs *would* be helpful...get in, spread out, poke around, get out...it'll go faster."

Liam said, "I'll go, too."

With one glance in his direction, I saw the ever-present concern for me that was flaring in his eyes, and there was no need to question him.

"Me too," Luke spoke.

I heard Claire nervously whisper, *"Luke, you sure?"*

"Uh huh—no way I can sit still through this shit."

I thoroughly understood that feeling.

"Okay...Zoey," Claire called to her, "come sit with me while they go—you can watch up the street, I'll watch down."

"Mhm," she returned, apprehensive. "If—if there's any movement at *all* out here, even neighbors, y'all are getting the *fuck* out of there, okay?"

Her tone was laced with her usual protective mentality.

"Assuming there are multiple exits, this should be fine," Colton noted.

"Liam."

He twisted to look back at Zoey, and as their eyes locked, they seemed to share a silent conversation. I looked away from them and back to the house to give them a means of privacy, and Colton pressed:

"Y'all good?"

"Good," Liam instantly replied.

"'Kay," he returned in an exhale. "Let's get this over with—we'll go around back and see if there's an easy entry.

Front door's just askin' for trouble if he has a doorbell cam. Y'all ready?"

There was no verbal confirmation from any of us. We all just began to move—out of our respective vehicles, hoods on our jackets up in mock protection from the falling snow, and casually across the street. A car door opened and shut twice behind us as we all walked along, and I knew it to be Zoey going to sit with Claire and keep watch.

When our feet met the sidewalk, Colton reached into his hood, up by his ear with one hand, and then let it fall back to his side.

"Hello, Claire," he cooed. "I…did not see that. Observant—cockiness doesn't become you, though." He nodded toward the fencing on the left side of the house and told us, "Gate to the back."

We all followed the gesture of his head, the black hinges visible along the light wash of the wooden fence that enclosed the backyard, and we stepped through the snow to reach it. It opened with no trouble, and Luke glanced up and around.

"Private back here," he remarked.

Greenery encompassed us, planted just inside the fence line—the pine trees stood tall, and I felt myself breathe out a sigh of relief because Luke was right. The neighboring houses were invisible to us here...and I assumed that meant that *we* were invisible, as well.

"Good," I muttered.

The remainder of the backyard was small, with just enough space for a wooden deck on our right. Three small steps led to the patio, and as we all looked it up and down, Liam voiced:

"Back door on the porch?"

"Maybe," Colton responded. "Windows, too."

He pointed at the one situated next to the sliding glass door. Similarly to the one in front and unlike the door beside it, there were no blinds drawn, though we were at such an angle that I couldn't view the inside.

We trailed behind Colton as he walked up the steps, Liam at my back and Luke at my front, and I barely heard the wood creak before he pointedly pulled his hoodie sleeves to stretch over his hands, grabbed the handle, and gave it a gentle tug to the left.

It didn't budge.

"Locked," he murmured. "Figures."

"Well, *unlock it,*" Luke requested.

"I'm not a dog performing a trick, man," Colton chuckled. "Just take it easy—other options first." I moved past Luke and Colton, to the left, up to the window, and just as

I began to reach for it, Colton chastised, *"Ah-bup-bup-bup,* no-no. Cover up like I did—*fingerprints."*

I yanked my hands away, rapidly pulling down my sweatshirt's sleeves, and pressed the heels of my palms against the bottom edge of the pane. Wetness from the snow immediately melted through the cuffs that protected my hands, and when I pressed upward to usher the window along its track, they slipped. I caught them as quickly as I could, leaning the weight of my body into my touch on the glass, and tried once more.

This time, it gave way, leaving an inch-wide opening.

"Fuck, yes," Colton spoke. "In—window." I grasped along the crack, pushing up as far as I could manage, and it slid easily. "I know." He continued murmuring to Claire, "Lookin' good out there?" His head bobbed up and down as he seemingly nodded to her, confirming all was well, and he sidled up to me. Peering inside, he saw all that I did—an empty kitchen—and set both of his hands on the sill. *"After me."*

He boosted himself inside with a catlike balance that I hadn't expected from him, and once he was on his feet within the house, he brushed his sleeves against his pants. Pulling them up past his wrists, he outstretched one of his hands in an offer to me.

I looked at him, to his hand, raised my eyebrows, and let his offer hang in the air while I let myself in just as he did. Colton's shoulders shook in a silent laugh as I stepped lightly on the floor below and stood beside him.

His hand fell, and he sarcastically whispered, "Stripping made you graceful."

I waved away his comment that should have been amusing, muttering back, "I've always been graceful," as I looked around the kitchen while Luke and Liam made their way through the window.

There was little I could absorb about the space aside from the fact that it was alarmingly white. White cabinets. White countertops. White tile backsplash. Though the lights were off everywhere, the color rendered the area anything but dark, and it was apparent that it was rather clean. No dishes were out—no magnets affixed anything to the front of the stainless-steel fridge.

We all looked about, wordlessly pondering our next steps and where to go—where to look. To the left was a dining area, similarly clean with more white accents. To the right was the living area that we were able to see from the front window.

Colton quietly walked around the island, opening drawers with his hand that was once again covered by his sleeve and shutting them as he ruled them out. Luke followed suit and began to do the same, and as I moved to the right, Liam followed me. Entering the living room to gain my bearings, I saw the front door and a staircase to my left, and noted that I could see right past those stairs to the dining area.

Realizing that there were no dead ends to the main floor—the dining room wrapped around to the living and kitchen and vice versa—I returned to the kitchen with Liam. Colton seemed to have found a small stack of mail. Luke was standing beside him, and envelopes were scattered on the island before them both.

I asked, "Mail? What did you find?"

"Well, we're definitely in the right house," Luke remarked, pointing at the papers all addressed to an *R. Dowler.*

On the latter end of his hushed sentence, something rustled from above, and we all stopped our actions. As unnecessary as it was, Colton still held out an index finger as a request for everyone to cease speaking, and all of our eyes shifted upward.

It was a murmur.

A deep muttering that neither I nor anyone else could understand.

That aside, it was still *someone*...which meant that we weren't alone.

Colton let out a nearly inaudible, *"Shit,* someone's here—*yes,* Claire—upstairs—*stop-talking-stop-talking-stop-talking."* He ordered all of us, "Out. *Out.* Back through the window."

Liam grabbed my arm and tugged me toward the exit. Luke's wide eyes bounced around the room, landing on nothing as if he were considering his next moves. Colton swept all the mail into a pile to be taken with us, but he didn't get a chance to pick it up because his incoherent words were replaced by something else:

A guttural scream.

Clearly coming from the depths of a man's diaphragm, the raw, pleading tone grated on all of our ears, causing us to freeze. The hair on the back of my neck rose. Nausea swirled in my gut. I could feel the man's desperation through his initial screams, and when they abruptly cut off, we were all stuck in place, absorbing the sound of silent horror from above. There was no way to be sure how long it lasted—five seconds? Ten? Even twenty could have been possible, but there was no way to tell because those *seconds* dragged on.

Then, finally, the silence stopped.

"Fuck. OFF!"

The voice was quavering yet steadfast. *Angry.* Gritty as all hell.

And it was James.

There was no question in my mind that it was him—I felt it in my bones—and the realization was a shot of adrenaline. My heart raced, my palms shook, and I felt the dire instinct to sprint in the direction of his voice. To...I don't know...sneak up from behind and grab the man that I assumed to be Officer Randy Dowler by the head. To twist my grip so quickly that his neck snapped. To snatch a knife from somewhere in the kitchen and slash his throat.

That idea was unreasonable, of course. Not because of killing Randy. *I wanted to fucking kill Randy,* and if it came to it, well...I would happily see myself on the other side and evaluate my options after the deed was done. But because I had no idea of the layout of the upstairs and racing to find him could lead me to be face to face with the man in question, I was stuck in this goddamn kitchen, glued to the spot.

Luke, however, was not.

With an exhaled, *"Oh my God, he's here,"* he attempted to take off, but was abruptly met with Colton's attempted resistance.

Liam let me go and took his place, forcibly holding Luke back with a tight grip on either one of his biceps. Colton rapidly stepped aside as it was clear that he was only interfering with Liam's brawn, and Liam looked Luke in the eye as they spoke to each other in quiet murmurs.

"Take a breath, Luke."

"Do you fucking *hear James up there?*"

"I get that, man, *I do,* but—"

James began to scream again, and Luke's face contorted as if he were in pain.

"If we're not running up there to get him out, what the fuck else are we here for?!"

Colton ripped the headphone out of his right ear, holding it between his fingers as he told Luke quickly, "I'm all about busting in to fuck shit up, but he's a *cop.* He's probably strapped. You're about to bring fists to a gunfight, *and fists lose.* We can go upstairs, but we have no idea where we're going. It..." he hesitated, "it'd actually be better if he were looking for us and we could split up or something—if we could just get him down here, we..."

Before Colton could finish or Luke could speak further, my lungs had swollen to the point of pain on their own volition, and in an act of insanity to get the man away from James, I let it all out in a shrieked:

"HEEEYYY!"

Everyone flinched.

James' screaming stopped.

It was silent save for our loud exhales when Colton berated me in a hiss, "What. The *fuck*. Is *wrong with you?!*"

Liam let go of Luke, bringing his hands to his hair. "Jesus *Christ*, Cassandra."

I retorted, *"Colton said it*—it'd be better if he's looking for us rather than the other way around so we can split up and—"

"In a *planned manner!*" Colton whisper-yelled back. "With. Fucking. *Communication!* Not screaming like a goddamn banshee and leading him to us all in the place where he likes to eat his breakfast!"

James' voice sounded once more, this time the words indistinguishable and muffled.

I seethed through my teeth, *"Then. Fucking. Scatter."*

Colton had already begun to frantically search the area around him mid-way through my demand, quietly sliding drawers and opening cupboards before he whined:

"Why the *fuck* are there no knives in this kitchen?!"

Bending down to look underneath the sink, he grabbed a red aerosol canister, appraising it for the shortest moment, and footsteps creaked from above.

Liam's breath shook. "Cassie, I need you out of here."

"No."

Taking the container with him, Colton grabbed a handful of Luke's sweatshirt, tugging him along as he ordered in a hushed tone, "Move—*crouch.*"

They tip-toed to the left, choosing appropriate shadowed areas to hide.

"Cas—"

"I said *no,* Liam!" I whispered angrily. "I am *not* leaving here without getting Jay."

There was no time to speak of, and the desperation in my tone could have been sensed by the deaf, but Liam still ensured to catch my eye. With so much to see within his dark gaze, the split second that we glanced at each other stretched on for what felt like far longer, and I could read him thoroughly. There was fear—*naturally.* Confusion, for the briefest moment. Attempted understanding, then. And, finally, begrudging acquiescence.

Liam squeezed his eyes together tightly and replied, "Fuck, okay—*go.*"

His head tipped where I had intended to walk in the first place, and I scurried with light steps to the living area on the right. Liam's hands touched either of my shoulders as if he were shielding me, and when slow, careful footsteps walked down the staircase, our bodies shrank to the left, sinking into the wall.

Reaching the bottom, it seemed as though the man paused. Perhaps he was listening for something—*someone*—but none of us would have known. And then his steps grew slightly quieter, pointedly walking away from us. I let out a ragged breath, and it was only two more of the man's steps later that Liam nudged me with his arm.

I looked to him, and he gestured with his head to the upstairs as he mouthed silently, *'Go find Jay.'*

It was a tactic to lure me away from the maniac that was most likely Randy Dowler—I knew that for sure—and though my initial instinct was to vehemently shake my head and demand my involvement, I didn't. By my own doing, this had escalated to an immediate extraction attempt...and we had no idea if this man would be subdued in the midst of that attempt. We did, however, need someone to locate James—to try to free him from whatever madness this was.

I was more than up to the task, and I noiselessly demanded back, *'Be careful.'*

Liam gave me a curt nod along with what I took as a silent insistence for me not to come back downstairs until the coast was clear. I neither agreed nor argued, and I took off.

The stairs creaked as I took them two at a time, the carpeting below doing little to disguise my leaping up them. I didn't hesitate, though, nor did I look back, and I heard nothing else as blood roared in my ears rather than any potential noises from below or behind. The landing had scant hallway to speak of, with a single door to the left and right, and the only reason I ran through the former was because it was already ajar.

There was no furniture. No paint or decorations on the walls. In fact, if it weren't for the closet being cracked open, I would have left and sprinted for the other bedroom. I moved to the space instead, seemingly being pulled by gravity rather than my own two feet, and I pushed the door open.

I saw his legs first.

Sitting on top of a grey padding that covered the rest of the area, they were still covered in the brown slacks and loafers that he dressed in that morning. My heart jammed into my throat, and my eyes moved over his shirt. The material was a lighter, cool-toned blue, just as I remembered, but the top half clung to his shoulders for it was sopping wet. His face was obscured by a white hand towel, jerking from side to side as he grunted with each motion. It stayed stuck in place, what I assumed to be the same wetness making it heavy, and he only had time to take one panicked breath before I lurched for him.

Life often moves in both fast and slow motion when pulses race—when bullets fly—hell, when a boy unexpectedly shows up at your front door. It's moments like *those* where time is merely a construct—toying with the perception of reality by passing in the blink of an eye and subsequently slowing to the rate of pouring molasses.

This was one of those moments.

I yanked the fabric from his face, and time whipped back into hyper-speed.

I expected...fear in his eyes, maybe. Shock at my sudden arrival. Maybe even a whispered, *'Cassie?'* I didn't know...maybe I wasn't sure what to expect under the towel at all, but it most certainly wasn't *this.*

Bruising along his left temple and cheek had yet to darken to a purple, but I knew that it would in due time. The areas were angry—swollen to the point that the skin had split on his brow, and blood had dripped from the wound down his face. In some areas, it had washed away or smeared because of the wet material that was previously covering him, but in others, it had coagulated enough that it would require a generous scrubbing to remove it from his skin...over his eyelid...all the way into his beard.

James had flinched when I removed it, a metal clinking sounded from behind him, and as soon as he realized that it was me, his gaze turned to one of abject horror.

"*No,*" he exhaled, his voice strained, "no, *please,* no—where is he? *Why are you here?*"

The way he asked it was tortured, and I could only assume that he thought Randy had taken me at some point, as well.

Seeing James in such a state boiled my blood, and any fear that I had at the dire situation at hand just...*vanished.*

My vision tinged in various shades of red, my teeth threatened to crack under the strain of my clenched jaw, and I felt as though I began to vibrate in place with white-hot rage. I lifted an index finger, pointing it toward the floor, and it twitched as I brought it up to my lips.

He watched me carefully, his chest still heaving as gusts of air ran through him, and when I knelt before him to inspect whatever was clearly binding him, he was looking at me in realization-induced bewilderment.

I entirely understood why he was staring at me with a wide-eyed embodiment of the one-worded sentence, *'How?'* but there was no use for me to explain how I was here in this exact moment. Feeling for his wrists, I found the cold steel around them and quickly realized that he was shackled through the padding and into the wall. I gave it a rough tug, groaning as its hold on him was all too strong.

The floor shook with a scuffle breaking out from below, and I whipped my head back and forth in search of something—*anything* that could free him that was located nearby.

I found nothing, and I hissed, "God dammit!"

James anxiously murmured, "Cassie, you can't—"

Clutter rang out. Heavy items crashed to the ground.

"I—I don't—" I stammered, pulling on the chain with more desperation, "I don't know how to..."

He rapidly told me, "The cuffs aren't going anywhere unless we can cut them off, Cas. He'll be back. You need to go—"

"AH!"

A male voice let out a shriek, another yelled, *"MOVE!"* and heavy stomps from multiple pairs of legs joined the chaos.

"Oh my God," James whispered. *"Who else is here?!"*

I couldn't answer him, for there was more. *So* much more to be heard as I considered searching through the second room for something to aid in freeing him. The noises buzzed in my brain—general clatter of rushing feet, deep-voiced words, and something I could only describe as angered fighting—but then, it all stopped.

Loud enough to rattle an eardrum from afar, a gunshot rang out, and there was no time for us to freeze and listen to the reaction of whoever was downstairs. No time for me to do the impossible and free him from his handcuffs without severing either his wrists or the chains that bound them. No time to *think*.

"FUCK!"

I couldn't tell who had screamed it, for their voice was disguised by a pained grit that could only have been caused by someone being horribly wounded, and I knew.

I knew that my options were fight, flight, or freeze...and because there was no realistic way to escape with James without cutting the chain that bound him, cowering in a corner was useless, fleeing without him or anyone else was *fucking unacceptable,* and everyone downstairs sounded to be in the midst of mayhem with an armed man, my plans had drastically changed.

And despite the fact that it could very well have been a death sentence, I couldn't stay here. I couldn't sit aside and listen to the others, let alone *Liam,* in the face of danger without at least trying to come to their aid.

Without meeting James' eyes, I leaned toward his right side rather than his left to avoid his wounds and launched myself at him, kissing him with all I had in me. It only lasted a split second, and the moment that I separated from him, I leaped to my feet.

"Cassie, what are you—" James halted his words the moment that I allowed myself to look at him, and he seemed to instantly understand my intent. "No," he muttered, and as I spun on my heel, I heard him yell, *"No, NO—PLEASE!"*

Chains clinked as James forcefully yanked against his constraints, continuing to scream pleas for me not to run toward the living hell below us. His anguished begging instantly blurred my vision with tears as I reached the top of the stairs, and I quickly swiped them away. I bit the insides of my cheeks, willing the pain and the sounds from below rather than behind to fill my mind.

Stooping low into a crouch as I moved down the stairs, I listened intently. In the dining area on my left, the pained shrieking had turned to vicious grunts with every breath the individual was taking. Steps scurried from the kitchen. Everyone else appeared to continue around the layout to my right, and I made my move by sprinting to the dining space.

I had only just now realized that the tile on the floor was white, much like everything else—I wouldn't have noticed that at all if it weren't smattered with red. Trying not to hesitate but failing miserably, I noticed the splatters and smears along with the wreck of the dining furniture. Chairs looked to have been thrown. The table itself was askew and thrown on its side. A short hutch had been knocked over; two lamps that must have previously sat upon it were toppled to the ground but not broken. What was most notable, though, was just past the wreckage.

The blood had pooled on the tile to the point that it was akin to dark ink, and Colton sat within it with his back against the wall on the threshold to the kitchen. His left leg was stretched before him, black jeans darkened even further from the hole made near his knee, and his hands gripped either side of it as if he were attempting to hold his limb together.

Skin paled to the point that it was grey and clammy, Colton caught my eye, shook his head rapidly, and moved his lips, baring his teeth to silently shush me as he gestured with a nod to his right.

I moved as quietly as I could along the tile, edging past the hutch that was face down on Colton's left, and without stopping to question it, I grabbed one of the lamps. Holding it by the neck just under the bulb, I felt that the heaviness of it came from the gold stand on its wide base—not the white ceramic that I gripped. Twisting the power cord around it several times so the wire wouldn't hang loose, I held it in place just below my fingers and continued on.

Past where Colton huffed and puffed, I peered into the kitchen to find it empty. All had gone silent, and as I reached the living area, I thoroughly understood why.

Tall, dark-haired, dressed in policeman's blues, and facing away from me, he stood just before the couch with his gun pointed in my brother's direction. Liam was near the window, hands up to show that he had no weapon, and he was frozen to the spot.

My heart slammed in my chest, stemming from my anger—my *rage*—rather than anxiety, and I secured both of my hands on the lamp as if it were a makeshift bat, squeezing so hard that my fingers went numb.

Luke attempted to back away, nearing the staircase with a single, careful step when Randy whipped the gun to him instead. Both he and Liam nearly jumped in place, and Luke held up his hands in a similar fashion to how Liam was. The only difference was that he was holding the red canister that Colton had previously grabbed in the kitchen.

"Ah-ah, you try to go upstairs, I shoot," he told him, and I tread forward slowly. "You move, I shoot." Shaking his head and hissing through his teeth as if something had burned his eyes, he bit out, "You fucking spray me with that shit like your friend did, *I shoot.*" Luke kept his focus on him and nodded, and Randy instructed, "Put it down, kick it to me."

Luke did as he asked, setting the can on its side on the tile floor. He nudged it Randy's way, and it was when he moved slightly to the left to stop its motion with his foot that Liam noticed me creeping up.

What little color was left in his face drained away, his arms trembled as he held them up, and the breath that he pulled through his mouth was audible from across the room. His petrified look toward me was a mere glance, but the shift of his eyes back to Randy was still too slow.

He looked to Liam, rapidly turned to see me stalking behind him, and I didn't wait.

I just swung.

Lining myself up as if I were a first-string batter on a baseball team, the lamp cracked across his face, the recoil from the blow shook down my arms and into my chest, and though both Luke and Liam began to lurch forward, Randy went down. Following the momentum of the lamp, his body twisted, his expression went entirely slack, and he collapsed to the ground so quickly that his knees didn't even bend. He fell to his side, landing so close to Luke that he had to jump out of his way, and while he and Liam stopped mid-motion, I was winding up for another swing.

"*Shit,*" Liam cursed, running to stand before me. "Stop—" He placed his hands over mine to cease my actions, assuring me, "You got him, just stop!" He ripped the lamp from my grasp, I snarled in response, and he stated,

"We can't leave a string of bodies wherever we go, Cas, *fuck!*" Liam blew out a loud exhale. "He's—" Looking to Randy, he waited for him to move, and Luke spoke for him:

"Breathing—he's breathing."

"LUKE?!" James shrieked.

Luke took off, shouting, *"Where are you?!"* as he was halfway up the stairs, and almost immediately followed it up with a stammered, "Oh—oh my God, *Jay!"*

He yelled down to us regarding handcuff keys at the same instant that Colton called to us from the other side of the house:

"He down?"

His voice slurred slightly on the second word as Liam kneeled to roll the officer onto his back. I internally noted that it didn't appear that the lamp had broken his skin, but the red lump near his temple was practically forming before our eyes. He didn't stir as Liam patted along, searching his chest pockets and duty belt for the keys to James' cuffs.

"Yeah!" He called back. "Racked out. You good?"

Colton's sinister laugh was biting and tired. "He blew off my *fucking kneecap,* so *no..."* Seemingly focusing on his breathing, he heaved through the sass, "Could use a towel...tourniquet...surgery...amputation and prosthesis..."

I had intended to run straight back to James, but as I recalled the sheer amount of blood surrounding Colton, I made way for him instead, for there was no one else here to assist him.

"Jesus," Liam groaned, "Cas, go—"

"Already on it," I told him over my shoulder as I rounded the corner into the kitchen.

Rapidly pulling open any drawer that I could find, I finally reached the one to the right of the sink and saw an assortment of kitchen rags. Snagging the largest towel I could find in hopes that it could be tied around his leg, I half-jogged to meet him on the floor.

"Are you coming to help me?" Colton cooed, and I caught a hint of a smirk on his sweat-ridden face.

"You've been shot," I remarked. "How are you smiling right now—what is *wrong* with you?"

"Mostly," he panted, "blood loss—*oop,*" he voiced in a high pitch, "speaking of...you're kneeling in it..."

"Leg, Colton," I chastised.

He deliriously chuckled, "I can't lift it," and his head fell back to the wall with a dull *thump.* As gently as possible, I placed my hand on the backside of his knee, and he spoke, "This is gonna hurt like a bitch—*AHHH!"*

"I barely touched it—"

"I've been *fucking shot!* I don't think it matters how hard ya touch it!"

Sliding the towel underneath his leg and aligning it right over his kneecap, I warned him, "It's about to get worse," and I gave him no warning before I tied the fabric in a knot and gave it the swiftest of pulls.

The scream he let out was so loud that it made my ears ring.

"Sweet MOTHER OF CHRIST!"

Wincing at his decibel, I whined, *"Ow,"* tying it a second time for good measure before I sat back to look at my handiwork. "Are you good?"

He laughed once more, this time in a disbelieving, pained manner, and I instantly deduced that it was either a coping mechanism, wound-induced delirium, or shock.

"Good," he told me through his heavy breaths and odd cackling. "Get...your guy. Get...*out of here."*

"You bleed out before I'm back, and I'll *kill you*—don't make me deal with a corpse."

Colton's weak giggle caught in his throat. "Not today. *Go."*

Obeying immediately, I dashed for the stairs again.

Liam stood over Randy, watching him intently, and he noted, "You *really* got him—startin' to wonder how much he's gonna remember when he's up."

I only slowed enough at the base of the staircase to ask:

"Did you..."

"Get the key?" he questioned without taking his eyes from him. "Uh huh. Threw it up to Luke while you were with Colt."

I pointed with a thumb over my shoulder in reference to Colton. "He's fucking out of it, we need to—"

"Get out of here?" Liam finished my sentence for me. "Yeah—how much is he bleeding?" Splaying my red palms out for him, I gestured toward my pants, which had been soaked through the knees. A quick glance to me made his eyes widen. "Holy *shit*...how are we supposed to clean up and not leave all his blood behind?"

"You...don't!" Colton yelled.

Liam called back, "The hell do you mean *we don't?!*"

Colton continued to speak with his weighted inhales and exhales, but I didn't hear him, for Luke ran across the landing to enter the bedroom on the right-hand side. He said nothing as he burst through the door, and I had no chance to question him before James appeared at the top of the stairs.

On his own two feet and anything but weary despite the wounds decorating his face, he rounded the corner, frantically racing down the steps. His eyes locked on me, he looked to be flooded with relief, and he embraced me so roughly that his wet shirt made a loud *smack* against me.

Arms enveloping me around my waist and shoulders, he was squeezing so tightly that my lungs strained for air. I craved the feel of him more than the oxygen, though, so I returned it—my head tucked into his shoulder and my fingers digging into his back.

"Fuck, Cassie," James choked. "You *crazy* woman." He leaned away from me first, just enough to allow our gazes to meet and his fingers to brush over my tear-stained cheeks. "Are you hurt at all?"

"No." One of my hands left his back, skating up his shirt to land on the left side of his chest. Finding him tachycardic, I whispered, "Breathe, Jay."

His expression twisted, and he pulled me back to him once again.

Tone stripped and welling with emotion, he murmured into my hair, "I don't know what I would've done if you weren't okay…"

As his words yanked at my insides, I opened my eyes to see Liam watching us carefully. He cleared his throat loudly, quickly shifting his focus back to Randy as if he hadn't intended to see a damn thing, and the noise prompted James to abruptly release me, whipping around to turn his attention on Liam.

James muttered, *"Oh,* um..." as it was clear that though he was no longer looking our way, my brother had witnessed our dramatic embrace.

A bang erupted from upstairs, one much like the sound of the crashing furniture that had occurred earlier. Our heads all snapped to the stairway, and Luke could be heard from above:

"Oh, *God—*" High pitched whimpering cut him off, and he assured, "No, no-no-no, you're okay, I'm—"

"GET AWAY FROM ME!"

The woman's scream was terror-laced and shrill, turning my veins to ice.

James' shoulders sagged as he uttered, "He found her."

I questioned him, "Jay?"

"I'm here to help you," Luke's muffled voice comfortingly spoke. *"Look—*key—it's for your cuffs. I can—"

It didn't seem as though the woman heard a single word he spoke, for she shrieked, *"NO!"*

The vowel carried on for long enough that it turned into a pleading cry.

James somberly confessed, "I—*fuck,* I should have gone myself—come on." He grabbed my wrist to lead me upstairs, and he told me in a rush, "She'll probably calm down more with seeing you, too."

"Who?"

ELIZA MODISTE

"Sky."

Chapter 24

James

Racing to leave Officer Dowler's home was a necessity that we weren't granted the ability to perform for there were too many questions.

Did the neighbors hear the commotion?
Will Randy have amnesia?
Did anyone nearby call for emergency services?
How much evidence, aside from Colton's blood, would we be leaving behind?

Those were only a handful of the concerns swirling around us now that we had managed to get Skylar downstairs, and though we all felt as though we needed to run and never look back...we couldn't. The metaphorical ice that we stood on was not only thin...it was already cracked beneath us—and if we weren't careful, our next steps could plunge us all into the depths below.

Standing among the wreck of a dining room, Cassie still had a hand comfortably placed on Skylar's upper back as she sneered at us all:

"It's not too late to just fucking kill him."

Liam admonished her from the next room over, *"Cassandra!"*

Skylar simply wrapped her arms around her torso, and I couldn't decipher whether she truly believed Cassie's vicious suggestion or not.

I did, though, because the fury that had flared in her eyes when she tore the fabric off of my face was still there in all of its crazed, beautiful glory...and I could *feel* the anger that was boiling beneath her skin. Despite her clearly being relieved at finding me alive—and shock at realizing that Skylar was here—she was still all too genuine with the intention of her wrath.

"Cassie," I exhaled her name, "we aren't doing that, and you know it."

"Why the *fuck* not?" she hissed.

"Bad idea," Colton spoke from our left, still sitting in a pool of his own blood. His words were slow, as if he had to focus on forming them, and he heavily slurred, "A-Plus for enthusiasm, though."

One of our most abundant concerns announced itself in Colton's ragged breathing, and I rapidly noted, *"Shit, we need to get you out of here and to a hospital."*

Cassie stated, "We can get him in my car, I'll—"

"It's snowing," Colton reminded her bluntly. "Red...white..."

The mention that his spilled blood would clearly be seen on the snow made us all take pause, and all that could be heard for a moment was Luke. Pacing behind us, he had been assuring both Claire and Zoey that everyone was alive with one of Colton's headphones secured in his ear. From what I could tell from his side of their conversation, no neighbors had left their houses to investigate, and it was still, simply, *quiet*. It was odd to me, truly, for we had all screamed at some point—hell, the single gunshot followed by Colton's reaction to it would be burned into my memory for quite a while—and I knew that any of those sounds would carry. But, that being said, it was midday in suburbia...and the snow was beginning to pick up once again. Even if there *were* individuals who weren't away from their homes, hard at work, they were most likely inside with all doors and windows closed, and it was highly plausible that they could have only heard a single *bang!*

Perhaps because the sound wasn't repeated, there was no cause for concern. Perhaps, if anyone heard, they attributed it to a car backfiring. Or, perhaps, no one heard at all.

None of us would know unless the police inevitably arrived, of course...and Skylar was the one to ask:

"Why has no one called 911?"

Cassie gestured to the other room, where Randy still remained unconscious. "He *is* the police, Sky...we can't call the authorities."

"They can't all be like him," she replied in a shaking tone that matched her shivering body. "He—he said he couldn't have the rest of the force getting the calls from the dancers who—who were worried about the other ones like..." Skylar paused, her voice growing quieter as she said, "Like me."

"He did say that," I agreed, "but we can't know for sure. Last thing we want is to be in *more* hot water because other people know that we're aware of horrible shit he's done—"

"So, we just...leave him here?" she asked in disbelief. "I—he'll find me again. He'll find *you* again. I—" Skylar's voice hitched in her throat, and she brought her hands to her eyes. "I can't believe this is happening. There's a man," she waved toward Colton, *"bleeding out in the corner!"*

I wasn't sure how long it had been since Colton had been shot—my best guess was five minutes, at the maximum—and though Cassie had tightly wrapped his knee with a towel, it appeared to have bled through. His breathing was turning heavier with each second passed, and when we all stopped talking to glance his way, the pause in conversation made Liam nervously call out from around the corner:

"Colton?!"

One side of Colton's lip pulled up in an exhausted smirk. "Present."

I heard Liam exhale a relieved, *"Fuck."*

"Not dead yet," he returned wearily. Rolling his head, his brow pinched together as he took in the damage done to Skylar's face. "Skylar, right?"

She watched him hesitantly. "Uh huh."

"You have your phone?"

Skylar shook her head. "He took it, I—"

"Is it blue?" Liam called out.

"Yes!"

"It was on the cop," he replied. "Jay, yours is here, too."

"Oh," I muttered, for I hadn't exactly been thinking about my cell. "Thanks."

"Skylar," Colton tried to speak to her, but his tone was too soft, and her head had ping-ponged from Liam to me, and then back to Liam. "Skylar? *Skylar.*" Her mirror eyes danced around the room, finally landed on Colton, and he instructed her, "Call 911."

"We—" Luke paused, taking the headphone out of his ear to focus on us all rather than the conversation he had been plugged into. "No. We can get you out of here with us, there's gotta be a blanket or something to wrap you up better here, we can—"

"Carry me out?" Colton suggested in a wry rasp.

Liam interjected, "His blood's everywhere, Luke—"

"Have the whole gang...drop me at a hospital...with a gunshot wound?" Colton continued.

"Well, we can't be here when an ambulance shows!" Luke bit back. "We will be interrogated. *Immediately—*"

"You'll be interrogated eventually...if you drop me off, too." Colton announced, "Y'all can't...stay here."

"I don't," Luke rapidly shook his head, "I don't understand."

Colton looked to Skylar. "You were kidnapped."

She nodded, her voice small as she replied, "Yes."

"No one else was here...but you and the cop," he told her slowly—purposefully. *"That is what you tell the police*...no one else was here but you two...until I came in."

Her wide, guileless eyes simply blinked in his direction, and she asked with a weak wave to us all, "They can't be here?" Colton shook his head in a silent *no,* and she pressed, "Why?"

"If he's with another cop...if someone else is dirty...they can't be involved."

Realization of what he was attempting to do sank in for me—presumably for all of us, as we stared at him, stunned—and I argued:

"You'll be questioned."

"And...*unlike you*...I have no connections...my DNA is everywhere here...I'll be brought in...no matter what," he explained his train of thought, and we all listened. "Skylar...do you understand why you're here?"

Confusion written on her face, Skylar's eyes watered as she said, "No...not—not really."

"Look at me," he spoke to her consolingly through deep breathing. "For this to work...you need to listen...*you were kidnapped.*"

Skylar kept her gaze on him, and she nodded, repeating his telling of the story for emergency services. "I was kidnapped."

"You have no idea why he took you."

"I—I don't, I have no idea—"

"He did. Not. Tell you. Anything. About other...missing dancers."

"Wha—" Skylar looked around the room once more. "Why, I—I don't—"

Seemingly understanding, Cassie told her, "If there *are* other dirty cops, they can't know that you know."

Her palms flew to her eyes again. "I—*um*—okay, okay-okay—"

"We're friends," Colton spoke to her.

Skylar's hands fell away, tears trailed down her cheeks, and she cried, "We are?"

"Close friends." Colton nodded, and I even saw a sympathetic smile peek through his pain. "You went missing...and I noticed...*I came to find you.*"

"Y-you came to find me."

"I got to you upstairs," he told her.

Skylar confirmed, "You got to me upstairs."

"I tried to get you out...he saw us...he shot me...you hit him with the lamp...when he came after you."

"I-I," Skylar stammered, "okay. Okay. H-how did you know I was here?"

"Your phone's GPS," he clarified, "was on...I had your location."

"I—how do I even—"

Cassie interrupted Skylar, "Go get your phone from Liam. I'll show you how to share your location and give you Colton's number."

"Not the number you have," Colton instructed. "That's a burner...share to...colton-dot-langdon-at-icloud-dot-com."

Cassie nodded and began to lead Skylar toward the living area, her voice turning quieter as she began, "This is my brother..."

"Okay," my brain scrambled to keep up with his plan. "You're saying that we're all leaving and pretending that I was never even here?"

Colton gritted out, "Mhm."

Luke, still holding Colton's headphone pinched between his fingers, questioned:

"And if he *was* working with another cop? They'll know Jay was here, he's got a goddamn target on his back!"

I said, "If that's the case, then don't I have one on my back regardless?"

Colton remarked, "If there are any clean cops in this town...this is too big to bury. Kidnapping...assault...attempted murder at most, without anyone knowing...about the other dancers. Better to at least...*try* to get him...behind bars...without y'all involved."

Luke watched him with a slack jaw, the picture of disbelief, but none of us questioned this...this *plan* any further for it was the only one that allowed us to leave, Colton to not die from blood loss, and Randy to potentially be arrested.

Colton began to shiver, his teeth chattering loudly from what I presumed was shock.

"Shit," I hissed, "911 *now*, Skylar!"

She appeared to be already dialing, and just as she was greeting the dispatcher, Colton began to grimace and groan. Twisting his body as he retrieved the flip phone that he had described as a *burner* from his hoodie pocket, he looked to me as I was the person nearest to him. He extended his hand with his cell to me, and I quickly closed the distance between us to retrieve it from him.

Colton whispered, *"Lose this."* I nodded in response, pocketing it for future disposal, and he tipped his head toward the kitchen. A wave of shivers hit him as he muttered, "W-w-window."

My brow pinched together as I mouthed back, *'What?'*

Cassie came up from behind me, silently finding my wrist as she led me along to a window that had already been opened. The wind blew through it, the cold shockingly pleasant on my wounds, and I followed her out the way that I presumed they had all come in.

Though the palpable threat had gone, the minutes that passed after climbing through that window were ones that set my soul on edge. Not because of the unknown state of Office Dowler's comeuppance and whatever his memory retained, Skylar's questioning by the emergency services, or Colton's inevitable well-being—though those were certainly on all of our minds. No, it was because every living second was dragging by due to the need to repress our collective emotions.

Arriving back at our cars was horrid.

To mask the outward appearance to any onlooking neighbors, though I had begun to doubt that there were any at all, none of us could appropriately reunite.

Claire was unable to sprint to Luke mid-street, sobbing loudly as she threw her arms around his neck as I imagined she would, and he couldn't lovingly speak to her that he was okay.

Zoey couldn't go to Liam, embracing him with such velocity that he would have to sputter and cough, for I could imagine that her shoulder would hit him square in the diaphragm, and he couldn't wrap his arms around her in a bear-like fashion, picking her up and continuing to walk her to the car.

Instead, they remained sat in the two vehicles—invisible to us due to the falling snow, though I was certain that we were thoroughly visible to them.

Luke shot me a glance that I could have sworn was teary-eyed as I followed Cassie to her car, but he nodded in understanding as I tipped my head toward the Jeep to tell him that I was riding with them.

Liam didn't even ask—he just took the responsibility to drive—and when we were off, we were just...*off*. I sat in the back on Cassie's left while Zoey remained in the passenger seat, and because we felt as though we were being watched by some unknown force, none of us dared to so much as look at each other before we were long on the highway.

When Liam finally broke his stiff posture by reaching across the center console for Zoey, she let out all the air in her lungs as if she had been holding it in. Clasping onto his forearm so tightly that I knew her nails would make indentations in his skin through his sweatshirt, she rested her head against his bicep, cursing softly under her breath before placing a kiss there. Zoey cleared her throat as if her display of emotion were an embarrassment, rapidly pulling away from him, but he muttered a quiet, *"Come back,"* and she returned without hesitation.

I felt her, then.

Cassie's hand tentatively touched the top of mine, and my eyelids fluttered closed at the feel of her comfort, even if it were only from her fingertips. Heat swelled in my chest, and I looked to her to see that she breathed in deep alongside me as her warm eyes locked on mine. The moment that she whispered, *"Jay,"* I was quickly removing my seat belt. If I were being honest, I didn't even remember latching it in the first place...but that thought was neither here nor there. Cassie did the same, and the instant that we were both free, present company be damned, I pulled her onto my lap.

She cradled into me, her legs off to my left, her arms around my neck, and her head tucked into my shoulder...and the weight of her, along with the relieved breath that she let out against me, saved me from the repressive hell that we all had been momentarily bound to.

I held her to me as if she were sand running through my fingers—desperately and haphazardly—and I didn't relax my frantic, white-knuckled grip on her until she voiced in my ear, *"Shhhh."*

Neither of us moved until we arrived back at the complex, and when we did, there was no communication with the group regarding where we were all planning to go, nor were there any quietly spoken goodbyes. We all just walked straight into my apartment, shut the door behind us, and allowed ourselves to feel.

Holing up for the remainder of the day, there were occasional moments when we voiced aloud questions regarding the events past. They were mostly mutterings that we all wondered about but couldn't answer—like asking of the possibilities of Randy being charged or other police officers being dirty. The inquiries would fall away as quickly as they were spoken, but no one seemed to mind, for it was necessary that we aired out our worries.

The one that carried the most weight, though, came long after I had washed the blood from my face and intermittently iced my cheek for what felt like an appropriate amount of time. We all were attempting to eat ordered Chinese food. Gathered around the living area rather than the dining room, we hadn't even bothered to grab plates. Utilizing only the provided chopsticks, we silently passed around various paper containers. Sat on the opposite end of the couch from me, Luke appeared pensive as he stared forward at the coffee table.

Cross-legged and on the floor, for he didn't bother pulling up an additional chair, Liam had just impaled a piece of chicken on a chopstick and tossed it in his mouth when Luke spoke slowly:

"How...um...how do we know if Colton's alive?"

Liam's eyes widened as he coughed through his bite, and Zoey quickly pushed herself up into a kneeling position beside him to smack between his shoulders as he croaked, *"M'fine."*

From my right, Claire cleared her throat heavily, placing her head in her hands and miserably groaning a gritty, *"Oh, God."*

"Shit," Luke whispered, rapidly sitting up to stroke her back. "I—that's not what I meant, baby, *I think he's alive*—I meant we can't just...show up at the hospital. We've already been over this."

We had. And though we had thoroughly considered checking on Colton at the nearest emergency room, we all decided that it was far too risky for us to drop in for a wellness check. We knew that we needed to present as staunchly *uninvolved* with everything.

"I can call Skylar," Cassie quietly offered. "Just...just not yet, right?" I glanced her way to see her legs folded just as her brother's were, though she was in the green chair rather than on the floor. "I know it's been a little while, but I don't—I don't know if she's getting interrogated or something, and the timing feels..."

Claire murmured, "Yeah." She pulled her head from her hands and repeated once more, "Yeah."

"I'll call her in the morning," Cassie assured her.

I nodded, as did everyone else. Our appetites—which were scant to begin with—looked to wither down to nothing, and the leftovers were inevitably put in the fridge. And though it had been several hours since I had crawled out of the window at Officer Dowler's home, it seemed that none of us could bear to separate...so we shifted our seating, and everyone remained for several hours more.

Claire scooted to nestle under Luke's arm. I took the middle seat. Cassie wordlessly sat on my left, so closely that her arm brushed with mine, while Liam took her chair, and Zoey rested on the floor between his legs. Reruns of a sitcom played at a dull murmur on the television, and as every episode ended only for another to start in a marathon-like fashion, we all sank further into our seats—further into comfort.

On the first roll of the credits, I traced the backside of her hand with my fingertips. Having changed into a short-sleeved t-shirt and sweatpants, Cassie's arms were exposed, and I watched as goosebumps rose to her skin.

On the second, our fingers had begun to interlace, every slight movement causing the quietest intakes of breath from her or me, and I was sure that despite our eyes being on the screen, neither of us were watching it.

By the third, Zoey had wandered to the kitchen only to return with a glass of water. She set it on the side table next to Liam, glanced to me and Cassie to see our hands woven together, and silently walked to the light switch. Flipping off the one that glowed overhead while the kitchen lighting remained, our motions turned more private, and her grip squeezed mine.

The fourth played through, and at the fifth iteration of the theme song, Cassie looked my way.

"Hi."

It was a whisper, and I returned it. "Hi."

"You okay?"

"Mhm," I mumbled. "You?"

Her lips twitched in a barely-there smile, soft and somber. "Yeah." Slipping her hand from mine, she reached to brush my hair away from the left side of my face, lingering along the outside of my bruising. "Does it hurt?"

I exhaled bitterly through my nose because it did, and my previously taken ibuprofen had done little to take the edge off the aches.

"Mhm."

"Sorry." Her nails traced up to my scalp, gently scratching tiny circles and figures of eight. "This alright?"

The comforting gesture made my heart jump. I hummed quietly and contentedly, and as I moved to lovingly touch her cheek with the tips of my fingers, my actions felt predetermined, for I had seen this before. I had seen this look on her face while my palm cradled her with an emotional purpose that didn't need to be spoken.

It was another one from my dreams.

But instead of the usual feelings of horror and dread that came with my other visions coming true, I felt...*complete*. All of the sights—those from the past that occurred in a non-historical order, those with Cassie, those of Skylar, and the sensation of drowning—they had all come to fruition. The past had met the future, and all that haunted me had come to life as if it were inevitable. Now that I was here, holding her face in my hand, I felt that it was all over.

Dropping my hand back down to my lap, my eyelids fluttered closed as I relished in the sensation of her soft stroking through my hair, and I was at peace.

Cassie

The wood grain of his headboard tickled my upper back as I sat in his bed. His comforter was a soft sage green, and the sheets a few shades darker. Both of them were bunched at my hips, and I inspected the material. I idly rolled the fabric this way and that with my fingertips, finding the sheets to be more silken and the duvet similar to linen. I knew that if I were to sink into the bed, it would be remarkably comfortable. After all that we had just gone through, I supposed that anything would be, but this would be more so because James was by my side.

It was two o'clock in the morning, everyone in the group had long gone, and he was sleeping. He had been sleeping since he drifted off on the couch beside me a few hours earlier, and when I had ushered him awake to send him to bed after everyone's departure, he had hit the mattress with a heavy *thump* and instantly dozed once more. His breaths were heavily weighted now. Laying on his front with his inked arms stretched overhead and hugging his pillow, air was pulling into his lungs smoothly and letting out with loud huffs in a slow, metronomic fashion. His hair was hanging onto his face over his cuts and bruises, and while I had a strong urge to push it away and tuck the strands behind his ears, I knew that doing so would wake him...therefore, I resisted.

I didn't relax back into bed yet, though. I had been sitting, distracting my mind with everything and nothing—occasional phone scrolling and thoroughly examining the bedding around us being two of those things—but nothing would do. It wasn't that I couldn't sleep. I knew that I could. In fact, I was exhausted, and I was continually fighting the nod of my head. If I were to have slinked down into bed and wrapped my arms around him, I would have bet money that I would be gone within thirty seconds. So...*no,* my issue wasn't insomnia. Nor was it the terrors of what we had all seen.

Rather, it was the sensation of horror-ridden longing that I had experienced that continued to plague me.

He was here. For that, I was thankful, and if I allowed myself to settle, I knew that I would experience a rest like none other. However, when recalling the feeling of him being, for lack of a better word, *gone...*I couldn't do it. Every moment that my eyes would close, my head would sag down to my chest, my body would violently flinch, and I would look to him. Panicked and sure that my momentary lapse would cause him to evaporate like smoke, I would absorb his presence, breathe deep, and the routine would begin again.

It happened a countless number of times...and I was sure that I would be fine by morning. Though entirely sleep deprived, I would offer him a smile as he woke. Call Skylar to get a much-needed update on both herself and Colton. Demand that James take the day off work. Tend to the wounds on his face. Allow us to just...coexist.

I was thoroughly looking forward to that idea. However, because it was the dead of night, and I was convincing myself that all things do, indeed, go *bump* in the night...I was increasingly anxious with every iteration of my initial drift off to sleep.

My eyes closed. My head sagged down. I felt my breath pull, warm and heavy into my lungs. And the moment that my chin touched my sternum, I jerked awake.

"Ah!"

The uncomfortable whine that came from me was unable to be stopped. Eyelids snapped open and a hand covering my mouth, I glanced to James...and he looked back at me.

"What're y'doing?" he spoke in a sleep-filled voice.

I shook my head. "Go back to sleep."

He let out a dissatisfied grumble. "You're not in bed."

"Incorrect," I replied, despite the fact that I knew he was referring to me *lying* in bed and not my mere presence. "I'm sitting right next to you. *Go back to sleep.*"

James pulled his left arm—the one closest to me—out from beneath his pillow and reached for me. His hand wriggled its way under my shirt, found my waist, and squeezed as he groaned a wordless plea for me to come closer. His touch was alarmingly warm. So much so that it immediately made my eyelids droop and my body soften in his direction.

I sucked in a sharp breath through my nostrils.

"Sleep, Jay."

In a tone that could rival a teenage boy's, he mocked, *"No, you."*

"James."

"Come on," he begged with another squeeze of his grip. "Come here. I want you down here."

That, I unfortunately couldn't ignore—especially not when his vocal cords were adorably raspy. I exhaled heavily, shifted my way down to him, and we adjusted ourselves to be face-to-face. He laid one heavy arm over my waist, brushed his nose against mine once from tip to top, and sighed contentedly.

"Better?" I asked.

"Mhm." He murmured, "Why aren't you sleeping?"

I lied, "Just can't."

James let out a single chuckle. "Bullshit, you look exhausted."

Smiling at the sound, I replied, "Okay, *fine*. You're right. I'm tired."

"Knew it. So, why are ya sitting up in bed, then?" He jokingly ventured, "Is the bruising on my face too hideous? Ya don't want to sleep with the beat-up man? *I see how it is.*"

I rolled my eyes. "Oh my *God.*"

More seriously, he questioned, "Why aren't you sleeping, Darlin'?"

He was so obviously tired that I probably could have lied. His insistence, combined with his so well-spoken *Darlin'* weakened my will to the point that I considered the truth, though...and I couldn't withhold that from him. I reached gently—*so* gently—to usher away the strands of his hair that fell around his face and over his wounds. Tucking them behind his ear, I repeated the action three times to ensure that they were out of the way, and when I was finished, my hand lazily draped on his neck.

"Today was bad," I told him in a meek tone.

Making sure to lock his eyes on mine, he responded, "It was. You can't get it out of your head, can you?"

I shrugged. "I can deal with the screaming and fighting and...y'know...*everything.*"

He gave me the most minuscule of nods. "I know."

"You being gone, though...I can't. You're here, and it's over, but I—I was scared shitless, Jay."

His face pinched together as he breathed, *"Cassie."*

I admitted, "I just...I can't help but feel like if I fall asleep, I'll wake up, and you won't be here."

*"Oh...*come here," he consoled me, pulling me flush against him. "I'm not going anywhere."

He said the last sentence in my ear as my face nestled into the crook of his neck, and the scent of his bodywash invaded my nostrils. It was a smell that I was entirely too fond of—a musk that could only be described as *teak* or *mahogany*—and I allowed myself to feel as though I were being consumed by it. He sighed into me, and his touch began to comfortingly trail up to my head—down over my hair, and back again. The gesture made my chest tighten and my heart skip, and there was no hesitation as I murmured:

"I love you."

James' movements stopped, as did his breathing, and I supposed that should have made me nervous. Well...I supposed that speaking those three words at all should have been an altogether nervous affair, but it wasn't. Though the way that he froze against me could have been construed as him being taken aback or working up the courage to tell me that it was simply *too soon* for him to repeat the sentence back to me, I didn't care. I hadn't said it because I wanted to hear the words in return—I just needed to speak them aloud. Needed to tell him.

He pulled back, looking into my eyes with a hooded gaze that I knew wasn't caused by the pull of sleep, and he whispered:

"Say that again? I...don't know if I heard you correctly."

"I love you," I repeated, stressing the words with purpose. James blinked slowly, and I gently noted, "There are acceptable responses aside from *I love you, too,* y'know...*I care for you...I love being around you...you're special to me...*" Even in the dim lighting, his eyes sparkled while he smiled softly at my suggestions. I continued, *"Thank you* would also be...fine. Not the best, but fine. *Or,* you could just kiss me—"

His mouth sealed on mine quickly but delicately, and there was no pang of disappointment beneath my ribcage. Instead, there was a lightness within me as our lips moved against each other's because there was no rush. He had all the time in the world to repeat his *I love yous* back to me, and I would wait patiently until that time came—whether it was days, weeks, or months...it didn't matter.

It was after our third soft kiss that he quietly spoke against me, *"God,* I love you, too," and hearing it snatched the air out of my lungs.

"You're sneaky," I admonished him breathlessly, "waiting to say it back like that."

"Sorry," he chuckled. "You caught me off guard." James kissed me again. "I love you." Again. "I love you." And again. *"Fuck,* I love you."

I whimpered his name as my arms tightened around his neck. He snaked his arms down to squeeze me tight around my waist, and in the smoothest of motions, our drowsiness was whisked away, and our kiss turned deep. Our touches turned ever-greedy. His hands wandered under my shirt by the hem, his warm palms skating from the bottom of my spine to my neck, and I moaned into his mouth as he pulled me tight.

We devoured each other until heat was swelling between my thighs. My hips moved forward and back, his briefs-covered erection pressed hard against me, and James removed my shirt with a quick tug over my head. He immediately gave my breasts deft attention, tongue lolling over my nipples. My head fell back as my tone turned breathy, and with his hands pressed on either side of my ribcage, he pushed them upward, his beard scratching the flesh that rested in his palms.

I ushered him to take his time there, his movements, the soft sounds of his hums, and the smacking of his mouth a music that caused my eyes to roll back, and when I reached for his groin, he let out a pleasure-induced:

"Ahhh."

His motions ceased when I palmed him through his briefs, moving up and down as he gasped against my chest, and as I shifted to remove my bottoms, he did the same.

The fabric was kicked to the floor. My leg hitched over his hip. He pressed against me. We flexed into each other, and the feel of him stretching me was so magnificent that I lost my breath.

"Baby, I..."

"So good like this," he murmured as we moved slow.

"Yes."

We rocked away, on our sides and face to face. His lips at my throat, over my heated chest, and back to my mouth, I treated him in the same fashion, gently biting wherever I saw fit. As I nipped a particular spot over James' pulse point, he let out a satisfied, *"Ohh,"* and grabbed my jaw to lock my eyes on his. His grey smoldered as he kept me there, our tempo quickened, and he crooned, *"So* fucking good like this."

The noises we made were pleading as our movements into each other turned desperate, and I caught his lips for one open-mouthed kiss before exhaling:

"Are you right there for me?"

He thrust harder. *"Fuck,* yes."

Our tongues met roughly. I moaned into his mouth, and James brought us further, rolling me so I was on my back. I wrapped my legs around his waist, and he sank in deep, driving into me with enough force for the headboard to smack the wall over and again.

"Shit!"

"You like it hard like this?"

"Yes!"

"Cassie, *fuck."* Grabbing each of my wrists, he firmly planted my palms on the wood above me. *"Put those there."*

He let me go and reached up for the molding that was scraping against the drywall, pulling against it to cease its smacking as he used it for leverage to move faster. *Harder.* My hungry eyes dragged over him as the muscles in his arms flexed underneath his tattoos with every movement. I removed one of my hands from the headboard and—careful not to scratch—trailed it from his chest, over his abdomen, and down to my clit, nearly crying:

"God!"

His vocal cords rumbled, and as if he could take the sight of me touching myself no longer without closing the distance between us, he dropped back down to smash his mouth against mine.

"Are you gonna squeeze around my cock, Cassie?"

His filthy words were a jolt straight to the apex of my thighs, and I gasped, *"Yes."*

"Do it." James pulled back just enough to look into my eyes. *"Show me that you're mine."*

My thighs went weak, shaking as he continued to slam into me.

"James!"

"Ah," he moaned, trailing a hand down to my upper legs and flexing his fingers. "There's my girl. Give it up for me."

My tone turned sharp and shrill, and it was as if my body were waiting for permission because the moment his other grip moved to my mouth to stifle my noises of pleasure, I came with a garbled scream.

James watched me, drinking me in as I writhed beneath him, and his thrusts turned erratic—wild. My aftershocks repetitively continued, dragging on for long enough that I was nearly faint, and the bedframe rattled as he groaned:

"Fuck...*fuck*...oh, *fuck!*"

I felt the muscles clench in his back underneath my palms as he orgasmed, and his hand left my mouth only to be replaced with his lips. His kiss was tantric—tying me to him, body and soul—and we rolled to our sides once again, the gusts of air between us hot as our hearts hammered as one.

He held me and I him, stroking each other's hair, nuzzling noses, and humming contentedly until his breathing seemed to slow. I leaned back to look at him, knowing that I would find him fast asleep. Seeing him with his eyes closed and lips parted made my chest warm, and when I moved to kiss his forehead gently, he let out a drowsy grunt.

In a final attempt to evade my own rest, I slipped from his arms and wandered to the bathroom. I washed my face...debated taking a shower...legitimately considered making a pot of coffee. But I did none of those things.

I returned to bed, instead—climbing in beside him, allowing his arms to find me and pull me close, and I couldn't so much as blink before sleep took me.

James

This was the first morning that I had noticed how the window in my bedroom shined a perfect golden cast along my bedframe. Cassie lay facing away from me, the blankets bunched at her waist, and the ethereal glow lit her bare, tanned back in slits that ran through the blinds. My palms itched to touch her—to feel where the light had warmed her skin, tangle my fingers in her tresses, kiss the soft spot on her neck behind her ear, and wake her in the way that only a lover could.

Unfortunately, I knew that she needed the rest...and if I stayed in this bed for another minute, staring at her as she lay naked beside me, I feared that I wouldn't let her sleep much longer.

As gently as possible, I rose. Thankfully, Cassie didn't stir, and I padded about my apartment in the manner that I typically did on a day that was work-free. I found sweatpants and a loose shirt. Made a pot of coffee. Took some ibuprofen—though it was for my face rather than the twinge that historically shoots up my back when I sleep in a manner that my body deems unfit. The only notable difference in this morning compared to my usual ones as of late was that I felt...good.

Really good, which was saying something considering the aches and pains that lingered on my cheek, and I knew that part of it was just *her*. The other was mostly the feeling of upcoming closure with the knowledge that Cassie would contact Skylar whenever she was up and about. My anxiety would persist throughout time, I knew that...but I woke this morning without the sensation of foreboding that my nightmares would bring—and it gave me a spring in my step. A swelling, levitation-like floating within my chest.

It didn't feel entirely warranted as I had just come out of the haze of darkness, and some of it still lingered above us, but I reveled in it regardless.

I stood in my kitchen, leaning my backside against the counter while I waited for my coffee machine to finish gurgling away to my right, and a timid knock came from the front door. Moving to it and checking the view through the peephole, I saw his mop of a blond head before anything else.

Liam stood with his hands shoved in his sweatpants' pockets, short-sleeved shirt doing nothing to protect him from the cold as he patiently waited.

The door creaked on its hinges as I opened it. "Morning."

His eyebrows rose in mild surprise at the sight of me.

"Oh."

I held my hands out to the side, looking down at my body. "What *oh?*"

"Not," he blinked several times in succession and looked upward, "not *oh*, definitely not *oh*—um—just the, ah..."

Liam's nervous stammering had me wondering if he was here for his sister. If he had pondered how the remainder of our night had fared after he saw me run to her in a panic, embrace her as if she were life itself twice over, and subsequently witnessed her lovingly stroking my scalp as I drifted to sleep.

Over time, I had assumed that many saw Liam as how he looked—all brawn, no brains. Those who were actually graced with knowing him—*really* knowing him—knew that this wasn't the case, though.

I was happy to be one of those people. I was well aware that Liam was far from dim...and he would have had to have been a dumb man not to be cognizant of what was going on between me and his sister.

He continued, pointing at his own face in a circular motion, "The—*ah*—"

"Oh...the bruises."

Knowing that they had significantly darkened overnight, I stretched my neck to the right, angling my wounds in his direction, and he murmured:

"Jeez, man."

"Yeah," I sighed. "Not great, but, ah—ibuprofen, ice, all that. It'll go away."

"Right...right."

Liam seemed to be contemplating his next words as he shoved his hands into the pockets of his hoodie, rocking backward on the heels of his bare feet, to his toes, and back.

"Are you...here for Cas?" I slowly asked. "She's sleeping still."

"Huh?" He ceased his rocking, his dark eyes locking with mine anxiously. "Oh, no. No, I, ah—"

"Do you wanna come in, Liam?"

He smiled in a manner that seemed shy, and I noticed the scar on his lip stretch as his mouth did. The thin, white line marked him from the left side of his cupid's bow, jaggedly extending all the way to the underside of his nostril. I had no idea why I locked in on it now...maybe it was because I was more aware of his and Cassie's godawful childhood and teenage years...I don't know. But I did.

He chuckled. "My feet *are* cold."

I stepped aside to allow him in, joking, "It snowed yesterday. It's November. The hallway is concrete. Throw on some shoes or *at least* some socks if you're going out."

"You live across the hall," he countered as he walked through the threshold. "I figured it would be, *'Oh, good morning, Liam, come in,'* but—"

"But my face was off-putting," I mocked as I shut the door behind him.

He snorted. "No!" I shot him a raised eyebrow, and he corrected, "I mean...*yeah*. It's, ah...*very* purple."

"Thanks." I swiftly changed the subject as I moved to the kitchen, "You didn't bring coffee."

"Hmm?"

"Your French press," I clarified. "You didn't bring it."

"Oh, um...yeah, Zoey's not up yet." I heard him approach the island as I grabbed myself a mug and began to pour. He explained, "I'll make it fresh. I don't know how long she'll be out for."

"Very chivalrous of you," I commended, placing the pot back on the burner. "You want a cup?"

He scrunched his nose, and I knew that due to his coffee-aficionado tendencies, a simple drip would just *not do*.

"Nah."

I chuckled, *"Picky,"* as I took a tentative sip.

"Yeah, yeah, I know."

"So...what's up?"

"You, uh...you feeling okay?"

"I'm *fine*, Liam—*what's up?*"

Liam sighed. "Just fuckin' jump in, I guess—you and Cas have been, ah...*close.*"

Right.

I ignored the nerves that swarmed my gut and set my coffee down on the counter. "We have."

Eyes on the granite, he noted, "I mean, I thought it was just Cas being Cas...y'know, 'cause she's a lot sometimes?"

I couldn't help but smile as I replied, "She is."

"And that maybe she was just...I dunno...in your business a little more?" Liam began to ramble, "And I—I mean, ya didn't seem to mind, but then everything went down and I—" He looked at me seriously as he quietly stated, "Cassie fucking freaked, man."

My smile faded away. Of course, I had known her feelings during the chaos because she had shared them with me. But with Cassie being so...well...*choosy* about which emotions she decides to show, I had assumed that her nervousness—her abundant concern—her rage that I wondered if only I had seen—was all well hidden.

"Freaked?"

"Freaked," he repeated. "I mean, Zoey told me how she was before I got home from campus, and I don't—and Cas doesn't—and then we got to you, and I saw you both, and I—and then the drive back, and last night—" Liam shut his eyes for a second, *hard,* before opening them once

more. "I'm bad at this. I just—I can see it with you two, and I—I figured it'd be best to talk about it without everyone else, so..." He exhaled heavily. "Here I am."

There were many times over that I had contemplated speaking with Liam regarding his sister...and I had consistently waffled on exactly *how* I wanted to go about it. Do I dive in headfirst? Be bold and let him know that we've started seeing each other? Or...should I be more delicate about it? Tell him that after spending more time with her lately, we've just...*clicked?* That I like her? Which, I knew that both of those things would be massive understatements...but surely, it would be unwise to flat-out tell him that me and his only semblance of blood-related family are in it *deep.*

I mean...that would naturally bring up the question of, '*Oh...*so how long have you been fucking my little sister, exactly?' and I've seen how Liam typically reacts to most things involving Cassie. He's loud. Overprotective. Damn near paternal.

So...certainly, I couldn't go about screaming my love for her from the rooftops the moment that he noted we had been *close*...but he wasn't acting as he typically did regarding his sister and her personal affairs. And he also didn't seem to be *asking* whether or not we were involved...he was only voicing it aloud. Willing it to be spoken of.

Rather than beat around the bush of our relationship any further, I sympathetically said, "I wanted to tell you, but there was a lot going on."

"Puttin' it lightly," he mumbled.

"I..." *Love her?* My mind finished for me, but in the interest of not dramatically shouting my adoration for his sister into his face, I stated purposefully, "I care about her. *A lot.* This isn't some...some random fling, I swear—"

"Jay, it's *you.*" Liam let out a disbelieving laugh. "I didn't think it was random or ya didn't care. We're good."

I exhaled in relief. "Yeah?"

"To be fair, if I hadn't seen how you two were yesterday, I probably would'a felt a little different." He paused, rubbing the back of his neck. "I, ah, I'm not blind, but that was a surprise and a half."

I pressed my lips together tightly. *"Yeah...*sorry."

"Like I said, we're good, man." Liam waved my apology away. "I just wanted to clear the air."

I repeated, "Clear the air?"

"Uh huh—and for the record, I can tell that she cares about you, too."

My face instantly went hot.

"Oh," I whispered. "Thanks."

He smirked in such a way that I wondered if he noticed that my cheeks had flushed, but he gave me a curt nod that signified we didn't need to delve into nitty-gritty details.

"James?!"

Cassie's panicked call of my name rang out from my bedroom, interrupting Liam's large inhale in anticipation to speak once more, and I didn't get a chance to take in his reaction for my head had snapped to the noise so quickly that I should have been concerned about whiplash.

I understood in an instant—she woke, and I wasn't there.

My chest lurched as I cursed, "Shit."

Running for the door, I left Liam without a second thought, and the moment that I reached for the knob, it was yanked open for me.

Haphazardly dressed and hair frizzed and frazzled, Cassie's eyes were wild as she nearly sprinted into me. I caught her by the arms, holding her at length because she looked to not be absorbing what was around her, and stooped ever so slightly down to her level.

"Cassie."

"I..." Under eyes a bit purple, she was hellbent for the door until I spoke her name. When she finally saw me, she just blinked. "You're here."

"I'm here," I told her gently. "I was just making coffee—was letting you sleep."

"Right," she breathed. "Sorry…I—"

Liam cleared his throat loudly from behind me. Cassie caught sight of him immediately, and she looked to be caught with her hands painted red. I meekly glanced at Liam, grateful to find him less than shocked and looking at his sister with arms crossed and a half-lidded gaze.

"Oh…erm…hi, Liam."

"Good morning," he greeted her, no doubt amused at the lack of her usual confidence, his words less than casual and holding an undertone of, *'I know what you did.'*

She hooked her thumb over her shoulder toward my bedroom door.

"I…*um*—"

Rather than mention her entry or the fact that she had exited from my room, he asked, "Did you call Skylar yet?"

"Um…no? Not yet."

"Good—let me make some coffee for me and Zo', and she'll call Claire." Liam's thick brows pinched together. "I think she would want to be here…she looked worried."

"Yeah," Cassie quickly replied. "Of course."

Just as Liam passed me on his way to the front door, he spoke, "Jay," and clapped me twice on the shoulder so hard that it stung through my t-shirt. "Be back."

We watched him stroll out the door, Cassie with her jaw hung open, and when it clicked shut, she looked at me, bewildered.

"What—what the fuck just happened?"

I shook my head as I let out a quiet sigh. "Coffee?"

The ringing through Cassie's speakerphone was akin to a ticking timebomb. All six seats were filled as we gathered at the dining table—Luke and I at the heads with Claire and Cassie on our sides and Liam and Zoey on the other—and our breath was bated as it rang.

And rang.

And rang.

One would think that deciding to wait overnight to discreetly contact Skylar for an update would have been hard enough. While that period of time wasn't *great,* the majority of us—save for Claire, who appeared to be nearly sick—were clearly able to compartmentalize these particular emotions until the time came. Now that the time was upon us, though, those twenty or so seconds in which we were left in limbo were oddly torturous.

Skylar finally answered, "Hey," and we collectively perched on the edges of our seats.

Rapidly speaking, Cassie greeted her with, *"Sky*—how are you, what's going on, how's—"

"Who ya talkin' to?"

The voice from the background was deep but also somehow lilting in a sing-song manner, and it made us all deflate into our seats in massive relief because it was clear who it belonged to.

Luke leaned close to murmur to Claire, *"See?* It's okay," rubbing her shoulders while she held her face in her hands.

"Cassie," Skylar seemingly replied to Colton, her voice muffled as if she had covered the speaker.

We were still able to hear his shocked, "And company?!"

She exhaled heavily. "I don't know. Let me at least—"

"Are they checkin' up on me?"

"Colton," she replied calmly, as if she were speaking to a child, "I. Don't. Know. You have to give me a second to talk here—"

"I *knew* it," he boasted. "Tell them my knee's fuckin' *shot.*" Colton hesitated, and then giggled in a high-pitched tone that made us all squint toward Cassie's phone in the center of the table. "Which is funny! 'Cause it *was* shot!"

Skylar grumbled, "Oh, goodness."

"And I almost. Fuckin'. Died!"

"Colton, they know that—"

"Great drugs here, though," he simpered. "Y'know what's awesome? *Ketamine."*

Luke mumbled, "Oh, dear *God."*

"Alrighty," Skylar sighed. "Colton, I'll be right back—"

He cooed, *"Your hair's pretty."*

"Bye-byeee," she sang in a soothing tone as the sound of a door shutting emitted through the speaker, and then she groaned loudly. "If you heard all that and are somehow still on the line, you can tell that he's...*so* high. Fine now, but high as a kite off pain meds."

"Aren't those supposed to keep him level?" Luke questioned more to himself than anyone else. "You'd think he'd be knocked out instead of, ah...wired?"

She huffed out a single, *"Ha,"* before saying, "You'd think so. I swear I saw a doctor note in his file, *'wild on ketamine,'* but they closed the screen so quickly that I couldn't tell for sure. Anyway—no more ketamine for Colton."

We all had a brief moment of silent amusement, peeking at each other with raised eyebrows before Cassie asked, "And you?"

"Me?" Skylar asked as if she weren't sure why Cassie would say such a thing. *"Oh.* Er—one stitch above my eye."

"You're alright?" Cassie pressed.

"For the most part," she remarked. "Um...Jay?"

It was quiet for a beat before I told her, "I'm okay, Sky."

"Good," she nearly whispered.

All wanting to ask the obvious, we glanced around the table before I questioned, "Have the police talked to you at all?"

"One second...stepping outside." The metallic clack of a push bar on a large door sounded. *"Gosh,* it's cold," Skylar muttered. "Okay...long story short?"

All of us replied in a collective, "Yes."

"They've been around. Kinda why I've been staying here...plus, Colton doesn't have anyone else here with him, and we're...you know...*friends.* "She stressed the last word with a purpose that we didn't need to question. "Anyway...that police officer that took me, I—I don't think he remembers much. I mean, I haven't been told specifics...been eavesdropping, though...heard someone say *retrograde amnesia.*"

Liam glanced at Cassie, eyes wide as he mouthed, *'Shit.'*

"He's still in the hospital, but I *also* heard the officers that came in saying that he needs to be detained upon discharge, which...that means he's being arrested, right?"

"I think so," Claire remarked, her voice turning jovial, *"God,* I think so! At least until a trial?"

Zoey spoke up, "Did anyone question you?"

"Asked me, like...my telling of things," she replied. "Which you guys know, right?" We did know. The fabricated story that now only involved Colton and Skylar was embedded into all of our memories, whether we wanted it to be or not. "As for Colton, he's too looped up on medication to be reliable on any front, so they're circling back to him later." She continued, "I mean, one of you already mentioned it—I'm not doubting that we'll have to go to a trial for this, and those take time, so...long road ahead, right?"

It was interesting that she said so, for I was thinking the opposite, though I supposed that was because I was looking at the situation only in my shoes. As far as I had felt the night prior, my door had closed. The seemingly never-ending cycle of what haunted me, along with my family, was soon to be over. Long gone. Forever existing in our minds, but hopefully turning into a distant memory that we all buried with the purpose of living peacefully.

Our door *did* close—I felt it in my bones that it had—but I feared that upon its closure, a window may have opened.

Epilogue

Normal (adjective)

nȯr-məl

Conforming to a type, standard, or regular pattern. Characterized by that which is considered usual, typical, or routine.

Normal.
Normal.
I had said the word—both in my mind and aloud—so many times that it had begun to lose all meaning. *Normal* now sounded merely like a strange conglomeration of let-

ters. It was mush. A moving of lips that may as well have been incoherent babbling in the distance.

Hence why I had taken the time to Google search the word and find the literal definition within a collegiate-approved dictionary. I now knew it verbatim as I was attempting to settle the confusion in my brain, but it did no good. It was still just...noise.

That being said, I knew what my normal could look like.

The morning that I was to return to work, she was there. Flitting around my kitchen in a tiny pair of cotton shorts and one of my t-shirts, I had smiled as I watched her pour my coffee into a travel mug. Because she knew that my tastes varied from day to day, she had asked how I wanted it. I told her that it was fine as is, for I was recently enjoying the bitter tannins just as she did. Cassie searched for my lunch in the fridge, and I reminded her that I had already retrieved it. I patted the space where I had safely secured it in my work bag slung across my shoulder, and she nodded in response, promptly beginning to search for anything else I needed.

I told her, "I've got it all, Darlin'. I have to go."

Cassie blew a rough breath through her nose. "You sure?"

Stepping forward to stand before her, I gently joked, "You're too young to get worry wrinkles," as I traced the space between her brows that looked wrought with concern.

She pouted out her lower lip, and I traced my touch downward to brush my thumb against it.

"One more day?" she pleaded.

The way she said it made me want to throw all knowledge of the necessity of having a job out the window.

"You're very good at puppy-dog eyes," I murmured, "but I've gotta get back to normal at some point—you know that."

Her arms wound around my lower back. "You could be late?"

I chuckled, pulling her in for a single kiss, and just as she hummed against me, I mockingly whispered, *"Succubus."*

"Does that mean *yes?*" she cooed.

"You're trying to fool me into you fucking me all day?"

"Mhm."

Her giggle was quieted with my mouth, and it took all the power I had in me to note, "Unfortunately, I don't get paid to be in bed with you."

Cassie groaned loudly. Her frown returned, and I nipped at her lip.

"You'll call me?" she asked.

"Yes."

"Right when you get in the car?"

Her palpable nervousness squeezed at my chest, and I touched my forehead to hers. *"Right* when I get in the car."

"Okay."

Our lips brushed together one last time, and I muttered, "Love you."

She sighed. "Love you, too."

I released her, happily grabbing my coffee from the counter, and called over my shoulder to her, "Enjoy being willfully unemployed while you can!"

Cassie gave me a hefty eye roll and a playful, *"Uh huh,"* and I strolled out the door.

The last time I had been in my vehicle was when I went to retrieve it from the side of the highway the day before. Doing so had made my all-too-usual nervousness flare in my chest, and it was easily equated to someone staring over my shoulder. Or, perhaps, the feeling of being a child and running from a nonexistent monster—one that only lurked in the darkness after a light switch was flipped off, and you sprinted toward any remaining illumination.

Now was no different, but I pushed through, and there was no monster waiting to snatch me. I secured myself in the driver's seat, pulled out onto the road, and called Cassie as she had requested.

We spoke of her job options—of which, I heavily favored the salacious suggestion that she could be my own private, live-in dancer, though we both knew that option was one made in jest. She didn't care for the thought of returning to Gas Lamp or any other club, and neither did I—and I *swear* that wasn't due to my jealous tendencies. As much as it seemed that the threat in Salem and the surrounding area might end with Officer Dowler's arrest, we truly didn't know that for certain...so Cassie felt it too nerve-wracking to go back to dancing, no matter the location.

She read off job listings for accountants nearby, discouraged from the pay rate or necessity to gain further education in order to receive a decent salary. By the time I arrived in the parking lot at work, we were debating her monthly mortgage payment, the reality of how long her savings would last her during a job search, and whether or not she should expand her education. The mention of upcoming change had laced excitement in her voice, and as I walked into the office, the upturn of my lips remained until I reached my desk and Shawn nearly screeched:

"What the *fuck?!*"

The volume of his voice made me jump in place. Just having reached for my glasses in my work bag, I fumbled them by the stems, and they fell to the floor.

I clutched at my chest. *"Jesus,* Shawn!"

"Brooks!" Larry, who sat just two cubicles down from us and was approximately twenty years our senior, snapped from his seat, "Language!"

Picking up my glasses from the carpet, I began to polish the lenses with a pinch of the fabric on my shirt while Shawn stammered, "I—um—sorry, Larry."

Frames on my face, I glanced over to see his vibrant eyes wide as they trailed over my cuts and bruises. Not long enough to have begun to fade from the nasty purple to a more acceptable green, they remained marring my skin—dark and obvious—and Shawn looked no less than aghast. Stood at his full height in the entrance to his cubicle, his sweater-clad arms hung loose at his sides while he looked at me expectantly.

I sighed heavily. "Hi."

"Hi?" Shawn had begun to raise his voice in incredulity, but he managed to stop himself, glancing up and down the hallway of cubicles between us before he bustled over to mine. Hands on his hips as he stopped no further than a foot in front of me, he challenged with his decibel at a low murmur, "What happened?!"

"Mugged," I succinctly told the lie that I had been planning to. "I was mugged. Not exactly proud of it."

"God…I—how—you're not exactly a small guy, Jay, how does that even happen?"

"People have their means," I remarked, "I don't exactly want to do a play-by-play here."

Shawn clenched his jaw and released it. "Are you good?"

"*Look* at my face, man—"

He grumbled, "Kinda hard not to—"

"I'm as good as I can be," I assured him. "I've just…I've had a hell of a week, or—or less than that, I don't—I've lost track of time at this point. I don't wanna talk about it. Okay?"

His green gaze bored into me for two long, time-sucking breaths, and though he didn't seem to *want* to cease his questioning, he replied, "Okay. Fine."

"How about you tell me about what's going on with *you*," I offered.

"You think I have anything to say about my life?" Shawn finally broke into a weak laugh. *"You've been gone.* I thrive off your gossip, James, and I've been severely deficient in that. My life is…" He hesitated before he joked, "Pretty damn boring unless I'm going to strip clubs with you."

His mention of Cassie without even saying her name brought a smile to my lips.

And to give him the shred of gossip he desired, I said, "She quit, y'know."

Shawn squinted at me. "Don't tell me that was *your doing*. It's her job, Jay—"

I cut him off, "Different circumstances, damn—I'm not *that* toxic."

His eyes shot to the ceiling. "I doubt that you actually are. Just sayin' in this particular instance, you seemed a little blinded."

"Yeah, yeah—"

"By the glow-in-the-dark lights."

I groaned, "Shawn."

"Brooks," he insisted, as he always does. "And, in fact, those lights were so blinding that you broke. A. Man's," he whispered the last word, *"Fingers."*

"Which he deserved," I countered quietly. "Don't act like you don't agree—"

"I do, I do," he relented.

"And I'm assuming that he still fuckin' works here," I sneered. Shawn nodded while I muttered, *"Point—*my point...not that I was wanting to in the first place, but strip club trips are not in the cards for me in the future, 'kay?"

He chuckled, "I figured that already, man."

"And," I admitted in a somber tone, for I knew it would bring a frown to his face, "I don't want to talk about my last week 'cause it's been a *lot—*including anything with Cassie."

My assumption about his inevitable expression was correct.

"Jay, *please!*" he whined.

"We're good, we're together," I succinctly spoke. "'Kay?"

Shawn griped, "That's not *enough.*

"Beer, though?" I offered. "In Salem?"

As if his saddened expression had never existed, he smiled wide.

"Yeah?"

And I returned it. "Yeah."

Cassie and I arrived at Henry's together, the atmosphere pleasantly quiet with only a handful of other patrons sitting at the counter. She gave Garrett a friendly wave. He stopped his motions from behind the bar, buzzed blond head lifting as he saw her greeting in his periphery. He happily waved back...and I tried my damnedest not to bark to defend my territory.

Not that she was my territory.

She was her own territory.

She *was*.

But she was mine.

Cassie glanced at me with playfully narrowed eyes as if she had read my every thought, and I immediately thanked my good graces that I hadn't spoken anything along those lines aloud. Throwing Garrett a begrudging waggle of my fingers in greeting, he returned it with a megawatt smile that made me chew on my tongue, and without skipping a beat, he turned to grab my usual whiskey. He held up the bottle in question with a raised brow. I nodded, and he went to work.

At the table that we used whenever Luke and Claire were off the clock, we sat in our usual seats, her on my left and I on her right. Already having arrived and received their own drinks, Luke and Claire spoke a simultaneous:

"Hey."

We returned it—me with an uptick of my head and Cassie with a chipper, "Hi," and once again, they talked at the same time.

"You still staying at Jay's, Cas?" had come from Claire's mouth, while Luke had merely asked how my day went as he had known that it was my first shift back at work.

Luke tipped his head to the side as he looked to her with a disbelieving smile.

"Claire," he laughed her name.

She hummed back, "Mhm?"

"Didn't we talk about this?"

"Whatever do you mean?" she coyly replied. "It's a simple question. They've never shown up somewhere *together*...so I'm asking."

"Not prying," he stated as if it were a reminder. "We're *not* prying—weren't *you* the one to say that we shouldn't be prying?" Luke feigned, waiting for Claire to reply. She opened her mouth to do so, and he mockingly cut her off, "I *distinctly* remember—"

"Yes, I'm still at Jay's," Cassie admitted, matter of fact.

Claire high-beamed on her. "Is that right?"

"A *lot* happened to make me bunk there for a bit, no?" she responded with a single, high eyebrow. "I'll get back to my place soon."

"No rush," I told her, and she shot me a crooked grin.

My drink was set before me, and we all looked to Garrett as he remarked, "Cas, I have to go grab another bottle of Jack from the back, so give me a sec—"

Without hesitation, she reached for my glass, took a hefty sip, smiled as if her insides were immune to fire, and took it as her own.

"That's okay, Garrett—Jay's gonna have another."

Garrett murmured an understanding, *"Right,"* as he turned to move to the bar. "Be back."

"I'll buy your next one?"

Cassie was looking at me with a glint in her warm eyes that challenged me as she always did, and as I had done in the past, I imagined tucking the stray strands of hair behind her ear, pulling her to me, and kissing her so deeply that I could taste my whiskey.

Only this time, there was no need to sit back and imagine. My gaze wandered down to her mouth, her teeth bit at her lower lip, and I did it all—basking in every movement. Her hair was silky between my fingertips. The deep pull of whiskey she took had already seemed to bring a flush to her cheeks that I could feel on my palm. Her husky chuckle as I ushered her toward me with a curl of my hand on her neck played in my ears like soft music, and my whiskey on her lips—and oh-so-briefly on her tongue—sent me soaring.

Claire squealed, "AH!" as Luke groaned:

"Good *God*, Jay."

At my brother's complaint of our expressive public display of affection, I pulled away.

"Yes," I told Cassie. "You're buying my next one."

She giggled, my hand fell back to my lap, and Claire announced:

"I have been *waiting* for this to be official public knowledge!"

"Waiting for what to be public knowledge?" Shawn's voice came from my right, and I turned to him, surprised.

"Oh—hey."

"Hi, everyone," he greeted the table, and then fixed his gleeful gaze on me. "What, did you not hear me come in? Didn't hear that little ring of the bell above the door 'cause you were all..." He mimed embracing someone, his arms hanging in thin air as he comically moaned, closed his eyes, and *licked*.

Luke chortled, and as Shawn moved to sit down beside me in the third chair gathered around the head, I mumbled, "It wasn't *that* brazen, but something like that."

Shawn pointed at Claire. "If you're talking about Jassie—"

I grumbled, *"Oh, God."*

Cassie laughed—*loudly.*

Claire's eyebrows shot up as she questioned, "Jassie?"

"Mhm," he hummed, moving his finger to gesture toward me and Cassie. *"These two.* If you were talking about waiting for *them* to be public knowledge, ya should have been hanging with me."

She replied, "What is *that* supposed to mean?!"

Shawn shrugged. "Let's just say that I like to be in the inner circle of all things Jassie."

Claire squinted. *"Inner circle* as in..."

"As in, if ya wanted to debrief—"

"Shawn."

Without taking his eyes from Claire, he casually chastised, "Don't first-name me, Jay," and didn't skip a beat before continuing, "I've got notes. *Receipts.* Happenings over the last two...three weeks?"

Claire nearly yelled, *"Weeks?!"*

Shawn bobbled his eyebrows at her. *"But* the last few days or so? Zip. Zero. *Nada.* Sounds like you're not getting the full story from these two, either—*we should compare notes."*

"We're happily living in the *present,* thank you," I reminded him. "No need to gossip here."

"Well, *go on,* then!" she ushered him.

"Ah-ah," Shawn stopped her with an index finger in the air. "Not now—I'd hate to activate his grump gene."

Claire snatched her phone from the table. "Give me your number, Shawn."

"Brooks," he corrected her quickly and began to rattle off his cell number. He then asked Luke in an all-too-playful coo, "You wanna join in on the fun?"

Beer half-lifted to his mouth, Luke snorted, took his time taking his sip, set his glass down with a clunk, and upon realizing that Shawn was expectantly awaiting a response, he responded:

"Oh, you were serious. Ah—no. No." Seeing the side-eye that Claire shot his way, he gently added, "No, *thank you."*

"Suit yourself," Shawn told him with a shrug. "Now—more importantly—*this.*"

He waved a hand so close to my face that he almost struck me, and I flinched out of his way.

"I told you," I chastised him. "I was mugged."

"Yes, you said so," he remarked with skeptical eyes. "But *where?* When? How? Weren't you sick? Someone mugged a poor, sick guy?"

"You didn't hear?" Garrett piped up as he set my new whiskey down before me, and Shawn's focus whipped to him. "In an alley in downtown Roanoke. Few days ago, right?"

"Thank you," I mumbled, clarifying the story that I knew Luke and Claire had planted for me, "Yeah. Few days."

Shawn's attention stayed on Garrett for a beat, as if his presence had momentarily rendered him a deer in the headlights, and he shook his head rapidly before pressing, "So...you *weren't* sick?"

Garrett questioned with a cock of his head, "You were sick?"

"No—"

"Wait, no," Shawn backtracked, "if you got mugged when you started taking off work, your bruises wouldn't be so fresh."

"Was." I rapidly clarified the lie, "Was sick. Took off work. Wasn't sick anymore. Got beat up in a goddamn alley for my credit card and a spare twenty." Turning to Cassie, I simpered, "I forgot, I can't buy that first round...still waiting for my card's replacement. You wanna get my drinks for me, Darlin'?"

She smiled wide. "Chivalry is genderless, I suppose."

Claire threw her head back, incredulously murmuring, *"Darlin'?"* to the ceiling.

"What are we talking about?" Zoey's dainty voice chimed in as she and Liam arrived and slid into their seats.

"Pet names?" Liam guessed with a smirk that seemed *extra* lopsided.

"Wait, do you know?" Claire asked Liam.

Luke muttered, "How could he not?"

"Know what?" Liam returned.

"Is the bell above the front door broken?" I griped, not answering their ponderings as I grabbed my glass. "I mean, *shit.*"

"You're distracted," Cassie quipped quietly.

Garrett pointed at Cassie first, stating the past events in chronological order, "Whiskey stealing," he moved to me, "tongue down throat of said whiskey stealer—"

"James!" Liam admonished me, though it held little to no weight, and he maintained his smirk throughout it. "In *public?*"

I thanked my lucky stars that I had already swallowed my sip, for I knew I would have choked otherwise, and my face heated alongside my throat.

"He knows," Claire monotonously deduced.

"That my sister's a gravedigger?" Liam innocently asked Claire, and Cassie shrieked:

"LIAM!"

He ignored her. "Yeah," he noted with a wide grin as Claire and Zoey tried to keep their laughter under their breath. "I know."

Garrett chuckled, inserting himself back into the conversation as he shifted his finger to Shawn, "Asking about Jay's face," and Shawn assumedly smiled at the recognition.

"Oh," Zoey told Shawn, "mugged—he was mugged."

"Yeah," he replied with a heavy eye roll, *"I got that."*

"And," Garrett moved his focus back to me. "Darlin'."

His alarmingly white, straight-toothed smile remained, and I was surprised to see no hint of jealousy or contention in his eyes.

Reluctantly softening toward him, I sighed, "I think ya covered it, Garrett. Thank you."

"I'll be of service any time," he remarked. "Liam—amber. Zoey—cider?" They both nodded, and Garrett set his eyes on Shawn. "Shawn?"

"You remembered my name?" Shawn questioned him in delighted disbelief. "We met *once.*"

"I've got a good memory." Garrett's teeth flashed us all once more. "Turn of events, drink orders, names. Y'know. All that."

"Right," he murmured. "Stout?"

"You got it, Shawn," he returned, chipper, and spun around to return to the bar.

Lighthearted conversation continued. My family around me smiled. Our night went on. In small, gentle acts of affection, Cassie occasionally brushed my thigh—or hooked her pinky through mine and gave it a tug—or reached up to move an out-of-place strand of my hair to where it belonged. My cheeks inevitably ached from overutilization of the muscles used to smile, and Cassie returned home with me.

I couldn't help but think once again how strange it is how life can toy with a person because this felt *normal.*

I knew what my normal was before. Although, it didn't feel as such because I had forced myself into a routine of *sleep, eat, repeat* to try to dull what plagued me—whether that be horrific memories or the attempt to quiet my thoughts of all things Cassie Cohen.

Going about existence as if I were simply living on a rock that flew through space did nothing to ease it all, though...and now that life had shifted for me once again, I considered my metaphorical reforging as I had done in the past. Melted down by any hard comings—any trauma in life—I believed that I was not poured into an attractive mold. Instead, I was left to dry just as I was, and I remained damaged—scarred.

That was still abundantly true...and I won't go as far as to say that my love for Cassie and her wholehearted return of it had boiled me down and rendered me a new, damage-free man.

It didn't.

I was still damaged. I mean...we all were.

But she made it easier—and *God,* I loved her for that. Cassie smoothed my jagged edges time and again, assisting me with feeling normal however I could.

Normal.

Somehow, the word made perfect sense now.

Dear Reader

Thank you so much for reading *Shattered Veil!* I adored writing James and Cassie's story, and I thoroughly hope you enjoyed it. The Veiled Series is most definitely not over. Find my Amazon author page or website on the next page to learn more about the continuation of The Veiled Series!

I would love to hear from you, so feel free to drop me a message on my website or you can follow me on Facebook, Instagram, or TikTok under the user handle elizamodiste. I also would thoroughly appreciate a quick review if you are so inclined to do so!

Thank you, again—and happy reading.

Eliza

ELIZA MODISTE

SHATTERED
Veil

THE VEILED SERIES BOOK THREE
ELIZA MODISTE

https://www.amazon.com/author/elizamodiste

www.elizamodiste.com

Made in the USA
Las Vegas, NV
15 July 2024